Praise for Val McDermid's Lindsay Gordon series

"One of my favorite authors."   —Sara Paretsky

"There's a vividness and energy to this tale that makes it satisfying and convincing."

—*Washington Post* on *Booked for Murder*

"Her real skills in creating compelling characters, as well as a mystery that is profoundly twisted . . . , blossom in this dark, chilling novel."   —*Bay Area Reporter* on *Final Edition*

"McDermid cannot write an uninteresting sentence."
—*Women's Review of Books* (UK) on *Final Edition*

"The writing is tough and colorful, the scene setting excellent."   —*Times Literary Supplement* (UK) on *Booked for Murder*

"The macho world of the whodunnit has never seen a sleuth like Lindsay Gordon."
—*Manchester Evening News* (UK) on *Booked for Murder*

"Full marks for plot, atmosphere, character, dialogue, politics, humour—Oh hell, full marks for just about everything. I don't know how Val does it, but I'm bloody glad she does."
—*Crime Time* on *Booked for Murder*

REPORT FOR MURDER

AND

COMMON MURDER

Also by Val McDermid

A Place of Execution
Killing the Shadows
The Grave Tattoo
A Darker Domain
Trick of the Dark
The Vanishing Point
Northanger Abbey

TONY HILL/CAROL JORDAN NOVELS

The Mermaids Singing
The Wire in the Blood
The Last Temptation
The Torment of Others
Beneath the Bleeding
Fever of the Bone
The Retribution
Cross and Burn
Insidious Intent

KAREN PIRIE NOVELS

The Distant Echo
A Darker Domain
The Skeleton Road
Out of Bounds

KATE BRANNIGAN NOVELS

Dead Beat
Kick Back
Crack Down
Clean Break
Blue Genes
Star Struck

LINDSAY GORDON NOVELS

Final Edition
Union Jack
Booked for Murder
Hostage to Murder

SHORT STORY COLLECTIONS

The Writing on the Wall and Other Stories
Stranded
Christmas is Murder (ebook only)
Gunpowder Plots (ebook only)

NON FICTION

A Suitable Job for a Woman
Forensics

VAL McDERMID

REPORT
FOR
MURDER

AND

COMMON
MURDER

Grove Press
New York

Report for Murder was first published in Great Britain in 1987 by The Women's Press Ltd.
Paperback edition in 2004 by HarperCollins UK. First published in the United
States in 2005 by Bywater Books.

Common Muder was first published in Great Britain in 1989 by The Women's Press Ltd.
Paperback edition in 2004 by HarperCollins UK. First published in the United
States in 2005 by Bywater Books.

Printed in the United States of America
Published Simultaneously in Canada

Text Design by Norman Tuttle at Alpha Design & Composition
This book was set in 11.5 Bembo with Charlemagne
by Alpha Design & Composition of Pittsfield. NH.

First Grove Atlantic edition: March 2018

Library of Congress Cataloging-in-Publication data is available for this title.

ISBN 978-0-8021-2776-1
eISBN 978-0-8021-4666-3

Grove Press
an imprint of Grove Atlantic
154 West 14th Street
New York, NY 10011

Distributed by Publishers Group West

groveatlantic.com

18 19 20 21   10 9 8 7 6 5 4 3 2 1

INTRODUCTION TO THE GROVE EDITION

I grew up reading mysteries. From Agatha Christie to Ruth Rendell, from Rex Stout to Chandler and Hammett, I devoured them all. But what started me working on the first Lindsay Gordon novel, *Report for Murder*, in the mid-1980s was the chance to march to a different drum.

There was a new wave breaking on the shores of crime fiction, and it was led by women. Even though there had never been any shortage of female protagonists in the genre, you'd have been hard pressed to find many you could call feminists. But by the early eighties, a new breed of women had emerged.

They were mostly PIs, though there were a few amateurs among them. What marked them out was their politics. Whether they called themselves feminists or not, they were strong, independent women with a brain and a sense of humour, but most of all, they had agency. They didn't shout for male help when the going got tough. They dealt with things on their own terms.

Another key difference was that these stories were organic. They weren't random murders bolted on to a random setting. The crimes grew out of their environment—the particular jobs people did, the lives they led, the situations and recreations they were involved in.

I devoured every one of those books I could get my hands on. Sara Paretsky, Barbara Wilson, Sue Grafton, Marcia Muller, Mary Wings, Katherine V. Forrest and a dozen others showed me how to write about real lives within the framework of murder and suspense. Their protagonists took on the male establishment when they had to, and they didn't back down. They didn't shy away from confronting difficult issues either. I loved them.

I wanted to write my own version of those women. A Scottish version, a woman as firmly rooted as her American sisters, but one who would have to accommodate different laws, different customs, different politics and different histories. I didn't have the nerve to make her a PI because I didn't know any at the time. And I suspected women PIs in the UK would have very different professional lives to their US counterparts.

What I did know was journalism. I became a journalist after I graduated from Oxford, just to bridge the gap until I could support myself writing fiction. (I always had the absolute conviction that day would come, a conviction not shared by anyone else back then…) I thought if I made my character a journalist, I'd be on safe ground. I knew what journalists were capable of and how we went about circumventing the doors that were closed to us. I knew the rhythm of our working lives and what made a good newspaper story.

In other respects, Lindsay Gordon has congruences with my own background. She's Scottish, she shares my politics, and she's a lesbian. It would, however, be a mistake to conflate us. Our personalities are quite different. (Except that we both have a fondness for fast cars and good whisky . . .) She's far more headstrong and stubborn than I am, for example, and much more willing to take risks.

I'm proud to say that Lindsay was the first out lesbian protagonist in UK crime fiction. It never crossed my mind that she wouldn't be a lesbian, because those American novels had given me permission to put whoever I wanted centre stage. But the books were never "about" being a lesbian. Lindsay doesn't wrestle with her sexuality or her gender, nor does she ever apologise for it. It's only one part of her identity and it's not one she has a problem with. The gay characters in the books are part of a wider landscape, one that accommodates all sorts and conditions of people.

That was a very deliberate choice on my part. When I was growing up on the East Coast of Scotland, there were no lesbian templates for my life. No books, no films, no TV series, and certainly no lesbians living open lives. I decided that if I was going to write fiction, I was going to give the next generation of gay women a character they could celebrate. I never describe her physically and that's deliberate too. I wanted her to be a chameleon, to take the form of whatever her readers needed. They could identify with her if they wanted. They could fantasise her as lover or friend or colleague.

Report for Murder was published in 1987 and the Lindsay Gordon books have never been out of print in the UK. I think those early choices I made go some way to explaining why the books have remained so popular. This series is all about character and story, not special pleading or righteous argument.

Each of the books is set in a different world—a trick I learned from reading P. D. James! My own experiences were the springboard for my imagination in the creation of those environments. *Report for Murder* is set in a girls' boarding school; *Common Murder*, at a women's peace camp; *Final Edition*, in the world of newspapers; *Union Jack*, in the milieu of union politics; *Booked for Murder* in publishing; and *Hostage to Murder* moves between Glasgow and St Petersburg in the course of a tense kidnap and murder thriller.

I never intended to write so many Lindsay Gordon novels. Originally I planned a trilogy. (Mostly because the book I really wanted to write was the third one but I couldn't figure out how to get there without writing the first two.) I even packed her off to live in Half Moon Bay with a view of the ocean so I wouldn't be tempted to write about her any more.

But she wouldn't let me go. As soon as I'd despatched her, I had a great idea for another book that gave her the starring role. And then another, and another . . .

Lindsay Gordon took a hold of me and for almost twenty years, she wouldn't let me go. I hope she has the same effect on you.

Val McDermid, 2017

REPORT
FOR
MURDER

For Gill

PART I

OVERTURE

1

Lindsay Gordon put murder to the back of her mind and settled down in the train compartment to enjoy the broken greys and greens of the Derbyshire scenery. Rather like home, she decided. Except that in Scotland, the greens were darker, the greys more forbidding. Although in Glasgow, where she now lived, there was hardly enough green to judge. She congratulated herself on finishing the detective novel just at the point where Manchester suburbia yielded place to this attractive landscape foreign to her. Watching it unfold gave her the first answer to the question that had been nagging her all day: what the hell was she doing here? How could a cynical socialist lesbian feminist journalist (as she mockingly described herself) be on her way to spend a weekend in a girls' public school?

Of course, there were the answers she'd been able to use to friends: she had never visited this part of England and wanted to see what it was like; she was a great believer in "knowing thine enemy," so it came under the heading of opportunities not to be missed; she wanted to see Paddy Callaghan, who had been responsible for the invitation. But she remained unconvinced that she was doing the right thing. What had made her mind up was the realisation that, given Lindsay's current relationship with the Inland Revenue, anything that had a cheque as an end product couldn't be ignored.

The fact that she cheerfully despised the job she was about to do was not a novel sensation. In the unreal world of popular journalism which she inhabited, she was continually faced with tasks that made her blood boil. But like other tabloid journalists who laid claim to a set of principles, she argued that, since popular newspapers were mass culture, if people with brains and compassion opted out the press would only sink further into the gutter. But in spite of having this missionary zeal to keep her warm, Lindsay often felt the chill wind of her friends' disapproval. And she had to admit to herself that saying all this always made her feel a pompous hypocrite. However, since this assignment involved writing for a magazine with some credibility, she was doubly pleased that it would avoid censure in the pub as well as provide cash, and that was enough to stifle the stirrings of contempt for Derbyshire House Girls' School.

Paddy, with the contacts of a life membership of the old girls' network, had managed to persuade the features editor of *Perspective* to commission a piece from Lindsay about a fund-raising programme about to be launched by the school with a Gala Day. At that point, Lindsay was hungry for the cash and the prestige, so she couldn't afford the luxury of stopping to consider if it was the sort of project she'd actually choose to take on. Three months ago she'd reluctantly accepted redundancy when the *Daily Nation* discovered it needed fewer journalists so that it could pay its print workers their "pound of flesh." Since then, she had been applying for unlikely jobs and frenetically trying to make a living as a freelance. That made the call from Paddy all the more welcome because it meant a relatively quiet weekend away from the demands of the telephone—which would soon stop disrupting her life altogether if she didn't earn enough to pay the last quarter's bill.

At that unwelcome thought, Lindsay reflected with relief on the money she would receive from the Derbyshire House job.

It seemed poetic justice that such a bastion of privilege should stake her. Good old Paddy, she mused. Ever since they'd met in Oxford six years before, Paddy had not only been a tower of strength in emotional crises but the first to offer help when life got Lindsay into one of its awkward corners. When Lindsay's car staged a break-down on a remote Greek mountainside it was Paddy who organised the flying out of a spare part. When Lindsay was made redundant it was Paddy who found the cousin who told Lindsay the best thing to do with her less-than-golden handshake. And when Lindsay's lover died, it was Paddy who drove through the night to be with her. The daughter of two doctors, with an education begun at the "best" schools and polished off at Oxford, Paddy Callaghan had shaken her family by deciding to become an actress. After four years of only moderate success and limited employment, however, she had realised she would never make the first rank. Always a realist, and fundamentally unaffected by four years of living like a displaced person, she reverted to type and decided to make sure that the rising generation of public schoolgirls would have a better grounding on the stage than she'd had. When the two women first met, Paddy was half-way through the teacher training that would take her back to her old school in Derbyshire to teach English and Drama. It had taken Lindsay quite a long time to realise that at least part of her appeal for Paddy was her streak of unconventionality. She was an antidote to the staid world Paddy had grown up in and was about to return to. Lindsay had argued bitterly with Paddy that to go back to her old environment was copping out of reality. Though the argument never found a solution, the friendship survived.

Lindsay felt sure that part of the reason for the continuation of that friendship was that they had never let their separate worlds collide. Just as Lindsay would never drag Paddy off to a gay club, so Paddy would never invite Lindsay to one of her parents' weekend house parties. Their relationship existed in a vacuum because they understood and accepted the gulf that separated so much of their lives. So Lindsay was apprehensive about encountering Paddy on what was firmly her territory. Suddenly all her fears about the weekend crystallised into a panic over the trivial issue of what she was wearing. What the hell was the appropriate gear for this establishment, anyway? It wasn't something that normally exercised her thoughts, but she had gone through her wardrobe with nervous care that morning, rejecting most items on the grounds that they were too casual, and others on the grounds that they were too formal. She finally settled on charcoal-grey trousers, matching jacket and burgundy shirt. Very understated, not too butch, she'd thought. Now she thought again and considered the vision of the archetypal dyke swaggering into this nest of young maidens. God help her if St George hove into sight.

If only she'd brought the car, she could have brought a wide enough selection of clothes to run no risk of getting it wrong. But her crazy decision to opt for the uncertain hands of British Rail so she could get some work done had boomeranged—you could only carry so much for a couple of days, unless you wanted to look like the wally of the weekend tipping out at the school gates with two cabin trunks and a holdall. As her paranoia gently reached a climax, she shook herself. "Oh sod it," she thought. "If I'm so bloody right-on, why should I give a toss what they think of me? After all, I'm the one doing them a favour, giving their fund-raising a puff in the right places."

With this bracing thought, the train shuddered into the station at Buxton. She picked up her bags and emerged on to the platform just as the sun came out from the autumn clouds, making the trees glow. Then through the glass doors she caught sight of Paddy, waiting and waving. Lindsay thrust her ticket at the collector and the two women hugged each other, laughing, each measuring the other for changes.

"If my pupils could see me now, they'd have a fit," laughed Paddy. "Teachers aren't supposed to leap around like lunatics in public, you know! My, you look good. Frightfully smart!" She held Lindsay at arms' length, taking in the outfit, the brown hair and the dark blue eyes. "First time I've ever seen you fail to resemble a jumble sale in search of a venue."

"Lost weight. It's living off the wits that does it. Food's a very easy economy."

"No, darling, it's definitely the clothes. Who's the new woman, then?"

"Cheeky sod! There's no new woman, more's the pity. I went out and bought this all by myself. At least six months ago, too. So there, Miss Callaghan."

Paddy grinned. "All right, all right. I'll take your word for it. Now, come along. I'm parked outside. I've got to pick up a couple of things from the town library then we can shoot back to the school itself and have a quick coffee to wipe away the strain of the train."

In the station car park, they climbed into Paddy's battered Land Rover. "Not exactly in its prime, but it's practical up here," she apologised. "Highest market town in England, this is. When the snow gets bad, I'm the only member of staff who can make a bid for freedom to the local pub. You still got that flashy passion wagon of yours?"

Lindsay scowled. "If you mean my MG, yes I have."

"Dear, oh dear. Still trying to impress with that retarded status symbol?"

"I don't drive it to impress anyone. I know it's the sort of car that provokes really negative reactions from the 2CV brigade, but I happen to enjoy it."

Paddy laughed, "Sorry. I didn't know it was such a sore spot."

"Let's just say that I've been getting a bit of stick about it lately from one or two people who should know better. I'm seriously thinking about selling it just for a bit of peace and quiet from the purists who think you can only be right-on in certain cars. But I think I'd miss it too much. I can't afford to buy a new sports car. I spend a lot of time in transit and I think I've got a right to be in a car that performs well, is comfortable and doesn't get like an oven in the summer. Plus it provokes interesting reactions from people. It's a good shorthand way of finding out about attitudes."

"Okay, okay. I'm on your side," Paddy protested.

"I know it's flash and pretentious," Lindsay persisted. "But then there's a bit of that in me anyway. So you could argue that I'm doing women a favour by forewarning them."

Paddy pulled up in a Georgian crescent of imposing buildings. "You are sensitive about it, aren't you? Well, if it's any consolation, I've never thought you were flash. A little over the top sometimes, perhaps . . ."

Lindsay changed the subject abruptly. "What's this, then?" she demanded, waving an arm at the buildings.

"Not bad, eh? The North's answer to Bath. Not quite on the same scale. Rather splendid but slightly seedy. And you can still drink the spa water here. Comes out of the ground warm; tastes rather like an emetic in its natural state, but terribly good for one, so they say. Come and see the library ceiling."

"Do what?" demanded Lindsay as Paddy jumped down. She had to break into a trot to catch Paddy, who was walking briskly along a colonnade turned golden by the late afternoon sun. They entered the library. Paddy gestured to Lindsay to go upstairs while she collected her books. A few minutes later she joined her there.

"Hardly over the top at all, dear," Lindsay mocked, pointing to the baroque splendours of the painted and moulded ceiling. "Worth a trip in itself. So where are all the dark satanic mills, then? I thought the North of England was full of them."

"I thought you'd appreciate this," said Paddy with a smile. "You're in altogether the wrong place for dark satanics, though. Only the odd dark satanic quarry hereabouts. But before you dash off in search of the local proletarian heritage, a word about this weekend. I want to sort things out before we get caught up in the hurly-burly."

"Sort out the programme, or my article?"

"Bit of both, really. Look, I know everything about the school goes right against the grain for you. Always embraced your principles so strongly, and all that. I also know that *Perspective* would be very happy if you wrote your piece from a fairly caustic point of view. But, as I tried to get across to you, this fund-raising project is vital to the school.

"If we don't raise the necessary fifty thousand pounds we'll lose all our playing fields. That might not seem any big deal to you, but it would mean we'd lose a great deal of our prestige because we've always been known as a school with a good balance—you know, healthy mind in a healthy body and all that. Without our reputation for being first class for sport as well as academically we'd lose a lot of girls. I know that sounds crazy, but remember, it's usually fathers who decree where daughters are educated and they all hark back to their own schooldays through rose-tinted specs. I doubt if we'd manage to keep going, quite honestly. Money's become very tight and we're getting back into the patriarchal ghetto. Where parents can only afford to educate some of their children, the boys are getting the money spent on them and the girls are being ignored." Paddy abruptly ran out of steam.

Lindsay took her time to answer while Paddy studied her anxiously. This was a conversation Lindsay had hoped would not have had to take place, and it was one she would rather have had over a drink after they'd both become accustomed to being with each other again. At last she said, "I gathered it was serious from your letter. But I can't help feeling it wouldn't be such a bad thing if the public schools felt the pinch like everyone else. It seems somewhat unreal to be worrying about playing fields when a lot of state schools can't even afford enough books to go round."

"Even if it means the school closing down?"

"Even if it means that, yes."

"And put another sixty or seventy people on the dole queue? Not just teachers, but cleaning staff, groundsmen, cooks, the shopkeepers we patronise? Not to mention the fact that for quite a lot of the girls, Derbyshire House is the only stable thing in their lives. Quite a few come from broken homes. Some of their parents are living abroad where the local education isn't suitable for one reason or another. And others need the extra attention we can give them so they can realise their full potential."

"Oh, Paddy, can't you hear yourself?" Lindsay retorted plaintively, and was rewarded by scowls and whispered "shushes" from around the reading room. She dropped her voice. "What about all the kids in exactly the same boat who don't have the benefit of mummies and daddies with enough spare cash to use Derbyshire House as a social services department? Maybe their lives would be a little bit better if the middle classes had to opt back into real life and use their influence to improve things. I can't be anything but totally opposed to this system you cheerfully shore up. And don't give me those spurious arguments about equal opportunities. In the context of this society, what you're talking about isn't an extension of equality; it's an extension of inequality. Don't try to quiet my conscience like that.

"Nevertheless . . . I've had to come to the reluctant conclusion that I can't stab you in the back having accepted your hospitality. Shades of the Glencoe massacre, eh? Don't expect me to be uncritically sycophantic. But I won't be doctrinaire either. Besides, I need the money!"

Paddy smiled. "I should have known better than to worry about you," she said.

"You should, really," Lindsay reproached her. "Now, am I going to see this monument to the privileged society or not?"

They walked back to the Land Rover, relaxed together, catching up on the four months since they had last seen each other. On the short drive from Buxton to Axe Edge, where Derbyshire House dominated a fold of moorland, Paddy gave Lindsay a more detailed account of the weekend plans.

"We decided to start off the fund-raising with a bang. We've done the usual things, like writing to all the old girls asking for contributions, but we know we'll need a bit of extra push. After all, most of our old girls are the wives and mothers brigade who don't exactly have wads of spare cash at their disposal. And we've got less than six months to raise the money."

"But surely you must have known the lease was coming up for renewal?"

"Oh, we did, and we budgeted for it. But then James Cartwright, a local builder and developer, put in a bid for the lease that was fifty thousand pounds more than we were going to have to pay. He wants to build timeshare holiday flats with a leisure complex. It's an ideal site for him, right in the smartest part of Buxton. And one of the few decent sites where he'd still be able to get planning permission. The agents obviously had to look favourably on an offer as good as that. So our headmistress, Pamela Overton, got the governors mobilised and we came up with a deal. If we can raise the cash to match that fifty thousand pounds in six months, we get the lease, even if Cartwright ups his offer."

Lindsay smiled wryly. "Amazing what influence can do."

Although Paddy was watching the road, Lindsay's tone of voice was not lost on her. "It's been bloody hard to get this far," she complained mildly. "The situation's complicated by the fact that Cartwright's daughter is one of our sixth-formers. And in my house, too. Anyway, we're all going flat out to get the money, and that's what the weekend's all about."

"Which is where I come in, yes?"

"You're our bid to get into the right section of the public consciousness. You're going to tell them all about our wonderful enterprise, how we're getting in gear, and some benevolent millionaire is going to come along and write us a cheque. Okay?"

Lindsay grinned broadly. "Okay, yah!" she teased. "So what exactly is going to happen? So far you seem to have avoided supplying me with any actual information."

"Tomorrow morning we're having a craft fair, which will carry over into the afternoon. All the girls have contributed their own work as well as begging and scrounging from friends and

relations. Then, in the afternoon, the sixth form are present-
ing a new one-act play written especially for them by Cordelia
Brown. She's an old girl of my vintage. Finally, there will be an
auction of modern autographed first editions, which Cordelia
and I and one or two other people have put together. We've got
almost a hundred books."

"Cordelia Brown? The chat-show queen?"

"Don't be snide, Lindsay. You know damn well she's a good
writer. I'd have thought she'd have been right up your street."

"I like her novels. I don't know why she does all that telly
crap, though. You'd hardly believe the same person writes the
books and the telly series. Still, it must keep the wolf from the
door."

"You can discuss the matter with her yourself. She's arriving
later this evening. Try not to be too abrasive, darling."

Lindsay laughed. "Whatever you say, Paddy. So the book
auction rounds the day off, does it?"

"Far from it. The high point is in the evening—a concert
given by our most celebrated old girl, Lorna Smith-Couper."

Lindsay nodded. "The cellist. I've never seen her perform,
but I've got a couple of her recordings."

"More than I have. I've never come across her, as far as
I know. She had left before I came to the school—I didn't get
here till the fifth form. And it's not my music, after all. Give me
Dizzy Gillespie any time."

"All that jazz still the only thing you'll admit is music,
then? You'll not be able to help me, in that case. I'd love to get
an interview with Lorna Smith-Couper. I've heard she's one
of the most awkward people to get anything out of, but maybe
the good cause together with the old school ties will make her
more approachable."

Paddy turned the Land Rover into a sweeping drive.
She stopped inside the heavy iron gates, leaned across Lindsay
and pointed. "See that folly on the hill over there? It's called
Solomon's Temple. If you look straight left of it you can just

see a corner of the stupid green acres that all this fuss is about."
There was an edge in her voice and they drove on in silence.
Ahead of them stood Derbyshire House, an elegant mansion
like a miniature Chatsworth. They swung round a corner of
the house and dropped down into a thick coppice of birch,
sycamore and rowan trees. After a hundred yards, they emerged
in a large clearing where six modern stone blocks surrounded
a well-tended lawn.

"The houses," said Paddy. "About half of the girls sleep
in the main building and the more senior ones sleep here," she
pointed as she spoke, "in Axe, Goyt, Wildboarclough and my
house, Longnor. The two smaller ones, Burbage and Grin Low,
are for teachers and other staff."

"My God," said Lindsay, "the only thing this verdant near
my school was the bloody garden of remembrance behind the
local crematorium."

"Very funny. Come on, Lindsay, do stop waving your
origins around like a red flag and have a drink. I can feel this is
going to be a good weekend."

2

Paddy and Lindsay were stretched out in Paddy's comfortable sitting-room. It was furnished by the school in tasteful if old-fashioned style, but Paddy had stamped her own character on it. One wall was completely lined with books and the others were covered with elegant photographs of stage productions and a selection of old film posters. The chairs were upholstered in leather and, in spite of their shabbiness, they were deep and welcoming. By the window was a large desk strewn with piles of papers and exercise books and in the corner near the door was a cocktail cabinet, the only piece of furniture that Paddy had carted around with her everywhere for the last ten years.

Lindsay nursed her glass and drawled, "So what's this one called?"

"Deep Purple."

"Great hobby, making cocktails. Of course, I'd never have your flair for it. What's in this, then?"

"One measure Cointreau, three of vodka, blue food-colouring, a large slug of grenadine, a measure of soda water and a lot of ice. Good, isn't it?"

"Dynamite. And it goes down a treat. This is certainly the life. What time's dinner? And should I change?"

"Three quarters of an hour. Don't bother changing, you're fine as you are. Tomorrow will be a bit more formal, though; best bib and tucker all round. We'll have to go over to the staffroom shortly, so I can introduce you to the workers."

Lindsay smiled. "What are they like?" she asked, slightly apprehensive.

"Like any collection of female teachers. There are the super-intelligent, witty ones; the boring old farts; the Tory party brigade and the statutory radical—that's me, by the way. And a few who are just ordinary, unobjectionable women."

"My God, it must be bad if you're their idea of a radical. What does that mean? You occasionally disagree with Margaret Thatcher and you put tomato sauce on your bacon and eggs? So am I going to like any of this bunch of fossils?"

"You'll like Chris Jackson, the PE mistress. She comes from your neck of the woods, and apart from being a physical fitness freak is obsessed with two things—wine-making and cars. You can imagine what we have in common, and it isn't overhead camshafts."

Lindsay grinned. "Sounds more like it. I don't suppose . . . ?"

Paddy returned the grin. "Sorry. There's a large rugby player in the background, I'm afraid. You'll also like Margaret Macdonald, if she can spare enough time from this concert to say hello. She's head of music, and a good friend of mine. We sit up late and talk about books, politics and what passes for drama on radio and TV."

Lindsay stretched, yawned, then lit a cigarette. "Sorry," she muttered. "Train's tired me out. I'll wake up soon."

"You better had. You're due to meet our magnificent head-mistress, Pamela Overton. One of the old school. Her father was a Cambridge don and she came to us after a brilliant but obscure career in the Foreign Office. Very efficient and very good at achieving what she sets out to do. High powered but human. Talk to her—it's always rewarding, if unnerving," Paddy observed.

"Why unnerving?" Lindsay was intrigued.

"She always knows more about your area of competence than you do yourself. But you'll enjoy her. You'll have a chance to judge for yourself tonight, anyway, before the guest of honour gets here. Ms Smith-Couper has not said when she'll be arriving. Her secretary simply said some time this evening. Really considerate."

Paddy got to her feet and prowled round the desk, her strong, bony face looking puzzled. "I'm sure I left myself a note somewhere . . . I've got to do something before tomorrow morning and I'm damned if I can remember what it is . . . Oh, found it. Right. Remind me I have to have a word with Margaret Macdonald. Now, shall we go and face the staffroom?" They walked through the trees to the main house. In a small clearing over to one side, a few floodlights illuminated a building site.

"New squash courts," Paddy explained. "We have to light the site because we kept having stuff stolen. It's very quiet round that side of the school after about ten—an easy target for burglars. Chris Jackson is champing at the bit for them to finish. Pity we can't hijack the cash for the playing fields, but the money came to us as a specific bequest."

The two women entered the main building by a small door in the rear. As they walked through the passages and glanced into the classrooms, Lindsay was struck by how superficially similar it was to her own old school, a crumbling comprehensive. Both had had the same institutional paint job done on them; both used pupils' artistic offerings to brighten the walls; both were slightly down at heel and smelled of chalk dust. The only apparent difference at first sight was the absence of graffiti. Paddy gave Lindsay a quick run-down on the house as they walked towards the staffroom.

"This is the kitchen and dining room. The school has been in the building since 1934. Above us are the music rooms and assembly hall—it was a ballroom when Lord Longnor's family had the house. There are classrooms, offices and Miss Overton's flat on this floor. More classrooms on the second floor, and the top floor is all bedrooms. The science labs are over in the woods, on the opposite side from the houses. And this is the staffroom."

Paddy opened the door on a buzz of conversation. The staffroom was elegantly proportioned, with a large bay window through which Lindsay could see the lights of Buxton twinkling in the darkness. About twenty women were assembled in small groups, standing by the log fire or sitting in clumps of unmatched and slightly shabby chairs. The walls were occupied by a collection of old prints of Derbyshire and a vast noticeboard completely covered with bits of paper. The conversations did not pause when Lindsay and Paddy entered, though several heads turned briefly towards them. Paddy led Lindsay over to a young woman who was poring over a large book. She was slim but solidly built, and seemed bursting with a vitality that Lindsay only dreamed of these days. Her jet black curly hair, pink and white complexion and dark blue eyes revealed her Highland ancestry and reminded Lindsay painfully of home.

Paddy interrupted the woman's concentration. "Chris, drag yourself away from the exploded view of a cylinder head or whatever and meet Lindsay Gordon. Lindsay, this is Chris Jackson, our PE mistress."

"Hello there," said Chris, dropping her book. She still had the accent Lindsay had grown up with but had virtually lost under the layers of every other accent she had lived amongst. "Our tame journalist, eh? Well, before everybody else says so without meaning it, let me tell you how grateful I am for any help you can give us. We need to keep these playing fields, and not just to keep me in a job. We'd never get anything nearly so good within miles of here. It's good of you to give us a hand, especially since you've no real connection with the place."

Lindsay smiled, embarrassed by her sincerity. "I'm delighted to have the chance to see a place like this from the inside.

And besides, I'm always glad of work, especially when it's commissioned."

Paddy broke into the pause which followed. "Chris, you and Lindsay are from the same part of the world. Lindsay's from Invercross."

"Really? I'd never have guessed. You've hardly any trace of the accent. I'd have said yours was much further south. I'm from South Achilcaig myself, though I went to school at St Mary Magdalene in Helensburgh."

The two women launched into conversation about their origins and memories of the Argyllshire villages where they grew up, and discovered they had played hockey against each other a dozen years before. Paddy drifted off to talk to a worried-looking woman seated a few feet away from Lindsay and Chris. Only minutes later their reminiscences were interrupted by raised voices from Paddy and the other woman.

"I had every right to excuse the girl. She's in my house, Margaret. On matters of her welfare, what I say goes," Paddy said angrily.

"How could you blithely give her permission to opt out when it's so near to the actual concert? She is supposed to have a solo in the choir section. What am I supposed to do about that?"

Startled, Lindsay muttered, "What's going on?"

"Search me," Chris replied. "That's Margaret Macdonald, head of music. Normally Paddy and her are the best of pals."

Paddy glared at Margaret and retorted, "Far be it from me to put my oar in, but Jessica did suggest the Holgate girl could perfectly well handle an extra solo."

The other woman got out of her chair and faced Paddy. "I make the decisions about my choirs, not Jessica Bennett. If the girl had come to me with her demands, I would not have given her permission to skulk in a corner and avoid her responsibilities. She's not the only person who has reasons for wanting to have nothing to do with this concert. But some people just have to struggle on."

"Look, Margaret," said Paddy more quietly, realising the eyes of the staffroom were on them, "I'm sorry this has put you out. I know how much you've got on your plate. But in my view it would be far worse if I'd sent the girl off with a flea in her ear and she ended up throwing a fit on the concert platform. And in my view that would have been quite possible."

Margaret Macdonald opened her mouth to retort, but before she could speak the staffroom door opened and a tall woman entered. As she moved into the room, the conversations gradually started up again. The music teacher turned sharply away from Paddy, saying only, "Since you have told the girl it will be all right, I must abide by your decision."

Looking slightly stunned, Paddy returned to Lindsay and Chris. "I've never known Margaret to behave like that," she murmured. "Incredible. Hang on a minute, Lindsay; I'll go and bring the head across." She walked over to the tall woman who had just entered and who was now chatting to another mistress.

Pamela Overton was an imposing woman in her late fifties. She was dressed in a simple dark blue jersey dress and wore her silver hair over her ears in sweeping wings which flowed into an elaborate plaited bun on her neck. Paddy went over to her and exchanged a few words in a low voice. The two women joined Lindsay and Chris.

Paddy had scarcely finished the introductions, with Lindsay lost in admiration at Pamela Overton's beautifully modulated but unquestionably pukka voice, when there was a knock at the door. It was opened by one of the staff who stepped outside for a moment. Returning, she came straight to Miss Overton's side and said, "Miss Smith-Couper is here, Miss Overton."

Pamela Overton had hardly reached the door when it was flung open to reveal a woman in her early thirties whom Lindsay recognised instantly. Lorna Smith-Couper was even more stunning in the flesh than in the many photographs Lindsay had seen of her. She had a mane of tawny blonde hair which descended in a warm wave over her shoulders. Her skin was pale and clear, stretched tightly over her strong bone structure. And her eyes shone out from her face like hard blue chips of lapis lazuli.

As Lindsay watched her sweep into the room, she was aware of Paddy turning to face the door. And she sensed her friend's body stiffen beside her. Only Lindsay was close enough to hear Paddy breathe, "Jesus Christ Almighty, not her!"

3

After dinner, Lindsay and Paddy skipped coffee in the staffroom and walked back through the trees to Longnor House. All Paddy had said was, "They'll be too busy with the superstar to notice our absence. And besides, we've got the excuse of having to be back in case Cordelia arrives early." Lindsay was struggling to remain silent against all her instincts both as a friend and as a journalist. But she realised that to press Paddy for information would be counter-productive.

Dinner had not been the most comfortable of meals. Lorna Smith-Couper had greeted Paddy with an obviously false enthusiasm. "Dearest Paddy, whoever would have expected to find you in such a respectable situation," she had cooed. Paddy had smiled coldly in return. Her attempts to drift away from the group that had immediately formed around the cellist had been thwarted by Pamela Overton, who had suggested in a way that brooked no argument that Paddy and Lindsay should join Lorna and her at high table. Lorna had ignored Paddy from then on and had devoted herself to her conversation with Pamela Overton, after pointedly saying to Lindsay, "Anything you hear is completely off the record, do I make myself clear?" As it happened, she said nothing that anyone could have been interested in except Lorna herself.

The meal itself had come as a pleasant surprise to Lindsay, whose own memories of school and college food had left her disinclined to repeat the experience. A tasty vegetable broth made with a good stock was followed by chicken and mushroom pie, baked potatoes and peas. To finish there was a choice of fresh fruit. She remarked on the quality of the food to Paddy, but her friend was too abstracted to do more than nod.

Back in Paddy's room, Lindsay stretched herself out in a chair while Paddy brewed the coffee. From the kitchen she called out, "Sorry I've not been much company."

Lindsay saw her chance to dig an explanation out of Paddy and immediately called out, "Dinner was a bit of a strain. I could hear my accent becoming more and more affected with every passing sentence. But I thought you said you'd never met our guest of honour?"

There was a lengthy silence filled only by the sound of the percolating coffee. When Paddy eventually spoke there was deep bitterness in her voice. "I didn't realise I had," she said. "I only ever knew her as Lorna. In that particular circle, first names were all we ever seemed to exchange."

She returned to the living-room and poured coffee for them both. "You make it sound like a John Le Carré novel," Lindsay said.

"Nothing so dramatic."

"You don't have to tell me about it unless you want to. No sweat."

"I'd better tell someone before I blow up. It goes back, oh, eight or nine years. I was doing bit parts in London and the odd telly piece. Looking back at it now, the people I used to hang around with were a pretty juvenile lot, myself included. We thought we were such a bunch of trendies, though. We were heavily into nightclubbing, getting stoned, solving the problems of the world, and talking a lot about permissiveness without actually being particularly promiscuous. A depressing hangover from the sixties, our crowd was. It was all sex and drugs and rock and roll. Or at least we tried to convince ourselves it was."

Paddy looked Lindsay straight in the eye as she spoke, not afraid to share her shame with someone she trusted. "An expensive way of life, you see. And not easy to sustain on the sort of money I was making. But I found a way to finance it. I started dealing dope. No big-time hard stuff, you understand, but I put a fair bit around, one way or another. So there were always people coming round to my flat to score some dope. Regular customers, word of mouth, you know." Lindsay nodded. She knew only too well the scenes that Paddy described. "One of my customers was a musician, a pianist. William. Came several times with his girlfriend. The girlfriend was Lorna."

Lindsay pulled out two cigarettes from her pack and lit them. She passed one to Paddy who inhaled deeply. "You see what this could mean?" she asked. Lindsay nodded again as Paddy went on. "All she's got to do is drop a seemingly casual word when there are other people around and bang, that's my job gone. I mean, okay, most of our generation have dabbled with the old Acapulco Gold at one time or another but nobody talks about it now, do they? And no school, especially a public school, can afford to be seen employing a teacher who is known to have dealt in the stuff. It's no defence to say I've never so much as rolled a joint on school premises. What a story for you, eh?"

Paddy abruptly rose and poured two brandies. She handed one to Lindsay and paced the floor. Lindsay sensed her anguish. She knew Paddy had worked hard to achieve her present position. That hard work hadn't come easily to someone who was used to having the world on a plate. So it was all the more galling that even now it might come to nothing because of a way of life that hadn't seemed so risky at the time. Lindsay ached for Paddy. She tried to find words that might help.

"Why should she say anything? After all, she'd be admitting her involvement in the drugs scene and she'd surely be loath to damage her own reputation," was all she could manage.

"No, she wouldn't do herself any damage. You see, she never used the stuff herself. Always took the deeply self-righteous line that she could feel good without indulging in artificial stimulants. As to why she should say anything—well, why not? It might be her idea of fun. She could always say she had the best interests of the school at heart."

Lindsay was silent. She got to her feet and went to Paddy. They held on to each other tightly. Lindsay prayed Paddy could sense the support she wanted to offer. Then, relieved, she felt the tension begin to seep out of her friend.

The moment was broken by a single peal of the telephone. They smiled at each other, then Paddy went to her desk and picked up the phone, pressing the appropriate button to take an internal call.

"Miss Callaghan here . . . Oh good, I'll be right over." She put the phone down and started for the door. "Cordelia's arrived. I'll go and collect her from the main building. There's some cold meat and salad in the fridge. Could you stick it on a plate for me? She'll doubtless be starving. Always is. Dressing's on the top shelf, by the tomatoes." And she was gone.

Lindsay went into the kitchen to carry out her instructions. Her mind was still racing over Paddy's problem, though she knew there was nothing she could do to improve the situation. She was also considering the more general problem of how to persuade Lorna Smith-Couper to grant her the sort of interview that would provide more than just a piece of padding for her feature on the school. Then there was Cordelia Brown. She might also be good for a feature interview to sell to one of the women's magazines.

Lindsay had never met the writer, but she knew a great deal about her from what she had read and from what mutual friends had told her. Cordelia Brown was, at thirty-one, one of the jewels in the crown of women's writing, according to the media. She had left Oxford half-way through her degree course and worked for three years as administrator of a small touring theatre company in Devon. Then she had gone on to write four moderately successful novels, the latest of which had been short-listed for the Booker Prize. But she had broken through into a more general public awareness with a television drama series, *The Successors*, which had won most of the awards it was possible to be nominated for. A highly acclaimed film had followed, which had appeared at precisely the right moment to be described as the flagship of the re-emergent British film industry. All of this, coupled with an engaging willingness to talk wittily and at length on most subjects, and an acceptable quota of good looks, had conspired to turn Cordelia into the darling of the chat shows.

As she shook the dressing and tossed it into the bowl of salad, Lindsay had to admit to herself that she was looking forward to their meeting. She had no great expectations of finding the writer sympathetic; on the other hand, she might be considerably more pleasant than her television appearances would lead one to imagine. She heard the door opening and the sound of voices. She went to the kitchen door just as Cordelia dropped a leather holdall to the floor. The woman had her back to Lindsay and was speaking to Paddy. Her voice sounded richer face to face than it did coming from the television set which managed to strip it of most of its warmth. The accent was utterly neutral, with only the faintest trace of the drawl Lindsay had become familiar with at Oxford and with which she had renewed her acquaintance earlier that evening at dinner. "There's four or five boxes, but I'm too bloody exhausted to be bothered with them now. Let's leave them in the car till tomorrow."

Then she turned and took in Lindsay standing in the doorway. The two women scrutinised each other carefully, deciding how much they liked what they saw, both wary. Suddenly the weekend seemed to hold out fresh possibilities to Lindsay as Cordelia's grey eyes under the straight dark brows flicked over her from head to foot. She felt slightly dazed and weak with something she supposed was lust. It had been a long time since she had felt the first stirrings of an attraction based on the combination of looks and good vibes. Cordelia, too, seemed to like what she saw, for a smile twitched at the corners of her wide mouth. "So this is the famous Lindsay," she remarked.

Lindsay prayed that her face did not look as stricken as she felt. She nodded and smiled back, feeling a little foolish. "Something like that," she answered. "Nice to meet you." She found herself desperately hoping that what she'd heard about Cordelia's taste in lovers was true.

She was spared further conversational efforts just then by the demands of Cordelia's stomach.

"I say, Paddy, any chance of some scoff?" she demanded plaintively. "I'm famished. It took much longer than I thought to get here. The traffic was unbelievable. Does the entire population of London come to Derbyshire every weekend? Or are they simply all desperate to see the new one-act play by Cordelia Brown?"

Paddy laughed. "I knew you'd be hungry. There's some salad in the kitchen. I'll just get it." But before Paddy could make a move, Lindsay had vanished into the kitchen. Cordelia shot a look at Paddy, her eyebrows rising comically and a smile on her lips. Paddy merely grinned and said, "I'll fix you a drink. What would you like?"

"A Callaghan cocktail special, please. Why the hell do you think I was prepared to come back to this dump?" As Paddy mixed the drinks, Lindsay returned with Cordelia's meal. She promptly tucked in as though she had not eaten for days.

Paddy strained a Brandy Alexander out of the shaker and passed it to Cordelia, saying, "Lindsay is writing a feature about the fund-raising."

"Poor old you. But you're not an old girl, are you?"

"Do I look that out of place?" asked Lindsay.

"No, not at all. It's simply that I knew that I'd never seen you before either at school or at any of the old girl reunions.

I'd have remembered. I'm good at faces. But you're not one of us, are you?"

"No. I know Paddy from Oxford. I was up when she was doing her teacher training. And she talked me into this. I'm freelancing at the moment, so it's all grist to the mill." Lindsay's response to the assurance of the older woman was to adopt the other's speech pattern and to polish up her own accent.

"And what do you make of us so far?"

"Hard to tell. I haven't seen enough, or talked to many people yet."

"A true diplomat." Cordelia resumed eating.

Paddy chose a Duke Ellington record and put it on. As the air filled with the liquid sounds, Lindsay thought, I'm always going to remember this tune and what I was doing when I first heard it. She was embarrassed to find she could hardly take her eyes off Cordelia. She watched her hands cutting up the food and lifting the glass; she watched the changing planes of her face as she ate and drank. She found herself recalling a favourite quotation: "A man doesn't love a woman because he thinks her clever or because he admires her but because he likes the way she scratches her head." She thought that perhaps the reason her relationships had failed in the past was because she hadn't looked for such details and learned to love them. She was surprised to find herself saying rather formally, "I was wondering if there was any chance you could be persuaded to give me half an hour during the weekend? I'd like to do an interview. Of course, I can't guarantee that I'd be able to place the finished feature, but I'd like to try if you don't mind me asking on a weekend when you're intent on having fun with your old friends."

Cordelia finished eating and put her plate down. She considered her glass for a moment. She turned to Paddy and said in a tone of self-mockery familar to her friend, "What do you think, Paddy? Would I be safe with her? Is she going to lull me into a false sense of security and tempt me into indiscretions?

Will she ask me difficult questions and refuse to be satisfied with easy answers?"

"Oh, undoubtedly!"

"Very well then, I accept the challenge. I will place myself in your hands. Shall we say Sunday morning while the school is at church?" Lindsay nodded agreement. "And don't feel guilty about dragging me away from old friends. The number of people here I actually want to see can be counted on the fingers of one thumb. And there are plenty of others I'll be glad of an excuse to avoid. Such as our esteemed guest of honour."

"You're not alone there," said Paddy, struggling unsuccessfully to make her words sound lighthearted.

"You another victim of hers, Paddy?" asked Cordelia, not waiting for a reply. "That Smith-Couper always had the charm and rapacity of a jackal. But, of course, she'd left before you arrived, hadn't she? A fine piece of work she is. Beauty and the Beast rolled into one gift-wrapped package. Do you know what the bitch has done to me? And done it, I may say, in the full knowledge that we were both scheduled for this weekend in the Alma Mater?" There was a pregnant pause. Lindsay recalled that Cordelia had started her career in the theatre.

"She's suing me for libel. Only this week I got the writ. She claims that the cellist in *Across a Crowded Room* is a scurrilous portrait of her good self. Though why she should go out of her way to identify herself with a character whose morals would not have disgraced a piranha fish is quite beyond me. That aside, however, she is looking for substantial damages, taking into account the fact that the bloody thing made the Booker list and is about to come out in paperback. If she was going to get in a tizz, you'd think it would happen when the book came out, wouldn't you? But not with our Lorna. Oh no, she waits till she's sure there's enough money in the kitty. Infuriating woman." Having let off steam, Cordelia subsided into her chair, muttering, "There you are, Lindsay, there's the peg to hang your feature on. The real-life confrontation between the Suer and the Sued. By the way, Paddy,

I hope I'm not bedded down within a corridor's length of our Lorna. The temptation to get up in the night and commit murder most foul might be altogether too much for me!"

Through her infatuated daze, even Lindsay could detect the acrimony behind the self-mocking humour in Cordelia's voice. "Luckily not," Paddy replied quickly, "she's in Pamela Overton's flat." She went on to explain that Cordelia was to occupy the guest room in Longnor, while Lindsay was to have the room next door, its occupant having volunteered to give up her room to the visitor in return for the privilege of sharing her best friend's room for the two nights.

"Fine by me," yawned Cordelia. "Oh God, I must have a shower. I feel so grubby after that drive, and I need something to wake me up. Okay if I use yours, Paddy?" Paddy nodded. Cordelia opened her holdall and raked around till she found her sponge-bag, then headed for the bathroom, promising to be as quick as possible.

"Another drink?" Paddy demanded. "You look as if you could use it. Quite a character, isn't she?"

"Wow," said Lindsay. "Just, wow. How do you expect me to sleep knowing she's only the thickness of a wall away?"

"You'll sleep all right, especially after another Brandy Alexander. And if you're really lucky, maybe you'll dream about her. Don't fret, Lindsay. You've got all weekend to make an impression! Now, just relax, listen to the music and don't try too hard."

With those words of wisdom, Lindsay had to be content until Cordelia returned, pink and glowing from her shower. She apologised for her lack of manners in dashing off. "If I hadn't taken drastic action, I'd have been sound asleep inside five minutes. Which would have been remarkably rude. Besides, I did want to talk," she added with a disarming grin, as Paddy announced that, since it was ten o'clock, she was going on her evening rounds of the house to check that all was well and everyone was where they should be. Left alone with Cordelia, Lindsay found herself at a complete loss. But Cordelia was too generous and perceptive to let the younger woman flounder, and before long they were talking avidly about the theatre, a shared passion. By the time Paddy returned half an hour later, Lindsay's nervousness had been subdued and the two were arguing with all the affectionate combativeness of old friends. Paddy was quickly absorbed into the conversation.

In the small hours of the morning, she eventually saw her two friends to their respective rooms and made a last circuit of the house before she headed back to bed. Cocktails and conversation had driven away her earlier fears about Lorna. But as she prowled the dark corridors on her own, her thoughts returned to the cellist. Somehow Paddy would have to make sure that Lorna's presence could not leave a trail of wreckage in its wake.

4

Lindsay was drifting in that pleasant limbo between sleep and wakefulness. A distant bell had aroused her from deep and dreamless slumber, but she was luxuriating in her dozy state and reluctant to let the dimly heard noises around her bring her up to full consciousness. Her drifting was abruptly brought to an end by a sharp knock on the door. Her nerves twitched with the hope that it might be Cordelia and she called softly, "Come in."

But the door opened to reveal a tall young woman carrying a tea-tray. She was wearing a well-cut tweed skirt and a fisherman's sweater which engulfed the top half of her body. "Good morning Miss Gordon," she said brightly. "Miss Callaghan asked me to bring your tea up. I'm Caroline Barrington, by the way, second-year sixth. This is my room. I hope you've been comfortable in it. It's not bad really, except that the window rattles when the wind's in the east." She dumped the tray on the bedside table and Lindsay struggled into a sitting position. Caroline poured out a cup of tea. "Milk? Sugar?" Lindsay shook her head as vigorously as an evening of Paddy's cocktails would permit.

Caroline walked towards the door, but before she reached it, she hesitated, turned and spoke in a rush. "I read an article in the *New Left* last month about women in politics—that was by you, wasn't it?" Lindsay nodded. "I didn't think there could be two of you with the same name. I enjoyed it very much. I was especially interested, you see, because I might go into politics myself after university. It's rather given me a boost to realise that there are other women out there with the same sort of worries."

Lindsay finally managed to get her brain into gear. "Thanks. Which party do you favour, by the way?"

Caroline looked extremely embarrassed, shifting from one foot to the other. "Actually, I'm a socialist," she said. "It's something of a dirty word round here. I just think that things ought to be changed—to be fairer. You know?"

Half an hour later, Lindsay felt she had been put through an intellectual mangle. Never at her best in the morning, she had had to struggle to keep one step ahead of Caroline's endless stream of questions and dogmatic statements about everything from student politics to the position of women in Nicaragua. Trying to explain that things were never as simple as they seemed without bruising the girls idealism or patronising her had not been easy, and Lindsay wished they'd been having the conversation over a cup of coffee after dinner, the time of day when she felt at her most alert. Finally, the buzz of a bell made Caroline start as she realised that this was neither the time nor place for such a discussion.

"Oh help," she exclaimed, leaping off the end of the bed where she had settled herself, "that's the breakfast bell. I must run. You don't have to worry—staff breakfast is pretty flexible, and Miss Callaghan's waiting to take you across. Blame me if she moans on at you about being late—I'm always in trouble for talking too much. See you later."

"Thanks for the tea, and the chat. Oh, and the use of your room. Maybe we'll have the chance to talk again. And if we don't, enjoy the weekend anyway," said Lindsay, wondering to herself how quickly she could manage to wash and dress. She almost missed Caroline's words as she dashed through the door.

"Sure. But don't ask me to join the fan club for our concert star." And she was gone, her footsteps joining the general background clamour that the bell had released.

Over a breakfast of scrambled eggs and mushrooms, Lindsay told Paddy about her early morning visitor. Paddy laughed and said, "She's full of adolescent fervour about the joys of socialism at the moment. She was always an idealistic child, but now she's found a focus, she's unstoppable. Her parents' marriage broke up last year, and I think we're getting a bit of referred emotion in the politics."

Lindsay sighed. "But she's not a child, Paddy, and her views are perfectly sound. Don't be so patronising."

"I'm not being patronising. But in a closed world like ours, I don't believe the opinions of one individual make a blind bit of difference."

Lindsay, who should have known better after six years' friendship with Paddy, allowed this red herring to set her off into a familiar fight about politics. It was an argument neither would ever win, but it still had the power to absorb. In spite of that, Lindsay found herself continually glancing towards the door. Paddy finally caught her in the act, grinned broadly and relented.

"She's not coming in for breakfast. She always does an hour's work first thing in the morning, then goes for a run. She even did it when we went on holiday to Italy four years ago. You won't see her much before ten-thirty, I'm afraid," said Paddy.

"What makes you think I'm looking for Cordelia?"

"Who mentioned Cordelia?" asked Paddy innocently. Lindsay subsided into silence while Paddy started reading her morning paper. Lindsay felt fidgety, but was not certain if this was simply because she was in an alien environment, or because of Cordelia's disturbing effect on her. She found herself studying the half-dozen or so other women at breakfast. Chris Jackson was deeply engrossed in a book about squash, and the two other women at her table were also reading. Lindsay's gaze moved to Margaret Macdonald who was sitting on her own. A magazine was open by her plate, but although she kept glancing at it, she was obviously not reading. She was not eating either, and the eggs and bacon on her plate were slowly congealing. A bright red sweater emphasised the lack of colour in her face. Every time someone passed her or entered the room, she started, and her eyes were troubled.

As they rose to leave, Lindsay quietly remarked, "She looks scared stiff."

"Nervous about tonight, I suppose. Who wouldn't be? There's a lot hanging on it," Paddy replied in an offhand way before bustling off to put her cast through their paces one more time before the afternoon's performance. Left to herself, Lindsay thought again about Margaret Macdonald. Paddy's explanation didn't seem to go far enough. Not knowing the woman, however, there was nothing Lindsay could do to find out what was troubling the teacher so.

She strolled back to Longnor House, revelling in the magnificent colours of the changing trees against the grey limestone and the greens and browns of the moorland surrounding the school. There were even patches of fading purple where the last of the heather splashed colour on to the bracken. Lindsay decided to run upstairs for her camera bag so she could take some photographs before the day became too crowded. After all, if she waited till the quiet of Sunday, she might miss the sunshine and the extraordinary clarity of the Derbyshire light.

A few minutes later, she was wandering through the grounds, pausing every now and again to change lenses and take a couple of shots. She took her photography seriously these days. It had started as a hobby when she'd been a student, and she had gradually built up an adequate set of equipment that allowed her to work on all sorts of subjects in most conditions. She had also picked the brains of every photographer she had ever worked with to the extent that she could now probably do the job as well as many of them. Her favourite work was portraiture, but she also enjoyed the larger challenge of a landscape. Now, looking at the contours of the land, she realised that a short scramble up the hillside would give her the perfect vantage point to catch the main building, its gardens, and the valley leading down to Buxton. Thankful that she was wearing jeans and training shoes, she began the steep climb up through the trees. After ten minutes' brisk walking, she was out of the woods and on top of a broad ridge. From there, it was all spread before her. She took several shots, then, just as she was about to descend, her eye was caught by a splash of colour and movement in a corner of the gardens. In a sheltered nook, invisible from the school, two women were standing. Lindsay recognised the vivid scarlet of Margaret Macdonald's sweater.

Hesitating only for a moment, she quickly grabbed her longest lens and slotted it into the camera body. She flicked the switch from manual to motor drive and set her legs apart to give herself more stability. Swiftly she focussed and began to shoot. She could see clearly who was with the teacher now. Margaret looked as if she was pleading with Lorna Smith-Couper, who suddenly threw her head back in laughter, turned and stalked off. The music teacher stood looking after her a moment, then stumbled blindly into the wood. Lindsay had been surreptitiously photographing people without their awareness or consent for a long time. Journalists called it "snatching." But for the first time she felt she had behaved shabbily—had in fact spied on what did not concern her.

Before she could ponder further on what she had seen, her attention was distracted once again. She had caught the flash of a running figure in the direction of the main gates. She swivelled round and could tell even at the distance of half a mile or so that the runner was Cordelia. She waited till Cordelia was nearer, then swung the camera up to her face again and steadily took a couple of pictures. Like the earlier photographs, they would be no great shakes as portraiture—they'd be too grainy for that. But as character studies, they'd do very well. Even the familiar barrier of the camera, however, could not distance Lindsay from the surge of emotion she felt at seeing Cordelia. There was nothing for it but to go back down the hill and hope the craft fair would bring the chance to talk to her. Lindsay knew that Paddy wouldn't be there this time to interrupt because she would be busy with her dress rehearsal. And she also knew that Cordelia would not be watching the run-through. One of the last things she had said to Paddy the night before was that she never attended rehearsals. "I always prefer to wait for the finished product," she had said. "Any changes or cuts I can sort out with the director. But I've served my time dealing with the bumptious, egocentric shower of know-alls that make up such a large part of the acting profession. There is one in every cast who always knows better than you how the damn thing should be written."

Her rich laughter echoed in Lindsay's memory as she scrambled quickly down the hillside. She noticed she wasn't as nimble as she used to be and resolved to start going to the gym again as soon as she got back to Glasgow. She was back in her room with twenty minutes to spare before the start of the craft fair. She had just slipped out of her jeans and into a skirt when there was a knock at her door. She called out permission to come in as she squeezed into a pair of court shoes, expecting Caroline to breeze in. But when the door opened, it was Cordelia who appeared.

"Hi there," she said. "I heard you come in as I was changing. Are you coming down to the hall to have a look round ahead of the hordes? The front drive's already filling up with cars. I suppose the locals can't resist the chance of a good poke around. Amazing how curious the great unwashed are about the supposed mystique of public schools."

"Yes, aren't we, though! That's part of the reason why I agreed to come. I feel extremely curious about how the other half is educated," said Lindsay wryly, smiling to take the sting out of her words.

"But you went to Oxford! Surely that must have given you some idea, even if you didn't have the misfortune to spend your childhood in one of these institutions," Cordelia remarked as they walked down the corridor.

"Yes, but by that stage, one is well on the way to being a finished product. You forget, I'd never come across people like you before. I wanted to see how young you'd have to catch kids before their assumptions and preconceptions become ingrained. How much comes from schooling and how much from a general class ethos imbibed at home along with mother's milk and Château Mouton Rothschild."

"And how much of what made you the woman you are comes from home rather than education?"

"I suspect about equal amounts from each. That's why I'm a mass of contradictions." By now they were walking through the woods and Lindsay was well into her stride. "Sentimental versus analytical, cynical versus idealistic, and so on. The only belief that comes from both home and education is that you have to work bloody hard to get what you want."

"And do you?"

"Sometimes—and sometimes."

They fell silent as they entered the main building, neither willing to pursue the conversation into more intimate areas. A large number of people were milling around the corridors, ignoring the arrows pointing them towards the main hall. Lindsay and Cordelia struggled through the crowds and nodded to the girls as they slipped into the hall. But even here there was no peace. All the stalls were laid out in readiness, and behind most of them schoolgirls were making last-minute adjustments to the displays. Lindsay looked around and from where she stood she could already see stalls of embroidered pictures, knitted garments, stained-glass terrariums and hanging mobiles, handmade wooden jigsaws and pottery made in the school's kiln. As Lindsay and Cordelia stood admiring a stall of patchwork, the senior mistress called out from her vantage point by the doors, "Two minutes, girls. Everyone get ready."

Lindsay had moved on to look at a display of wooden toys when she saw Chris Jackson hurrying through the hall. She made straight for Lindsay and spoke to her in a low voice. "Do you know where Paddy is?"

"She's rehearsing with the cast in the gym."

"No, they're having a half-hour break. I thought you might have seen her. I've got to get hold of her now."

"Hello, Chris, long time no see. Hey, what's up?" asked Cordelia, joining them.

"I've got one of the sixth in floods of tears behind the stage. She's just had a stand-up row with a couple of other sixth-formers. The girl is absolutely hysterical, and I reckon Paddy's the only one who can deal with her. There'll be chaos if we don't sort it out. And soon."

Immediately, Cordelia took control. She grabbed a couple of passing juniors and said, "I want you to find Miss Callaghan for me. Try Longnor, or her classroom or the staffroom. Tell her to come to us at the back of the hall as soon as possible, please." The girls scuttled off at top speed. "I wasn't Head of House for nothing," she added to the other two. "Wonderful how they respond to the voice of authority. I say, Chris, sorry and all that, I hope you didn't think I was trying to usurp you?"

"No, you were quite right. I lost my head for a moment when I couldn't find Paddy."

"But what on earth happened?" asked Cordelia, putting the question that Lindsay was longing to ask.

Chris said, "Sarah Cartwright's father is the developer who's trying to buy the playing fields. Apparently she said something about it being a real bore to have to give up Saturday morning games for this, and the others rounded on her and told her straight out that if it wasn't for her rotten father we wouldn't have to do it at all. That set the cat among the pigeons and it ended with Sarah being told that her classmates take a pretty dim view of what has happened; she's more or less universally despised, they informed her. So she's weeping her heart out. Paddy's the only one who can help; she's the only one that Sarah lets near enough. In spite of the fact that I spend hours in the gym with the girl, I may say.

"She's gymnastics mad. She wants to teach it, but you need temperament as well as talent for this job. Mind you, this is the first time I've seen her lose her cool. I'd better get back there now till Paddy comes, in case the girl makes herself ill. Besides, I've had to leave her with Joan Ryan, who is neither use nor ornament in a crisis."

"Do you want either of us?" asked Cordelia. "No? Okay, we'll wait here for Paddy and send her through to you as soon as she appears." At that moment, the doors opened and people surged into the hall, separating Lindsay from Cordelia. She saw Paddy arrive and be hustled off to the rear of the hall. It seemed to Lindsay as she browsed round the stalls that there was no need for Cordelia's play; there were altogether too many mini-dramas taking place already. So much for her quiet weekend in the country.

PART II

EXPOSITION

5

The play was an unqualified success, Cordelia had used the limitations of cast and sets and turned them into strengths in the forty-five minute play which dealt wittily, sometimes even hilariously, with a group of students robbing a bank to raise money for a college crèche. As the audience sat applauding, Cordelia muttered to Lindsay, "Always feel such a fraud clapping my own work, but I try to think of it as a way of praising the cast." There was no time for more. Even before Lindsay could reply, the young local reporter intent on reviewing the play was at Cordelia's side.

"Any other plans for this piece, Cordelia? Are we going to see it again?"

"Certainly are," she replied easily, switching the full glare of her charm on him. "Ordinary Women start rehearsing it in a fortnight's time. They're doing it for a month as half a double bill at the Drill Hall. Though I doubt if even they will be able to give it more laughs. That was a remarkable performance, wasn't it?" And she drifted off with the young man, giving Lindsay no chance to produce the detailed critical analysis of the play she had been preparing for the past five minutes.

She couldn't even discuss it with Paddy who, with her young cast, was surrounded by admiring parents and friends from the nearby towns. So she perched in a corner of the hall as

the audience filed out and scribbled some notes in her irregular
shorthand about events and her impressions. So far, she had no
clear idea of the shape her feature was going to take but, by
jotting down random thoughts, she could be reasonably sure
of capturing most of the salient points. She had also found that
this method helped her to find a hook for the introductory
paragraphs and, in her experience, once the introduction was
written, the rest fell neatly into place. The problem here was
going to be striking the right tone, she mused as she stared out
of the window into the afternoon sunlight. Beneath her was the
flat roof of the kitchen block, surrounded by a sturdy iron railing which enclosed tubs of assorted dwarf conifers. She admired
the mind that could appreciate details such as the decoration of
an otherwise depressing expanse of flat roof. Beyond the roof,
the woods stretched out, and she caught a glimpse of one of the
other buildings as the breeze moved the trees.

Lindsay was roused from her reverie by Cordelia's voice
ringing out over the public address system. "Ladies and gentlemen, please take your seats. The book auction is about to begin
and you really mustn't miss any of these choice lots."

The hall was filling rapidly again. Paddy wove through
the crowds and made her way to Lindsay's side. "We're doing
very well so far," she said. "And I recognise at least a couple of
book dealers among that lot, so perhaps we'll get some decent
prices. There are one or two real rarities coming up. Shall we
find ourselves a seat?"

Bidding was slow for the first few lots, all newish first editions by moderately successful writers. But it soon became brisk
as the quality began to improve. An autographed first edition
of T. S. Eliot's *Essays Ancient and Modern* fetched a very healthy
price, and a second edition of Virginia Woolf's *Orlando* with a
dedication by the author climbed swiftly and was bought for
an outrageous amount by the doting mother of one of Paddy's
fifth-formers. Paddy whispered in Lindsay's ear, "That woman
will try anything to get her Marjory to pass A level English."

Lindsay bid for a couple of items, but the things she really wanted were beyond her means. After all, she reasoned, it was crazy to spend more than she would earn this weekend on one book. Her resolution vanished, however, when it came to lot 68.

Cordelia grinned broadly and said, "Ladies and gentlemen, what can I say? A unique opportunity to purchase an autographed first edition of a priceless contemporary novel. *The One-Day Summer*, the first novel of Booker prize nominee, yours truly. A great chance to acquire this rarity. Who'll start me at a fiver?"

Lindsay thrust her arm into the air. "Five pounds I am bid. Do I hear six? Yes, six. Seven over there. Ten from the gentleman in the tweed hat. Eleven pounds, madam. Eleven once, eleven twice . . . twelve, thank you, sir. Do I hear thirteen? Yes, Thirteen once, thirteen twice, sold for thirteen pounds—unlucky for some—to Lindsay Gordon. A purchase you'll never regret, I may say."

An embarrassed Lindsay made her way over to the desk where the fourth-formers were collecting the money and wrapping the purchases. She didn't feel much like facing Paddy's sardonic grin right away, so she slipped down to the end of the hall by the stage and crossed through the heavy velvet curtains to the deserted backstage area where all the music rooms were situated. As she rounded the corner of the corridor, she saw Lorna Smith-Couper coming up a side corridor. The cellist did not notice Lindsay, because she was turning her head back to talk to someone coming round the corner of the corridor behind her. Without thinking, Lindsay slid through a half-open door and found herself behind the heavy backdrop of the stage. She could hear every word of the conversation in the corridor. Lorna Smith-Couper was speaking angrily.

"I don't know how you could have the nerve to put such a proposition to me. I may be many things, but shabby I'm not—and to let this place down now would be shabby in the extreme. You think money can buy anything. That's astonishing for a man your age."

The reply was muffled. But Lorna's retort came over loud and clear. "I don't care if your life depends on it, never mind your pathetic little business. I intend to play tonight and no amount of money is going to change my mind. Now, take yourself out of here before I have you removed. Don't think you've heard the last of this, I'm sure the world will be delighted to hear how you conduct your business affairs."

The man stormed off furiously down the corridor, past Lindsay's hiding place. She leaned against the wall, exasperated with the melodramatic excesses that the weekend seemed to be producing. All Lindsay wanted to do was to get inside the skin of this school to write a decent piece. But every time she thought she was making some headway, some absurdly histrionic confrontation spoiled her perspective. Either that or, as happened even as the thought came into her head, Cordelia Brown appeared out of nowhere and reduced her to a twitchy adolescent.

Cordelia had just finished the auctioneering and had decided to slip out through the backstage area and down the back stairs behind the music rooms. "Hey," she said when she saw Lindsay, "the only reason I came through this way was to avoid you journos. But here I am, caught again."

"Sorry, it's my nose for a scoop. I just can't help it. But I wasn't actually looking for you, honestly. Simply poking around," said Lindsay contritely.

"Don't apologise. I was only joking. You must never take me seriously; I'm incorrigibly frivolous. Lots of people hate me for it. Don't you be one, please." Cordelia smiled anxiously, yet with a certain assurance. She was sharp enough to see the effect she had on Lindsay, but was trying not to exploit it; she never found it easy to guard her tongue, however. "By the way," she went on, "what on earth possessed you to spend all that money on my book? I'd have given you a copy if you'd asked."

Lindsay mumbled, "Oh, I don't have the book—though I've read it of course. It seemed to be for a good cause at the time."

"Oh-oh, the young socialist changes her tune!" A glance at Lindsay's face was enough to make her add, "Sorry, Lindsay, I don't mean to be cheap. Look, hand it over and I'll stick a few words in it if you want."

Lindsay gave the book to Cordelia who fished a fountain pen out of her shoulder bag. Above the scrawled signature on the flyleaf, she scribbled something. Then she closed the book, embarrassed in her turn, said, "See you at dinner," and vanished down the side corridor where Lorna and the man had come from. Lindsay opened the book, curious. There she read, "To Lindsay. Who couldn't wait. With love." A slow smile broke across her face.

Twenty minutes later, she had changed into what she called her "function frock" for the evening's activities and was again firmly embedded in Paddy's armchair, clutching a lethal-tasting cocktail called Bikini Atoll, the ingredients of which she dared not ask. Paddy had relaxed completely since the previous evening. After all, she had argued to herself, the day had gone off well: much money had been raised and no one had so much as mentioned the word dope. Now she was gently teasing Lindsay about Cordelia before an early dinner. The meal had been put forward to six because of the evening's concert, and Cordelia bounced into Paddy's room with only ten minutes to spare. She looked breathtaking in a shiny silk dress which revealed her shoulders. She was carrying a shawl in a fine dark blue wool which matched her dress perfectly.

"Hardly right-on, is it, my dears?" she said as she swanned across the room. "But I thought I'd better do something to bolster the superstar image."

"We'd better go straight across; you've missed out on the cocktail phase, I'm afraid. We've been invited by my house prefects to sit with them tonight, so we'll be spared the pain of eating with dear Lorna," said Paddy.

"Terrific," said Cordelia. "I've managed to avoid her so far. If it weren't for the fact that she plays a heavenly cello, I'd give this concert a miss and make for the local pub for a bit of peace. Oh, by the way, Paddy, how is the Cartwright girl?"

As they walked through the trees, Paddy said that Sarah was feeling somewhat embarrassed after her earlier outburst. She had decided to go to bed early. "I popped up earlier with some tea and I'll take a look later on," said Paddy. "She's very overwrought. I worry about that girl. She keeps too much locked up inside herself. If she'd let go more often, she'd be much happier. Everything she does is so controlled. Even her sport. She always seems to calculate her every move. Even Chris says that she lacks spontaneity and goes too hard for perfection. I think her father is probably very demanding, too."

The subject of Sarah was dropped as soon as they entered the main building by the kitchen door. Cordelia remarked how little it had changed in the thirteen years since she had left. She and Paddy were deep in the old-pals-together routine by the time they arrived at the dining hall; it was only the presence of the Longnor House prefects and their friends which changed the subject. On sitting down to eat, Lindsay was immediately collared by the irrepressible Caroline who demanded, "Do you mostly work for magazines like *New Left*, then?"

Lindsay shook her head. "No, I usually write for newspapers, actually. There's not a vast amount of cash in writing for magazines—especially the heavy weeklies. So I do most of my work for the nationals."

"Do you write the things you want to write and then try to sell them? Is that how it works?"

"Sometimes. Mostly, I put an idea for a story to them and if they like it, either I write it or a staff journalist works on it. But I also work on a casual basis doing shifts on a few of the popular dailies in Glasgow, where I live now."

Caroline looked horrified. "You mean you work for the gutter press? But you're supposed to be a socialist and a feminist. How can you possibly do that?"

Lindsay sighed and swallowed the mouthful of food she'd managed to get into her mouth between answers. "It seems to me that since the popular press governs the opinions of a large part of the population, there's a greater need for responsible journalism there than there is in the so-called 'quality' press. I reckon that if people like me cop out then it's certainly not going to get any better; in fact, it's bound to get worse. Does that answer your question?"

Cordelia, who had been listening to the conversation with a sardonic smile on her face, butted in. "It sounds awfully like someone trying to justify herself, not a valid argument at all."

A look of fury came into Lindsay's eyes. "Maybe so," she retorted. "But I think you can only change things from inside. I know the people I work with, and they know me well enough to take me seriously when I have a go at them about writing sexist rubbish about attractive blonde divorcees. What I say might not make them change overnight but I think that, like water dripping on a stone, it's gradually wearing them down."

Caroline couldn't be repressed for long. "But I thought the journalists' union has a rule against sexism? Why don't you get the union to stop them writing all that rubbish about women?"

"Some people try to do that. But it's a long process, and I've always thought that persuasion and education are better ways to eradicate sexism and, come to that, racism, than hitting people over the head with the rule book."

Cordelia looked sceptical. "Come on now, Lindsay! If the education and persuasion bit were any use do you think we'd still have topless women parading in daily newspapers? I know enough journos to say that I think you're all adept at kidding yourselves and producing exactly what the editor wants. You're all too concerned about getting your by-line in the paper to have too many scruples about the real significance of what you are writing. Be honest with yourself, if not with the rest of us."

Her remarks had the salutory effect of injecting a little reality into Lindsay's attraction towards her and she scowled and
said, "Given how little you know about the work I do and my
involvement in the union's equality programme, I think that's a
pretty high-handed statement." Then, realising how petulant she
sounded, she went on, "Agreed, newspapers are appallingly sexist.
Virginia Woolf said ages ago that you only had to pick one up to
realise that we live in a patriarchal society. And the situation hasn't
changed much. But I'm not a revolutionary. I'm a pragmatist."

"Ho, ho, ho," said Cordelia hollowly. "Another excuse
for inaction."

But Caroline unexpectedly sprang to Lindsay's defence.
"Surely you're entitled to do things the way you think is best?
I mean, everybody gets compromises thrust upon them. Even
you. Your books are really strong on feminism. But that television series you did didn't have many really right-on women. I
don't mean to be rude, but I was . . ."

Whatever she was was cut off by Paddy interjecting sharply,
"Caroline, enough! Miss Brown and Miss Gordon didn't come
here to listen to your version of revolutionary Marxism."

Caroline grinned and said, "Okay, Miss Callaghan, I'll
shut up."

The conversational gap was quickly filled by the other girls
at the table with chatter about the day's events and the coming
concert.

As they finished their pudding, Pamela Overton came over
to their table. "Miss Callaghan," she said, "I wonder if I might ask
for your help? Miss Macdonald and the music staff are extremely
busy making sure that everything is organised for the girls' per-
formances in the first half of the concert. I wonder if, since you
seem to know Miss Smith-Couper, you could help her take her
cello and bits and pieces over to Music 2 so that she can warm up
during the first half?"

Paddy swallowed her dismay and forced a smile. "Of course,
Miss Overton."

"Fine. We'll see you in my flat for coffee, then. Perhaps Miss Gordon and Miss Brown would care to join us?" With that, she was gone.

Caroline sighed, "She's the only person I know who can make a question sound like a royal command."

"That's enough, Caroline," said Paddy sharply. The three women excused themselves from the table and walked through the deserted corridors to Miss Overton's flat, Paddy muttering crossly all the way. Fortunately, Lorna was in her room changing, so coffee was served in a fairly relaxed atmosphere. Miss Overton reported on the success of the day and revealed that, by the end of the evening, she hoped they would have raised over £6,000. Lindsay was impressed, and said so. Before anything more could be said, Lorna appeared and announced she was ready to go over to the music room. Paddy immediately rose and grimly followed her out of the room, as Pamela Overton apologetically revealed that she too would have to leave, to welcome her special guests. Lindsay and Cordelia trailed in her wake and made their welcome escape up to the gallery where they settled in among the sixth form and those of the music students who were not directly involved in the concert.

Cordelia said, "That woman makes me feel like a fifteen-year-old scruff-box, I'm so glad she wasn't head when I was here; if she had been, I'd have developed a permanent inferiority complex."

Lindsay laughed and settled down to enjoy the concert. In the hall below she saw Margaret Macdonald scuttling through the side door to the music rooms. Members of the chamber orchestra were taking their places and tuning up their instruments. Caroline and several other seniors were showing people to their seats and selling programmes which, Paddy had told Lindsay, had been donated by a local firm of printers. Caroline also slipped through the curtains, returning five minutes later with a huge pile of programmes. Cordelia leaned over and said to Lindsay, "I'm going to the loo, keep my seat," and off

she went. Lindsay absently studied the audience below, and
noticed a girl with a shining head of flaming red hair go up
to Caroline, who pointed to the door beside the stage. The
redhead nodded and vanished backstage. About eight minutes
later, she re-emerged with Paddy. They left the hall together.
"One damn thing after another," thought Lindsay "I wonder
what's keeping Cordelia?"

The lights went down and the chamber orchestra launched
into a creditable rendering of Rossini's string serenade No. 3.
Half-way through it, Cordelia slipped wordlessly into her seat,
Lindsay surfaced from the music and smiled a greeting.

Then the senior choir came on stage and performed a selection of English song throughout the ages, with some beautifully
judged solo work conducted by Margaret Macdonald. The first
half closed with a joyous performance of *Eine Kleine Nachtmusik*
and the audience applauded loudly before heading for the refresh-
ments. Lindsay and Cordelia remained in their seats.

Cordelia leaned over the edge of the balcony. Suddenly
she sat upright and said, "Hey, Lindsay, there's something going
on down there." Lindsay followed her pointing finger and saw
Margaret Macdonald rushing up the hall, looking agitated. The
velvet curtains were still swinging with the speed of her passage.
She headed straight for Pamela Overton and whispered in her
ear. The headmistress immediately rose to her feet and the two
women hurried off backstage.

"Well, well! I wonder what that's all about? Something
more serious than sneaking a cigarette in the loos, by the look
of it." As Cordelia spoke, the bell rang signalling the end of the
interval, and the audience began to return to the hall. Mean-
while, Miss Macdonald came scuttling back through the hall,
gathering Chris Jackson and another mistress on her way.

"Curiouser and curiouser," mused Cordelia. At that moment,
Pamela Overton emerged on to the stage. So strong was her presence that, as she stepped towards the microphone, a hush fell on
the hall. Then she spoke.

"Ladies and gentlemen, I am deeply sorry to have to tell you that Lorna Smith-Couper will be unable to perform this evening as there has been an accident. I must ask you all to be patient with us and to remain in your seats for the time being. I regret to inform you that we must wait for the police." She left the stage abruptly and at once the shocked silence gave way to a rumble of conversation.

Lindsay looked at Cordelia, who had gone pale. When she met Lindsay's eye, she pulled herself together and said, "Looks like someone couldn't stand any more of the unlovely Lorna."

"What do you mean?"

"Come on, Lindsay, you're the journalist. What sort of 'accident' means you have to stay put till the police get here? Don't you ever read any Agatha Christie?"

Lindsay could not think of anything to say. Around them, the girls chattered excitedly. Then Paddy came down the gallery to the two women. Her skin looked grey and old, and she was breathing rapidly and shallowly. She put her head close to theirs and spoke softly.

"You'd better get backstage and see Pamela Overton, Lindsay. We've got a real scoop for you. Murder in the music room. Someone has garrotted Lorna with what looks very like a cello string. Pamela reckons we should keep an eye on our journalist. You've been summoned."

Lindsay was already on her feet as Cordelia exclaimed, "What?"

"You heard," said Paddy, collapsing into Lindsay's seat, head in hands. "No reason to worry now, Cordelia. Dead women don't sue."

6

Lindsay hurried on down the hall, aware that eyes were following her. She pushed through the swathes of velvet that curtained the door into the music department. Uncertain, she listened carefully and heard a number of voices coming from the corridor where she had seen Lorna quarrelling with the unknown man earlier. She turned into the corridor and was faced with a door saying "Music Storeroom." The passage turned left, then right, so she followed it round and found Pamela Overton and another mistress standing by a door marked "Music 2." Beyond them was a flight of stairs.

Even in this crisis, Pamela Overton was as collected as before. "Ah, Miss Gordon," she said quietly. "I am afraid I have to ask another favour of you. I was not entirely truthful when I said there had been an accident. It looks as if Lorna has been attacked and killed. I don't quite know how the press operates in these matters, but it seemed to me that, as you are already with us, it might be simpler for us to channel all press dealings through you. In that way we might minimise the upheaval. Does that seem possible?"

Lindsay nodded, momentarily dumbstruck by the woman's poise. But her professional instinct took over almost immediately and she glanced at her watch. "I'll have to get a move on if I'm going to do anything tonight," she muttered. "Can I see . . . where it happened?"

Miss Overton thought for a moment then nodded. She walked to the door and, with a handkerchief round her fingers, delicately opened it, saying, "I fear I may be too late in precautions like this, since others have already opened the door. By the way, it was locked from the inside. The key was on the table by the blackboard. There was some delay while Miss Macdonald searched for the spare key."

Lindsay crossed the threshold and stood just inside the room. What she saw made her retch, but after a brief struggle she regained control. It was her first murder victim, and it was not a pleasant sight. She realised how wise she'd been to avoid it in the past when she'd reported on violent death. Then, there had always been someone else to take over that aspect of the job. But this time it was up to her, so she forced herself to look, and to record mentally the details of the scene. There had been nothing peaceful about Lorna Smith-Couper's end. She had been sitting on a chair facing the door, presumably playing her cello. Now she was slumped over her instrument on the floor, her face engorged and purple, her tongue sticking grotesquely out of her mouth like some obscene gargoyle. Round her neck, pulled so tight that it was almost invisible amidst the swollen and bruised flesh, was a wicked garrotte. It did indeed seem to be a cello string, with a noose at one end and a simple horn duffel-coat toggle tied on to the other end to enable the assassin to tighten the noose without tearing the flesh on his—or her—fingers.

Lindsay dragged her eyes from this horror and forced herself to look around with something approaching professional detachment. She noticed that all the windows were shut, but none of the casements appeared to be locked. Then she turned, revolted and overcome, and went back to the corridor. "Where can I find a quiet telephone?" she demanded.

"You'd be best to use the one in my study," said Miss Overton. "Ask one of the girls to show you the way. I must stay here till the police arrive. Is there anything else you need?"

"To be perfectly blunt, I need a comment from you, Miss Overton," Lindsay replied awkwardly.

"Very well. You may say that I am profoundly shocked by this outrage and deeply distressed by the death of Miss Smith-Couper. She was a very distinguished woman who reflected great credit on her school. We can only pray that the police will quickly catch the person responsible." With that, Miss Overton turned away. Lindsay sensed her disgust at the situation in which she found herself and understood it very well.

She walked back down the corridor towards the hall. Just before she re-emerged into the public gaze, she paused and took out her notebook. She leaned on the window ledge to scribble down the headmistress's words before her memory of them became inaccurate. For reasons which she didn't understand at all, she was more determined than usual to be completely precise in quoting the headmistress. Then she stared briefly out into the night. The last thing she had expected was to find herself caught up in a murder and part of her resented the personal inconvenience. She was also aware of her own callous selfishness as she thought to herself, "Well, this is really going to screw up any chance I might have had with Cordelia."

Then Lindsay pulled herself together, gave herself a mental ticking-off for her self-indulgence, reminded herself that as sole reporter on the spot she stood to make a bob or two and resolutely shoved the vision of the dead musician to the back of her mind. There would be time later to examine her personal feelings. She glanced up at the gallery, but Cordelia and Paddy were no longer there. Lindsay looked around her for a face she recognised and spotted Caroline half-way up the hall. She went over to her and asked to be shown the way to Miss Overton's study. Caroline nodded and set off at a healthy pace. Half-way down the stairs, she turned and said conversationally, "I say, not wishing to talk out of turn and all that, but what has happened to the Smith-Couper person? I mean, everyone staff-wise is running around in circles like a bunch of chickens with their heads cut off. What's all the fuss in aid of? And why are the police coming?"

"Sorry, Caroline, it's not for me to say. I'd like to tell you, but I'd be breaking a confidence."

"Oh, I see, grown-up conspiracies, eh? Anything to protect the kiddiewinks," the girl retorted, smiling.

Lindsay laughed in spite of herself. "Not quite. It's just that it's not right for me to pass on what I've been told in confidence." A little white lie, she thought, and that's not going to fool Caroline.

"I see. So you're not actually dashing to the phone to tell the world's press about murder most foul, then?" Caroline said mischievously. They had reached Pamela Overton's quarters, so Lindsay managed to avoid giving an answer by vanishing through the door indicated and into the study with only a word of thanks. Caroline shrugged expressively at the closed door then took herself off. Lindsay turned on a side-light and sat down at a desk which was fanatically tidy. All that adorned its surface was a telephone, a blotter and a large pad of scribbling paper. Lindsay pulled the paper towards her and roughed out two introductions. "A brutal murderer stalked a top girls' boarding school last night (Saturday). A star cello player was found savagely murdered as she prepared to give a concert before a glittering audience of the rich and famous," read the first, destined for the tabloids. The other, for the heavies, was, "Internationally celebrated cellist Lorna Smith-Couper was found dead last night at a girls' public school. Her body was discovered by staff at Derbyshire House Girls' School, just before she was due to perform in a gala concert." Then she jotted down a series of points in order of priority; "How found? When? Why there? Overton quote. No police quote yet."

Within minutes she was on to her first newsdesk and dictating her copy to one of those remarkably speedy typists who perform the inimitable and thankless task of taking down the ephemeral prose of journalists out on the road all over the world. It was well after ten when she finished. A good night's work, she thought, but tomorrow would be a lot tougher. She'd have to file copy again with more detail to all the dailies, and act as a liaison for Pamela Overton, her staff and the girls. And some time within the next few hours, she would somehow have to develop the roll of film in her camera. Someone would pay a good price for what were almost certainly the last photographs of the murder victim. She would, of course, have to crop Margaret Macdonald right out of the frame. No one wanted a photograph of an unknown music teacher.

She sat smoking at Pamela Overton's desk, using the waste-paper bin as an ashtray. She was strangely reluctant to return to the centre of events where a good journalist should be. The police would be here by now, and she would have to get a quote from the officer leading the investigation. But that could wait. The police would be too busy at present to be bothered with her questions. She was jotting down a few notes to herself about her course of action in the morning when there was a knock at the door. Before she could answer, it opened and Cordelia came in.

"I hoped I'd find you here," said Cordelia. "Paddy reckoned Pamela Overton would have sent you here to do your stuff. I'm not interrupting you, am I?"

"No, I'd just finished phoning copy over. It's debatable how much any of the newspapers will be able to use at this time of night. But the radio news will give it plenty of airtime, and I'm afraid that by tomorrow morning we'll have the whole pack of journos on the doorstep. And how Pamela Overton imagines I'm going to cope with that lot, I do not know," Lindsay replied wearily.

"Paddy says the boss will probably ask you to stay for a couple more days."

"Not beyond Monday, I'm afraid. I've got a dayshift on Tuesday on the *Scottish Daily Clarion*, and I can't afford to let them down since they are my major source of income at the moment. Still, tomorrow will be the worst, the fuss should have died down by Monday, especially if they make a quick arrest."

Cordelia sat down on the window seat and looked out into the darkness. She spoke quietly. "The police are here now. Going into their routines. They've got a batch of coppers on the door of the hall. Taking down the names and addresses of all the audience, and then letting them go off. They've pulled Paddy and Margaret Macdonald and Pamela Overton off to one side and a very efficient-looking Inspector is questioning them one by one. They'll be tied up for a while yet, I suspect. Another bunch of plainclothes men are questioning girls and staff. Anyone who's got anything interesting to contribute will no doubt be winnowed out and sent through to the Inspector. Pamela Overton still hasn't turned a hair. But then you probably guessed all that anyway."

Lindsay said nothing. She went over to the window and gave Cordelia a cigarette. She noted with a clinical eye that the hand that took it was shaking. Cordelia slowly smoked the cigarette. When it was burned half-way down, she gave a nervous laugh and said, "It's not always like this, you know. Most of the time it's pretty civilised. We don't go around killing old girls on a regular basis, no matter how obnoxious."

"I didn't for one moment think you did."

There was another pause. Then Cordelia said, "Lindsay— I've got to ask a favour. Or, rather, ask your advice."

"Ask away."

"You know when we were sitting together before the concert and I went off to the loo?" Lindsay nodded. "Well, I didn't only go to the loo. You probably noticed I was gone for quite a while. You see, I thought that just before the concert might be the best time to tackle Lorna. You know, I thought she'd have her mind on what she was about to do and might just be a little less vindictive than usual.

"I know one is supposed to leave all that wheeling and dealing to the lawyers, but I simply thought that a few words, woman to woman, appealing to the old better nature and all that, might do the trick and we could come to a civilised agreement that would avoid going to court."

Cordelia nervously stubbed out her cigarette. She ground it so fiercely that it broke and shreds of tobacco scattered in all directions. She went on, her voice rising. "I ducked down the stairs, through the ground floor, down to the back stairs beyond this flat. I knew she was in Music 2 and I knew I could get there without being seen. I went up and knocked on the door. There was no reply, so I tried the door handle. It was locked. There was nothing else I could do but come back. I swear that's all. I didn't hear a sound. I didn't call out to her or anything."

A sudden coldness gripped Lindsay's chest. With icy clarity she realised that she could be listening to a murderer laying down her first line of defence. But surely not Cordelia? Lindsay broke the silence that followed Cordelia's outburst, forcing herself to speak calmly and quietly. "You're going to have to tell the police. I think you knew that really."

"But nobody saw me. I'm sure of that."

"You can't be certain. At the very least, there must be other people in the gallery who saw you leave and return later. And remember, you tried the door. There's an outside chance that your prints are still on the handle, though that's been handled enough since to make that unlikely. Also, it is material evidence. At the time you say you knocked, it was all quiet in there. So presumably she was dead by then, or there would either have been music or some response from Lorna. You can't withhold evidence like that, Cordelia."

She put her hand on the other woman's shoulder. Cordelia gripped it tightly. "I'm afraid," she said. "I'm afraid they'll think I did it."

Lindsay replied quickly, trying to convince herself as much as Cordelia. "Don't be silly. How on earth could you have got into the room, killed Lorna and got back to your seat, having locked the door behind you, replaced the key and not shown the slightest sign of upheaval? At the very least you'd have been out of breath and I'd have noticed that. Besides, whoever killed her must have had the weapon ready, and you couldn't hide anything in that dress," she ended, realising even as she spoke that the garrotte could easily have been hidden in the music room in advance. But she desperately didn't want to consider seriously the proposition that a woman she'd fallen for could have murdered someone. So she wanted to offer what reassurance she could. When the police made any move towards Cordelia, that was the time to worry. Not before.

"Look, it's okay. Don't worry. Nobody could think for a moment that it was you. You've hardly got a motive, after all. Oh, I know dead women don't sue. But the case was by no means a foregone conclusion, and surely she would have come out of it at least as badly as you. At worst, it would have given the book a lot of publicity." Lindsay squeezed down on the seat beside Cordelia, who rested her head on Lindsay's shoulder.

She sighed and said, "You're right. I suppose I'll have to face them. Sorry, I'm not normally such a wimp. Oh God, I really don't want to go through with this. I wish I could just climb into bed and pull the covers over my head. Just sleep long enough for it all to go away."

"That's not really on, though, is it?"

"No. Instead, I've got to go and tell all to some tedious plod who will doubtless trip me up and proceed to arrest me for murder on the spot. Will you come with me?"

Lindsay nodded. "Of course. They'll not let me stick around while they take your statement, though, particularly with me being the resident hack."

Cordelia chuckled softly. "Oh no, they wouldn't want witnesses when they start pulling out my fingernails to get a confession." They both laughed, and the tension evaporated. Lindsay felt slightly hysterical with a mixture of jubilation that her doubts about Cordelia had vanished, and shock in reaction to the events of the past few hours. She got to her feet and Cordelia followed her out of the room.

On the way upstairs, Lindsay asked Cordelia, "Do you know if there's a darkroom in the school?"

"Yes. Some of the seniors do photography as a hobby. There's a little darkroom in the science block, over at the back of the tennis courts. Why?"

"I took a couple of candid camera shots of Lorna this morning when she was out walking. I was up the hill. I wanted to take a look at them to see if they were at all saleable. Mercenary to the last, you see."

"No, just professional."

"Not a professionalism to be proud of, particularly. However, it does keep the emotions at bay."

By then they had reached the doors of the hall. Most of the girls had left, but there was still a handful of staff members and a few of the girls Lindsay recognised as ushers and programme sellers. When they entered, Chris Jackson looked up and beckoned them over. They sat down on either side of her, a little way off from the nearest schoolgirls.

"How is it progressing?" asked Lindsay.

"Quite quickly, considering. They've finished with the head and Paddy, but Margaret's still in there. A lesser copper is interviewing the others—a 'preliminary chat,' he says. They'll be back tomorrow for more, I gather. At least they've got the decency to see everyone here instead of dragging us all down to the nick. The young copper's got Caroline Barrington in there just now. I know who I feel sorry for, and it's not Caroline." Chris's nervous chatter suddenly ground to a halt.

"I want to have a word with one of the boys in blue," said Cordelia, trying to appear nonchalant but failing. "How long is she likely to be?"

Just then, Caroline bounced into the hall, calling out, "Next please for the Spanish Inquisition."

"That girl is impossible," said Chris, exasperated. "Why don't you go in now? That way, you and Lindsay can get off back across to Longnor at the first opportunity. Paddy asked me to say she'd see you over there. She's gone back to try to get the girls into some sort of order. Most of them seem to be behaving remarkably well, but one or two are going right off their trolleys." Cordelia nodded and went off, Lindsay calling, "Good luck," softly after her. Cordelia disappeared through the swing doors with a nervous smile.

"Quite an upset," Lindsay remarked, realising as she did so the banality of her words.

"Horrific, Lindsay, absolutely horrific. As soon as word of this gets out, there will be a mass exodus of girls from the school. If James Cartwright doesn't close us down, this certainly will," said Chris Jackson sadly.

"It certainly closed Lorna Smith-Couper down," said Lindsay drily.

"Oh, don't think I'm being callous. But I never knew the woman, so it would be hypocritical of me to pretend I'm heartbroken about her death. What worries me is that no one seems to be able to work out quite how it was done. I mean, from what I can gather—though we probably shouldn't be gossiping about it—there's no question of it being an outsider. It had to be someone who knew the layout of the building. I hope to God they clear it up quickly. I mean, no responsible parent would leave their child at a school with a homicidal maniac on the loose, now would they?"

Lindsay changed the subject as diplomatically as possible and managed to get Chris chatting casually for a while about other topics. They were interrupted by Caroline, who breezed up to them, excusing herself perfunctorily. "I was wondering, Miss Jackson, could we beetle off back to Longnor now? The coppers have seen all the girls from the houses; it's only main building girls who are left. And Miss Callaghan said we shouldn't come back on our own. I suppose it's in case we get bumped off *en route*. So can you or Miss Gordon take us across?"

Chris looked a question at Lindsay, who nodded, "Of course I'll go back with you. If you don't mind waiting a few minutes till Miss Brown is finished with the police, then we'll all go together."

"Fine, that's that solved at least," said Chris, "Now if you'll excuse me, I'll just go and check there are no girls hanging about in the music department. Thanks, Lindsay."

She strode off, leaving Lindsay once more with the effervescent Caroline. Nothing, not even murder, seemed to take the bounce out of her. "How did you get on with the police?" Lindsay asked quickly, hoping to avoid diving deep into dialectical dialogue.

"Oh, they were okay. I was surprised. I expected them to be a lot heavier. They asked all the questions you'd expect. About who was where and when, and if I'd been down to Music 2. I told them I'd only been as far as the storeroom for more programmes and that I didn't see a sausage. Mind you, I told them they'd probably find no shortage of people with axes to grind about Lorna Smith-Couper, judging by the stories you hear. That woman left a trail of human wreckage in her wake. Not entirely surprising that someone finally did her in, really," she said, barely pausing for breath.

"What makes you say that?" asked Lindsay, more to pass the time than from any strong curiosity. But before Caroline could elaborate any further, the double doors swung open and Cordelia appeared, looking drained but relieved. There was nothing in Lindsay's world at that moment except concern for Cordelia. She immediately rose and went to her. "Okay?"

Cordelia nodded. "Tell you later," she said, as Caroline found her way to their sides.

"Can we go now?" she asked. "Only, we're all dying for a coffee."

Lindsay nodded and briefly explained the situation to Cordelia as Caroline shouted, "Okay, anyone for Longnor, Axe, Goyt, Wildboarclough. Come now or face the psychopath alone."

Half a dozen girls peeled off from the group and followed Lindsay and Cordelia out into the back drive and down the well-lit path through the woods to the houses. As they left the main building behind, Lindsay glanced back at the window of the room where Lorna had been killed. A light still burned at the window as the police scene-of-crimes officers worked on. Something was nagging at the back of her mind, but she dismissed at once any idea that the killer could have come through the window. Only a chimpanzee could have made that climb without being instantly visible from the hall or the music corridor. She turned back, and followed the file of chattering girls, headed by Cordelia and Caroline who were already deep in animated conversation.

7

Having seen their charges safely stowed, Lindsay and Cordelia escaped to Paddy's sitting-room. Lindsay headed straight for the gas fire and warmed her hands, while Cordelia made for the cocktail cabinet.

"I don't suppose Paddy would mind if we fixed ourselves a drink," she said. "I could certainly use one." She tried the door. "Damn! It's locked."

Lindsay stood up. "She keeps it locked when she's not here. I noticed her unlocking it last night. I suppose there's always the chance that it might get raided by some adolescent alcoholic. I've got an Islay malt upstairs in my bag if you fancy that."

"If that's some kind of whisky, yes please, I feel the need for some calming alcohol. Say, a couple of bottles for starters!"

Lindsay smiled to herself as she went to collect the drink. When she returned, she found Cordelia crouched by the fire, shivering. She immediately went over to her and put an arm round her shoulders.

"Silly, really. I can't stop shivering. Must be reaction. Be an angel and fix me a drink, would you? Water in it, please, about the same amount as whisky."

Lindsay went through to the kitchen and poured out the two drinks, mentally scoring another plus point to Cordelia for drinking her whisky properly—in other words, as Lindsay preferred it. Cordelia followed her and took her tumbler gratefully. She gulped down a large slug of whisky and water, shuddered convulsively as the fire in the peaty spirit hit her, then relaxed.

"Better?" asked Lindsay.

"Much. Let's go back into the warm."

They sat on opposite sides of the fireplace. Lindsay offered her a cigarette and they both lit up. "Thank you," sighed Cordelia. "Not just for the cigarettes and whisky. Thanks for making me pull myself together earlier on. You were right; it was foolish even to think of any other course of action. I was in a state of shock, I suppose. I couldn't believe I was off the hook about the libel suit, and I simply didn't want to involve myself in Lorna's death at all. I panicked.

"I felt sure I'd be the prime suspect—you know, one sees and reads so much that makes the police look both bent and stupid that one comes to believe that every encounter with them will inevitably end in disaster.

"But it wasn't too bad at all. I mean, they were actually quite reasonable, when you consider that I must be one of their suspects. The detective sergeant took my statement and asked me not to leave the school premises until the Inspector has had the chance to interview me in the morning." She smiled wanly. "He also told me, very politely, that there will be a police guard on the main gate. 'To keep out undesirables,' he said, though I suspect it's more to keep us in."

Lindsay was about to question Cordelia more closely when Paddy came in. She greeted them with a brief, "Hi," and headed for the drinks cupboard.

"Three minds with but a single cliché," said Lindsay. "If you're going to expose us to murder on a regular basis, Paddy, you'll have to give us a spare key to the booze cupboard."

"Oh God, I'm sorry," groaned Paddy. "Have one now?"

"We're all right, thanks," said Cordelia, "Lindsay has come to the rescue for the second time this evening. She does a good impersonation of the US Cavalry. I'll have to make her a permanent feature at this rate."

"Drinks, fags and a shoulder to cry on. All part of the service," Lindsay replied, trying to cover her blushes.

Paddy sprawled out on the couch, clutching a large brandy. "What a bloody day," she complained and then fell silent.

"How did you get on with the local constabulary?" Cordelia asked, "I found them remarkably pleasant, in spite of my having to confess to being on the spot during what seems to be the crucial period."

"Were you? Well, if you were there after I left her, they've probably crossed you off their list already. I seem to be the odds-on favourite at the moment. If they knew I had the shred of a motive, I'd probably be under arrest by now," Paddy replied, bitterness in her voice.

"Why is that?" asked Lindsay.

"Because nobody admits to seeing her, speaking to her or even hearing her warm up on her cello after I took her up there. I showed her up to the room and went in with her to make sure she had everything she needed. I took the opportunity to thank her for keeping her mouth shut about the circumstances of our previous acquaintance. She smiled like a fox and said she saw no reason so far to break her silence, but she'd have to consider the good of the school."

Paddy sighed deeply and went on. "I left it at that and took off. I was around the backstage area till right before the concert when Jessica Bennett came to fetch me because one of the fifth form in Longnor was sick and Jess didn't want the responsibility of dealing with it. By the time I got back, the first half was in full swing, so I went straight backstage again via the back stairs to avoid disturbing the audience.

"So I'm there. For all they know, I might have had a reason for murdering her, and I had a better chance than anyone else of getting to her. Because, you see, she locked the door behind me as I left. She said she wanted to be sure of getting some peace."

"But if you're supposed to have done it, how do they think you got the key on the table through a locked door?"

"There's a spare key in Margaret Macdonald's room, which was unlocked all evening. The key for Music 2 wasn't where it should have been, either. Whoever put it back last put it on the wrong hook. But it could have been like that for weeks because those keys were hardly ever used. On the other hand, I or almost anyone else could have done it tonight. Everyone was milling around backstage. I doubt if anyone could positively say I didn't slip into Margaret's room."

There was a moment's chill silence. Then Lindsay spoke with quiet excitement. "But there would be no point in you killing Lorna while she was at the school. Not just to silence her. Her murder will surely mean the end of the school's chances of raising the money for the playing fields. It's bound to mean hard times or even closure for the school itself, so you won't have a job in any event."

"Agreed. But the police wouldn't necessarily see it like that," Paddy argued. "After all, if I felt sufficiently threatened, I wouldn't necessarily think things through to their logical conclusion."

That set the three of them off in a discussion about motive. Lindsay put forward her line of argument, but Cordelia countered that, in the heat of the moment, the murderer could well have panicked and seen no further than the immediate, short-term benefit.

There was a deep hush, broken by Cordelia's forced cheerfulness as she said, "But there must be others besides you—and to a lesser degree, me—who were on the spot and have reasons for hating Lorna. Let's face it, she'd never have won a popularity contest, would she?"

"That's right," said Lindsay, "Caroline Barrington seems to have hated her guts—and seems to think there were others in the same boat."

"I can imagine people hating, but I can't imagine anyone killing her," said Paddy dubiously. "Not killing her."

"Well, what about this property developer?" asked Cordelia. "It would definitely be in his interest to get rid of Lorna and discredit the school in the process."

"He wasn't there tonight," said Paddy. "They're still going to find me firm favourite if they come up with a motive."

"But we've come up with Caroline and the property developer guy in just a few minutes and we scarcely know the people involved," Lindsay protested, alarmed by her friend's defeatism. "There have got to be others. Listen, I heard someone having an argument with Lorna only this afternoon. I don't know who it was, but they were going at it hammer and tongs."

"What about?" demanded Cordelia.

"I don't really know. He wanted her not to play at the concert or something and she wasn't having any."

"You should tell the police about that," Cordelia urged.

"Yeah, I'll get round to it when I see the Inspector tomorrow," Lindsay replied. "So that's another one to add to the list. And if we're talking about people who knew the terrain and had access to keys and cello strings, what about Margaret Macdonald? She's seemed really uptight all weekend."

"She wouldn't hurt a fly," said Paddy positively. "I know the woman; God damn it, if anyone is incapable of murder, it's Margaret."

"No one is incapable of murder," said Lindsay vehemently. "This particular murder may just have been the one that she was capable of."

And they were off again. None of them seemed to be able to hang on for long to the idea that this was a real murder. None of them was willing to face the fact that, once the first horror had worn off, there would be fear, suspicion and isolation left. No one seemed keen to make the first move towards bed, afraid, perhaps, of sleeplessness and speculation in the early hours.

It was after two when they reluctantly decided to end their talk. Paddy went off to make her last checks of the house, having promised to wake Lindsay early and take her across to the darkroom so she could process her film.

Cordelia and Lindsay sat in a companionable quiet, broken only by the hiss of the gas fire. Finally, Cordelia got to her feet and stretched languidly. "I'm off," she said. "You coming now or staying up a bit?"

"I'll be up in a little while. I'll have one last smoke before I get my head down."

"Okay. See you in the morning. And thanks—again."

"Don't mention it. It was little enough."

"One day, when all this horrible business is over, I shall cook you a special banquet as a thank you. I'm famous among my friends for my cooking, I promise you."

"I'll look forward to that."

"Goodnight, then." And she was gone, leaving Lindsay alone to stare into the fire and conjure her own dreams out of its flickering light. It was very late indeed when she finally climbed the long stairs to her bed.

⚜

Sunday dawned dull and misty on Axe Edge. Lindsay shivered as the raw cold bit through her jacket when she and Paddy emerged from the warmth of Longnor House at a quarter to eight. They were both silent on their walk through the trees, wrapped up in their own thoughts. Paddy unlocked the science block and led Lindsay to a compact but well-equipped darkroom on the first floor.

"There you are," she announced. "Hope you've got everything you need. I'll leave the keys so you can lock up after yourself. Sorry it's so cold in here; we always turn off the heating in this block at lunchtime on Saturday. How long will you be?"

"Half, three-quarters of an hour? No longer."

"Okay. I'll see you in my rooms at around half-past eight, then." Paddy left her curiously illuminated by the black-out lighting.

Lindsay quickly checked the light-proofing, then started work on her film. She pulled it from its cartridge and shoved it into the tray of developer she had laid out. She moved it round, then put it into the fixer, washed it, and snapped on a lamp to look at it more closely. Even in an unfamiliar darkroom she worked swiftly and efficiently, slotting the frames one by one into the enlarger, fumbling the photographic paper out of its light-proof envelope, and then exposed her prints. Half an hour later, she was looking at a dozen prints of Lorna Smith-Couper with her head thrown back in laughter.

It was not a bad picture, thought Lindsay. Though it was rather grainy, it would still reproduce quite well. It didn't look too much like an unauthorised snatch.

She had also printed a couple of copies of the full frame with Margaret Macdonald in profile looking remarkably upset— almost on the verge of tears, Lindsay thought. And, for her own amusement, she had printed up the shots she had taken of Cordelia. They were not particularly flattering, but they were good likenesses and very different from the other, posed photographs she had seen. There was a grittiness and determination in the face that casual acquaintance with Cordelia gave no hint of. Lindsay smiled to herself and cleared up. She let herself back out into the woods, carefully checking that all doors were locked behind her.

She slipped upstairs and sorted out the photographs. The ones of Lorna she put into a large envelope scrounged from Paddy, the others she put straight into her bag. Then she went downstairs to join Paddy.

"Mission accomplished," she said.

"Good," Paddy replied. "Pamela Overton has just been on the phone. She's already had two calls from newspapers and has told them that you're the only journalist who will be given any co-operation by the school, also that you'll be supplying a story later today. She would like you to have breakfast with her, and after that she's arranged for you to speak to Inspector

Dart—he's the one we all saw last night; he's running the show as far as I can see."

That was the last minute of peace Lindsay had all day. Breakfast with Pamela Overton was sticky and uncomfortable for both of them, and afterwards, Lindsay felt she had been professionally stalled on every question apart from the purely superficial. She did know for sure that the fund-raising would go on and that Pamela Overton was anxious to get across the message that she was convinced it was the work of an outsider and that none of the girls was in danger. But that was all Lindsay had gathered in terms of fresh information.

She walked slowly up to the hall where the police had taken over a small classroom and asked a uniformed constable if she could have a word with the officer in charge. After a brief wait she was ushered in. Over by the window, a young plain-clothes officer was sitting at a desk with a sheaf of paper around him. Behind the teacher's desk stood a tall lean man whose face would have been handsome were it not for a mass of old pitted acne scars. He looked in his mid-forties, with greying sandy hair and sleepy grey eyes at variance with his sharp features and lined face.

Lindsay introduced herself and he looked keenly at her over the bowl of a pipe he was lighting. When he spoke, his voice was rich and slow. "I'm Inspector Roy Dart," he said. "I'm running this investigation. What are you after?"

"Miss Overton has asked me to handle press liaison for her. I'll be putting out copy to all the dailies later on today, so I would appreciate anything you're in a position to give me."

"I'll not be saying anything to you that I won't be saying to any reporter who picks up a phone and calls me. You get no special favours here, I'm afraid. And I expect information to be a two-way street, understood? Anything you dig up that I should know about, I want to hear from you, not read in the papers. Now, officially you can say we are treating Lorna Smith-Couper's death as murder. We are pursuing several promising avenues of inquiry."

With an air of finality, he picked up some papers from the desk. Lindsay refused to accept dismissal and asked, "Do you anticipate a quick arrest? Obviously, with a school full of young girls, there's a lot of anxiety about a murder like this . . ."

"We're doing everything in our power to bring this matter to a swift conclusion. There are policemen on the school premises at all times and I do not expect any further incidents," he retorted forcefully. "The girls are being looked after properly. Rest assured on that point. Now, if there's nothing else?"

This time the dismissal was explicit. Lindsay moved towards the door. Just as she was about to leave, she turned and tried again. "Off the record, I take it you expect to mop it up soon?" She smiled warmly.

She might as well have saved her charm for Cordelia, where it could have done her some good. Dart looked up from under his eyebrows and said, "You're wasting your time, Miss Gordon. Don't waste mine."

Lindsay walked back down to Pamela Overton's study ruefully, thinking of all the reasons why she hated having to be polite to senior police officers. The headmistress had left the study free for Lindsay to work in, and she started putting together a holding story that she could send out early to the wire services for the radio news bulletins. She noticed with a wry smile that an ashtray had appeared since the night before. She made a couple of attempts to speak to Margaret Macdonald, to inject a bit of colour into her story, but the music mistress steadfastly refused to say anything, pleading pressure of work.

She phoned over a factual piece to several papers, promising more material later. Then she set about trying to sell the dramatic last pictures of Lorna. The first paper she rang didn't want to know because of the price she was asking, but the next tabloid she rang seemed keen.

"They're the last pics taken of her, and I'm offering them exclusive," she explained.

The picture editor at the other end of the phone spoke with all the false enthusiasm of his breed. "That's terrific. What do the pics show?"

"The murdered woman is standing in the garden of the school where she was killed. She's laughing in a couple of them, and there's one pic of her just straight-faced. The laughing ones are a good line to go for—carefree musician enjoying a joke unaware that within twelve hours she'll be dead; that sort of routine. I can let you have a deep caption to go with it, say five or six paras," persuaded Lindsay.

"Who took these, then? What's the quality like?"

"I took them with a telephoto zoom. They're a bit grainy, but they'll reproduce all right."

There was a pause. "And you've got them to yourself? What sort of price are we looking at?"

"Two hundred fifty pounds seems reasonable to me."

"Including syndication rights?"

"I suppose you've got to get your money back somehow."

"It's a deal, then. Two-fifty. How are you getting them to us?"

"I'll put them on a train to Manchester. Your desk there can pick them up, can't they?"

"Sure thing. Phone them and let them know what train they're on. Thanks again, Lindsay."

She called a taxi to take her down to the station. As soon as she put the phone down, it pealed. She picked it up to hear a crime reporter baying for details. Four months ago she would gladly have given him all she had. But her brief spell as a freelance had taught her the hard fact that staff reporters don't do favours to anyone except themselves. The only way she could be sure of making her information work for a living was to keep it to herself. As she put the phone down after a heavy exchange, she sighed. Another potential ally lost for a while. She was pleased when the taxi arrived for the small oasis of calm the trip to the station provided in the chaos of the day.

Back at the desk, she got to work again. Lunch and dinner were snatched meals eaten from a tray in the study. The desk had lost its formal tidiness. Now it was covered with scribbled sheets of paper as Lindsay drafted out the various versions of the story tailored to each paper. Used coffee cups and cigarette packs added to the general clutter. She had escaped from the smoke-filled room a couple of times to collect some quotes for her stories. But for the rest of the day she was confined to the study, with a phone jammed to her ear for most of the time. Paddy stuck her head round the door a couple of times to make sure she had everything she needed, but it was after nine before she could call a halt to her work on the "mystery killer grips school with fear" stories for the next morning's papers.

She walked back alone through the woods to Paddy's room without giving a thought to the lurid prose she had despatched about the hand of terror that made schoolgirls go everywhere in groups. She found Cordelia watching the television news and sipping brandy. "What's happening, then, ace reporter?" she demanded.

"Police have gone home for the night, leaving the statutory constable to repel boarders, journos and ghouls. No arrest has been made. No one has been held for questioning. They have been taking statements all day and as yet are not in a position to make any comment. Several parents are arriving tomorrow to remove offspring. James Cartwright is unavailable for comment. The body has been removed and the music room sealed. The funeral will be on Thursday in London, with a memorial service to be arranged. Cause of death thought to be asphyxiation. Or whatever it is when you are garrotted. End message," Lindsay rattled off.

"Looks as though you've had a busy day."

"You're not wrong. What about you?"

"I had a brief chat with the charming Inspector Dart who doesn't seem terribly interested in me except in so far as I seem to provide an end point in his timetable. He seems to think she was dead by then. Since which time, I have been sitting around reading Trollope and avoiding human contact like the plague, apart from dear Paddy who looks more harassed with every hour that passes. She's at a staff meeting just now, they're all wondering what the hell to do next. I just wish the bloody police would get a move on and arrest the bloody murderer," said Cordelia, trying unsuccessfully to force some lightness into her voice.

"Are you leaving tomorrow?"

"I should really. I'm supposed to have lunch with my agent, and I've already put her off once. I'm torn, I must admit, between hanging on to see if I can be of any help and wanting to put as much distance as possible between me and the school. I expect I'll go, though. Good agents are hard to find! What about you? Heading back tomorrow?"

Lindsay shrugged. "I'm aiming to get a train about three at the latest, so I can be back in Glasgow at a decent time of night. Then I'm going to get well pissed in my local. Put all of this out of my mind."

"You seem to be doing that rather well anyway," Cordelia commented drily.

"What do you mean?" asked Lindsay indignantly.

"Well, I couldn't have sat on the end of a phone all day rattling off sensational stories about Lorna's murder. I don't know how you can be so cool about it."

Lindsay shook her head, disappointed. "It's the job I do. I've been trained to forget my feelings and do the business. And I do it very well. Don't think I've enjoyed today."

"That's exactly what I do think. You came in here like you were coming off a high. Like you'd got a real buzz from doing the business, as you call it. I find that very strange, quite honestly."

The remark stung Lindsay, who was not about to admit its truth. She took a deep breath and said angrily, "Look, Cordelia, at the end of the day, I have to make a living. Lorna's murder cost me money, to be brutal about it. The feature I was supposed to write would have cleared me a hundred fifty pounds. Now,

I've got to earn myself at least that this weekend otherwise things start happening in my life that don't appeal to me. Like the phone gets cut off. Like I can't afford to have the car exhaust repaired so I can't work. I didn't know Lorna, so I'm not personally devastated by her death. By doing what I'm doing, I do myself the favour of earning a bit. I'm also doing the school a favour. Make no mistake about it, whether I supply the raw copy or not, all the papers are going to have their sensational stories. But at least this way, we know they're getting accurate copy to start with. And if they get it wrong, well, Pamela Overton knows who to blame and where to find me.

"It's easy to criticise the job I do, but most people never have to make the moral decisions I take as a way of life. And whatever they may think, few of them would make a better job of it than me. I could have a go at you about the anti-feminist slant of your telly scripts. But that's none of my business because I don't know the pressures on you. Until you understand the pressures on me, don't knock me."

Cordelia looked stunned by the onslaught. "I didn't realise you were so sensitive about it," she said huffily. Conversation died there. They both pretended to watch television, each reluctant to bridge the gap and swallow her pride. Eventually Lindsay rose and poured a drink. "I'm taking this up to bed with me," she announced. "I feel like flopping with a good book and trying to forget the day I've had."

"Okay. Listen, Lindsay—I may not get much chance to talk to you tomorrow because I'll probably be off about nine. I haven't forgotten that meal I promised you. So when are you likely to be in London next?"

Lindsay shrugged. "I don't know. I've no firm plans. It's hard for me to take a weekend off because Sundays especially are good days for me and I can't really afford to turn down work at the moment. But I'd like to come down soon and see some magazine editors—I give myself till the end of the month to get organised. That'll probably be in the middle of the week."

"That's no problem for me. I can easily arrange my work schedule to fit round your visit. Do you have somewhere to stay?"

"I've got friends in Kentish Town I usually stay with."

"Well, if you're stuck, you're welcome to stop over at my place. I've got plenty of room and it's good to have company."

"Thanks," Lindsay said shyly. "I might take you up on that." There was an awkward pause. "Well. Goodnight, Cordelia."

"Goodnight. Sleep well."

In the morning, Lindsay again breakfasted with Pamela Overton. She was nervous about the encounter, having risen early and made a trip into Buxton in Paddy's Land Rover to pick up a full set of the morning papers. Most of the tabloids, being a little short on alternative tales of shocking horror, had gone to town on Death at Derbyshire House. But Lindsay was put at her ease at once by Pamela Overton's praise for her efficient and unobtrusive work.

"I can't pretend that I particularly enjoyed the sensational aspect given to the story by most of the newspapers," she remarked, "but I do realise how much more difficult things would have been for us if we had had to deal with a whole battery of reporters. As it is, we have managed to keep them all out of the school, thanks to the joint efforts of yourself and the police, and have retained some measure of control over the stories that have appeared. I am only sorry that you can't stay longer to defend us, but Miss Callaghan has explained the position to me, and I do realise that you have commitments you must stick to. I want to say again how grateful we are, and if ever I can be of any help to you, don't hesitate to let me know."

Lindsay went on to ask about the future of the school and the playing fields fund. The headmistress looked troubled for the first time since Saturday's horrors.

"I am very much afraid that we'll have to give up the idea of saving the playing fields—and concentrate instead on saving the school. Already, seventeen girls are being withdrawn, and I fully expect more to follow. One can scarcely blame the parents.

I hope the police will deal swiftly with this business so we can reassure parents that their girls are in safe hands. I care about this school, Miss Gordon. I very much hope that we shall not be destroyed by what has happened."

Lindsay felt the strength of the other woman's determination, and it stayed at the back of her mind as more than just an angle for the news story of the day while she went for a walk on the ridge that Monday morning. She looked down on the privileged panorama of Derbyshire House Girls' School and resented the fact that Pamela Overton had infected her with her determination. She knew that whether she liked it or not, she, too, was in some degree involved with the school. She realised that in spite of herself she cared what happened to it.

8

Few assignments appealed less to Lindsay than royal visits. To be stuck with the rest of the pack, trailing behind some lesser scion of a monarchy she despised, festooned with badges of different colours to tell the security guards where one could and couldn't go, was not her idea of a good day's work. And as a common freelance she could not even complain as bitterly as the rest of the press were doing, for she was glad of a day's work, tedious though it might be. And on that Tuesday, tedious it certainly was, particularly after the excitements of her weekend in Derbyshire. A children's hospital, an art exhibition and a new youth club on a housing estate had all been superficially visited and the correct rituals observed. The photographers had taken their pictures, the reporters had scrambled their words together, everyone had kept in their rightful places. So, as she stood watching the royal jet take off through the rain in the late afternoon, Lindsay felt an enormous sense of relief. Another day, another dollar.

She said goodbye to her photographer and found a phone. It was after five by the time she had finished dictating copy, but she was nevertheless surprised when the newsdesk told her not to bother coming into the office for the last couple of hours of her shift and to call it a day. "See you tomorrow, then," she said, quickly putting down the phone before they could change their minds. There was a spring in her step as she walked over to the car park and climbed into her MG. Being in love made a difference, she thought wryly. Even with a possible murderer.

Twenty minutes later she was unlocking the front door of her top-floor tenement flat. She sighed with pleasure as she closed the door behind her. There was something on the answering machine, she noticed, but she ignored it, went through to the living-room and poured herself a generous whisky. She took her glass over to the window, sat down and lit a cigarette as she gazed over the trees to the distant university tower which stabbed the skyline to her left. She always relished returning to her eyrie, and loved the view that had nothing to do with the Glasgow of popular mythology; that hard, mean city composed of razor gangs and high-rise slums was not the city that most Glaswegians recognised as their home. Sure, there were bits of the city that were barely civilised. But for most people Glasgow now was a good place to live, a place with its own humour, its own pride.

After a while, she got to her feet with a sigh and went back through to the hall to listen to her messages. She switched the machine to playback and rewound the tape. The voices came through. "This is Bill Grenville at the *Sunday Tribune*. Can you do the eleven o'clock shift for me on Saturday? Ring and let me know as soon as possible." Bleep. "Lindsay, Mary here. Fancy a pint tonight to get the royal dust out of your throat? I'll be in the bar about nine." Bleep. "This is Cordelia Brown. I'm catching the six o'clock shuttle. Meet me at Glasgow Airport about quarter to seven. If you're not there, I'll wait in the bar."

"Hellfire!" Lindsay exclaimed. "It's five past six now. What the bloody hell is she up to?" There was no time to shower, but it took only five minutes to change from her working uniform of skirt, shirt and jacket into a pair of jeans, a thick cotton shirt and a clean sweatshirt, and to give her face a quick scrub. Then she was running down the three flights of stairs, shrugging into a sheepskin jacket and into her car again. She had deliberately not allowed herself to wonder what was bringing Cordelia to Glasgow for fear that hope would betray her. To keep her mind off the subject, she turned the car radio on to hear the tail-end of the news. She drove fast down the expressway and over the Kingston Bridge, trying to convince herself that the day's financial report was truly fascinating. Then, in the middle of the news headlines, she had her second shock of the hour, a shock so acute it caused her to take her foot clean off the accelerator momentarily, to the consternation of the driver behind her, who flashed his lights as he swerved convulsively into the outside lane.

Lindsay could hardly believe that she had heard correctly. But the newsreader's words were branded on her brain: "Police investigating the brutal murder of cellist Lorna Smith-Couper at a girls' boarding school at the weekend have today made an arrest. Patricia Gregory Callaghan, aged thirty-two, a house-mistress at the school, has been charged with murder and will appear before High Peak magistrates tomorrow morning." Now she understood why Cordelia had jumped on the first plane to Glasgow. Lindsay threw the car round the bend in the airport approach road and parked illegally outside the main entrance, grateful for the royal visit sticker which still adorned her windscreen.

The arrival of Cordelia's flight was being announced as she ran up the escalator. She resisted the temptation to slip into the bar for a quick drink and headed for the Domestic Arrivals gate. She could see the first passengers in the distance as they walked up the long approach to the main concourse. They were only about twenty yards away when she spotted Cordelia. Then Cordelia was through the gate; without pause for thought, the two fell into each other's arms and held on tight.

"You've heard, then?" asked Cordelia.

"Yes. Only just now, on the radio in the car."

"I thought you would have heard at work."

"No, I've been out on the road all day. Look, we can't talk here. Let's go back to my flat."

Lindsay picked up the leather holdall which Cordelia had dropped when they met and led the way back to the car. Cordelia was silent till they were roaring back down the motorway. Then she said, "I'm not just here off my own bat. I did want to come up to see you because I know you love Paddy as much as I do, but I wouldn't have had the nerve to do it without being prodded. Pamela Overton rang me not long after the police took Paddy away. She wanted to enlist your help, and mine, in trying to find out what really happened. Can you believe it? She put it perfectly, though—just enough flattery to pull it off. 'With Miss Gordon's talent for investigative journalism and your novelist's understanding of human psychology, you might be able to ensure there is no miscarriage of justice.' You see, she knows Paddy couldn't have done it."

"She's got a way of making people do things, hasn't she? I can't imagine why she thinks we'll be able to succeed where the police have made an absolute cock-up," said Lindsay. She was focusing on the road ahead and talking about Pamela Overton, but her thoughts were on Cordelia and the nagging fear at the back of her mind.

"I suppose she thinks that our personal interest in Paddy will make us that bit sharper," Cordelia replied. There was silence as they swung off the motorway on to the Dumbarton road. Lindsay pulled up alongside an Indian grocer's. The street was as busy as midday, with people shopping, gossiping and hurrying by to keep out the cold of the raw autumn weather.

"Won't be a tick," she promised, hurrying into the shop. She returned a few minutes later, clutching a cooked chicken, some onions, mushrooms and natural yoghurt. "Dinner," she muttered as she drove off again.

Lindsay pulled up outside her flat. "But this is beautiful," Cordelia exclaimed. "I didn't know Glasgow was like this!" She gestured in the sodium-lit darkness at the crescent of trees outside Lindsay's door, at the Botanic Gardens and the River

Kelvin beyond, at the newly sandblasted yellow sandstone tene-
ments elegant under their dramatic lighting.

"Most people don't," Lindsay replied defensively as she
led the way upstairs. "We've also got eighteen parks, some of
the finest art collections in the world, terrific architecture and
Tennents lager. It's not all high-rise flats, gap sites and vandals.
But don't get me started on my hobby horse. Come on in and
have a drink and something to eat."

Lindsay lit the gas fire in the living-room and poured them
both a drink. She said, "Now, come through to the kitchen
with me while I get some dinner together and tell me exactly
what you know."

As Lindsay put together a quick chicken curry, Cordelia
spoke, pacing up and down the kitchen floor. "The first I knew
about it was when the phone rang this afternoon. It was Paddy.
She used her one permitted phone call to ring me because she
knows I have a good solicitor and she wanted either her or someone local recommended by her. She wasn't able to tell me much
except that she'd been arrested and charged, and that somehow
the police had found out she had some sort of motive.

"So I called my solicitor who put me on to a firm in
Manchester who got someone out there right away. It's a very
bright-sounding young woman called Gillian Markham who
specialises in criminal work. I'd just got all that organised, plus
phoning Paddy's parents to break the bad news, when Pamela
Overton rang.

"She told me they'd had Paddy in for questioning for most
of last night. Obviously, she doesn't know all the details of why
they've arrested Paddy, but she did tell me this much. You see,
no one saw or heard anything of Lorna after Paddy had left her.
And now they've got a couple of other bits of evidence which,
as far as they're concerned, tie the murder to Paddy. They have
statements from several people, saying Paddy was hanging around
in the music department for ages for no apparent reason. And

the toggle on the garrotte comes from Paddy's own duffel coat. It normally hangs in the cloakroom just outside her rooms."

"How can they be sure?"

"It's got special horn toggles, not ordinary wooden ones."

"Oh God, they've tied her up well and truly, haven't they? It's all circumstantial and I doubt if they'd get a conviction before a jury if that's all they've got. But it hangs together, especially since, from what you said about motive, they obviously know all about the drugs business," said Lindsay, slicing onions savagely.

"What drugs business?" Cordelia interrupted, bewildered.

"Paddy's supposed motive. I thought from what you said that you knew all about it," Lindsay replied, and proceeded to tell Cordelia the depressing tale. As she led the way back to the living room, she added, "So what are we going to do? How do we go about making this mess any less chaotic?"

They sat down. Cordelia stretched out on the faded chintz sofa and looked appraisingly round her at the spacious, high-ceilinged room. Lindsay had painted the walls chocolate brown, with cream woodwork, picture rail and ceiling. The room was big enough, with its huge bay window, to stand it. On the walls were Lindsay's black and white photographs of buildings and street scenes in Edinburgh, Oxford, Glasgow and London. Book cases stretched the length of one wall; along another was a massive carved oak sideboard which Lindsay had inherited when she bought the flat and which she feared she would have to leave behind if she ever left as it was so enormous. There was a stereo which Lindsay had built into a series of cupboards under the bay window, with shelves for records and cassettes alongside. She said, "I like this room. But it seems very heartless of me to be relaxing here while Paddy languishes in some spartan bloody cell. How could they be so stupid? Any fool can see that Paddy couldn't hurt a fly. She might demolish people verbally, but violence is something she'd simply find beneath that dignity of hers. Not her style at all."

"So what are we going to do about it?"

"Will you come back to Derbyshire with me? When we were talking on Sunday night, you seemed to have one or two ideas about other people with motives. We can see Paddy and find out if there's anything she can tell us. If we can get people to talk to us, maybe we can find out things the police have missed. I know it all sounds a bit *School Friend* and *Girl's Crystal* stuff, but perhaps we can just pull something off. After all, we're starting from a different premise. We know Paddy didn't do it."

Lindsay thought for a moment. "I can't go anywhere till tomorrow night. I've got to work tomorrow. I can cancel Thursday and Friday, but I can't afford to let the *Clarion* down tomorrow. We could go down then."

"Fine. A few hours can't make that much difference. Besides, I've no idea how to go about this. What should our plan of campaign be?"

Lindsay shrugged. "I've no experience of these things. Usually on investigative stories, you have a source who tells you where to look for your information. Or at least you have an idea where to find some background. This is a very different set-up. It always seems so easy for the Hercule Poirots and Lord Peter Wimseys of this world. Everyone talks their head off to them. But why should anyone want to talk to us?"

"Because people love being interviewed. It makes them feel important, and besides, no one who knows Paddy would want her to go to prison."

"No one except the murderer. And I hope whoever it is can sleep easy tonight. Because he or she won't have many easy nights once I get after them, that's for sure."

9

An hour later, after food, more whisky and wrangling, they had produced a sheet of A4 paper covered in the following:

1. James Cartwright. Motive: wants the playing fields to turn into expensive development. Opportunity: poor—not at concert. Where was he? Access to weapon: presumably knew Longnor House since daughter is there. Anyone could get hold of a cello string. Find out about financial position.
2. Margaret Macdonald. Motive: unknown but seen in emotionally charged discussion with Lorna on Saturday morning. Opportunity: excellent. In all the bustle, could easily have slipped into the room after Paddy left. Access to keys and weapon: good—even though she lives in a different house; any member of staff could presumably wander in and out of Longnor without raising any suspicion.
3. Caroline Barrington. Motive: not clear, but makes no secret of her hatred for Lorna. Opportunity: took a long time getting programmes from music storeroom, only yards from murder room. Access to weapon: lives in Longnor, probably knew music-room stock, and likely to know where keys are kept.

4. Sarah Cartwright. Motive: love of father, deserted by friends over playing fields. Opportunity: unknown. Supposedly asleep in Longnor. Access to weapon: lives in Longnor. No known connection with music rooms.

5. Cordelia Brown. Motive: to avoid unsavoury and costly libel action. Opportunity: reasonable. She was away from her seat for a significantly long period around the crucial time. Hard to believe she could have done it without being spotted. Access to weapon: spent the night in Longnor and knew her way round the music rooms. Would have had difficulty concealing weapon as she was wearing close-fitting dress with no bag. If her, action must have been premeditated—weapon must have been secreted in music room earlier.

6. Paddy Callaghan. Motive: to avoid exposure of drug dealing in the past. Opportunity: best by far. Was in the music room alone with Lorna. Last person known to have seen her alive and speak with her. Access to weapon: excellent.

7. Who was the man quarrelling with Lorna?

"Of course," said Lindsay, "I only include you and Paddy for the sake of seeming objective."

Cordelia smiled wanly. "Thanks for your confidence. Don't think I don't feel the cold wind at my neck. If Paddy weren't such a convenient choice, they'd be looking very hard at me. So are you suggesting that these are the people we should concentrate on?"

"They're our only starters so far. But enough of this, we're going round in circles. We can't actually get any further till we've spoken to the people concerned. And one thing I've learned from newspapers is that when you can't get any further, you go for a drink. We could nip down to my local and have one or two before closing time. It's only five minutes' walk. There's usually a couple of my mates in there. Fancy doing that?"

Cordelia looked doubtful. "I'd be just as happy staying here with you. I'm not one for pubbing it, normally. But if you really want to . . ."

Lindsay looked at her suspiciously. "You're doing the 'English fear of the Scots drinking' number, aren't you? What you're really saying is that if this was some bijou wine bar with a rather nice house Muscadet, that would be okay, but some wild Glasgow spit and sawdust bar is really not what you have in mind—am I right?" She grinned to take the sting out of her mockery.

Cordelia had the grace to look sheepish. "All right, all right. I'll come to the pub. But I'm warning you now, the first drunk that accosts me with, 'See you, Jimmy' and I'm off."

When they walked into the Earl of Moray Tavern, Cordelia felt all her worst fears had been realised. The floor was bare vinyl, the furnishings in the vast barn of a room were rickety in the extreme and had clearly never been much better. There was not another woman in sight, apart from the calendar girl on the wall. But Lindsay walked confidently through the bar, greeting several of the men at the counter, leaving Cordelia with no option but to follow. Let this be her baptism of fire, thought Lindsay grimly. At the far end of the bar, they went through a glass-panelled door into another world. The lounge bar was cosy, carpeted and comfortable. Lindsay piloted Cordelia to a table where a blonde woman in her early thirties was staring glumly at the last inch of a pint of lager. She looked up and smiled at Lindsay. "I'd given up hope of seeing you tonight," she greeted her. "Everybody's either out of town or washing their hair or on the wagon."

"Would I let you down?" Lindsay retorted.

"Not if there was drink involved. Who's your friend, then?"

Lindsay sat down and, hesitantly, Cordelia followed suit. "This is Cordelia Brown. Cordelia, this is Mary Hutcheson, the best careers officer in Glasgow, an occupation rather like being lead trombone in the dance band of the *Titanic*."

Mary smiled. "Hello. What brings you to Glasgow? Surely not the company of a reprobate like Lindsay?"

Before Cordelia could reply, the barmaid, a gentle-faced woman in her forties, came across to them. "What'll it be, Lindsay? The usual?"

"Please, Chrissie. And one for Mary. What'll you have, Cordelia? Glass of the house Muscadet?"

Cordelia looked bewildered, not certain if she was the butt of Lindsay's humour. Seeing her confusion, Chrissie said, "We've got some Liebfraumilch too, or a nice Italian red if you like that better."

Lindsay, struggling to keep a straight face, said, "I think she'd maybe just like a whisky and water, Chrissie, that's what we've been on. Okay, Cordelia?"

She nodded. As Chrissie returned to the bar, Mary astutely demanded, "Lindsay, have you been winding this woman up?"

Lindsay smiled broadly. "Afraid so. Sorry, Cordelia, I couldn't resist. I've seen so many people come up from London and patronise this city of mine so thoroughly you wouldn't believe. So now we tend to get our blows in first."

Cordelia lit a cigarette and looked at Lindsay, considering her. "All right, I probably would have got round to deserving it. But just remember—one day you'll be on my patch and these games can cut both ways."

It was two hours and several drinks later when they staggered giggling up the three flights of stairs to Lindsay's flat. "Sorry about the stairs," she panted. "Top flats are always the cheapest, you see."

Lindsay shut the door behind them and fastened the bolts and chain, then turned to Cordelia with a diffidence far removed from the brash assertiveness she'd been displaying all evening and said, "I don't know what you want to do about sleeping arrangements. There's a spare bed in my study if you want it. It's up to you. I . . . I don't want you to feel anything's expected . . ."

She leaned against the door, shoulders slightly raised against the rebuff she felt sure was coming.

Cordelia stood, hands in pockets, looking far more casual than she felt. "I'd rather like to sleep with you," she said softly.

Lindsay's uncertainty made her scowl. "You're sure? You don't just feel you've got to?"

Cordelia moved to her and hugged her close. "Of course not. But if you're going to make an issue of it, I'll begin to think you don't want me."

Lindsay held her tight and laughed nervously. "Oh, I want you all right. Even if you do turn out to be the big bad murderer."

She felt Cordelia stiffen. "You still think I might have done it?" she demanded, pulling away.

Lindsay held on to her hand, refusing to allow her to escape, "I hardly know you. The fact that I turn to jelly every time you come near me doesn't cancel out what I know with my head. You were there. You had a motive. I don't believe you did it. But I'm still clear-headed enough about you to know that at least half the reason I don't believe it is because I don't want to believe it."

"You really know how to kill desire stone dead, don't you?"

Lindsay shook her head. "I don't want to do that. I've sat in that pub for the last two hours wanting you so badly it hurt," she said passionately. "The only reason I wanted to get out of the flat was that I didn't think I could sit all evening in a room alone with you and not make a bloody big fool of myself. Of course I want to go to bed with you. But it's going to mean something to me, you'd better be aware of that. And if it's going to mean something to me, then I'm not going to bed with you under false pretences. So let's spell it out. Yes, I still think you might have done it. With my head, I think that. But all my instincts tell me you're innocent."

They stood bristling at each other. Cordelia shook her head, wonderingly. "My God, you're honest. You don't spare anyone, do you?"

"If you start with lies, nothing you build can be honest. It's true in every area of your life. And I tell you now, honesty's the point at which my previous relationships have come unstuck. So if we're going to be lovers, let's do it with our cards on the table."

"All right, honest journalist." Cordelia moved back towards Lindsay. "Cards on the table. I didn't kill Lorna. I don't go to bed with people just for kicks. It'll mean something to me too. I'm not committed to anyone else. I have all my own teeth. I love Italy in the spring. I hate tinned soup, and I want you right now." She kissed her suddenly and hard. Lindsay tasted cigarettes and whisky and smelled shampoo. And was lost.

Glued to each other, they performed a complicated sideways shuffle into Lindsay's bedroom. Because it was the first time, the clumsy fumbling to undress each other lost its ludicrous edge in mutual desire.

They tumbled on to the duvet, both bodies burning to the other's touch. Lips and hands explored new terrain, hungry to commit the maps of each other's bodies to memory. Later, as they lay exhausted among the ruins of the bedding, Cordelia ran her hand gently over the planes of Lindsay's body where she lay face down, head buried between her new lover's small, neat breasts. Lindsay propped herself up on one elbow and licked her dry lips. She smiled and said, "I taste of you. You taste like the sea. That's what I miss, living in the city. I grew up by the sea. My father earned his living with what he could pull out of the sea. I've always associated the best times in my life with the smell and taste of the sea."

Cordelia smiled. "You saying I'm like a piece of seaweed?"

"Not exactly. Not everyone tastes like the sea. Everyone tastes different. Everyone smells different."

"Maybe you just bring out the best in me." They chuckled softly, and because it was the first time, they didn't move apart, but simply fell asleep where they lay, somewhere in the middle of their conversation.

Lindsay was wakened at eight the next morning with a cup of coffee. Cordelia stood by the bed, looking better in Lindsay's dressing gown than its owner ever did, and said, "I woke early. I always do. So I just made myself at home in a corner of your kitchen and did some work. I thought you might like a coffee."

Lindsay could tell at once that everything was all right between them. There was no constraint, no trace of regret for either of them. It had been the right thing after all, thought Lindsay with relief. She pushed herself upright and took the coffee. Cordelia sat down on the bed as if it was something she had been doing all her life.

"Anything in the papers about Paddy?" asked Lindsay.

"Just the bare fact that she has been arrested and will appear in court this morning. I wish I could be there to give her some moral support. I wish she knew where I am and why."

Lindsay smiled wryly. "No doubt she won't be in the least surprised to hear how things are between us. I suppose I should be feeling guilty that we've been enjoying ourselves while she's locked up."

"Paddy would be furious if she heard you say that," said Cordelia with a grin, getting up. She took a track suit and training shoes out of her bag and put them on, adding, "She knows that we'll be doing everything we can as quickly as possible, and if on the way we've found time for ourselves, well, that's nothing to be guilty about. Now, I'm going out for a run. What's the best way to go for a bit of scenery?" She jogged gently on the spot.

"Go down to the Botanic Gardens across the road, and down the steps to the river. There's a good long walkway by the banks of the Kelvin, whether you turn left or right."

"Terrific. Who'd have thought it in Glasgow, she says, sounding like every patronising Southerner who ever arrived here. Now, what time do you finish work?"

"I'll be through about quarter to seven. Can you meet me at the office to save time? All the taxi drivers know it—just ask for the back door of the *Clarion* building. I'll check the office library today for anything about Lorna that might help us. What are your plans?"

Cordelia carried on jogging and said effortlessly, "I'll make some phone calls to old girls, friends in the music business, anyone I can think of who might have some background gen. Have you some spare keys so I can get in and out—I presume you'll be gone by the time I get back?"

Lindsay yawned and stretched. "Unfortunately, yes. There are keys on the hook by the phone. I'll have to be off as soon as I've had a shower. Help yourself to food, drink, phone, whatever. There's eggs, cheese, bacon and beer in the fridge."

Cordelia shuddered. "What a disgustingly unhealthy diet. What about the fibre and vitamins?" She stopped running and leaned over Lindsay. "Have a good day. I'll miss you." They kissed fiercely, then Cordelia rose to go.

"By the way," said Lindsay, "I have a couple of pictures you might be interested in. The full frame of the snatch I sent out to the papers. I'll leave them on the kitchen table. See if they mean anything to you. Enjoy your run."

Lindsay lay back and luxuriated in thoughts of Cordelia as she listened to the front door closing behind her. Then she shook herself and jumped out of bed for her shower.

Half an hour later she pulled into the *Daily Clarion*'s car park and headed straight for the office library, pausing only to drop by the newsdesk and tell them where she was going. Their file on Lorna was not extensive but fairly comprehensive. Critical notices and a couple of profiles fleshed out what Lindsay already knew. She had jotted down one or two names without much hope that they might be worth talking to before she came across two clippings that seemed to provide more fertile ground. One consisted of a couple of paragraphs from the *Daily Nation*'s Sam Pepys's Diary linking her name with Anthony Barrington of the Barrington Beer brewing empire. The other was a few paragraphs long and reported that Lorna had been cited in the Barrington divorce a few months later. "Caroline!" Lindsay breathed.

She went back to the counter and asked if they had anything on file on Anthony Barrington. The librarian vanished among the high metal banks of the computerised retrieval system that still hadn't managed to render obsolete the thick envelopes of yellowing cuttings. He returned with a thin file and a current edition of *Who's Who*. Lindsay started with the reference book:

Barrington, Anthony Giles, m.1960 Marjory Maurice, m.diss.1982. 1 son 2 daughters. Educ. Marlborough, New Coll., Oxford. Managing Director and Chief executive Barrington Beers. Publ: *Solo Climbs in the Pyrenees, The Long Way Home—an Eiger Route*. Interests: mountaineering, sailing. Clubs: Alpinists, White's. Address: Barrington House, Victoria Embankment, London.

"Interesting," she mused. The file cuttings comprised the two she had already seen and a story about a climbing team he'd led reaching the Eiger summit by a new route. By no means a run of the mill businessman. Lindsay could see why Caroline might have good reason to hate Lorna if she had caused the break-up of the girl's family. Lindsay had no time for further thought, because the tannoy announced at that moment that she was wanted at the newsdesk.

Duncan Morrison, the news editor of the *Clarion*, was the typical Glasgow newspaper hard man with the marshmallow centre. Although he spent a lot of time winding Lindsay up about her views, she knew that he thought she was good at her job. He didn't seem to mind that she argued with him in a way that none of his staff reporters would dare. As she approached the newsdesk, he threw a memo to her and said, "Get busy on that. A real tear-jerker there. Just the job for you. What it needs is a woman's touch."

Lindsay flicked quickly through the memo. It had come from a staff reporter who had spotted the story in a local paper and noted the bare bones on a memo to the newsdesk, suggesting it be followed up. The story was about a woman who had given birth to twins after surgeons had told her she would never have a child.

"Wait a minute, Duncan," Lindsay moaned. "I'm not here to do this sort of crappy feature. Woman's touch, my arse. What this needs is a dollop of heavy handed sentimentality and you bloody well know that's not my line."

"Don't come the crap with me, lassie," he returned. "It's a real human interest story, that. I thought you'd be over the moon. The story of a woman who's fulfilled her destiny in spite of the setbacks. It's all there. Blocked fallopian tubes, thirteen miscarriages, doctors say she'll die if she gives birth—Christ, this woman's a heroine!"

"This woman's a head-case, more like."

"A head-case? Lindsay, you've got a heart like a stone. Can you not see how this woman's triumphed against all the odds?"

"By putting her life at risk? You'd think after thirteen miscarriages she'd have realised there's more to life than babies. There are plenty of kids up for adoption who need love and affection, you know."

"It's a good story, Lindsay." There was finality in Duncan's tone.

"Sure. Look, Duncan, I've been busy being a real reporter for the last three days, in case you hadn't noticed. You know, murder, heavy-duty stuff. I'm good at the serious stories. You should take advantage of that and use me on them. If you've got to run this sexist garbage, get someone who'll make a better job of it. What about James? He's a big softie."

Duncan put his head in his hands in mock sorrow. "Why do I employ the only reporter in Glasgow who thinks she knows better than me how to do my job? I give the girl the chance to be a superstar with her name in lights and what do I get? She wants me to go and set fire to an orphanage so she can be a real reporter. All right, Lindsay, you win. Away down to the Sheriff Court. There's a fatal accident inquiry on that guy that came off the crane at the shipyard. You cover that.

After all, I don't really want a feature about how male doctors conspire with husbands to convince women that motherhood is their finest achievement. Sometimes I wonder why I give you shifts."

They exchanged smiles and Lindsay set off. By five she was back in the office, writing her copy. Just before she left, at seven, Duncan called her over to the newsdesk. "Right then, kid," he said. "Now, you've got the rest of this week off as far as I'm concerned. Not that I'm paying you, mind. But one favour deserves another. You come up with anything good on the murder and I want first bite of the cherry. A cracking good exclusive, right? I know we're not usually interested in anything highbrow and south of the border, but she was at least born in Scotland and the scandals of the upper classes always sell papers. Is that a deal?" He fixed his bloodshot blue eyes on her and scowled.

"It's a deal," said Lindsay resignedly, "I don't mind cutting my financial throat for you, Duncan; you're such a charming bastard to work for."

"I'll make it worth your while, Lindsay. Don't worry about that. Now on your bike and get working. You've had a nice restful day to set yourself up. The next time I hear your voice, I want it to be saying, 'It's a belter, Duncan.'"

Lindsay chuckled to herself as she ran down the three flights of stairs to the back door. Cordelia was waiting for her there, and she again experienced that tight feeling in the chest on seeing her. She was glad to feel it, because it meant that this was more than just simple lust. Their eyes met and Lindsay could see that Cordelia was just as pleased to see her. They walked to the car arm in arm, Lindsay for once not giving a damn who might see and what they might think. It gave her immense satisfaction to stow Cordelia's bag in the boot beside her own.

"What kind of day have you had?" asked Cordelia.

"Busy," Lindsay replied, revving up the powerful engine. "I've only just had time to read the evening paper report of the remand hearing. Did you see it?"

"No, but I heard something on the radio at your place," Cordelia answered. "After that flat recital of Paddy's remand in custody without bail, I need something to lift my mood. Did you make any progress? For God's sake, say yes!"

"Well, I'm a bit further forward than I was this morning," said Lindsay, pulling out on to the urban motorway that cuts a broad concrete swathe through the heart of Glasgow. Cordelia scribbled down notes of what Lindsay told her she'd learned.

"I have a lousy memory," she explained. "I bought a notebook this morning, just for this business, and copied out what we jotted down last night. And now, do you want to know what I unearthed?" Cordelia continued without waiting for Lindsay's nod. "I picked up a fair bit of gossip, most of it general rather than specific to Lorna's death. The more we discover, the less I like her. There was one little gem I picked up, however.

"A lesbian friend of mine, Fran, plays the violin for the Manchester Philharmonic. She told me Lorna once said something to her that might just be relevant. She says she particularly remembered it because, for once, Lorna wasn't trying to score points or stage a put-down but was actually sounding human. It was along the lines of, 'I tried it your way once and I must say I found it all indescribably sordid. But then I was still at school and didn't know any better. Though the other person involved certainly should have known better.' That's all. Fran tried to get more out of her, but she clammed up. As if she regretted saying what she had and was determined to say no more. But I thought . . ."

"That a teacher might just fit the frame?" asked Lindsay. Cordelia nodded. "And the strong possibility for that would be Margaret Macdonald, wouldn't it? It would certainly explain that scene between them in the garden on Saturday morning." Lindsay went on. "They presumably had a lot of close contact, given Lorna's talent. I don't know who else is still at the school who was teaching when Lorna was a pupil, but her music teacher's got to have been close to her. We'll have to see what Margaret

Macdonald has to say about this. I hope to goodness we can rule that piece of information out as irrelevant. Now, did your researches produce any other results?"

"Lorna's current lover. He's a television producer for Capital TV, Andrew Christie. But they've only been together for a couple of months, so I don't know how much use he'd be to us. Still, I think we ought to see him anyway. If he can fit us in tomorrow night, we can shoot up to London and stay over at my place."

Lindsay agreed to this, and they both fell silent. As the car sped on through the night to Derbyshire, Lindsay put a cassette of *Cosi fan tutte* on the stereo and Cordelia sank back in the seat. It was shortly after eleven when they pulled into the forecourt of a small hotel where Cordelia had booked them a room. As they collected their bags, Cordelia said, "I thought it might be better for everyone if we didn't actually stay at the school. Pamela Overton is insisting on paying our bill, much to my humiliation, but who can argue with a woman like that? We can phone her from here and tell her we've arrived and that everything is under control."

"You really think you can make her believe that?" said Lindsay with a grin. "Tell her we'll be up in the morning. I want to see the music room again. I didn't really take it in on Saturday night. Lorna's body distracted me."

They took their luggage up to a large, rather spartan room at the top of the three-storey Victorian building, then went out in search of food. Eventually they found a fish and chip shop on the market place that was still open and returned to the car with fish and chips, Cordelia muttering all the while about cholesterol and calories. By midnight, they were in bed together, staving off their misgivings about what lay ahead.

10

Lindsay woke on Thursday morning to the sound of Cordelia pulling the curtains open. "Look at this view!" she exclaimed. All Lindsay could see was a square of grey sky.

"Do I have to?" she groaned crossly. "What time is it?"

"Half-past seven. I'm going for a run." Already she was dressed in the familiar training shoes and track suit. It occurred to Lindsay in her jaundiced frame of mind that Cordelia was certainly fit enough to have sprinted to the music department, garrotted Lorna and sprinted back again without even being out of breath, Cordelia added, "I'll be about half an hour. You can have a lie-in if you want."

Lindsay groaned again. "Some lie-in! I may as well get up. I'm awake now. I'll take a walk and see if I can pick up the papers."

"See you later." And she was off, running down the wide staircase.

Lindsay struggled out of bed, wondering if she could stand the pace and promising herself once again that the fitness programme should start soon. She walked over to the window to see the view and was impressed in spite of her drowsiness. The room looked out over a couple of football pitches to a broad sweep of mature woodland, and beyond that to distant hills folding into each other. Even in the grey morning light it was spectacular. She dressed hurriedly and went off in search of a newsagent, planning the interview with Margaret Macdonald as she walked.

It was shortly after nine when they arrived at Derbyshire House, and they went straight to Pamela Overton's study. The headmistress was dictating letters to her secretary but as soon as she saw them, she stopped and dismissed her. In the four days since Lorna Smith-Couper had died, Pamela Overton had aged visibly. Her face was grey and pale, and there were dark circles beneath her eyes. But her manner was as decisive as ever.

She greeted them in her usual formal manner, and faced them across her desk. "No one here can believe in Miss Callaghan's guilt. Her arrest is frankly incredible. And it hasn't stopped the rot, I'm afraid. Already we have lost twenty-one girls and I feel sure others will follow." She sighed deeply. "But I should not burden you with my problems. That will get us nowhere. How can I help you?"

Lindsay spoke first. "I think Cordelia mentioned that we would like to see the room where it happened. I want to get the scene completely clear in my mind, and it might suggest some possibilities. I take it the police have finished with it now?"

"There will be no problem there," said Miss Overton. "Their forensic people finished their work there on Monday. The room has, of course, been cleaned and put in order now that they have done with it, but we are not yet using it as a classroom. It's been locked up to avoid any ghoulishness, but I have the key here. You also want to question some people, don't you?"

"Yes, we do," Cordelia replied. "But we'd like to keep it on an informal basis as far as possible, especially where the girls are concerned. It's mainly a matter of details at the moment. We'd also like to talk to Miss Macdonald, since no one knows the business of the music department better than her. Can you tell us when she's free today? Also, we'd like a letter from you that we can use as an introduction to people outside the school, saying that we're inquiring into matters on your behalf and asking for co-operation. And finally . . . we'd like to use Paddy Callaghan's rooms as our base within the school."

Pamela Overton moved over to the wall where the time-tables were displayed. She studied them for a moment, then told them Margaret Macdonald had one free period later in the morning and another in the afternoon. "If she's not in her department, try her rooms in Grin Low House," she explained. She returned to her desk, took a sheet of headed notepaper from a drawer and wrote a few lines. She handed it to Cordelia, who read,

> To whom it may concern; Cordelia Brown and Lindsay Gordon are making inquiries on my behalf regarding the death of Lorna Smith-Couper. I would be grateful if you would give them the fullest co-operation, Yours faithfully, Pamela Overton.

Then Miss Overton gave Lindsay a handful of keys taken from another drawer. "The single key is for the music room, the bunch is Miss Callaghan's."

Cordelia nodded. "Thank you."

"One more thing," Lindsay chipped in. "What can you tell us about James Cartwright? This isn't a large community; you must know a fair bit about him. We have virtually no background, I'm afraid," she apologised.

The headmistress thought for a moment, a flicker of distaste appearing momentarily in her eyes. Finally, she said, "He is a very successful builder. He started off in a small way, as a one-man business working locally. He did general work, but began to specialise in buying old properties, doing them up and converting them into flats and selling them at a handsome profit. In the property boom of the seventies, he made some very shrewd deals and amassed a considerable amount of money. He expanded to employ a fairly large workforce and now takes on work throughout the Peak area. He is generally thought of as having done very well.

"He still keeps a close contact with the day-to-day running of the business—it's not unusual to see him up some scaffolding with a hard hat and a bricklayer's trowel. He is well liked locally, though some find him ostentatious. However, I must say there have been fewer signs of that lately. His wife left him and Sarah about nine years ago. I believe she left him for an American civil engineer, though I know little about the circumstances. Mr Cartwright has done his best to give Sarah a decent life—and not simply by spending money. He tries to spend time with her, though the pressures of his business don't allow him much free time. She in her turn worships him. He is ruthless, but not, I think, insensitive. Will that do?"

Lindsay smiled and said, "Admirably. Thank you. We won't take up any more of your time now."

As they moved towards the door, Miss Overton spoke again. "I will be here at all times to answer any questions. I know you may well be reluctant to discuss your progress with me, but I ask that if you think you have reached a solution you tell me before you communicate with the police." It was a command rather than a request.

"Of course, if that is possible," said Cordelia. Then they managed to leave. They walked down the corridor to the back stairs, Cordelia muttering, "She terrifies me. If I didn't have the evidence of my own eyes that she didn't budge from the hall, I'd swear she was the only person cool enough to get away with murder under everyone's nose."

Lindsay grinned, then said thoughtfully, "Yet whoever it was must have done just that. There were so many people flitting around it must have been an extremely dodgy exercise. It's hard to believe anyone could have got away with it completely unseen. Oh, and by the way, you've just fallen into the oldest trap. You said you have the evidence of your eyes that she didn't budge from the hall. But don't forget that you were out of the hall yourself during the crucial period. All you can say is that she was there when you left and there when you returned. For all you know, she could have slipped out, just like you did."

"Except that, by my own admission of where I was, we would have bumped smack into each other on the doorstep."

"Unless one of you was actually in there committing murder." Lindsay stopped on the stairs. "Now what am I saying? Oh God, I'm sorry, Cordelia. It's just my love of perversity . . . Look, I know it wasn't you. And I know it wasn't Pamela Overton, because I *do* have the evidence of my own eyes to go on there. Forgive my crassness."

Cordelia stood a couple of steps above her, smiling "Nothing to forgive. I don't expect two nights of passion to convince you that I'm above suspicion."

They were suddenly grinning at each other like schoolkids who have just discovered that they are best friends. Together they ran up the few remaining stairs. Only the sight of the music room door sobered them into rather frightened adults again. Cordelia put the key in the lock, then paused. "Ready?"

Lindsay nodded. Cordelia turned the key and opened the door. It swung open silently to reveal a completely ordinary music classroom. It smelled faintly of a mixture of polish, chalk and resin. In one corner was a neat stack of music stands. On open shelves along one wall were piles of sheet music. Glass-fronted cupboards beneath the shelves revealed boxes of strings, reeds, percussion instruments and piles of blank manuscript paper. There were about twenty chairs scattered around. At the far end of the room was a baby grand piano, the teacher's desk on a raised dais in front of the blackboard, and a walk-in cupboard whose open door revealed neatly ordered string instruments in racks; violins, violas, cellos, even a mandolin and two guitars.

The two women walked in and closed the door behind them. Cordelia wandered round slowly, uncertain of what she was looking for. After a moment, she joined Lindsay who was examining the windows. Below was a drop of about eighteen feet to the ground. There was no down-pipe within ten feet. The three windows were ordinary casements with pivoting catches. Lindsay took a Swiss Army knife from her handbag and selected the thinnest blade. She fiddled idly with one of the catches. It rose smoothly and fell back, allowing the window to swing open.

"Perfectly smooth. Not in the least stiff," she remarked. "Pity the murderer couldn't have got in that way. And a ladder's out of the question. It would have to be smack bang in the middle of the drive, which would have been more than slightly noticeable." She turned back to the room. "Lorna was sitting over there in front of the dais, facing the door, back to the windows. There was a music stand in front of her, overturned. Sheet music all over the floor. Her cello under her. Not a pretty sight." She pushed the window shut smartly and the latch promptly fell back into place. "Have you seen enough? It rather gives me the creeps, being here. I can still remember all too vividly how Lorna looked."

Cordelia gave her hand a squeeze and nodded. "Yes, I've seen quite enough. Let's go over to Paddy's room. We've got nearly an hour to kill before we can see Margaret Macdonald and we can use the phone in Paddy's room to see if we can set up a meeting with Andrew Christie."

Paddy's sitting-room looked as if she had only slipped out to take a class. The Sunday papers were still strewn around. On the table was a half-drunk cup of coffee, and there was still a record sitting on the silent turntable. Lindsay went through to the kitchen to brew up while Cordelia struggled with the television company switchboard.

She was replacing the receiver and sighing with relief when Lindsay returned with the coffee. "Will he see us, then?" Cordelia nodded. "You smooth-talking bastard! I could use your gifts of persuasion on the doorstep next time I've got a sticky one," Lindsay enthused. "What time, and where?"

"It was touch and go, but he'll see us at eight at his place in Camden Town. For God's sake don't tell him you're a journalist! He was very twitchy about it all, and no wonder. He's had the police and half your lot in the last few days, and as far as he's concerned, it all ended with the arrest."

"It might feel like that for him, but I'm bloody sure that's not how it feels for Paddy. I think we should try to go and see her this afternoon. Did the solicitor tell you what the score is on visiting arrangements?"

Cordelia shook her head. "Why don't you give her a call? I don't suppose we'll be able to visit, anyway—I mean, don't you have to have a visiting order or something?"

Lindsay shook her head. "Not when the prisoner is on remand. Paddy's legally entitled to a fifteen-minute daily visit from family or friends. Plus unlimited time with her legal advisor. Give me the number for this solicitor."

She was quickly connected with Gillian Markham, who sounded brisk and competent. As they talked, Lindsay's face grew more puzzled and angry. She finally put the phone down and said, "Well, there's no problem with the visit. We can see Paddy if we get there between three and half-past. Gillian thinks it will take us about an hour to drive to the remand centre. We can take food and cigarettes with us, and Paddy would apparently like some fresh clothes since she's opted to wear her own gear rather than prison uniform. Does that still give us time to get to London, assuming we get away about four?"

"Given the way you drive, I don't anticipate any problem with that," Cordelia replied tartly. "But what's the matter? You look as if you've just been kicked in the teeth."

"From what Gillian's just told me, I think it's Paddy who's been kicked in the teeth, not me."

"Meaning?"

"Gillian's just had a tip from a contact inside the force about a new piece of circumstantial evidence against Paddy. Remember all that carry-on with Sarah Cartwright on Saturday morning? Well, guess where Paddy took her to cool down?"

Cordelia looked dismayed. "If I said Music 2, would I be wrong?"

"You'd be spot on. As if that wasn't bad enough in itself, Sarah has given the police a statement saying that Paddy passed a remark along the lines that the room had been nicely spruced up for its VIP guest. Sarah also maintains that Paddy was wandering around idly opening cupboards and picking things up while they talked."

"Oh God, no! Surely the girl must be lying?"

"I suggest we check that out with Paddy before we confront the girl with anything. If she's telling the truth, it wouldn't in itself be damning. Those seem to me to be perfectly normal things to do and say, taken by themselves. But coupled with the other bits and bobs the police have against Paddy, it can only be seen as more evidence weighing the scales against her. If Paddy denies that those events took place, we're in a very different ball game. We'll have to look at the reasons why the girl might be lying."

"Surely she'd only tell that kind of lie against Paddy if she had something to hide," Cordelia protested.

"Not necessarily. It could be she's lying to protect herself. It could also be that she's lying to protect her father because she knows he was involved. Or it could simply be that she's made up this story because she only fears her father may be involved and she's trying to divert police attention well away from him. Either way, we need to talk to Paddy about this. And quite honestly, with the interview we've got next, I'd rather put Sarah and her motives right to the back of my mind."

They drank their coffee in a tense silence. Neither was looking forward to the forthcoming interview. Cordelia cleared away the cups, taking Paddy's with her to the kitchen, and called through, "Have you got the photo?"

"Yes, in my handbag. I did a couple of seven by fives of the heads. Let's hope I don't have to use it as a shock tactic."

Cordelia re-emerged. "I'm beginning to wish we'd never taken this on. I like Margaret Macdonald, for God's sake. She taught me to like music, to listen properly to it."

Lindsay got up and hugged her. "Just think of Paddy," she whispered. "It may be unpleasant but you're doing it for all the right reasons."

They walked through pale autumn sunlight to Grin Low House and mounted the stairs in silence. Margaret Macdonald's rooms were at the end of the first-floor corridor. Lindsay knocked on the door and was rewarded with, "Come in." They entered to find the teacher sitting at a desk correcting some music in manuscript. When she saw who it was, she seemed startled. It would have been easy to read guilt into her look. Neither Lindsay nor Cordelia set much store by her reaction, since they already knew she was hiding something.

"I was rather expecting you two," she said. "Miss Overton told me she'd asked you to help sort out this terrible business." She stood up and gestured towards the three armchairs that were ranged round her gas fire. "Let's be comfortable. Now, I suppose you want me to tell you about the concert and the music department, that sort of thing?"

Cordelia took this as a cue to begin gently probing. "When you were backstage on Saturday night, did you see anyone at all going down the corridor towards Music 2?"

"I don't really remember. I was rushing round so much organising the choirs and the orchestra. But I would have thought nothing of it even if I had, because the music storeroom is there too, and that's where the programmes were being kept."

"Did you go to your own room?"

"Several times, but I didn't stay there for any length of time, as I've already told the police. I didn't pay any attention to the keys, and I didn't see anyone else go in or out of my room."

"How many people knew that Lorna was going to be in Music 2 before her performance?"

Margaret thought for a moment. "It was no particular secret," she replied. "Most of the girls involved in the concert could have worked it out for themselves, since that room had been left free. I think I mentioned in the staffroom that I'd had the fifth form clearing it up on Friday so that it would be tidy for Lorna. I wanted to make sure that everything was just right, so there could be no criticism from her of my preparations. So the answer to your question is that anyone could have known. There's no way of narrowing it down."

"I suppose in theory you yourself could have taken the key, gone to Music 2, done what you had to do and put the key back in the wrong place—deliberately?" Cordelia inquired.

Margaret Macdonald's hands worked in her lap. There was fear inadequately hidden in her eyes and Lindsay noticed a trace of sweat on her upper lip. "I suppose I could have. But I didn't. Look, Lorna was the most distinguished pupil I've ever taught; she was about to give a concert in aid of the school. Why should I have wanted to kill her? This is nonsense!"

There was a pause. Lindsay could sense that when it came to questioning her former teacher, Cordelia had no killer instinct. But she was loath to take the hard line of questioning herself. For once she felt unhappy at subjecting someone to her professional probing. She didn't want to strip this woman's defences down because she was sure she was a sister of sorts. She should be offering her support, not giving her a hard time. Then she thought about Paddy, "I know you taught Lorna, and obviously she owed a lot to you," she said decisively. "Did you remain close?"

Margaret studied the carpet as if inspecting it for some clue as to how she should respond. She said quietly, "Not since she left school. We exchanged Christmas cards, that was all. She had a very hectic life."

"I'm surprised you didn't stay more closely in touch."

Again there was quiet in the room. It wasn't easy for Lindsay to become the interrogatory machine, but she stifled her feelings and continued remorselessly. "You went for a walk with her on the morning of the day she died, didn't you?" she demanded.

Swiftly, Margaret's head came up. There was no mistaking the fear now. "No!" she replied sharply. "No, I didn't go for a walk with her."

"You were with her in the gardens on Saturday morning and you were arguing."

"That's not true."

Lindsay slipped the photograph from her handbag and offered it to the music mistress who glanced at it then rose to her feet and walked to her desk where she collapsed in her chair.

Lindsay spoke gently. "I was up on the hillside taking some photographs. The red sweater you were wearing caught my eye. I haven't shown these to the police yet. There seemed to me to be little reason to do so. But now Paddy has been arrested, I think I might have to go to the police with them. Unless I am convinced that they have nothing to do with the murder and would therefore serve no purpose in helping Paddy."

Margaret Macdonald looked Lindsay straight in the eye. Her fear had been replaced by resignation. She shrugged, then said bitterly, "After all, why not? If anyone can understand it, maybe you two can. They say it takes one to know one."

Lindsay kept her eyes on the teacher, but on the edge of her vision she was aware of Cordelia turning away, whether from sympathy or embarrassment she could not tell. Margaret sighed deeply. "I've never told anyone this, and I hoped I would never have to.

"Fifteen years ago, Lorna was a seventeen year old with a blinding and brilliant gift. The cello was my own instrument, and though I could never play like she did, I'm a good teacher. I had experience and so much enthusiasm to pass on. She wanted to absorb all she could from me, and I was happy to show her every secret.

"We spent hours together, practising, listening to music, or just talking. I had always known I was different from most of my friends. I only ever felt emotionally attracted to my own sex. It's ironic really—everyone assumes that it was my love of music and teaching that made me choose this life. But for me it seemed the only option because it was a life I could lose myself in.

"I had never acted on my desires in any way before Lorna—it was a different world when I was young. It wouldn't have been possible to have fulfilled my dreams and still have done the things I wanted to in my career. It would have set me too far apart, and I'd never have got a teaching job. I was never attracted to the idea of living a secret life, I never had that kind of nerve.

"When Lorna came along, I was thirty-five. Suddenly I felt that my life was slipping past me without meaning. I needed love. Lorna was half my age, but she worshipped me for what I could give her.

"And I worshipped her talent. I knew I could never play like that, but to have Lorna to listen to was the next best thing. We were each obsessed by what the other could give." Margaret paused. "It only lasted a matter of a few months. Then Lorna left to go to the Royal College. And that was the end. The week after she left here, she wrote saying that she didn't want to see me again. She took everything she could then simply discarded me. As you can imagine, it has haunted me ever since. I've never dared to get close to a pupil again, for fear I would fall into the same trap. I got what I deserved. I betrayed the trust of my position and she betrayed my love."

Cordelia rose and held her hands up to the fire. It was warm in the room, but she felt cold as ice. Neither she nor Lindsay felt capable of further questioning. But Margaret Macdonald continued unasked.

"I didn't see her in all those years, apart from going to the occasional concert where she was playing. I never spoke to her. We did exchange Christmas cards and I bought all her records, but that was all. When Pamela Overton told me she had persuaded her to come here, I didn't know what to do or how to act. On Friday, I had no chance to be alone with her. But on Saturday, I saw her going for a walk and followed. God help me, I could still see in her the girl I had loved. I caught up with her when we were out of sight of the house. I didn't really know what I was going to say, but I didn't get much chance to speak." She let her head drop into her hands but kept talking in a low monotone.

"She taunted me for being pathetic and afraid of the consequences of my actions. She said she supposed I'd come to plead and beg for her silence; she said. 'If you'd said nothing, of course I would have kept quiet. But this sneaking out behind me, this cringing and crawling makes me despise you. It devalues a pretty worthless past. So why should I protect you?' I said that wasn't what I meant to do at all, but that yes, she could damage my present and future with a few words. Not to mention the damage she would do to both our memories of the past. She laughed in my face, then walked off. It was all disgustingly melodramatic. I found it sickening.

"You may think this gives me a reason for wanting her dead. But she was already dead to me. Her reaction that morning killed the last dreams I had about her. The school is a very important part of my life, and has been for many years. But not as important as my music. If I had been inclined to murder, I wouldn't have done it here, before the concert. I wanted to hear her play. I wanted to be sure that she could still play like an angel. And if she had told anyone of our past, well, so be it, I would have lost the school, but I could have made a new life for myself teaching privately. Lorna could only destroy a fragment of my life, I see that very clearly. I didn't kill her for that fragment. Besides, Paddy Callaghan is probably the closest friend I have. I couldn't sit back and watch her suffer if I had committed this crime. Whether you believe me or not, I didn't kill Lorna."

"I believe you," said Cordelia, turning back to the room, "I don't think there's anything more we need to ask. I'm sorry we've caused you pain."

"Thank you," echoed Lindsay. "You have helped us a great deal. I'm sorry I had to be so hard." The music mistress remained silent as they left. Then she subsided into heavy, silent sobbing.

Lindsay and Cordelia walked back over to Paddy's room without talking. Lindsay went straight to the drinks cupboard, unlocked it and poured two liberal whiskies. "I'm glad I wasn't born twenty years earlier," she said, furious. "And I hope to God I never have to find the kind of courage she's needed all these years."

"You did believe her, then?"

"My God, yes. I believed her all right. You don't lie like that. Not with so much obvious pain. She might well have felt like killing Lorna, but I don't believe she did it. She's had the guts to live like this for so long; she must have known inside herself that she could have dealt with any blow that bitch could hand out," said Lindsay bitterly. "She may not have chosen to deal with it, but she had the strength to. You know, suddenly, this has stopped being a game. I didn't really take it seriously till now."

"I know what you mean," said Cordelia, "we've been fooling ourselves into thinking this would be some civilised exercise in detection like it is in the books, without understanding that there are real emotions involved. While the only thing we had to think about was Paddy, it wasn't difficult to imagine being detectives. The great righteous crusade. All that sort of rubbish. But I'm not at all certain that I can handle this kind of thing."

Lindsay nodded. "I know," she said. "But we're committed now. We can't back out. And if we don't do something for Paddy, who will? None of us can afford proper private detectives—and anyway, would we have any notion how to find a good one? We've still got the advantage of knowing Paddy and knowing something about all these people, especially Lorna, and I'm hopeful that Paddy can give us some ideas. We have to keep pressing on, no matter how much we hate it. Haven't we?"

For answer, Cordelia took out her notebook and started scribbling rapidly in it. "You should be doing this," she complained.

"You're the journalist; you should remember what people say. Who's next for the Lindsay Gordon Spanish Inquisition?"

In spite of herself, Lindsay smiled at the echo of Caroline's words on Saturday night. She said, "James Cartwright. I feel like working off some of my spleen, and from the little I've heard of him, I reckon he's a prime candidate for that."

"But we've really got nothing on him at all. What the hell are we going to ask him?" Cordelia demanded.

"We'll just have to try an elaborate con job, I suppose, and hope I can rattle him enough with my penetrating questions."

"I'll leave it to you, then. After all, you've already displayed your professional interrogation skills today," said Cordelia drily.

"I didn't get any pleasure from that success, if success you choose to call it," said Lindsay. "Usually when I monster people like that in the course of getting a story, I know they're villains. It's not too hard to get heavy and put on the pressure when you know your victim is no stranger to putting the screws on somebody else. There's no satisfaction in hammering somebody like Margaret Macdonald, believe me. At least Cartwright should be sufficiently tough for me not to have any qualms about turning nasty if I have to."

"I feel sorry for the poor bloke," Cordelia mocked. "Almost as sorry as I feel for you, sweetheart. What a way to make a living!"

11

By any standards, James Cartwright's was an impressive house. Rather than choosing something he had built himself, he had opted to live in the dramatic flowering of another man's imagination. It was three storeys tall, built in extravagant Victorian Gothic in the local grey stone with twin turrets and superb views across open fields to the distant White Peak. In front, a Mercedes sports car and a Ford Sierra were parked. Even fortified by whisky and coffee, Lindsay felt daunted as she parked her car at the end of the semi-circular sweep of gravel. She switched off the engine and said, "Suddenly I feel I'm driving a matchbox. Just look at that garden! He must employ a battalion of gardeners. Have you got the letter from God?"

"It's right here," said Cordelia. "Now, let me check . . . have I got the thumbscrews, or have you?"

Lindsay scowled. "Very funny."

"Only teasing," Cordelia replied sweetly.

Lindsay opened the car door. "Sometimes I wish I'd become a bloody fashion writer on a women's magazine," she muttered.

They walked up the drive to the front door. Lindsay looked at Cordelia, pulled a face at her then pressed the doorbell. Its sharp peal was loud enough to make them both start. Cordelia stood almost to attention facing the door while Lindsay turned away, pulled up the collar of her leather jacket and tried to force a profoundly casual aspect on her appearance. As the door opened, she turned to face the young man who stood in the doorway. He was smartly dressed in a well-cut pinstripe suit and his hair was beautifully groomed. When he spoke it was with a strong Derbyshire accent.

"What can I do for you?" he demanded sharply.

Lindsay spoke. "We'd like to see Mr James Cartwright."

"Have you an appointment?"

"If we had, you'd be expecting us, wouldn't you?" she responded sweetly.

"I'm afraid Mr Cartwright is a very busy man. He doesn't see anyone without an appointment," said the young man brusquely. "Are you from the papers?"

"If you would take this letter to Mr Cartwright, perhaps he'll be able to fit us in," Lindsay replied nonchalantly, handing over the envelope containing Pamela Overton's letter. "We'll wait and see, shall we?"

The young man turned to enter and Lindsay nipped smartly into the porch behind him. Cordelia, surprised by this manoeuvre, took a moment to follow her. The inner door to the hallway was closed neatly in their faces by the young man, and Lindsay turned to Cordelia, saying, "Easy when you know how, isn't it?"

Cordelia muttered, "Brazen hussy!" They stood in an awkward silence till the young man reappeared a few moments later at the inner door. "He can give you a quarter of an hour. He's got to leave after that for an important meeting in Matlock."

"Talk about delusions of grandeur," Lindsay muttered to Cordelia, who struggled to swallow a nervous giggle as their footsteps clattered on the polished parquet of the wide hall in the wake of the young man. Cordelia sized up the stained pine doors and skirting board, the Victorian-style wallpaper dotted with framed photographs of sailing ships and nineteenth-century harbours, and the stripped pine church pew and pine chests that were the only furniture in the hall. The cushion on the pew matched the wallpaper. "Straight from the pages of a design catalogue," she remarked. At the end of the hall, the young man waited by a door. As they reached him, he opened it and gestured them to enter.

The room was painted white. On the walls were two calendars and three year-planners. The floor was covered with carpet tiles and the furniture comprised equally functional office equipment. There were two metal desks, filing cabinets the length of one wall, a large computer terminal with printer attached and, in the bay window, a draughtsman's angled desk with a battery of spotlights above it.

At the larger of the two desks, a man was working. As her eyes swung round to him, Lindsay felt as though she'd been punched in the chest. She recognised the man she had last seen storming through the music department on the afternoon of the murder. She rapidly revised the outline of what she was going to ask him.

He had not looked up when they entered but continued to write notes on a large plan laid out on his desk top. It was Cordelia's first sight of Cartwright and she was impressed in spite of herself. He was in his middle forties, a big man, at least six feet tall. His torso looked solid without being flabby and his hands were the strong tools of a man used to strenuous physical work. His dark hair was thinning and greying at the temples, and his skin was weathered and lined. When he finally looked up his eyes were surprisingly dull and tired.

"Sit yourselves down, girls," he said. Like his assistant, he had kept his local accent. "Now you tell me just why I should extend you my fullest co-operation. Why should I care what happens to any of that lot up there, apart from my Sarah?"

There was silence for a moment, Cordelia flicked a glance at Lindsay, who calmly took out her cigarette pack and offered it to Cartwright. "Smoke? No? Clever boy." She passed one to Cordelia and lit both. Then she answered him. "It strikes me that a businessman with your obvious acumen would not have kept his daughter on at Derbyshire House after the question of the playing fields came up unless there was some highly pressing reason. After all, it gave her an awkward conflict of loyalties, didn't it? I'd guess that you didn't remove her because the school has given her the security and friendship she never found anywhere else."

Cartwright slammed his hands flat on the desk. "You've got a hell of a nerve! My daughter was sent there for the best education, and she'll stay there till it's finished. Are you suggesting I don't treat her properly?"

Lindsay continued unflustered, "Quite the opposite," she said calmly. "I think you and Sarah are very close. I think you both care deeply about each other. But you're a very busy man. You must often be away from home, working late, whatever. Obviously, a growing daughter needs more than you can spare. If she's found something she needs at the school, it would be a very important reason for letting her stay there, in spite of the conflict of interests."

"They must be better off up there than I thought if they can afford smart-arsed psychological private eyes to try and clear their homicidal staff," sneered Cartwright, still angry but cooling fast.

"We're not private eyes, and we're not being paid," Cordelia retorted, no longer able to hold back her irritation. "We happen to be friends of Paddy Callaghan. And we're certain she didn't kill Lorna Smith-Couper. We intend to find out who did. Now, if you're prepared to help us, well and good. If not, also well and good. We'll simply have to get the answers we need by another route."

Lindsay managed to hide her surprise at this display of iron in Cordelia's soul. Cartwright sat back in his chair, considered them both for a moment, then spoke slowly. "All right," he said. "Bloody nosy women, that's what you are. I suppose you can ask me your damn questions. I don't promise to answer any of them, but I'll listen to what you have to say. Just remember one thing—I wasn't at that concert on Saturday night."

"I didn't see you, certainly," said Lindsay. "But I imagine you know the school well enough both as a parent and as a builder to know how to find your way around without falling over the audience at a concert."

"Point taken, young lady," he replied. "As it happens, I do know the school. I've done most of the building jobs there in the last fifteen years. Now, let's hear these questions."

"I suppose the police have already asked you, so it shouldn't be a problem to remember where you were on Saturday night between, say, six and eight-thirty."

"I was out walking on the moors late Saturday afternoon till about half-past six. I had a drink in a pub down near the Roaches, those rocks on the Leek road. The pub's called the Woolpack. Then I wandered over to the Stonemason's Arms near Wincle. I had a few pints there and something to eat. I left there about nine. You can check with the landlady; she'll probably remember—I'm a regular there." He leaned forward again, looking smug. "The police have already checked me out. Not that they were at all suspicious of me; they were just going through the motions. Roy Dart is a friend of mine. He told me it was just routine."

"Did you see Sarah at all on Saturday?" asked Lindsay.

"No. Why should I have? I wasn't near the place all day." He did not flinch at the lie. He kept his eyes fixed on Lindsay as she asked the next question.

"So you didn't know she had a set-to with her friends about your bid to get your hands on the playing fields?"

"No, I didn't. Not that it surprises me. Half those silly little girls at that school don't know what it means to live in the real world. They occupy some cloud-cuckoo land, where everything will be all right because someone will always make it all right for them. So, of course, they turn on my Sarah when the usual magic doesn't work."

Cordelia leaned forward and asked, "You're pretty sure about getting the land, aren't you?"

"I am now," he answered readily. "But don't go reading too much into that. I was anyway. This charade they're putting on about raising the cash is just that—a charade. It would never have happened, take my word for it."

Lindsay gathered together her bag and fastened her jacket. "Well," she said, "I think you've covered what we wanted to know, more or less. We won't keep you from Matlock any longer. Just one thing, though—you say you weren't near Derbyshire House on Saturday. Now that seems a little odd to me. Because I saw you there about five o'clock. Just when you were walking on the moors, according to what you've said." She got to her feet, as did Cordelia, who felt a little bewildered. "Funny that," added Lindsay. "You must have a double."

They got as far as the door before he spoke. "Wait a minute," he said uncertainly.

Lindsay half turned towards him. "Yes?"

"All right, dammit," he said, "all right. I did drop in at the school. I was looking for Sarah, if you must know. But I couldn't find her, so I just buzzed off again. I saw no point in mentioning it; it might have given the wrong impression."

"It certainly gives me a strange impression, Mr Cartwright. And I'm sure your good friend Inspector Dart would think the same, especially if I told him that I'd also seen the person you were talking to—or should I say arguing with? And it wasn't your Sarah."

If she had expected James Cartwright to collapse at her words, she was mistaken. His eyes suddenly came to life and there was venom in his voice. "Don't you sodding well threaten me! I don't have to explain myself to two bloody girls. If you heard so much, what's the need for your bloody questions? Unless you heard nothing and you're trying to bluff me. Well, I've news for you. I always call bluffs."

"Okay," said Lindsay. "Call mine, then. It won't take long to tell all this to Inspector Dart. It may not make him release

Paddy Callaghan on the spot, but it will provoke some hard questions and give her solicitor enough fuel to make a pretty bonfire at the committal hearing, especially if she asks for the reporting restrictions to be lifted. What price your business then, Mr Cartwright?"

She had opened the door and had gone halfway down the hall with Cordelia at her side before Cartwright caught up with them. "What did you hear?" he demanded.

Lindsay stopped. "So you want to talk, then?" He nodded and they all walked back to his office. He threw himself petulantly into his chair. The women remained standing.

"What did you hear?" he repeated.

"Enough to know that you tried to bribe Lorna Smith-Couper into pulling out of the concert. You can't have been so sure about Derbyshire House failing to reach their target. I also heard Lorna sending you off with a flea in your ear, threatening to expose you. And I saw the expression on your face. Murderous, I'd call it. None of it very edifying, is it?"

"All right, so I did try to bribe her. But that's no crime, not compared with murder. And I didn't murder her. I've already cleared this up with the police. I was in one of those two pubs at the time. Look, I'll write their names down. You can check up." He pulled a memo pad over, scribbled the names of the pubs with a thick, dark pencil and handed the paper over to Lindsay. "There you are, take it. Murder's not my way, you know. I may have been underhand, but I'm not one of your bully boys that believes violence is the answer."

"And you're sure you didn't see Sarah?"

"I didn't. I didn't go there to see her. I went to see Lorna Smith-Couper."

"How did you know where to find her?" asked Cordelia.

"I rang her up before she came to the school and asked for an appointment because she refused to discuss business over the phone. She agreed, and rang me on Saturday morning to arrange a meeting in Music 2 at quarter to five. I knew exactly where that room was—in fact, when I was just a little two-man operation, I replaced all the windows on that floor. Like I said, I've done most of the building work there. The woman was there, sorting out some strings for her cello. I put my offer to her. She laughed in my face. When I left, she left too. I don't know where she went, but I went straight to my car and drove around for a while. When the pub opened, I went in for a drink. I didn't feel like going home to an empty house—I often don't—so I went to the Stonemason's. I wanted to put my thoughts about the matter out of my head for a while, so I had a meal and a few pints. That's that. There's no need to tell the police after all, now is there?"

For a shrewd businessman, he was a shade too eager, thought Lindsay. She shrugged. "I make no promises," she said. "I don't see the need just at present. Thanks for your time, Mr Cartwright." Again, she and Cordelia left the office. This time, they made it out of the front door and back to the car.

"Phew!" Cordelia sighed. "So he's the man you saw arguing with Lorna. You sure as hell are good value for money. Nobody would guess you hadn't planned any of that. It must have been a hell of a shock when you recognised him. Do you normally eat villains for breakfast?"

"Come on, Cordelia. He told us hardly anything we didn't already know. He's only scared about more police inquiries and bad publicity. It's only a guess, but I think he might be in deep water financially. A lot of small and medium-sized builders are really strapped for cash now. And he didn't get that squash court contract. If that's the case, he would badly need the playing fields project. He's a worried man, but I'm not sure that's because he's a murderer."

"By the way," said Cordelia, "why were you so insistent about whether he'd seen Sarah?"

"Don't really know. It just seemed important. Journalist's nose, I guess."

Cordelia giggled. "That sounds like a particularly nasty complaint!"

"It leads to complications. Like broken legs. I'm told. Now . . . I want to check this so-called alibi of his. What time is it?"

"Just before two. We'd better get a move on if we're going to see Paddy."

"I'll drop you back at the school and you can sort out some clothes for her, if you don't mind. Then I can go into town and buy some sandwiches for us and some goodies and cigarettes for Paddy. And I want a good, large-scale map of the area. We're going to have to do some checking out on Cartwright's tale. It all sounds a bit too convenient to me."

Half an hour later, they set off. Cordelia navigated them across country for fifteen miles, then they shot up the motorway. They turned off in the depths of rural Cheshire and drove down country lanes for a few miles. Lindsay finally pulled into a car park beside a high wall. The two women got out and looked around them doubtfully.

They walked across to a high, forbidding gate and rang a bell. A small door opened and a prison officer appeared. Through the gap, Lindsay spotted an Alsatian guard dog chained to a security booth, Cordelia explained who they were and, after waiting for a couple of minutes while they were checked out, they were allowed in. Ahead lay twin inner rings of mesh fencing topped with ugly loops of barbed wire. Incongruously, this was succeeded by wide, beautifully trimmed lawns and flower beds, well stocked with mature rose bushes. Beyond that lay the red brick buildings, clean-cut functional, modern. They could have been offices, except for the barred windows and heavy double doors.

A woman prison officer walked them across the lawn to a square, three-storey building with a small plaque by the door reading. "Female wing. Hospital Wing." As soon as they entered the building they felt enclosed, almost claustrophobic, in spite of the bright colours of the paintwork and the occasional plant on the window sills. They were shown into a room that smelled of sweat and cigarette smoke. A listless man in his forties with a tired-looking teddy-boy haircut glanced at them without interest as they sat down at the opposite end of a long wooden bench. They sat in silence for more than ten minutes. Then another officer entered the room at the far end.

"Lindsay Gordon, Cordelia Brown," she said. They stood up. The officer indicated the door she had come in by and the three of them trooped through. Lindsay noticed that the door was locked behind them. The officer took the clothes, cigarettes, books and food that they'd brought for Paddy and showed them to a table. They faced a glass screen with strips of wire mesh at each side. At every corner of the room there were more prison officers. Even Lindsay, whose job had taken her to most extreme circumstances, found the atmosphere oppressive and alienating. She could barely guess at the effect all this would have on someone like Paddy.

After a few minutes, a door at the opposite end of the room opened, and the officer returned with Paddy. Already life behind bars had left its mark on her. Her skin had an unhealthy sallowness. There were dark bags beneath her eyes. But what was most striking was that she seemed to have lost all her self-confidence. Fewer than three days of living behind bars had cut her down to less than life-size. She looked uncertainly across the room. When she saw Lindsay and Cordelia, relief flooded her face. But even the eagerness with which she approached them seemed tempered with uncertainty. It was as if she expected them to have changed as much as she had and couldn't quite believe that they were still completely normal.

Cordelia spoke first. "My God, Paddy, this is dreadful. How are you managing to cope?"

Paddy shrugged and said, "You just have to, Cordelia. Most of the time, I try to switch off and project myself back home. It's not easy. It's routine that's the killer. Up at half-past seven, wash, breakfast in the dining-room with Radio One blasting out, then cleaning and sewing till lunch, then back to the workshops, unless Gillian's managed to get here. Then it's tea, then it's telly, and then it's bed. It's so debilitating. All you hear is Radio One and the sound of keys. You're not expected to think for yourself at any time; it's amazing how quickly you lose the habit."

Lindsay nodded sympathetically. "You must feel really shut off from everything. But don't think you're forgotten. Pamela Overton's got us working overtime to try and find out what actually happened. I know it must seem pretty pointless, expecting a pair of wallies like us to get to the bottom of things, but we're doing the best we can."

"Gillian told me. I appreciate it. It's not easy to feel optimistic in here, though. I feel condemned already. After all, what can you do against the combined forces of the police and the legal system?"

Lindsay pulled a wry face. "Probably not a lot. But we've got an advantage over them—we *know* you're innocent."

Paddy produced a tired smile. "Thanks for that. But you can't really know that for sure. I'm beginning to wonder if I didn't have a brainstorm and I just can't remember it now. You never think that a miscarriage of justice is going to happen to you, do you? I've spent all my life in a world where the police are the ones you call when the house gets burgled, or some drunk is falling through your hedge at midnight. Even when I was dealing dope I never really believed they'd touch me. You never expect them to get it wrong for you."

"You mustn't begin thinking like that," pleaded Cordelia. "Eventually they'll realise that they've made a terrible mistake. We're just trying to speed the process up a bit, that's all. You'll be out of here a free woman in no time at all."

Paddy shook her head. "I'll never be able to think of myself as a 'free woman' again, Cordelia."

Seeing that the conversation was moving into channels likely to depress Paddy even further, Lindsay interrupted.

"Look, Paddy, we're only allowed quarter of an hour. We need to pick your brains about the other people involved in this business. We've already talked to Margaret Macdonald about her relationship with Lorna—believe it or not, it turns out they were lovers years ago."

"Margaret? And Lorna?" Paddy interrupted. "That's incredible. I thought I knew Margaret well. But I'd no idea. My God, the skeletons are falling out of the cupboards now, aren't they?"

"You're not wrong there. But we think we'll have to rule her out and we don't want to have to drag her in as a red herring just to cast doubt on the evidence against you, not unless it's absolutely necessary. We've also got something on Sarah Cartwright's father that could be promising. But we need some other lines of attack. Who else might have wanted to see the back of Lorna?"

Cordelia butted in, "For example, did Caroline Barrington think that Lorna was behind her parents' marriage break-up?"

Paddy lit a cigarette before she replied. "Caroline blamed Lorna totally. I tried to talk her out of seeing it that way, but she wasn't having any. I don't know the full story, but apparently Lorna had an affair with Caroline's father which he was more wrapped up in than she was. The marriage broke up over it, but Lorna and he never really got it together. Caroline was very bitter at the time, and when she heard Lorna was coming to the school, she was furious. I was quite surprised when she volunteered for the programme selling at the concert."

"What about the girl who came to fetch you from Longnor? The one with the amazing head of red hair. Is there anything she might be able to tell us that could help?" Lindsay asked. Paddy shrugged again. "I doubt it. Though if there was, Jessica would certainly tell you. She's another one who hated Lorna's guts, you see. That's why she wasn't playing at the concert even though she's one of our best young musicians. You remember that row I had with Margaret in the staffroom, Lindsay? That was about Jessica. She'd come to me at the last minute and explained she couldn't go through with the concert with Lorna there.

"It was all to do with her brother, Dominic. He was a brilliant violinist, and Jessica worshipped the ground he walked on. There was some business between him and Lorna—she latched on to him and promised him the first vacancy in her string quartet. But things went wrong between them and she gave the post to someone else. Then there was some business about a reference she wouldn't give him for some other orchestral job, and he didn't get that either. The pressure of being rejected twice like that was too much for him—he killed himself. He clearly wasn't at all stable; in fact from what I've heard the blame was as much on his side as on Lorna's, but Jessica will never see it that way."

"I don't see how you can be so bloody charitable about Lorna," Cordelia burst out. "She was nothing but trouble to us while she was alive; and now she's dead, she's carrying on the good work."

"Leave it, Cordelia," soothed Lindsay. "What's the girl's full name, Paddy?"

"Jessica Bennett."

"Thanks, we'll have a chat with her. Now, what about Sarah Cartwright? Gillian tells us that she's given the police a statement about Saturday morning." Lindsay succinctly outlined what the lawyer had said on the phone. "What have you got to say to that, Paddy? Did it happen like she says?"

Paddy looked bewildered. "I don't know . . . It's true that I took her to Music 2 because I knew that nobody else would be using it and I wanted to get her on her own in the hope that she might open up a bit. I don't remember the other things she says happened—but then, I was very abstracted. I was worried about her; I had the play on my mind; and I was still twitchy about Lorna. So they might have happened. I honestly can't say definitely that they didn't take place. After all, there's no reason why the girl should lie."

"But of course there is," argued Cordelia. "She could be protecting either herself or her father."

Paddy shook her head. "I don't think she'd have deliberately done something that would cause me trouble. I'm closer to the girl than anyone else in the school. I can't believe she would calculatedly lie about me."

Lindsay interrupted gently. "I know it's hard to believe, Paddy, but try to think objectively. Don't you think that Sarah might just do anything for her father's sake? Even to the extent of killing?"

Paddy considered the question. "She's cool enough under normal circumstances to pull it off, I suppose. And she feels passionately protective of her father. Perhaps she might not be too worried about putting me in a spot if she looked at it as a straight choice between him and me. But when it comes to murder—I can't believe that. For one thing, I don't think she knew the music department well enough to set it up. And besides she was so upset after her row on Saturday morning, I doubt if she'd have been able to compose herself sufficiently to get it all together. No, I can't see Sarah as the killer at all."

Seeing that this line of conversation was upsetting Paddy, Lindsay decided on another approach. "Is there anything you can think of that might give us a new line to work on? Anything at all? Some little detail you might have noticed but not bothered about—in the room or in the music department?"

Paddy slowly shook her head. "Nothing springs to mind. Don't you think I've already been through it a million times in my head these last three days?" She rubbed her eyes with her fists. "After all," she sighed, "there's not a lot else to fill my head."

They all sat back in their chairs for a moment, Lindsay trying to hide her pity for her friend and her disappointment that nothing more substantial had emerged from the conversation. She leaned forward again and said reassuringly, "I've managed to come up with the goods on investigative stories before with less to go on than we've got here. And with Cordelia to keep me right, I'm sure we're going to crack this one too. I'm not giving up on you, Paddy, I owe you one."

For a moment, Paddy's face looked animated and she almost smiled, but at that moment the prison officer approached Paddy and said that their time was up. Immediately, Paddy's eyes became bleak again and she got to her feet. "Come again when you can," she implored before vanishing through the door once more.

When they emerged into the open space of the car park, Lindsay gulped air in as though that would somehow cleanse her. She leaned against the car, shoulders slumped and face full of dismay. Cordelia leaned against the wall, fighting back the tears. "It's so bloody unfair," she spat.

"I know," Lindsay sighed. "I feel completely inadequate. How the hell can we sort this mess out? I just don't know where to start."

"At least she's given us a couple of leads. We've got reasonable excuses for talking to Caroline and Jessica now."

Lindsay nodded wearily. "I suppose so. I kept on thinking there was something important I should have asked Paddy, but I don't know what it was. There's something which has been nagging at the back of my mind since Sunday and it won't surface for long enough to grasp it. But I know it's somehow significant, whatever it is."

Cordelia shrugged herself away from the wall. "Come on, we'd better get on the road to London. Maybe Andrew Christie will hold the key that will unlock all of this."

"I doubt it," Lindsay muttered. "But let's go anyway."

12

Andrew Christie ushered the two of them into the living-room of an elegant and expensive flat. It occupied the basement and ground floor of a tall, narrow Victorian house, and the large living-room was exactly what Lindsay imagined a slightly pretentious television producer should inhabit. The furniture was Habitat—inevitably tasteful without exhibiting any taste—three two-seater settees and a plethora of low tables piled with magazines, newspapers, scripts and half-full ashtrays. But the room was dominated by the electronic media. There was a giant television screen and a normal-sized set, two video recorders, an expensive hi-fi system and yards of shelves containing records, cassettes, video tapes and reel-to-reel tapes. Lindsay found it the least relaxing room she'd ever been in. Christie was in his late thirties, with shaggy blond hair, slim and wiry and dressed in tight olive green jeans, an open-necked plaid shirt and a shapeless hairy sweater. He looked the part.

"Sit down, do," he said in a voice like a radio announcer's. "I don't quite know how I can help you. Lorna and I had only been seeing each other for about three months and I can't say I was aware of her having enemies of sufficient seriousness to . . . well—to do this."

"We were hoping you'd be able to tell us a bit about her. Her personality, her lifestyle, her friends, that sort of thing,"

Lindsay responded gently. She knew she wouldn't be able to press this man as she had done Cartwright. She understood his grief too well. "The more we know about Lorna, the more chance we have of finding out why she was killed. And by whom. I know it's not easy to talk when it's only just happened and we do appreciate you giving us some time. I know we've got no official standing here, but it's important to us to establish who really did this. If you knew Paddy Callaghan like we do, you'd know that it would have been impossible for her to have committed such a cowardly crime."

For the first time, emotion flickered across his face. "I miss Lorna," he said. "I know a lot of people didn't care too much for her; she had a very cutting tongue at times. But to me she was always very tender. She used to make me laugh. She could be very funny at other people's expense. I don't think she especially meant to be cruel, but not everyone could see the humour behind what she said."

There was a pause. "How did you meet?" asked Cordelia. "I'd known her slightly for quite a long time—we had some mutual acquaintances and found ourselves at the same parties. Then I was producing a drama-documentary about Elgar and I needed someone to play the cello concerto. She seemed the obvious choice. I was very impressed by her attitude as I worked with her. She was the complete professional. I know she put people's backs up by criticising their talent and motivation, but that was simply because she was such a perfectionist herself. But no one gets killed for that. It makes no sense to me at all. I keep thinking about all that beauty gone out of the world just because of some evil bastard's inability to cope with life."

"Did she say anything about last weekend before she went? I mean, did she mention anyone in particular?" asked Lindsay.

He paused, then said, "She was looking forward to it. She said it should be good for a laugh, at least. She said there were one or two people she'd take pleasure in showing that she'd arrived and was somebody. She didn't mention any names. She also said it would be good for publicity because of the controversy about the fund locally. She hated talking to the press; she thought they were scum. But she was too good a businesswoman to ignore the value of publicity. Sorry, that's not much help, is it?"

"More than you think," said Lindsay. "Now, I'm going to ask you if some names mean anything to you, if you'd ever heard of any of them before the weekend. For example, had she ever mentioned Cordelia here?"

"Yes. At first, she was terribly amused that some people seemed to think that a nasty character in your last novel was based on her. She said it wasn't terribly likely, since you hadn't spent any time together for years. Then a few weeks ago when your novel was nominated for the Booker, it all flared up again and she began to get cross with people for making the same remark over and over again. She decided that if she was going to get all this stick, she should get something in return. So she set the wheels in motion to sue. She was amused that you were going to be at the school. She said—sorry about this—it would be fun to watch you squirm."

"Did she indeed!" said Cordelia through frozen lips.

"Had you ever heard her speak of Paddy Callaghan?"

"Never."

"James Cartwright? Or his daughter Sarah?" The mechanical recital of names was helping Lindsay relax into her questioning.

"Definitely not."

"Jessica Bennett, Dominic Bennett's sister?"

"She never mentioned a sister, but I know about Dominic, yes. He was quite a gifted young musician, Lorna said, and she'd encouraged his talent. She told him that one day she might be able to use him in her string quartet. But he wasn't quite up to scratch when a vacancy came up, so of course she had to turn him down. He was more distressed than she realised, and he killed himself soon after. Where does his sister come into this?"

"She's a pupil at the school. Does the name Margaret Macdonald mean anything?"

He shook his head. "Sorry."

"Caroline Barrington?"

"Barrington? Any relation to Anthony Barrington? He had a relationship with Lorna. She told me about him. Apparently he couldn't accept it when she cooled off, and went to the extent of divorcing his wife to try to force Lorna to marry him. But she wouldn't have it. They split up about six months before we got together. I got the impression that he caused her a lot of grief. But she never tried to make one feel sorry for her, for what she'd suffered in the past. She always said you start relationships with a clean sheet. God, I'm going to miss her," and he pressed the back of his hands against his eyes in a curiously vulnerable gesture. "The worst thing is that I can't get peace simply to sit and grieve. The police, the press and now you. Not that I blame you. I like to think that I'd do the same for a friend of mine. But there will be no peace until after the court case. And probably not even then. It makes me so bloody sad. A complete waste."

"And damage done to the living," said Cordelia. "There's been enough of that already and it's not finished yet. One last thing before we go—how many people knew she was going up to Derbyshire last weekend? Is there anyone else you can think of who might have had a motive for wanting to harm her—I mean in the widest sense?"

"Thousands of people knew where she was going. There were a few paragraphs about it in the *Daily Argus* diary column last week. As for motives—no, I don't know anyone who'd be crazy enough to want to harm her. It's all insane. All of it. It doesn't feel real. I've been working these last few days on the final stages of the Elgar documentary. It's going out in three weeks. It's very weird watching the film and hearing the soundtrack of her playing and knowing that's all that's left. I must have actually been working on that with the editor when she was being killed. It's hell."

"I know," said Lindsay. "I lost someone I loved once. You feel like part of you has been amputated. And nothing anyone says makes the slightest difference."

Cordelia cleared her throat. "Well, thanks for your help. We'd better be off now. I'm sorry if we've upset you."

He saw them to the door. His parting words as they climbed the shallow steps up from his basement entrance were, "Thanks, I wish you could have known her as I did."

They got back into the car. Lindsay had found the interview extremely painful. The man's grief had taken her back three years to the death of her lover. It was an experience she thought she had learned how to handle. But now she felt again the vivid pain that had filled her life for months after Frances's death had devastated her world.

"At least one person grieves for her," said Cordelia. "I can't decide whether she did a magnificent con job on him or whether he genuinely saw a side to Lorna that was hidden from the rest of us."

"Who's to say?" Lindsay replied. "Either way, it's not going to affect his memories. Unfortunately, however. I don't think our little chat has taken us any further forward. If anything, it only widens the field to the entire readership of the *Daily Argus*. Still, it was edifying to find out what Lorna apparently thought of Dominic Bennett and Anthony Barrington. Now, how do I get to your place?"

Under Cordelia's careful guidance, Lindsay drove them to a quiet cul-de-sac of tall Victorian terraced houses overlooking Highbury Fields. Feeling somewhat overawed by the fact that Cordelia's home was obviously one of the few three-storey houses that was not converted into flats, Lindsay followed Cordelia up the steps to the door. Cordelia caught sight of Lindsay's expression and grinned.

"Don't worry," she said, "it's not as grand as it looks. My accountant told me that property was the best investment, so I lashed out on this with the proceeds of my early successes in the mass media."

They stepped into the narrow hall. Cordelia flicked on the subdued lighting that revealed watercolour sketches of Italian landscapes. "In here," she said, opening one of the doors leading off the hall. Lindsay stepped through into an L-shaped living-room that was twice the size of her own in Glasgow. Four wooden-shuttered windows stretched from ceiling to floor. There was an enormous grey leather Chesterfield on one side of the fireplace and two matching wing chairs on the other side. On the polished wooden floor a couple of good Oriental rugs provided the only splashes of colour. Round the corner was the dining area, furnished with an oval mahogany dining-table and six matching balloon-backed chairs.

"My God," said Lindsay. "It's like living in a page out of *House and Garden.*"

Mistaking her contempt for admiration, Cordelia laughed and said, "As I spend an enormous amount of time in this place, I took a great deal of time and trouble to furnish it. I indulged myself completely. Do you really like it?"

Lindsay looked around her again in amazement. "To be honest, I don't think I'd ever feel at home in these surroundings, Cordelia. You could buy my whole flat in Glasgow with what you've spent on this one room."

"But what's wrong with being comfortable, for God's sake?"

"There's comfort and there's comfort. I feel comfortable in my flat with its tatty chairs that don't match and the threadbare carpet in the spare room. Put it down to my Scottish puritanism or my politics, but I find it a bit over the top."

"I'm sorry if you find it oppressive—I'll just have to re-educate you to appreciate it," Cordelia replied acidly.

"I'm sorry, I didn't mean to sound rude, I was just being honest. I get outraged about anyone spending so much money on a place to live. Though I suppose if I had the money I'd lash out a bit myself."

"But your flat's lovely. All the rooms are so airy. Now take my study. It has practically no light at all; even in sum-mer I have to have the desk lamp on most of the day. My mother keeps telling me it'll make me go blind. I tell her she's getting muddled and my eyesight is in no danger." They laughed. "Fancy a drink? I could do with one, and you must be exhausted after all that driving. There's whisky, sherry, gin, vodka, you name it . . ."

Lindsay settled for wine and together they went through to the kitchen. Cordelia said, "We'll have something to eat. The freezer's full of food. I have a binge every three months—I cook like mad, fill the freezer and live out of it."

The conspicuous consumerism of the kitchen took Lindsay's breath away. The units were oak, and the worktops bristled with gadgetry. "I love kitchen machines," said Cordelia as she tossed the chosen lasagne-for-two into the microwave.

"I never realised writing was so lucrative," said Lindsay wryly, picturing her own kitchen whose sum total of gadgetry was a liquidiser, a coffee grinder and a cooker, and whose decor consisted of theatre posters begged from friends.

"Well, to be fair, it's not all the proceeds of my sweated labour. My grandmother died three years ago and left me rather a large legacy. That went on the deposit for this place. Most of the rest of the money has come from telly, radio and the film I scripted last year. Crazy, isn't it? The novels are what I really care about, but they wouldn't allow me to live in a bedsit in Hackney, let alone here."

"You really are one of the obscenely privileged minority, aren't you?" remarked Lindsay. "I don't know what I'm doing with you at all. In my job, I see so much poverty, so much deprivation, so much exploitation, I can't help feeling that luxury like this is obscene. Don't you want to change things?"

Cordelia laughed and replied lightly. "But what would you have me do? Give all I've got to the poor?"

Lindsay saw the chasm yawning at her feet. She could leave the argument lying for a future day when there might be a strong enough relationship between them to stand the weight of disagreement. Or she could pursue the subject relentlessly and kill the magic stone dead. She turned away and deliberately picked up a cookery book.

⋰⋰❖⋱⋱

That night, the love-making was more tentative, less urgent than before. The reverberations of their earlier differences had died down as they had explored each other's history during the evening. Cordelia was already in bed by the time Lindsay came through from the kitchen with a tumbler of water. She undressed quickly. As she slid beneath the duvet, Cordelia turned on her side and they embraced. "All right?" she enquired.

"I feel a bit drained, to be honest. It's been quite a day. Margaret, Cartwright, Paddy in prison. And tonight. I haven't worked so hard for a long time." She smiled ruefully. "And then, boring you with my life story. Very exhausting."

"I wasn't bored. But I know what you mean. I feel pretty done in too."

"Not so tired that all you want is sleep?"

In reply, Cordelia leaned over and kissed her warmly.

More than the chaotic coupling of the previous nights it sealed them close. For the first time, neither was trying to prove anything. Lindsay lay awake as Cordelia slept. No matter how much she buried herself in the joyous sensation of making love with Cordelia, the uncomfortable thoughts wouldn't disappear without trace. And now that she'd actually seen for herself the way her new lover lived, those uncomfortable thoughts had a new element.

PART III

FUGUE

13

It was noon before Cordelia and Lindsay pulled in beside Paddy Callaghan's Land Rover at Derbyshire House on Friday. Lindsay had felt an increasing sense of unreality as the morning had worn on. The conversation of the evening before had all but restored her to her normal frame of mind, by recalling her past and awakening her desires for the future. Somehow that all seemed very distant from what had been happening in the last few days. It seemed absurd to Lindsay that she and Cordelia should have any pretensions about being able to solve the problem of Lorna Smith-Couper's death. She could not shake the increasing conviction that she was taking part in some elaborate but ultimately silly game. Only the presence of Cordelia made her determined to finish what they had started.

She was not even able to pause and collect her thoughts before they came face to face with Jessica Bennett at the door of Longnor House. The girl started when she saw them and a momentary panic flashed across her eyes before she regained her composure.

"Hello, Jessica. We haven't actually met, but Cordelia and I wanted to have a chat with you." Lindsay announced before the girl could escape. "We saw Miss Callaghan yesterday. She thought you might be able to help us with a couple of details. Are you busy at the moment?"

"Well . . . I suppose not. I'm meant to be in the library for private study, but no one will check up on me if I'm not there. They'll just assume I'm doing something else," the girl replied nervously.

The three of them went to Paddy's rooms. While Cordelia made some coffee, Jessica seemed apprehensive, so Lindsay tried to put her at her ease. "What are you studying for now? Is it A levels?"

"Yes. I'm doing music, history and maths. I know it sounds a funny combination—at least everyone says it is—but maths and music are very closely related in some ways, so it helps. The history I'm doing because I like it."

"That's a good enough reason. What comes next? After this place?"

"I'm not sure. I'd like to carry on with my music, but I don't know if I'll be good enough to get into one of the Royal Colleges. If not, I'll settle for reading music at university, I suppose. If my results are good enough. It's just a matter of working hard now, I guess."

Lindsay reckoned that Jessica was being so forthcoming because she did not want to come round to the subject of Lorna's death. So while the girl was still talkative, Lindsay started to slip in the more awkward questions. She said casually, "I shouldn't imagine anyone's getting much work done at the moment. The upheaval of the last few days must take a lot of getting used to."

Jessica's air of nervousness instantly returned. "It hasn't exactly been a help to anyone," she replied.

"If you'd known Miss Callaghan as long as I have, you'd know for certain she just couldn't have been involved in this," Lindsay said, throwing caution to the winds. "What are the girls saying?"

"No one—at least, no one I've heard—can believe it. Miss Callaghan's a marvellous housemistress. She really does have an instinct about the way people's minds work, and she gets under your skin to know how you feel underneath. She's always so understanding, you know? She tries to be a friend to us without being patronising, or playing favourites, like some teachers do. She gets angry with people sometimes and lets them know it, but nobody could imagine her being so . . . so . . . you know? We like her, you see," Jessica explained anxiously.

"And you didn't like Lorna Smith-Couper, did you?"

Jessica did not flinch. She did not respond at all. Lindsay continued slowly and quietly. "We have a problem. We're trying to get Miss Callaghan freed from prison, not just because Miss Overton has asked us to. We're not necessarily setting out to prove that any particular person did it. What we are trying to show is that there are other people against whom there is as much or as little circumstantial evidence as that which exists against Miss Callaghan. That way her solicitor can show up the weakness of the case against her."

Cordelia returned with the coffee and handed the mugs round. She took over from Lindsay, saying, "It seems to us, from what Miss Callaghan told us, that you might have some information about her movements that might possibly help. Let me repeat, we're not trying to pin the blame on you or on anyone else. We're simply trying to prove that other people were as likely—or unlikely, if you like—to have done this thing as Paddy. Now I think it's possible you didn't tell the police every detail of what you saw and heard. Perhaps you thought they might take it the wrong way because they don't know the people concerned. But you can tell us everything. You know whose side we're on."

For a moment there was stillness. Then Jessica nodded and said, "I don't mind talking to you. You could probably find out anything I have to tell you by asking other people, anyway. And Miss Overton asked us at assembly to co-operate with you as well as with the police. But I'd rather you heard what I have to say from me and not in a garbled version from other people. What do you want to ask me?"

The girl was still clearly very tense. There was little colour in her face and her freckles stood out like a rash. But as Cordelia asked the first question, she flushed an ugly scarlet. "How did you feel about Lorna?"

Jessica started to speak, but bit back her words. She struggled for control, then said venomously, "I hope she rots in hell. I hated her. And I despised her. I'm not surprised that someone killed her. I only wish it could have happened before she ever came near us. Then Dominic would still be alive now. I wished her dead, and I'm glad now that she is. I wish I'd had the nerve to think of doing it myself. I'd have enjoyed watching her suffer with the realisation that she was paying for what she did to my brother." She ran out of steam, seeming surprised and a little dismayed at her vehemence.

"What did she do to your brother, Jessica?" Lindsay pushed.

"They were going out with each other, and she promised him that she'd give him a job. She ran a string quartet and there was a vacancy for a violinist. He was really good, you know, more than good enough for her quartet. Anyway, they had a row and she ended up giving the job to someone else who wasn't anything like as good. So Dominic applied for a job with the Garden Chamber Orchestra as a second violin. And she was such a bitch that she gave him a reference that was so unenthusiastic it cost him that job too. After that, he found it really hard to get decent work. All he ever cared about was making the best possible music. But Lorna put a stop to that. And he killed himself." Her voice faded out, shaking and tearful.

"Was this the first time you'd seen her since your brother's death?" asked Lindsay.

"I didn't really see her, only across the room at dinner. I couldn't face going to the concert. I couldn't bear to hear her playing music I love. It would have hurt too much; Miss Callaghan saw that. That's why she left me in charge of Longnor, so I wouldn't have to be at the concert. And she sorted it all out with Miss Macdonald. I was supposed to be in the choir, you see, with a small solo. They got Karina Holgate to do it instead."

"But you did come across to the hall, didn't you? I thought I saw you talking to Caroline Barrington," said Lindsay.

Jessica nodded and took a gulp of coffee. "I thought the police would have asked me about that, but no one seems to have told them I was there. I told you I was left in charge of Longnor. Well, one of the fourth-formers was ill. She kept being sick, and I suspected she might have been drinking. I didn't want to be responsible for what might happen, so I thought it was best to come across to find Miss Callaghan."

"Did you see anyone hanging around outside, or anything else suspicious?"

Jessica shook her head. "There were quite a few people milling around outside the hall, but they all looked as if they were going to the concert. I recognised one or two of them because I've seen them in the town, and some of them because they're parents. I saw Caroline's father getting out of his car when I came across, but I don't think he can have stayed for the concert because his car had gone when I came back with Miss Callaghan. But you'd better ask Caroline about that."

Lindsay and Cordelia exchanged a look. Yet another complication had emerged. "What happened when you got to the hall?" Cordelia asked.

"I asked Caroline if she'd seen Miss Callaghan and she said she thought she was still backstage. I went through and asked one or two people if they'd seen her, but everyone was too busy to have noticed. I went down the side passage as far as the storeroom to see if she was there, but there was no sign of her. Then I went back to the main corridor and looked into the rest of the music rooms. I finally found her just outside Miss Macdonald's room, round the corner. I told her what had happened and she said I'd done the right thing and came straight back with me. She stayed in Longnor then for about half an hour." She ground to a halt.

"Did it seem to you as if Miss Callaghan had just come out of Miss Macdonald's room?" asked Lindsay cautiously.

"I don't think so. There are a few steps that lead down to the room. She was about half-way down them, looking out of the window down the front drive." She hesitated, then said in a rush, "She seemed to be miles away. I had to speak to her twice before she heard me."

Lindsay and Cordelia looked at each other, both filled with dread at the thought of how this new evidence could be made to sound by a good prosecuting counsel. Then Cordelia roused herself and said, "Did she seem upset or agitated at all, Jessica?"

"No, she just seemed to be very thoughtful. Preoccupied. Usually she's very lively and chatty. It was as if she had something on her mind. Not as if she'd just killed someone, if that's what you mean—not like that at all. She couldn't have done that, could she? Not someone like Miss Callaghan?"

"We don't believe so, no," said Lindsay. "Are you sure you didn't go any further down the side passage than the storeroom? You said you checked all the other music rooms on the main corridor. Didn't you check Music 2?"

"No, I definitely didn't go all the way down the corridor."

"Why not?"

"Because I knew that's where Lorna Smith-Couper had to be. I knew who was supposed to be in which room. I'd been involved with everything up to the last minute. I thought I could face her, so I'd taken part in the preparations. I knew the only room she could be in was Music 2 and she was the last person I wanted to see. If Miss Callaghan had been with her, I would just have had to wait till she came out again, or tried to find Matron. Nothing would have induced me to go anywhere near that room."

"Why didn't you get Matron in the first place? Why come to the music rooms for Miss Callaghan at all?" asked Lindsay.

"Because I thought the girl had been drinking. I thought Miss Callaghan would deal with it more sort of sensibly than Matron."

"Okay. Now, when you went down to the storeroom, did you see anyone outside Music 2?"

"I couldn't see round the corner of the corridor. But I did hear someone running down the back stairs. It sounded like someone wearing high heels. Could that be important, do you think?"

Cordelia replied, "I don't think that would tell the police anything they don't know already," she said, trying to sound nonchalant. The last thing she wanted was for the girl to think she had any ulterior motive in keeping her from giving information to the police. Lindsay and Cordelia exchanged a worried look. Almost certainly it was Cordelia that Jessica had heard. But if they encouraged her to go to the police with that corroboration, she might also tell them about Paddy's state outside Margaret Macdonald's room. The question of what to do for the best completely put out of their minds any other questions they might have wanted to ask Jessica.

"Is that all, then?" the redhead asked.

Lindsay nodded. "Yes, thank you. You've been quite a help to us. You'd better get off to the library now in case anyone's looking for you."

Jessica rose and went to the door. As she left, she turned and said shyly, "I hope you manage to clear Miss Callaghan. We all miss her." And she was gone.

"Not exactly a convenient witness," said Lindsay. "Prosecuting counsel would have a field day with her and Paddy's preoccupations. And your disappearing footsteps could get the police putting you in the frame as an accomplice. Let's hope we can clear Paddy without the police ever becoming aware of Miss Jessica Bennett's evidence."

"We're still not much further forward, though are we?"

"I don't know about that. We've got some hard questions to ask Sarah Cartwright, and now it turns out the jilted divorcee was on the scene too. We've got a decent list of possible murderers to present to Paddy's solicitor. But as I've said, I would rather tie

the whole thing up than leave loose ends and red herrings haunting the lives of a handful of people. Now, it's alibi-establishing
time. We can incorporate finding food with our examination
of James Cartwright's alleged alibi."

Cordelia smiled and said, "I can't help feeling that we are
mixing rather too much pleasure with our business."

"That's what you get for tying yourself up with a journalist.
We're great believers in looking after the comforts of the flesh
while we do the business."

"Okay, okay. I have heard that the Stonemason's at Wincle
does excellent food . . ."

Once in the car, to Cordelia's bewilderment, they drove
straight to the offices of the local paper. Lindsay left her sitting
there and reappeared ten minutes later clutching a photograph
of Cartwright. She said, "I managed to persuade one of the
local lads to let me borrow this picture. We might need it to
identify him. I promised the bloke I'd tip him off if there's any
change in the situation that might lead to fresh arrests. Which
of course I probably won't have the chance to do, but he's not
to know that."

They drove back to the school gates, where Lindsay turned
the car round in a spray of gravel. "Show-off," muttered Cordelia.

"Thank you. Now, I want to check some timings. Bear in
mind that that Mercedes of his is faster than my MG, and that
he knows these roads like the back of his hand. I want to see
if this alibi can be cracked. We'll have to check timings as far
as possible with the pubs, to see if he could have squeezed in
enough time for the killing. I'm not convinced by his injured
innocence routine. Done any rally driving, Cordelia?"

Cordelia looked aghast. "Certainly not," she replied.

"Well, you'll have to try and navigate for me. I've marked
what looks like the best routes on the map. You study that and
the terrain and tell me what's coming next. Okay?"

"I'll try. Have you done much rally driving?"

"Not a bit," said Lindsay blithely. "But I know the theory."

They set off back towards Buxton in an atmosphere of intense concentration, then turned down the Macclesfield road. Lindsay tore round the tight ascending bends in third, and as soon as they hit the straight stretch where they turned down the Congleton road, she flipped the switch that took the engine into overdrive. They turned off into a succession of country lanes and, after a hair-raising hurtle, they roared to a halt outside the Stonemason's Arms.

"Can I open my eyes now?" asked Cordelia mockingly. "Fourteen minutes and about five seconds."

The Stonemason's Arms was a long low stone building with a roof of heavy slate slabs. They found themselves in a clean, neat public bar, with matching wooden chairs, olde worlde wooden tables and chintz curtains at the windows. But the beer was real ale on hand pumps, so they perched on bar stools with a pint of best bitter for Lindsay and a dry white wine for Cordelia, having ordered two ploughman's special lunches. Lindsay wasted no time in eliciting information from the barmaid, a faded woman around forty who turned out to be the landlord's wife.

"I suppose you don't get much time off," she said sympathetically.

"Oh, we always take Tuesdays off," said the woman. "You have to get away from the place sometimes or else you'd go mad. It was always my husband's dream to retire to a country pub. When he was made redundant a couple of years ago, it seemed the obvious thing. Myself, I think it's a lot of hard work and not as much fun as people seem to think."

"Well, you certainly know how to please your customers. This is one of the nicest pints I've had in a long time. Actually, a friend of mine recommended this place to us. James Cartwright, I suppose you know him?"

"Oh yes, he's a regular in here. He often pops in for his evening meal. Living alone, with his daughter boarding at that school, I think he enjoys the company and not having to cook for himself. You'd think he'd have a housekeeper, really, but he seems to prefer looking after himself."

"Yes, he was just saying to me yesterday that it's just as well he's a familiar face in here. He was telling me the police had some daft idea he might have had something to do with the murder on Saturday night, but that since he'd been here at the time he was completely in the clear. He said it was a real blessing you knew him."

The landlady nodded vigorously. "That's right. We had the police here on Sunday asking about him. He came in about five to eight, I remember, because I'd been watching *Go for Gold* on the telly. I told the police, don't be silly, Mr Cartwright couldn't have anything to do with a murder! He was just the same as usual, chatty and cheery. He had something to eat—I think it was the grilled local trout—and two or three pints of his usual and then went off about ten."

"Lucky for him, really," said Lindsay. She was spared any further conversation by the arrival of their generous lunches, and the two of them retired to a distant table. As they ate, Cordelia talked between mouthfuls of cheese and bread.

"Let me see . . . now if he got here about five to eight . . . it would have taken him about quarter of an hour from the school. Say ten minutes to do what he had to do, give five to get there and get out again, and I'd give about ten to fifteen back to the Woolpack. So if he left the Woolpack before . . . say, about ten past seven, he's got no alibi and he could just have done it."

"Precisely. It all depends on what happened at the Woolpack. So eat, don't talk and we can buzz over there as soon as possible and suss them out."

Half an hour later they were in the bar at the Woolpack. In contrast with the suburban charm of the Stonemason's, the Woolpack was spartan and cheap. The plastic-covered benches and the chipped laminated table tops fitted well with the smell of stale beer and old tobacco smoke. A couple of farm labourers leaned against a corner of the bar. They fell silent when

Cordelia and Lindsay entered and stared blankly at them. Behind the bar was a bleached blonde in her twenties with too much eye make-up. "Really know how to make you feel welcome, don't they," Lindsay muttered to Cordelia as they approached the bar. This time Lindsay decided to drop the subtle approach and went straight to the point after she'd ordered her half pint of indifferent keg beer and a glass of white wine for Cordelia.

"Have one yourself," she insisted to the barmaid. "I wonder if you can help me? I'm a private investigator and I've been hired to look into this murder down the road at Derbyshire House School. I've been making inquiries into the movements of every-one connected with the case, and I want you to tell me if this man was in here on Saturday night." She took the photograph of Cartwright from her bag and handed it over.

"You're not the first, love," came the sullen reply. "Police've been here before you. But I may as well tell you what I told them. This bloke comes in here occasionally, and he was in on Saturday. We don't open while seven of a Saturday teatime, and he came in on the dot—same as a couple of hikers. I served him first and he went through the side parlour with a pint. I don't know how long he stopped; there's a door in there leads to the toilets and you can get out the back door that way. All I know is he was gone half an hour later when I went in to clear off the glasses. Now, if that's all, I'll get on with my work."

Without waiting for a reply, she disappeared through the door beside the bar. "A real charmer," said Cordelia. "Now do I have to finish this disgusting drink or can we push off?"

They left the pub and returned to the car for the second piece of timed driving. Lindsay drove the car to its limits and they shot into the drive a bare seven minutes later.

"I have the beginnings of a theory, thanks to you working out the times," Lindsay mused, cutting the engine. "Cartwright saw her sorting out strings, he says. Now, suppose she left them lying around in the room. He could fairly assume she'd be back there before she went on stage.

"He could have had a quick one in the Woolpack, raced back to the school, left his car in the trees beyond the houses, got the toggle from Longnor—after all, no one would have thought anything of seeing him there with Sarah doing her Greta Garbo routine. A quick dash through the trees to the main building. In by the side door, up the back stairs and into Music 2. He'd have had to go back home in the afternoon to pick up the school keys, by the way—I imagine he's got a set. Then he picks up a string—he's good with his hands, and strong. Then it's into the walk-in cupboard till Lorna arrives. As soon as Paddy goes, he's out and strangling her with one of the strings she's so conveniently left lying around. Then he's off, down the back stairs, drives like a madman and is back in the Stonemason's by five to eight. It could be done."

Cordelia looked doubtful. "It has its points. But you're assuming he has a set of keys. You're also assuming he could figure out her movements. I mean, it could have happened that Lorna didn't come into the room until just before she went on—he could have been stuck in the cupboard for over an hour, and where would his alibi have been then? And how the hell do we prove any of it?"

"You forget, we don't actually have to prove anything. We're not policemen, having to stand everything up in court. All we really have to do for Paddy's purposes is to demonstrate that she's far from being the only person with motive, means and opportunity."

"I suppose so. I rather like the thought of Cartwright as First Murderer. He could have given himself a bit more time by making his preparations in the afternoon—making the garrotte and all that. He couldn't be sure he'd get there ahead of Lorna, but it was a reasonable assumption. And the confusion over Margaret Macdonald's keys could simply be a fortuitous red herring."

"I don't know about you, but the more we find out, the more confused I get. We need to sit down and work out the permutations of what we know. What I need is a day off, to put all this to the back of my mind and do something completely different. But I know I can't walk away from this until we've at least got Paddy out of the mess she's in," Lindsay replied in a very tired voice.

"I know just what you mean," sighed Cordelia.

Back at the school, they drew up another of Cordelia's lists of essential information they'd picked up on their inquiries. As they suspected, the evidence still pointed in too many directions. Nothing had emerged that proved conclusively that Paddy could not have murdered Lorna Smith-Couper. Lindsay phoned Pamela Overton and asked her if Cartwright had a set of keys to the school. She promised to check up and let them know. Lindsay paced up and down Paddy's sitting-room, a worried frown on her face.

"There's something at the back of my mind that's got some bearing on the case. It's something I saw or heard. I can't even remember which. But some tiny thing has impressed itself on my mind and I've a feeling that it's the key to the whole damn business. Oh God, I wish I could remember! What a fool I am!" she exclaimed angrily.

"Relax," soothed Cordelia. "Try not to think about it and perhaps it will spring into your mind when you're doing something else."

"I've tried that. It hasn't worked so far. Do you know any good hypnotists?" asked Lindsay with a wry smile. "Now, we've still got things to do, you know. Shall we try to get hold of Caroline Barrington or Sarah Cartwright? It's almost four now, classes must be nearly finished."

"I suppose Caroline's the next person we should see," Cordelia sighed. "She might just know something that will help us put more pressure on Sarah Cartwright."

"Not until I've had another large injection of caffeine," Lindsay groaned. "Her heart seems to be in the right place, but she talks like a blue streak. I need to be fortified before we grill her or Caroline will end up grilling us."

She rose to go through to the kitchen, but before she could get there, Paddy's phone rang. Cordelia reached across the desk and picked it up. "Hello, Miss Callaghan's room . . . yes, that's right . . . Well, slowly at present, though I think we're making some . . . no, not as yet. No, we haven't been in contact with the police at all . . . well, I couldn't actually say. If you insist, we'll certainly do our best. Yes, four-thirty is fine. Yes, Lindsay knows that. Till then."

Cordelia put the phone down and muttered, "Damn and blast. That was Gillian. She wants to see us on Monday for a progress report. It looks as if the police are pressing for an early committal hearing and if she can demolish their case in the magistrates' court, she wants to have a go. So now we're battling against time, too."

Lindsay groaned. "That's all we need. We'd better cancel the coffee and find the garrulous Miss Barrington. Who knows, she might have the answers to the whole sorry business."

"If you were Hercule Poirot, she certainly would."

"Ah yes, but if I was Hercule Poirot, you wouldn't fancy me, would you?"

14

Longnor House seemed eerily silent as the two women climbed the stairs to Caroline's room on the top floor. Cordelia knocked. There was no reply, so they opened the door and entered. They had already agreed that if Caroline was not there they would wait for her. Lindsay walked over to the window and perched on the radiator beneath the wide sill. Cordelia sat on an upright chair by the desk, her legs propped against the waste-paper bin. They both studied the room as if seeing it for the first time, Lindsay checking off its features as she had not done when she was actually using it as a bedroom.

The basic furniture was institutional: a bed, table, chair, wardrobe, cupboard and chest of drawers. But Caroline's personality was everywhere. On the walls were a poster of Lenin, a large photograph of Virginia Woolf and a poster for a rally of peace women at Greenham Common. On the bookshelves were several textbooks. The rest of the space was taken up by dozens of books on politics, sociology and feminism. The table was untidy, but three things stood out. One was a desk calendar with photographs of sailing ships. But, as if by arrangement, both women's eyes reached out at the the same moment to the two framed photographs which were also on the desk. Cordelia picked them up. One was a family group, presumably consisting of Anthony Barrington, his ex-wife and their children. Caroline was between her parents, her brother and sister sitting on a sofa in front of them. The other was a photograph of the same man alone on top of a snow covered peak grinning into the camera. He was wearing climbing gear—old, stained clothes, heavy boots, ropes, a small rucksack. His face was lean and tanned, well-lined around the eyes. His eyebrows turned up slightly in the middle of his face, giving it a humorous cast. The rest of his face was unremarkable. But the eyes and their brows spoke of someone who might well be good fun to have around the place. No doubt Caroline thought so.

While Cordelia was studying the pictures more closely, the door opened and Caroline burst in, shouting over her shoulder, "Not tonight, I've got too much work to do." Cordelia started and almost dropped the pictures. Lindsay got to her feet as Caroline stopped in her tracks.

"Good Lord!" the girl exclaimed. "Murderers and burglars in the same week. Altogether too much for me."

In spite of herself, Lindsay smiled broadly. "Not exactly, no," she said. "We wanted to be sure of seeing you and your door was open. I promise we haven't been reading your letters and sifting through your worldly goods."

"Didn't for a minute think you had. Not that you'd find anything of interest if you did. I was just rather taken aback to find the super sleuths waiting to give me the third degree," Caroline replied, throwing herself down on the bed.

Cordelia remarked to no one in particular. "Good to see the old school grapevine is as efficient as it was in my day."

"Oh, everyone knows what it is you're here for. Her Majesty anounced it at assembly. I suppose you want to ask me about that bloody woman. I must say she caused enough trouble when she was alive without turning the world upside-down now she's dead. Really and truly, I think whoever put a stop to her should be congratulated, not punished. Still, that's a pretty antediluvian view, isn't it? I must say, though, that I think it's very dim of the police to have arrested The Boss. I mean, there are some pretty primitive people around who might think that killing people is some sort of answer, but really, she's not that sort at all. Not at all, truly." Caroline ground to a halt.

"The Boss?" queried Cordelia.

"Ooops! I mean Miss Callaghan," Caroline replied, blushing furiously.

"Why The Boss?" Lindsay asked.

"Because she lets you know who's in charge, I suppose. Hey, I hope you don't imagine I might have had anything to do with the murder? I mean, everyone's always telling me how hopelessly indiscreet I am, and I suppose I have rather been shooting the old mouth off about the ghastly woman's death being rather a blessing in extremely thin disguise. But honestly, do I look like a murderer to you?"

Lindsay found herself laughing out loud at the idea. Caroline sprawled on her counterpane, the picture of injured innocence. "Caroline," said Lindsay, "I can't honestly say that I think you're incapable of murder. But from what I've seen of you over the past week, I really have to say that if you had killed Lorna, you would have told the entire population of Derbyshire by now. If you're ever going to commit murder, you really must get laryngitis first."

Caroline grinned enormously, and suddenly Lindsay was struck by her resemblance to her father. It was her attitude—a sense of joy in risk-taking, a devil-may-care attitude—and at that moment, Lindsay saw that Caroline might indeed have killed Lorna and have managed to keep her mouth firmly shut. What better disguise for discretion than a reputation for logorrhoea?

"Okay, so if you know I didn't do it, what do you want me to tell you? Shall I start with what I told the police?" asked Caroline eagerly. It was hard not to see her as some enormously good-natured but clumsy young bear-cub.

"Tell us first of anything that struck you as at all unusual at any time all day Saturday," said Cordelia. Both women were conscious of the need not to waste the opportunity of a witness who seemed both talkative and observant.

"Well, the whole day was a bit funny, really. Miss Callaghan seemed a bit edgy, but I put that down to the general upheaval, plus she was responsible for both of you. Having a journalist on the loose about the place must have been a bit unnerving for everybody on the official side. I mean, only you know what you were going to say about us. You see, places like this are terribly insular, and being under constant attack from the forces of reason and equality make them even more on the defensive, you know? And then there was the business of Sarah Cartwright throwing a wobbler which upset more or less everybody—it threw Jacko into a perfect tail-spin and didn't exactly fill Miss Callaghan with good cheer.

"You were around, so I suppose you saw that carry-on. It was rather grisly, really. Sarah's a bit of a loner; I always get the feeling that she hasn't actually got much more to her life than this place, her father being so busy. I mean, my father is always up to his eyes in work, or climbing expeditions or whatever, but he always makes time to be with his children. It seems to me that Sarah's father puts work first—you know, if he's planned to take her off somewhere and work interferes, it's, 'Tough luck, old girl, we'll make it another time.' So although she doesn't really have close friends here, I suppose this place is more or less home to her. At least people are pretty impressed by her sporting ability.

"So of course, when those half-wits started to have a go at her it must have been pretty hellish. And, since Miss Callaghan is always frighteningly perceptive about what goes on inside our tiny heads, it's my guess that she must have been a bit upset on Sarah's account. All that would make her a bit iffy, wouldn't it?"

"Possibly," Cordelia replied. "Was she okay by the afternoon?"

"I don't know much about what went on then, because I was out with my father. I suppose you know all about him and that bloody woman by now?"

Cordelia said quickly. "We know a bit. Suppose you tell us what really happened."

"It's been the main event in our family over the last couple of years," said Caroline, her normal machine-gun delivery slowing down. "I'm not entirely clear how they met, but once my father got to know Lorna, he fell for her like the proverbial ton. He didn't say anything, but I think Mummy knew something was happening. Anyway, he decided that he didn't just want an affair, so he told Mummy he wanted a divorce. It was all extremely messy—and very painful for everyone because deep down, he loved us all really.

"When the whole sordid business of the divorce was over, he went to Lorna and asked her to marry him. He hadn't seen her for about a month because she'd been off touring in the Far East. She laughed in his face and told him not to be a fool, that she had no intention of marrying him. She didn't have the sense to see she was turning down the best man she'd ever meet. And he was devastated. Who wouldn't have been? I mean, he'd thrown his marriage away, torn up his own life and our lives too, and all for nothing." She paused.

"I can forgive him," she went on, "because everyone has the right to make at least one almighty blunder in their lives, and after all, he's still a part of my world. But I could never forgive her because, if she hadn't fooled him into thinking she wanted him, he'd have just let it be a stupid affair and that would have been the end of it. But no. She had to destroy his life. So I'm not sorry that someone killed her. Not a bit sorry." Lindsay detected a trembling in Caroline's voice as she finished her story.

"Was there any special reason why he came to see you on Saturday?" she asked, trying hard to avoid sounding eager.

"He was doing a bit of rock-climbing on Sunday down at Ilam," she explained. "That's a limestone gorge about twenty miles from here. He said he'd come up early and take me out on Saturday afternoon. He often does that. I'm sure that's half the reason he sent me to Derbyshire House. The school he chose for my brother is in Perthshire, so he can get up in the mountains when he goes to see him. I sometimes think he loves the mountains and rocks more than anything else. Mountains, music, his family and his job. In that order, I suspect. But he gives so much to all of us, he's never made me feel that a moment spent with me is a moment he'd rather spend doing something else. I'm very, very fond of my father," she added unnecessarily.

"How long did you spend with him on Saturday?" asked Cordelia.

"He picked me up at half-past two and we went for a walk in Chee Dale and Wye Dale. Then we went to have tea and he dropped me back here about a quarter to six. I told him about the concert, but he wouldn't come because she was here. I didn't expect him to. He said he'd send a cheque for the fund. He went off back to his hotel then, I suppose. He usually does. He has dinner, then sits in his room doing paperwork and listening to his Walkman."

"Do you know where he was staying?" Lindsay chimed in.

"I think he was at the Anglers' Retreat, in Thorpe Dale. That's where he usually stays. Anyway, I came back here, had dinner, and then it was time for the concert."

"And you didn't see him again on Saturday night?"

"No, how could I have?"

"Have you told the police any of this?" asked Cordelia cautiously.

"They didn't ask about anything except the concert. I suppose I was a bit nervy about them thinking my father might perhaps have had something to do with it. They don't know him like I do, after all. Should I have told them, do you think? Could it help Miss Callaghan?"

"I doubt it would have meant anything to them, Caroline. Don't worry on that account. Can you tell us what you remember about the rest of the evening?"

"Well, after dinner I went straight to the hall and collected a load of programmes from the music storeroom. I didn't see anyone around who shouldn't have been there, I'm afraid. I went back later for some more programmes, and went to the loo as well. But I wasn't paying too much attention; it was pretty chaotic except for the actual corridor down to Music 2, because the only people going down there were the people selling programmes. Jess Bennett turned up in the hall at one point looking for Miss Callaghan and I sent her backstage because I'd noticed Miss Callaghan there when I came out of the loo, ticking off one of the choir for the state of her hair. That's about all I remember.

"It's pretty frightening, really, isn't it? I mean, it's got to have been someone who knew the place well, hasn't it? And that more or less means someone we all, or at least some of us, know." Caroline dried up finally. She suddenly looked very young.

"I'm inclined to think so," said Lindsay. "Tell me, did you see Sarah Cartwright or her father at all on Saturday after the business at the craft fair?"

Caroline thought for a moment. "I didn't see him," she said positively. "He certainly wasn't at the concert. As for Sarah—I plodded along to her room when I got back from tea, just to see if she felt like coming in for dinner and wanted a bit of moral support. I knocked at her door, but there was no reply. I tried the handle, but the door was locked. I just assumed she was either asleep or not in the mood for company, so I buzzed off again."

Lindsay reckoned there wasn't much more they could hope to find out from Caroline, so she flicked a glance at Cordelia, got to her feet and said, "Thanks for being so honest with us. If you fancy a chat about anything. I expect we'll be sticking around for a few days. Okay?"

Cordelia's mouth twisted into a sardonic smile as she followed her friend on to the landing and she said drily, "The working-class hero never gives up the struggle, does she?"

By now Lindsay was beginning to take Cordelia's mockery in her stride. It forced her to keep her wits about her. So she replied mildly, "This place is so well defended that you can't expect me to ignore a chink in the armour. Now: do you want a conference, or shall we go straight on to see Sarah Cartwright? We should get her out of the way, I suppose."

Cordelia shrugged. "I haven't anything to say that won't keep. No flash of genius that will vanish for ever if I don't give it shape and form immediately. Let's see her and have done for today. Then we can go and have dinner somewhere and sort out what we've got so far."

"That should see us through the aperitifs," said Lindsay wryly. "Now, where do we find her?"

"It's just down the corridor here. I checked with Paddy's list." Cordelia led the way to Sarah's room and knocked. After a short pause a low voice invited them in.

Sarah Cartwright's room was furnished exactly as Caroline's, and had a splendid view of the trees that cut Longnor House off from the bleak moorland behind. But there were few of the personal touches that made Caroline's room so individual. The walls were bare except for a large black and white framed photograph of a gymnast on the beam who Cordelia identified as Nelli Kim, the Russian Olympic medallist. The books were all school textbooks except for several on gymnastics, and the desk was almost pathologically neat. On it there was one small framed wedding photo. The man was clearly a younger version of James Cartwright. Lindsay assumed the dark-haired, vivacious-looking woman by his side was Sarah's mother.

The girl was sitting cross-legged on her bed reading a newspaper. As they entered, she folded it carefully and put it down. She had dark brown hair cut short and neat with a straight, heavy fringe, contrasting with pale skin untouched by the ravages of adolescence. She had an air of extreme self-possession, but her dark eyes were watchful. Unlike her father, she seemed prepared to let other people make the running. She looked inquiringly at them.

Lindsay felt instantly uncomfortable, as if she were an unwelcome intruder on someone else's private territory. "I'm sorry to butt in on you," she said, "but I wondered if perhaps you could help us." Sarah said nothing. Lindsay glanced at Cordelia in a mute appeal for help.

Cordelia took up the hard job of communication. "Miss Overton has asked us to see if we can uncover anything that might establish Miss Callaghan's innocence. We've been talking to a lot of people in the hope that they might be able to come up with something to help and, basically, you're next on the list."

"I know all about you," said Sarah. Not surprisingly, there was nothing of the local accent in her tones. She might never have been north of Ascot. "You've been to see my father. How absurd of you to think he could have anything to do with this. I don't know what you think I could tell you either. I was here all the time on Saturday. I saw no one apart from Miss Callaghan. She came over at tea-time with some sandwiches and fruit for me. Anyone else who knocked I just ignored. There was no one I wanted to see. Except possibly my father, but he wasn't here."

"You must have been very upset by what happened in the morning," Cordelia probed.

The girl acknowledged this sally with raised eyebrows. "Of course I was. It's not terribly thrilling to have people attacking you because of something your father is quite properly doing in the course of his business. Especially when you're supposedly among friends. All the same, it was quite a useful experience in one sense. It's helpful to know who your real friends are."

"Like Caroline Barrington?" asked Lindsay quickly.

"Why her in particular?"

"Well, she did call round to see if you felt like going to dinner."

"Did she? I don't remember. One or two people came by. As I said, there was no one I wanted to see. I locked the door and only let Miss Callaghan in because I felt it might be rather more trouble not to." The girl's hostility was now becoming palpable.

"So you neither saw nor heard anything that might have any bearing on Lorna Smith-Couper's murder?"

"Correct. Now, if that's all, I have things to do. I was about to go down to the gym to run through some floor work before you arrived. Do you mind if I get on with that now?"

"If you don't mind, there are a couple more questions I'd like to ask," said Lindsay pleasantly.

The girl's eyebrows flickered and she threw a look of contempt at Lindsay. "If you've time to waste, go ahead and ask."

"You told the police that Miss Callaghan took you to Music 2 on Saturday morning?"

"Correct. I told them that because that's exactly what she did."

"Any idea why she took you there?"

"She was trying to be helpful. I was very upset, as I'm sure you understand. Miss Callaghan had the sense to see that the best thing for me was to be somewhere quiet till I felt all right again. She said, 'Let's go to Music 2 because I'm sure it will be empty. It's been spruced up for our celebrity guest, so no one will be using it today.'"

Lindsay's eyes bored into the girl. "Are you sure she said that the room had been set aside for Lorna?"

"Yes, I'm sure."

"Miss Callaghan doesn't remember anything of the sort."

"I'm sorry about that. But it doesn't alter the fact that she said it."

"You also told the police that Miss Callaghan had been opening cupboards in the room and picking stuff up. You're still sticking to that, are you? Because Miss Callaghan has no recollection of that happening either."

Sarah's eyes flashed as she replied angrily, "Yes, I'm still sticking to the truth. Why should I lie, for God's sake? I like Miss Callaghan."

"I can think of several reasons why you might be telling less than the truth." Lindsay paused, but Sarah refused to take up the challenge. Lindsay shook her head sorrowfully and said, "Sorry we've been such a nuisance, I hope we haven't put you off your exercises." Then she turned and walked out, followed by Cordelia. She marched down the stairs in a state of frustrated fury then suddenly saw the funny side and whirled round on Cordelia with a grin, saying, "There is something about me that seems to get right up the Cartwrights' noses. I can't have gone to the right school."

Cordelia dissolved into a violent fit of giggles, much to the amazement of a couple of sixth-formers who passed by as the two women staggered into Paddy's room.

15

Cordelia sat at Paddy's desk scribbling furiously in her notebook, while Lindsay wandered round the room, smoking and fiddling with the assortment of objects on the mantelpiece. Eventually she headed for the drinks cupboard and poured herself a small whisky. "You want one?" she asked.

"That depends. Are we going out for a meal? And if so, when?"

"Must we go out? I'm just not in the mood tonight for all the palaver of menus and waiters and posing about the wine list. I thought I'd go off in search of an Indian takeaway. Buxton may not be the cosmopolitan centre of the universe, but it must have some kind of fast food apart from fish and chips. Unless you have any other ideas?"

"I was rather hoping we could find a nice little restaurant and splash out a bit."

"Every day I spend down here is a day when I'm earning precisely zilch. I don't feel much like splashing out. Especially since I've got Paddy on my Presbyterian conscience."

"My treat, Lindsay. I've got it, we might as well spend it."

Lindsay looked outraged. "No way," she retorted. "We have to know each other a lot better before I let you pay for me. If you feel the need to go out and spoil yourself, fine. But

I'll settle for what fits in with my lifestyle, if it's all the same to you."

Cordelia looked thunderstruck. "My God," she complained, "you're so bloody self-righteous sometimes. Why the hell don't you just relax? There's no need for all this puritanical shit."

"What do you mean, puritanical shit? Just because I've always paid my own way and I'm not about to stop now. I've worked hard to keep my independence and I'm not about to throw it away."

Cordelia shook her head in bewilderment. "Look, I only offered to buy you dinner, not become your sugar momma. You can let someone buy you a meal without becoming a kept woman, you know."

Lindsay scowled. "In my business, you learn quickly that there's no such thing as a free lunch."

"God, you're impossible. All right, go and get a bloody curry if it makes you feel better. We'll split the cost to salve your conscience."

Lindsay stormed out, slamming the door behind her. By the time she returned with an assortment of Indian food, she was regretting the scene. She found Cordelia lying on the sofa with a glass of wine, reading one of Sunday's papers, ignoring her return. Lindsay began unpacking the tinfoil containers of chicken, lamb and vegetable curries and rice, and said gruffly, "I'm sorry. I was out of order."

Cordelia didn't put the paper down. "How much do I owe you?" she remarked coldly.

"Look, I said I'm sorry. Let's forget it, eh? Come and eat. Then we can talk about the information we've dug up."

Cordelia folded the paper and got up. "Okay," she said quietly. "We'll forget it. But don't push your luck, Lindsay. You should have the sense to know I'm not trying to buy my way into your life. You going to behave now?"

Lindsay nodded. She launched straight into her analysis of their current position, eager to re-establish their previous closeness. "If we look at our original list," she expounded, "we can cross off Paddy, of course. And you."

Cordelia smiled. "That's very generous of you. But you haven't been able to prove I didn't do it. You're simply reacting on instinct. And that goes for Paddy too."

"Not entirely," said Lindsay. "This crime has to have been premeditated to some extent. The fact that Paddy's duffel-coat toggle came from Longnor proves that. It means that the murderer had decided in advance what the murder method would be. It wasn't just a spontaneous reaction of anger in the music room. Now, Paddy didn't know until dinner was nearly over that she would have any opportunity to be alone with Lorna. After that, she had no chance to go back to Longnor to fetch the toggle.

"Paddy is not a member of the music staff and wasn't directly involved in the plans for the concert. Indeed, if she hadn't been asked by Pamela Overton to look after Lorna, she could reasonably have expected to spend the entire evening sitting with you and me. And there would have been no opportunity for her to go sailing off and commit murder. Also, I think we can rule out any conspiracy theory between Paddy and Pamela Overton. No, if Paddy had been planning to have a go at Lorna, she would have picked a different time and place. She'd have made sure she had some kind of alibi. But this way, she'd have had to go ahead with it knowing she'd be the prime suspect. And Paddy's not daft enough for that." Cordelia slowly nodded agreement.

Lindsay went on. "The same argument really applies to you. There is no reason why you should have imagined that any opportunity would arise that evening to kill Lorna. So it's highly unlikely that you'd be wandering around with a garrotte stuffed down your cleavage on the off-chance. Now, I know you're very fit, but I don't think you'd have had time to run to Longnor House and back and still get to the music room in time to kill Lorna. Anyway, in both your case and Paddy's, why go all the way back to Longnor when there were dozens of coats in the cloakrooms in this building, amongst which there must have been the odd duffel coat?"

Lindsay broke off and loaded dhal into her mouth with a chunk of nan bread. Cordelia tasted the lamb curry suspiciously and said grudgingly, "Not bad, this. Okay, then, Sherlock. Let's have the rest of your reasoning."

Between mouthfuls, Lindsay continued. "Up to now, we've rather been looking at this crime as if it had been a completely opportunist exercise. In reality, I think quite a bit of foreknowledge and forward planning was involved. On that basis alone, I'm prepared to exclude you and Paddy. Of the others, I feel strongly that Margaret Macdonald is out of the running. It would have been a completely unnecessary crime for her. As she said to us, her life wouldn't have been destroyed by any revelation Lorna could have made.

"Also, look at the actual nature of this murder. It was a very nasty way to kill someone. There was a lot of hatred in whoever did this. It wasn't done in a simple moment of anger or fear. The crime was vindictive; it had real unpleasantness in it, and a pretty gruesome irony in garrotting her with a cello string. Talk about hoist with your own petard! If Margaret Macdonald was going to kill Lorna, she wouldn't have murdered her like this. Their affair was dead, all passion spent far in the past. Margaret has lived for ages with the risk that Lorna might tell someone what had happened, and she made very sure that she lived a life whereby she could cope with the knowledge of that risk."

Cordelia frowned and said, "But look at it this way. Probably the only thing that kept Lorna silent in the past was fear for her own reputation. But now it's become rather fashionable to have had a bijou gay fling, so there was less need for her reticence. Surely the risk must have increased recently, and Margaret Macdonald must have realised that?"

"Not necessarily. I don't think Margaret moves in that kind of world. And besides, why would she take a duffel-coat toggle from Longnor? She wouldn't implicate Paddy, who's supposed to be her best friend here."

"Ah," said Cordelia with satisfaction, "but at that stage she wouldn't have specifically been incriminating Paddy, would she? She would just have been diverting suspicion away from herself in a general sort of way. We've probably got enough of a case against her to cast sufficient doubt on Paddy's guilt to get the charges dropped, don't you think?"

"But if we clear Paddy and don't prove who really did it, people will always assume that it was Paddy. And I don't really think Margaret, if she were the guilty party, would allow that state of affairs to continue."

Cordelia thought for a moment and gnawed a chicken leg. Then she said, "You're presuming too much on friendship. I don't think I'd speak out to save a friend if my own freedom were at stake."

"That's very candid of you. And you're probably right. Okay, leave Margaret in the running, but only as a rank outsider. Now, there's James Cartwright. We're cutting it rather fine as regards time, as well as assuming that he had access to a key to the music room. Not that that's a very big assumption, given the amount of work he's done there in the past. From their meeting in the afternoon he could have picked up that she'd be there again later. If we could only place him on the scene, we'd have a damn good case."

"It would certainly be an excellent choice from the school's point of view," Cordelia remarked.

"That's the least of my worries, to be perfectly blunt," Lindsay replied with asperity.

"Fair enough, but it would be nice for Paddy to have a job to go back to if we ever manage to get her out of this," said Cordelia. "So how do we place him on the scene?"

"I don't know. If I could answer that we'd have a case to put to the police. Cartwright is certainly my favourite on balance. To be honest, I can't really see any of the girls having done it."

"Even though any one of them might have had motive, means and probably foreknowledge of the opportunity? Be fair, you're being sentimental again. Don't forget that a growing-up process which includes incarceration in a place like this gives a certain hard edge to one's character that most people don't acquire till much later in life. I wouldn't mind betting that young Caroline Barrington has enough guts to have carried out that murder if she had had a mind to," Cordelia speculated.

"No, no, wrong timing again," Lindsay parried. "Caroline might have done it before her parents' divorce, while there was still a chance of salvaging her family. But I can't see her as the vindictive avenger of her father's lost face and her mother's lost pride."

"Come on, Lindsay, you can't use that as a valid argument against Caroline as a suspect," complained Cordelia.

"Why not? Look, I believe that we all have the capability to commit at least one murder. Fortunately, the precise set of circumstances never actually come together for the overwhelming majority of us. And since I believe that, I find the only way I can deal with the problems of a crime like this is to look at the psychological probabilities. I simply don't think that Caroline's psychology—in so far as I've seen it at work—matches the facts of this crime. I rule out Caroline, just as I rule out Margaret."

Cordelia pulled a face. "I'm still not utterly convinced," she said.

Lindsay leaned back in her seat, lit a cigarette and continued her lecture. "I can't say I feel so definite about the other two girls we've seen because I know even less about them than Caroline. But since you've told me not to be sentimental, let's look at them. Of the two, I'd say that Jessica was less likely, but with Sarah only marginally more so. Jessica might have killed out of immediate anguish for her brother, but I don't see her having the nerve for this crime. And I don't believe she really had time to do it. Remember—she'd have had to get the spare key to Music 2 and return it to Margaret Macdonald's room. The first part of the exercise wouldn't necessarily have been awkward, because she probably would have been able to do it in the afternoon. But if Paddy was a few steps away from Margaret Macdonald's room, where Jessica said she was when she found her—and it would have been too risky for Jessica to lie about that—then I don't see how such an obtrusive girl, with that mane of red hair, could have got it back unnoticed.

"As far as Sarah is concerned, from what we've seen of her so far, I'd say she might—just might—be capable of this killing. But we've no evidence at all to link her with the crime. Really, the only reason why she should be a suspect—apart from my nasty mind—is that we believe she's lied to the police in her statement about Paddy. But even that isn't certain, since Paddy seems to be suffering from amnesia on the subject."

"And what about the latest addition to the list?" Cordelia demanded.

"Anthony Barrington. Well, he's in the locality. He comes fairly often, so he knows the layout of the school pretty well. Must do by now. He had a very large axe to grind with Lorna. He's a man of action, too, not the sort who'd sit back calmly and shrug off being crossed. However, there's the difficulty he'd have with the keys and remaining unseen. I suspect we're going to have to engineer a talk with him. Which I don't especially relish."

Cordelia went through to the kitchen and made coffee. Lindsay followed her and said shamefacedly, "There's one major problem. I'm committed to working next week in Glasgow. Wednesday to Friday. To be quite blunt, I can't afford not to."

"I'm sure we can work something out with Pamela Overton if you're losing out by being here," Cordelia said sympathetically.

"It's not just the money, though obviously that's a major consideration. It's the goodwill. The *Clarion*'s my major source of income right now, and if I don't keep up my availability for shifts, they'll find someone else. There are plenty of hungry freelancers around ready to snap up the holes in the *Clarion* shift rota. Also, I think I've got a strong chance of getting the next full-time staff job that comes along, and I can't pretend that I wouldn't jump at the chance. So far as this business is concerned, after Tuesday night I'm back on part-time only. Which makes me feel a bit of a shit."

"That gives us four whole days. We'll see how we get on, and maybe the *Clarion* will give you more time if you need it. Don't despair yet. I'm sure we can do it. We've got to."

Later, back at their hotel, Lindsay lay awake, listening to the deep breathing that signalled Cordelia's quick drift into sleep. The endless searchings of her restless mind would not let her drop off. She knew that somewhere there was a key that would unlock the closed book of Lorna's death. But the more she wrestled to find it, the more frustrated she became. After an hour's fitful turning and tossing, she slipped out of bed.

Moving softly, she dressed in jeans and a warm sweater. She searched in her bag till she found Paddy's bunch of keys. Then, by the moonlight, she wrote a note for Cordelia:

> If I'm not here when you wake up, I'll be up at the school, prob-
> ably in Paddy's rooms. Come up and get me in the car. Keys
> inside the boot. Love you dearly. Lindsay.

She propped the note up against Cordelia's alarm clock and quietly closed the door behind her. She crept downstairs and out into the car park. At the car, she unlocked the boot and took out the heavy walking boots and windproof jacket that she always kept there. She slipped the jacket on, then swapped her trainers for the boots. Finally, she pocketed the Ordnance Survey map, dropped the keys into the boot, closed it and set off.

In the moonlight, she climbed steadily through the wood above the town till she emerged on high moorland at the foot of the Victorian folly Paddy had pointed out to her nearly a week before. She climbed the squat stone tower, blessing the almost full moon that made it possible, and gazed over the landscape. The site had been well chosen. In the moonlight, she could see for miles in all directions. Lindsay unfolded her map and gazed out over the terrain. She soon located her target and set off with regular, easy strides across the darkened landscape. The going was not difficult for it had been a fairly dry autumn and the ground was soft, but not as boggy as she expected moorland to be at this time of year. The only sounds were the occasional owl, the sudden quiet whispering of small animals in the tussocks of rough grass and the distant rumble of the odd car engine.

Forty minutes later, she was striding up the drive of Derbyshire House. It was after two by then, and the only lights visible were the dull glow of corridor night-lights. When she reached the main house, she walked all the way round, pausing several times to study the building. Finally, she let herself in by the door near the kitchens, using Paddy's master key. Once inside, she slipped off her boots and moved silently through the corridors. She climbed the back staircase to the music department, using the tiny pencil torch she always carried in her walking jacket, along with her compass, whistle and Swiss Army knife. She unlocked the door to the music room and closed it behind her.

Slowly she walked all round the room, not focusing on any one detail but letting her eyes and mind absorb everything around her. At the end of her circuit of the room, she sat down on the teacher's chair. She closed her eyes and forced herself to recall the scene she had witnessed when she had arrived in answer to Pamela Overton's ominous summons. Again she conjured up details of the room she had seen then and compared it with what she could see now. Nothing came to mind of any significance at all. She sighed, cursed herself for her incompetence, and got to her feet.

Lindsay locked up the music room behind her and prowled round the rest of the music department. But nothing struck her. She even probed around the recesses of the stage area, but still there was no echo in her mind. In despair, she wandered back down the corridor to the hall.

Then, as she had done on the night of the murder, she paused to stare out of the window to collect her thoughts. Not far away, she could see the lights of the squash courts building site. But everything else was in darkness. Below her was the roof of the kitchen area, with its sturdy iron railings and its tubs of miniature trees. And suddenly, Lindsay knew what her mind had been stubbornly hiding from her for the past six days.

16

There were two of them sharing the cell. At least being on remand meant they had certain privileges. For a start, Paddy had books to read and her own clothes to wear. Either Gillian Markham or her clerk visited daily, on Cordelia's instructions, bringing fresh reading supplies, tempting food and the half bottle of wine that Home Office regulations allow remand prisoners. But although these small luxuries made life a little more tolerable, it was just as hard for Paddy to submit to the indignities of prison life as it was for every other woman on the wing. Her plight had not really sunk in while she had been in police custody. The remand hearing in the magistrates' court had seemed unreal. But when she had arrived at the remand centre, she had started to feel like a condemned animal arriving at the abattoir. Nevertheless, the strip search, degrading in its intimacy, had humiliated but not broken her. What prison food she had eaten had only disgusted her.

What was pushing her perilously close to breaking point was the isolation. Her cell-mate, who was on remand for receiving stolen goods, was pleasant enough to her. But there was no real point of contact between them. Marion was understandably obsessed by the problems facing her three young children and her unemployed live-in boyfriend. Despite that, she still found it impossible to understand how Paddy could exist happily without a steady man and a family. That inability undermined Paddy even further, making her question why she had never been able to settle for any of the men who had been part of her life for varying lengths of time. But at least Marion was not hostile, unlike many of the other women on the wing, who seemed to take positive pleasure in seeing a middle-class woman facing the same degradation they endured.

At the same time as Paddy was awakened by the bang on her cell door that heralded Saturday morning, Cordelia was wakened by the buzz of her alarm clock. She rolled over and switched it off in one movement, then turned over to where Lindsay should have been. At once she shot upright, taken aback by the sight of a rumpled, empty space. She had known Lindsay for long enough by now to realise just how slim were the chances of her rising early for the hell of it. It took her a moment to become aware that she was clutching a piece of paper in the hand that had switched off the alarm.

Cordelia read the note and instantly leapt out of bed. She dressed quickly, raced downstairs and out into the freezing morning air. She found the car keys where Lindsay had left them and climbed into the driving seat. She turned the keys in the ignition and nothing happened. Cursing, she tried again. Nothing. Then she remembered Lindsay telling her about the engine immobiliser she had installed. "Bloody stupid gadgets," she swore, fumbling under the dashboard for the switch. She tried the ignition again, and the engine started at once. It took her only six minutes to reach Longnor House. She burst into Paddy's living-room and began to panic when she saw no sign of Lindsay. Then she remembered the bedroom.

Lindsay's clothes were strewn on the floor by the bed, where she was sleeping deeply. Cordelia stopped to let her heartbeat return to normal. In sleep, Lindsay lost half her years. Her face was gently flushed, her hair tousled, her features completely relaxed. Then her instincts told her she was no longer alone, and she began to wake up.

"Morning," Lindsay muttered sleepily. "What time is it?"

"Twenty past seven."

"Oh God, is that all? I thought you'd at least have your run before you arrived. I didn't imagine anything could come between you and your early morning exercise."

"You leave me a note like that and expect me calmly to go for a run and have breakfast too, I suppose, before I do anything about it?" demanded Cordelia incredulously.

Lindsay propped herself up on one elbow and nodded. "Why not?" she asked. "I didn't say anything about it being urgent."

"But what are you doing here?"

"Oh, I didn't think Paddy would mind. I simply didn't feel like walking back at three o'clock in the morning. Exhaustion came over me in a wave, so I thought I'd kip down here. Very comfortable I was, too," she smiled.

"God, you're exasperating," said Cordelia. "I meant, what possessed you to get up in the middle of the night and walk up here? I presume you did walk?"

"Yes, I walked. It's not far—only a couple of miles across the moors. I couldn't sleep, so I thought that if I came up here and wandered round on my own in the silence of night I might get some answers."

"And did you, you tantalising pig?" Cordelia appealed.

Lindsay leaned back on the pillows and smirked. "You really want to know?"

Cordelia jumped on the bed and grabbed her shoulders in affectionate annoyance. "Of course I want to know!"

"I've remembered what it was I had forgotten."

There was a pause. When Cordelia spoke it was almost a whisper, as if she did not want to tempt fate. "And it's important? As important as you thought it might be?"

"I think so. If I'm right, it shows how the murderer committed the crime without being spotted in the music department. And it also narrows the field down considerably. But we'll have to talk to Chris Jackson this morning to see if my theory will hold water."

"Well then, tell me; don't keep me guessing!"

"Okay. But only after you've made me a cup of coffee."

"Oh, Lindsay Gordon, I could strangle you," yelled Cordelia as they tussled on the bed. Finally she sat back and declared, "All right. If coffee is your price, I'll pay. Besides, I could do with a cup myself." She slipped through to the kitchen and set the percolator going. Then she returned to the bedroom.

"I've done my bit," she reported. "Now, while we're waiting, you can tell me what it is you've remembered. Who did you see or hear doing or saying what? If you see what I mean."

"Nobody. It's not quite that simple. On Saturday afternoon, after the play and before the book auction, I sat at the very front of the hall, at the side, and stared out of the window in between jotting down some notes. Those windows look down on the kitchen roof and the woods. The curtains were drawn in the evening by the time the concert began. But at that time, it wasn't quite dusk, so no one had got round to shutting out the view. I could see the flat roof of the kitchen. I noticed the pots of conifers. And I noticed that strong iron railing going all round the roof.

"Later, after Lorna had been murdered, I was going back from the music room to the hall. The two windows in the corridor didn't have curtains at them, so again I could look out and see the kitchen roof, though at an angle because it doesn't come along as far as the music department. I was thinking about what Pamela Overton had said, and about what I'd just seen, so I was looking without really noticing anything.

"I subconsciously registered that there was something different about the roof, but I didn't really focus on what it was because it was too far from the room where Lorna died to have anything to do with the murder, I thought at the time. Last night, however, I stood at the same window and I remembered what I'd seen. It hadn't been there on Saturday afternoon, and it wasn't there when I looked out again on Tuesday. But it was on Saturday night."

The percolator burped loudly as Lindsay paused for dramatic effect. She grinned and went on. "Four scaffolding poles and a pile of clamps. And I thought, what if someone put them together and clamped them to the railings? They could clamber along the frame, wait till Lorna was making enough noise to cover small sounds, slide up the window catch almost silently, as I did the other day with my knife, get into the room, creep up on her and kill her. All the setting up could have been done while everyone else was having dinner. The garrotte could have been made at any time during that afternoon, or even at dinner time. I also had a wander round the building site for the squash courts. There's lots of scaffolding poles there that look just the same as the bits on the roof."

There was a pause as Cordelia considered these new possibilities. "I think we both need that coffee now," she said softly. She left the room and returned with two steaming mugs.

"That certainly answers one or two questions," she sighed.

"All of them except the crucial one," Lindsay replied. "It explains why no one saw the murderer entering or leaving the room. It also explains the problem of the locked door. All the murderer had to do beforehand was to arrange the chair and music stand so that Lorna had her back to the window, to check out the window catches and to collect a cello string—a gruesome little touch. And if I'm right, it also cuts the suspects down considerably."

"I suppose so," said Cordelia meditatively. "I haven't had long enough to assimilate the idea yet. Surely, though, it lets out Paddy and Margaret for a start?"

"I reckon it eliminates everyone who was visible or alibied at dinner and during the first half of the concert. That does mean Paddy and Margaret—and also Caroline and Jessica. And of course, you. There's no way you could have been shinning up scaffolding in that outfit! And much to my irritation I think we may have to exclude James Cartwright. It's got to be someone who had motive, means and opportunity, but also the skill and nerve to contemplate that particular murder method. Right now I can think of only one person who fits the bill."

"The one man we haven't seen yet."

"Well, who else really? Anthony Barrington is known for his climbing feats. He's got nerve and skill. He's a successful businessman, which means he must have a streak of ruthlessness in his make-up. Lorna had cost him a great deal in personal terms, and I'd guess from the way Caroline has spoken about him that his family was pretty important to him. Losing that would rankle deeply with such a man. We've got to see him, Cordelia, and soon."

Cordelia thought for a moment. Then she said, "I imagine the school secretary will have an address and telephone number for him. If we're lucky, we may track him down today without having to ask Caroline."

"That would be all to the good. If we ask her, there's every chance that she'll tip him off and I'd like to hit him unprepared. So you try the school office and see what you can come up with. We'll also have to have a word with Chris Jackson to see if we can run a little experiment quietly. What normally happens on a Saturday morning?"

"Hockey and lacrosse matches for the games players. The rest are supposed to be involved in their hobbies — photography, woodwork, orienteering, you name it."

"Are there many people drifting around?"

"There shouldn't be any, but there's always the odd one or two. It's probably quietest around half-past ten. Most people are busy by then. But don't forget Chris will almost certainly be refereeing some games match. It would be best to go into school breakfast and try to catch her there. Maybe she can get someone to stand in for her."

Lindsay agreed to this, and while she showered and dressed, Cordelia sat scribbling in her notebook. When Lindsay reappeared, the other woman mused, "I don't think you've thought it through completely *vis-à-vis* James Cartwright. He would have had to take something of a risk, but I think he's still in the frame. He wasn't at the Woolpack till seven, don't forget. He could have made the preparations while everyone was at dinner—in the same way as Caroline's father could have done. There's hardly any leeway in terms of time. But I think Cartwright's still a possibility if we have to give Barrington a clean bill of health."

She waved her notes at Lindsay. "Look. I've worked it out. Six o'clock he comes back to the school. He collects the scaffolding—don't forget, he was bound to know it was there, which Barrington may not have done. Then it's up the fire escape to the kitchen roof, where he assembles the frame. He would also know what he was doing, he's been a builder for years. If anyone knew how to erect that frame, it was him. He's still a strong-looking bloke. And he installed those windows. He'd know exactly what he was about, breaking in through them without making a noise.

"So he bolts the scaffolding to the railings. Then he nips into the music department and makes his preparations. I'm not sure why he took the toggle from Longnor—maybe he'd parked his car near there and it was only on his way back that he realised he'd need something to protect his hands. Anyway, he drives to the Woolpack, has a very quick pint and shoots back here. Along the scaffolding he goes, flicks open the window catch, pulls himself over the sill, and bingo! Even if Lorna had heard him and there had been a struggle, he's strong enough to have overpowered her easily. Then it's off into the night, pausing only to dismantle the scaffolding. He could have come back and taken it away at any time. What do you think?"

Lindsay grimaced wryly at Cordelia and lit a cigarette. "Listen, sunshine," she said, trying but failing to keep her voice light and jokey, "I'm supposed to be the Sherlock Holmes around here. You're supposed to be the dumb Dr Watson who stands back in amazement when the great investigator propounds her extravagant but impeccable theories. Your role is to provide an appreciative audience for my little grey cells, not to steal my thunder. Nevertheless . . . you're absolutely right. I was too hasty in ruling him out. It's just as well one of us is cautious."

Cordelia made a mocking bow at Lindsay. "Your humble servant acknowledges her menial role. But I must be allowed at least one good idea per case. Is that what I'm supposed to say?" She looked hard at Lindsay. "I don't care what you think you've got to prove, Lindsay. Don't try to do your proving on me. It's not necessary."

Lindsay flushed. "I was only joking," she muttered defensively.

Cordelia winked broadly at her. "Better luck next time," she said, gently.

Together they walked across to breakfast and were lucky enough to find Chris Jackson sitting alone at a table ploughing her way through a mound of toast and bacon. They sat down beside her after collecting boiled eggs and rolls.

The Scottish gym mistress scarcely looked up from her morning paper and gave them a monosyllabic greeting. A moment later, she took in who was sharing her table, for she put down the sports pages and focussed sharply on the two women.

"How's it going, then?" she asked. "I'm surprised you're still around. I thought you'd dropped poor old Paddy down the plughole since I hadn't seen you around for a couple of days."

"No chance," Lindsay replied. "We've been chasing around like blue-arsed flies. There's no way I'm giving up till I've got somebody in the cells in place of Paddy Callaghan."

"And have you got anybody in mind?" Chris asked, trying to appear nonchalant but failing dismally.

"Let's just say we've eliminated certain possibilities and we've considerably narrowed down the field. I could even go so far as to say that we reckon we'll soon be able to prove that Paddy Callaghan could not have killed Lorna. We'd like your help to do that. It's a matter of assistance with a little experiment we've got in mind," said Lindsay.

Chris thought for a few seconds before she replied. "Provided I'm not top of your list of suspects I'll do anything I can to help," she said, a nervous undertone in her voice.

Lindsay grinned widely, and Cordelia declared quickly, "Not at all, Chris. It's just that we need a bit of help and you were the only person we could think of with the necessary skills. Are you busy this morning?"

"Well, I'm supposed to be umpiring the First Eleven's match against Grafton Manor. I don't see how I can get out of it because I can't think of anyone else who's available to do it."

"That is something of a problem. I was afraid you might be tied up," said Cordelia with regret.

"No problem at all," Lindsay interjected brightly. "I know just the person. She's fighting fit for all that running around—and she knows the rules. Don't you, Cordelia?"

Cordelia's mouth dropped open as she struggled for something to say.

Lindsay grinned. "I know you don't want to miss out on our experiment, but after all, you did suggest that this morning was the best time. Now, I've done a spot of climbing in the past and Chris is a gymnast. We should be able to manage it. So if you don't mind relieving her, we might be able to wrap this whole thing up nice and quickly. Besides, you missed your run this morning," said Lindsay in a rush.

"You rotten sod," Cordelia muttered. "You've got the cheek of the devil."

"Ah well, where we come from, the sparrows fly backwards to keep the dust out of their eyes, don't they, Chris? Seriously, now, is that okay with you both?"

"It's fine by me. At least it's a home match, so you won't have to travel with the girls," Chris replied. She quickly filled

Cordelia in on her duties at the hockey match and turned to Lindsay. "What exactly are we going to do?"

"I'll tell you when we meet," said Lindsay. "It's vital that you keep this to yourself. The murderer mustn't know what we're up to. I'll see you at about quarter past ten in Paddy's rooms."

Chris agreed to this arrangement, so Lindsay and Cordelia left her alone as they went off to obtain information from the school secretary. As they walked down the corridor, Cordelia spluttered with good-natured grumbles.

"That was some bloody stroke you pulled on me," she complained. "Umpiring a bloody hockey match while you have all the fun. I could kill you, Gordon. You just better cover all the angles, that's all I can say."

In the secretary's office they were lucky again. The files produced a weekday and weekend address for Anthony Barrington, complete with phone numbers. They were about to leave when the other door to the office opened and they found themselves confronted by Pamela Overton who ushered them into her office and asked them to sit down. Like mesmerised first-formers, they sat.

"It has been almost a week now since the murder, and Miss Callaghan is still unjustly imprisoned. Have your inquiries borne fruit so far?"

Cordelia shifted uncomfortably in her seat and gazed at Lindsay with mute appeal. Lindsay pulled herself together, trying desperately to feel like a mature adult instead of a naughty schoolgirl caught doing unspeakable things behind the bike sheds.

"We've made a certain amount of progress," she said. "We drew up an initial list of people we felt might have some possible motive for killing Lorna. We've managed to eliminate several people on that list. Right now we're taking some steps which we hope will produce results within the next forty-eight hours. We believe we'll be able to establish Paddy's innocence beyond question. I'm bound to say that the way things look at the moment, the criminal is neither a pupil nor a member of staff. We'll do our very best to let you know the results before the police are informed, if that's possible."

There was a silence while Miss Overton digested this information. At last, she said, "I hope you'll be able to bring this affair to a speedy end, and one that is satisfactory to the school. Now, some time ago you asked me a question about keys, and this I can now answer. As far as the Bursar is concerned, when Mr Cartwright does any work in the school, he is issued with the keys he needs and he returns them when the job is completed. We have no reason to suppose there are any of the school keys permanently in his possession. I hope this information will help. I won't keep you any longer, but I do hope to hear from you soon."

Thus dismissed, they left hastily. "She reduces me so," complained Cordelia. "I simply can't respond to her. You amaze me, you stay so composed."

"All a front, I assure you. Inside, I feel fourteen and guilty as hell. I feel she can read my mind; she knows exactly what I want to do with you!"

Slowly they walked back to Longnor, discussing their plans for Anthony Barrington. They decided that Lindsay should phone his weekend cottage to try to find out if and when he would be there. Back in Paddy's rooms, she dialled the number. On the third ring, the phone was answered by a woman who sounded middle-aged.

"Llanagar 263," she said with a strong Welsh accent.

"Hello," said Lindsay, "is Mr Barrington there?"

"I'm sorry," said the voice, "he's gone out on the hills."

"Oh, that's a pity," said Lindsay. "I had hoped to catch him. Do you know what time he'll be back?"

"He's usually back about four this time of year. Who shall I say called please?"

"Oh, it doesn't matter. I'll call again later," Lindsay replied, hanging up before she could be questioned further. "I think I got the cleaning woman," she said to Cordelia. "He'll be back around four. Shall we shoot over there this evening? I'd like to see Paddy again this afternoon. How long do you reckon it will take to get to his place?"

"I suppose between two and three hours driving. I'm game if you are."

They smiled at each other and began to prepare for their various morning activities.

PART IV

FINALE

17

Cordelia left just after nine-thirty to drive the hockey team in the school minibus to the pavilion on the threatened playing fields. As she drove, she mused on the irony of a conservation policy that meant the town had nowhere to expand, being surrounded by Country Park and National Park. The result was that any piece of land inside the boundaries immediately shot up in value so fast that soon there would be no green left inside the town at all except pocket-handkerchief gardens.

Left to herself, Lindsay put a Charlie Mingus album on Paddy's stereo and settled back for a solitary think. She reviewed all she knew about the case, from its beginning to the present, to make certain she had not missed some glaringly obvious piece of evidence. But eventually she was satisfied that no other vital fragment of information was lurking in the corners of her mind. All the evidence seemed to point inexorably to Anthony Barrington. She was forced to accept Cordelia's hypothesis that Cartwright was still a possibility, but she had reservations about him. She made a mental note to see if she could find out anything firm about the financial status of his business. If he turned out to be sufficiently solvent, his motive would be virtually demolished.

She thought for some minutes about how she could easily discover the relevant information, but there seemed no obvious answer. She would ask Paddy that afternoon, she thought. Paddy always seemed to have her finger on the pulse of life around her.

She shrugged and reminded herself that, in any event, Cartwright was only second favourite. Anthony Barrington was the horse she fancied. As the phrase formed in her mind, she brought herself up with a jolt. This was no horse race, no game. It was a sick and serious business that had already cost one life and would damage others before it was over. All she could hope to do was to limit the damage by helping to clear the woman she knew in her bones to be innocent.

"And," she thought wryly, "if I can't manage this, there's no hope on God's earth for Cordelia and me. We'll never be able to build any relationship with the shadow of Paddy perpetually before us. And I do want this one so very much."

She was interrupted by a knock at the door. Chris's curiosity had fired her to arrive ten minutes early. She clearly had difficulty in holding back questions as Lindsay deliberately took her time in making coffee for them both. As she came through with two mugs, Chris could hold back no longer. "What's all this about?" she demanded.

"I have an idea as to how the murderer got into Music 2," Lindsay replied. "And I need your help to try out my theory."

"But I thought it was obvious how it was done. Surely whoever did it just pinched the key and put it back afterwards," said Chris, frowning.

"I don't think so. Something's been puzzling me all week. There were dozens of people milling around backstage. But not a soul admits to seeing the key being taken or put back. Not a soul admits to seeing anyone in that corridor except Paddy. It seems impossible that anyone could have got in that way unseen. Now, I noticed some scaffolding poles on the kitchen roof. They hadn't been there earlier in the day and they were gone a couple of days later. I believe they were used to enter the murder room. Via the window. I want to check that it can be done."

Chris looked stunned. "You've got to be joking!"

Lindsay shook her head.

"Have you told the police about this?" Chris asked.

Lindsay sighed. "They'd never believe me. You see, I knew there was something I couldn't remember and it only came back to me last night. They know I've been trying to find out what happened. They'd be bound to think I was making it up to put Paddy in the clear. Besides Cordelia and I believe it's not enough just to clear Paddy. We've got to find the real culprit if we really want to help her. I think we're very close to the truth now. So, can I count on your help?"

Chris looked worried. She said, "I still think you should tell the police, but if you're dead set on doing it this way I'll help all I can. What do we do?"

Fortunately, both of them were properly dressed for their task, Lindsay in jeans, sweater and training shoes, Chris in the track suit and trainers she'd been wearing in preparation for the match. As they left Longnor, Lindsay picked up a selection of spanners and an adjustable wrench from her car tool box. They walked across to the squash court building site as Lindsay explained her theory more fully to Chris, carefully skirting round the subject of possible suspects. At the site, the gates were padlocked together, but it took Lindsay and Chris only a few moments to climb them. Then Lindsay selected the four poles she wanted and the clamps that would fasten the frame together. Back at the gate, they puzzled for a moment about how to get the equipment out, till Chris pointed out gaps between the fencing and the ground that would allow them to be pushed through.

They quickly clambered back over the gates, Chris complaining, "I hope to God none of my bright sparks is watching this carry-on."

Lindsay laughed, saying, "There's worse to come. Let's go." She insisted on carrying all four poles, though it was an awkward struggle. She was determined to do it herself, to prove that one person could do it alone. When they reached the main building, she nearly came to grief several times on the fire escape, that led up to the kitchen roof. Chris attempted to help, but when Lindsay explained the need for struggling on alone, she subsided. To Chris's surprise, she finally managed it, and the two women ended up on the roof in a confused heap of poles, joints, spanners, arms and legs.

The journalist lay breathing heavily and sweating. "Bloody hell," she moaned. "That was a lot tougher than I anticipated."

"That's because you did it all wrong," said Chris. "You should have roped the poles together, then they would have been a lot easier to carry. Then you could have fastened another rope to them and hauled them up to the roof. Much simpler."

Lindsay looked at her with new respect. "Thank you, Chris," she panted. "You have just resurrected my theory. Thank God for the practical mind. Now, onwards and upwards."

After a few failures, they managed to bolt the poles together in a rectangular frame. Then Lindsay realised that the frame was too heavy and unwieldy for one person to place in position and bolt to the railings.

So painstakingly they took it apart again, and Lindsay prepared to clamber over the railings on to the narrow ledge to fit the poles together one by one to form the frame. Before she could go ahead, however, Chris stopped her.

"Wait there," she commanded, all the authority of her position in her voice for the first time since the two had met. "Don't you dare do anything till I tell you." And she rushed off down the fire escape. Lindsay kicked her heels crossly for about five minutes till Chris returned, carrying two sets of yachting harness. "There," she said, handing one of them to Lindsay. "You put that on and clip the hook to the railings. I'm not having you splattered on our drive if I can help it."

Strapped in, Lindsay gingerly climbed over the railings and bolted one short strut to them vertically. Then, after a struggle with the heavy and unwieldy equipment, she added a long horizontal pole, to which Chris had previously bolted the other upright. That turned out to have been another mistake, since the extra weight was almost too much for Lindsay. Finally, with muscles that were beginning to tremble in protest, she managed to bolt on a second horizontal pole at a height that came just below the window sill of the music room windows.

"Jesus," Lindsay gasped, "I'm even less fit than I thought I was. This is where you do your stuff. I don't think I'm agile enough for this bit. You go along the scaffolding till you get to the end window. Then you use a knife blade to slip the catch and climb into the room through the window. Be careful not to damage the paintwork. Do you think you can do that?"

Chris grinned. "No bother at all. I'm a gymnast, you know, not just a lump of brawn. You'd need to be pretty sure-footed to do this by the way and pretty strong, given the fetching and carrying involved."

At first she inched her way gingerly along, but soon she was moving with assurance along the lower bar. As she reached the window she pulled herself up and on to the upper bar. There she crouched, leaning against the window frame as she slipped out the knife Lindsay had given her. It took heart-stopping moments fiddling around with the blade before the catch slipped open, but once she had managed it, she unclipped her harness and was inside the music room in seconds.

A few moments later, she re-emerged on the window ledge. She leaned over and hooked her gear back on to the pole as a precaution. Then she slammed the window shut with surprisingly little noise and tested it to make sure the catch had dropped back into place.

Next she swung back on to the lower pole. She called to Lindsay, "I may as well dismantle as I go," and came back crabwise for the necessary tools. It was only a matter of a few minutes before they were both staggering back through the grounds to the building site to replace the bits and pieces. It was still not long after eleven.

They returned to Paddy's rooms to wait for Cordelia, and collapsed into armchairs. "There's one thing," she said.

"Whoever did that was definitely on the strong side, and very fit. I feel quite tired and I didn't even carry the scaffolding over. Unless whoever did it took more than one trip to get the stuff there."

Lindsay agreed whole-heartedly. She knew just how heavy and how awkward the poles were. These were problems, however, that could be overcome by Chris's suggestions of more than one trip, and of using rope to get them on to the roof. Not wanting to discuss the details further, Lindsay steered the conversation into other channels, and when Cordelia returned just after twelve, they were deep in discussion about the relative merits of Lindsay's MG and other sports cars.

Chris broke off immediately to ask the score. "They won three-two," Cordelia reported. "Sarah Cartwright played a fine game. She scored twice and laid on the third. Very impressive."

"So she should be. She's playing for the county again this season and she should get a trial for the England schoolgirl side, though I doubt if she'll make it. She's not really a team player. Anyhow, who else played well?"

"The left half—is it Julia, Juliet?—had a good game. Caroline Barrington plays hockey like she does everything else—masses of energy, tearing off in all directions at once, unstoppable. I imagine she played her usual game—a little short on strategy but with endless goodwill. And you've got a bloody good goalie there. She only let the second one in because she slipped in the mud. They're not a bad side at all," Cordelia replied.

"Good, good," said Chris vigorously. "Thanks again for standing in."

"I don't think I made too many blunders."

"I'm sure you didn't—but if you did I'm sure Caroline will let me know!" Chris said with a grin. "Well, if you'll excuse me, I'll be on my way. I have to see the team captains about their matches and I'm sure you two have got plenty to talk over. Be seeing you. Thanks for the coffee." She got to her feet.

"Don't thank me, thank Paddy," said Lindsay. "She'll have a fit when she gets back and sees the state of her coffee jar and drinks cupboard."

"Listen, if you two get her out, that'll be the least of her worries," said Chris as she left.

Cordelia slumped into the vacant armchair and immediately demanded information. "Are you going to tell me how the intrepid mountain goats got on while I was tearing up and down the sidelines risking my reputation? Can it be done?"

"It can be done, yes. It would need a certain amount of strength and skill. Cartwright would certainly have known where the stuff was kept and would have had the skill to erect the scaffolding, while Anthony Barrington would undoubtedly have had the strength and skill to perform the actual feat. But I'm not at all sure that Cartwright would have had the agility to get from the scaffolding into the room. And we don't know how much Barrington would have known about the availability of materials on the building site. Certainly while we were up there I had a good look at the masonry and there were no signs of anyone having driven pitons into the pointing or stonework so Barrington couldn't have done it that way—which would have been the natural method for him to have used."

"Well, we'd better get ourselves down to Wales tonight and see what Barrington's got to say for himself," said Cordelia, reluctantly dragging herself to her feet. "It must have been one of those two. I've never believed that a woman could kill another woman as Lorna was killed. The murder's got a man's psychology written all over it; your evidence with the scaffolding just proves what I've felt in my heart all along."

⚓

It was just before three when they pulled up in the car park at the remand centre. It was busier than when they'd been before and there were a dozen other visitors by the gate when they arrived.

Everyone looked depressed by their surroundings; Lindsay thought again how appalling it must be for those locked up inside. Any politician who made cheap jibes about luxury prison conditions only proved that a brick wall had more sensitivity, she thought bitterly. After a short delay at the gate, they were allowed in with a group of other visitors and escorted to the room they'd sat in before. This time, they had to wait longer for Paddy—there appeared to be too few officers to deal with a busy visiting period.

Paddy seemed to have retreated further inside herself. She forced a smile when she saw them, but it stopped at her lips. Lindsay felt anger rising in her when she saw the damage done to her friend. If she'd had any doubts about carrying on, they died then. Sod the *Clarion*, she thought, if there was still work to be done for Paddy, she wouldn't be travelling north on Tuesday night.

"How are you?" Cordelia asked.

Paddy shrugged eloquently. "Anything becomes bearable after a while. Having something to read helps. And I've been doing some work in the laundry, which passes the time. My cell-mate is a pleasant enough soul; she keeps me entertained with tales of family life. Somehow she manages to stay cheerful in spite of being in here. God knows how she does it."

"I don't want to build your hopes too high," said Lindsay, "but we're beginning to make some progress. We think we've worked out how the murder was committed, and if we're right it lets you right off the hook. We'll give Gillian a ring first thing on Monday morning and see what can be done."

A slow smile spread across Paddy's face and this time it reached her eyes. "Tell me about it," she demanded.

Lindsay and Cordelia swiftly outlined the scaffolding theory, and when they came to the part about the experiment on the roof Paddy laughed out loud. "I wish I'd been there to see you and Chris leaping around like a pair of moorland sheep. You must have given the girls fuel for weeks of jokes. Poor old Chris. They won't let her forget that in a hurry."

"Fortunately, I don't think there were any girls around to see what we were doing," said Lindsay.

"Don't you believe it. In a rumour factory like Derbyshire House you only need one person for a story to be all over the school in a matter of hours," Paddy replied.

"We're still not sure who did it, however," sighed Cordelia. "The more information we get, the harder it seems to be to prove anything."

"Which reminds me," said Lindsay, "do you happen to know anything about James Cartwright's financial position, Paddy?"

Paddy's eyebrows shot up. "Not a lot," she replied. "The word is, he's not as flush as he used to be. Not getting the squash court contract was a bad blow. And he hasn't changed his car this year. I have heard this playing fields development is make or break for him, but I do find that hard to believe."

After a moment's thought, she went on. "Speaking of the Cartwrights, I've been thinking about what you were asking me the other day. About Sarah's statement. I think she's got it wrong, you know. In fact, it was the other way round. When I took her to Music 2, I stopped at the storeroom to have a quick word with a couple of juniors who shouldn't have been there at the time, and Sarah went on ahead. As I entered the room Sarah was standing by the cupboards looking through some sheet music. Which is slightly odd because the girl has no interest in music except as an accompaniment to gymnastics. I told her to be sure she put it back in the right place because the room had been tidied up for Lorna. I don't think one can read anything into all that but, just for the record, that's what happened."

"I see," said Lindsay thoughtfully. "I think we're going to have to have another little chat with Miss Cartwright. I don't like people lying to me. Not when it's a question of murder. It makes me start asking myself what they're trying to hide."

"Don't be heavy, Lindsay," Paddy warned. "She's not a very happy kid and I feel responsible for her."

"She'll have to be spoken to, Paddy. There are more important things at stake here than Sarah Cartwright's finer feelings."

"I know that, but take it gently. You'll get a pretty hostile reaction if you bully her."

"You've got to be joking," Cordelia said scornfully. "The last time we saw her, the only monstering that was going on was her giving Lindsay a hard time. She's the only person, apart from Pamela Overton, who has succeeded in squashing your favourite journalist."

Paddy laughed again and a little colour crept back into her cheeks. But before Lindsay and Cordelia could capitalise on this, the officer was there to take Paddy back to her cell. "We'll soon have you out of here, don't forget that," called Cordelia, as Paddy vanished through the door again.

They walked back to the car, arguing. Cordelia was all for heading straight down to Wales to talk to Anthony Barrington, but Lindsay had changed her mind and was determined to get her own way. "I want to talk to Sarah right away," she argued. "Barrington's still going to be there later on tonight. Or we could go down tomorrow early. But I want to straighten out Sarah Cartwright as soon as possible. She's lying and I want to know why."

"We can talk to her any time. Now we know she's lying, we only have to get at the reasons why. But we should get to Barrington as soon as we can. He's the only person who could have had a hand in this that we haven't talked to so far. And you seem to think he's the likeliest candidate. A little while ago you were desperate to get down to Wales to see him."

"But don't you see? Sarah's answers could change everything. It may be that after we've talked to her again there will be no reason for us to talk to Barrington at all. We may manage to wrap the whole thing up. We lose nothing by seeing Sarah first—and we could gain a lot. I just *know* it's important."

Cordelia sighed. "You're like a bloody steamroller. You flatten the opposition. You just don't listen, do you?"

"I know I'm right," said Lindsay stubbornly.

"Well, I still think you're wrong." Cordelia argued.

"We'll see," said Lindsay. "Now, is there a phone around here anywhere?"

"I think we passed one about a mile down the road towards the motorway. Who do you want to call?"

"I just want to leave a message for Sarah. To let her know we're coming. That should make her sweat a little. I want her nice and worried about what we may or may not know." She got in the car.

"My God, you really can be a bully, can't you," said Cordelia crossly to the empty air.

18

They parked the car outside Longnor House and marched straight up the stairs to Sarah's room. On the door a "Do Not Disturb" notice was hanging. Cordelia said curtly, "These notices are supposed to be sacrosanct, but for once we'll break the rules. After all, she should be expecting us." She rapped on the door. There was no reply. She looked questioningly at Lindsay, who nodded encouragement. Cordelia turned the handle, opened the door and stepped inside.

What she saw made her gasp and turn away, her hand to her mouth. Lindsay caught hold of her and held her tightly. She looked over Cordelia's shoulder and took in a vision of absolute horror. She said harshly. "We mustn't touch anything." Lindsay gently released Cordelia and steered her on to the landing before forcing herself across the threshold. She quickly glanced around, feeling her chest tighten, then spoke commandingly to Cordelia. "Go down to Paddy's room. Get Pamela Overton here and call the police." Cordelia stood numbly, seeming not to have heard. "Do it now," Lindsay cried. Cordelia shook herself and stumbled down the corridor.

Left alone, Lindsay somehow steeled herself to look at the appalling scene inside the room. She desperately wanted to see if there was anything obvious to explain the significance of what had happened there.

Sarah Cartwright—or what remained of her—sprawled half on the floor and half on the bed. Her left arm was slashed almost to the bone at wrist and elbow; her right arm had a matching cut, though far less deep, at the wrist. A sheath knife lay on the floor. She had obviously cut herself leaning over the washbasin for it was filled with a grisly mixture of blood and water. As consciousness had slipped away, she had fallen back and her blood had splashed the walls and soaked the carpet and bed. Lindsay badly wanted to be sick, but from somewhere came the strength to carry on her examination. She moved across to the desk, careful to avoid the blood.

On the top of the desk was a single sheet of foolscap paper, covered in neat handwriting. It was what she had half-expected to find. Across the top was written in block capitals, "To anyone who has an interest in the death of Lorna Smith-Couper."

The message continued,

I want to say first of all that I am sorry for all the trouble that I have caused, especially to my father, Miss Callaghan and the school. At the time, I thought I was doing the best possible thing and I did not think anything could be proved. I did not mean to incriminate Miss Callaghan.

I killed Lorna Smith-Couper. I fetched scaffolding from the squash courts and used it to climb from the kitchen roof to the music room. I climbed in the window and strangled her while she was playing. I knew she would be there because Miss Callaghan told me that morning when we were there together. I did it for my father. I wanted him to get the school playing fields to save his business, especially now I know what people at the school really think of me.

I thought Miss Callaghan would get off and I'd get away with it. But Lindsay Gordon and Cordelia Brown are coming to see me and I know they were messing about with scaffolding this morning. They must know I lied to Miss Callaghan, and it's all bound to come out now because I'm the only person who could have climbed up the scaffolding like that. And I couldn't face prison. I'm sorry for the pain I've caused my father. I did it because I love you, Daddy. Sarah Cartwright.

The tragic waste outlined on the paper angered Lindsay. She turned to look coldly at the body of the young woman. She had not liked Sarah Cartwright, had been irritated by her condescension, but no one deserved to die like this. There was no dignity in this death, only fear and degradation. Lindsay could stomach no more of it. She walked out of the room, feeling appallingly guilty for having been so slow to the truth.

When she emerged into the corridor she saw Pamela Overton coming up the stairs towards her. The headmistress looked shaken and walked tentatively like an elderly woman as she approached Lindsay, who took a deep breath, feeling suddenly exhausted. "I'm sorry," she sighed. "I was too slow. Sarah has killed herself."

"Cordelia told me," Miss Overton said bleakly. "It's to do with Lorna's death?"

Lindsay nodded wearily. "I'm afraid so."

"But surely not Sarah? Not one of my girls?" It was an extraordinary plea, thought Lindsay.

"She has left a confession," Lindsay replied. "I can't imagine a worse way to clear Paddy's name."

The headmistress said nothing. She looked coldly at Lindsay and walked a few steps down the corridor so she could stare out of a window. Lindsay leaned against the wall and closed her eyes. She could not have said how long it was before she heard heavy feet on the stairs and a murmur of voices as Inspector Dart arrived with a group of policemen, some in uniform and some in plain clothes.

"Miss Overton," he said gently, "I'm very sorry about this. I wonder if you'd be good enough to wait downstairs while we do what's necessary? And Miss Gordon—I'll want to talk to you and Miss Brown when I'm through. Will you wait downstairs with her?"

"Shouldn't someone inform Mr Cartwright?" asked Miss Overton.

"That is being taken care of," Dart replied. "Now, ladies, if you'll just go downstairs."

The two women made their way in silence to Paddy's room. When they entered, Cordelia looked up from an armchair and said shakily, "You shouldn't have phoned, Lindsay." She burst into tears.

Lindsay hurried to her and crouched beside the chair, putting an arm round her shaking shoulders. "How could I know?" she asked desperately. "I thought she was lying to protect him. I didn't know if she was doing it because she knew he was guilty or because she only suspected he might be. I really didn't think she had killed Lorna."

Cordelia's head came up. "She killed Lorna?"

"She left a confession. I think we'd better prepare ourselves for a sticky session with the police."

Pamela Overton moved over to them. "Do you mean to say that you may have had something to do with Sarah's suicide?"

"We uncovered some new information today. We also discovered that Sarah had lied in her statement to the police. I rang and left a message about an hour ago to say that we wanted to talk to her again. That's all."

The headmistress stared hard at Lindsay. "I had thought you were a reasonably sensitive and civilised human being," she said. "Please tell Inspector Dart that I will be in my study in the main building when he wants to see me." She turned on her heel and left.

Cordelia wiped her eyes and blew her nose noisily. "We really screwed up, didn't we?"

"I suppose so," said Lindsay angrily. "And since I'm now credited with being uncivilised and insensitive as well as just stupid, I'll put the finishing touches to everyone's low opinion of me." So saying, she went to the phone and dialled through to the *Daily Clarion*'s sister Sunday paper's copy room.

"Hello? Lindsay Gordon here. I've got a belter for you. Ready? Murder squad detectives were called in today after a pupil at a top girls' boarding school was found dead. The detectives were already investigating the murder of internationally famous cellist Lorna Smith-Couper at Derbyshire House Girls' School a week ago. A teacher at the school, Miss Patricia Callaghan, has been charged with the murder, but sources close to the police investigation revealed today that there was some doubt as to whether the killer was still at large. The dead girl was Sarah Cartwright, eighteen, whose father James Cartwright is a builder in the nearby town of Buxton. He is currently locked in a dispute with the school over his proposal to turn the school's playing fields into a luxury timeshare development.

"Sarah was found dead in her study bedroom at the school where she was a sixth-former. She had knife wounds to both arms. A keen gymnast and hockey player, Sarah hoped to become a PE teacher. Police said last night there were no suspicious circumstances. No one is being sought in connection with her death. End copy. Note to newsdesk; the girl left a note confessing to the Smith-Couper murder."

Lindsay repeated the process to three other papers, then put the phone down. "Bet you think I'm a real shit, don't you?"

Cordelia looked at her. "I couldn't have done what you've just done."

Lindsay shrugged, her face a mask. "It's a way of dealing with what's happened. A way of hiding, a way of postponing."

"It's your job, Lindsay. You chose it. I certainly couldn't have. However you cut it, what it comes down to is you doing your job. If you didn't go about it in a cold-blooded way, I suppose you'd be no use to your bosses." There was no approval in Cordelia's voice, only coldness.

Before Lindsay could reply, the door opened and Inspector Dart came in, followed by the young detective Lindsay had seen with him before. He looked grim, his lean face set in hard lines. He walked over to Paddy's desk and sat down behind it. The young detective sat down on a straight-backed chair near the door and took out his notebook. Dart said nothing, but continued to glance from Lindsay to Cordelia and back again. Lindsay felt extremely exposed.

Finally he broke the silence. He spoke slowly and his deep voice had become a growl. "I hate bloody waste," he said. "And I hate bloody pillocks who fall for the line spun by the media: that the police are not only woodentops but also corrupt and vicious. You know why I hate them? Because they think they know better than we do how to catch criminals. Usually, they never get the chance to put their crass little theories into practice. Just as well, wouldn't you say, on the evidence of today?"

Lindsay said nothing. She felt she deserved most of what was coming, and she resolved to bite on the bullet and not let this man see how upset she actually was.

"I've got what seems to be a confession here. A confession to a murder for which I already have someone in custody. The note mentions you, Miss Gordon, a couple of times. I also have a note found in the girl's waste-paper bin which seems to be a phone message saying you intended to call on her after seeing Miss Callaghan. All this suggests to me that you've been pissing about with things which are none of your bloody business. Am I right?"

Lindsay shrugged. He looked expectantly at her, but when he saw there was nothing more forthcoming, he went on. "I've one or two questions arising from the confession. You have read it, I take it?"

Lindsay nodded. "I have, but Miss Brown hasn't."

"For your sake, I hope I'm not going to find your fingerprints all over it. Quote: 'I know they were messing about with scaffolding this morning.' Unquote. Now, I want the explanation, please."

Lindsay looked up. "It was clear to Miss Overton that since you had already made an arrest that fitted the circumstances, you wouldn't be looking for alternative solutions. So she asked Cordelia and me to take a look at this business to see if we could come up with anything that would help clear Paddy Callaghan, whom all three of us believe is innocent.

"I have been a journalist for some years now," she went on, finding her stride. "I've done a fair number of investigations, a couple of which have resulted in arrests. I have qualifications both in English and Scottish law, and I know quite a bit about the burden of proof. If I didn't, I'd be too expensive a risk for newspapers to employ. I'm not as much of a fool as you seem to think, Inspector. And neither is Cordelia. I thought we might just manage to come up with one or two things that you and your experienced team had missed, especially since people seem to find it easier to talk to us. As for messing about on the kitchen roof with the scaffolding—it was testing a theory which seemed to cover all the salient facts."

"Spare me the speeches," he said caustically.

She ignored him and continued. "I don't particularly expect you to believe this, but all week I've had something nagging away at the back of my mind. I had a feeling it was important, but it just wouldn't come to me. I only remembered what it was in the early hours of this morning."

Then she explained the sudden realisation of what she had seen so briefly the week before. She went on to relate the events of the morning. When she came to the end of her tale, he looked aghast.

"God preserve me from amateurs," he said bitterly. "And just how many fingerprints, footprints and other forensic traces do you think you obliterated this morning? What in heaven's name possessed you to take the law into your own hands to this extent? Answer me, woman!"

"I didn't think there would be anything on the building site. After all, the workmen have been there all week. As far as the rest of it is concerned, I supposed the criminal would have been wearing gloves. It wasn't a spur of the moment crime, and everyone knows about fingerprints these days. And Chris Jackson made sure she didn't do any damage to the paintwork. There weren't any marks on it before, anyway. I checked early this morning when I realised what it was I'd seen last Saturday."

"Your stupidity is staggering," Dart groaned. "That corpse upstairs is a bloody monument to your stupidity. I suppose it never occurred to you to come to us with your information? If you'd done that, I can guarantee Sarah Cartwright would still be alive. Instead, you have to do things your way, and now she's just a lump of dead flesh. You say the girl lied in her statement. She admits that in her confession. If, instead of phoning to put the frighteners on her, you'd come to me, she'd still be alive. I've known that girl since she was in her pram. Now I've got to go and tell her father that not only was his daughter a murderer but that because of the sheer stupidity of a couple of so-called amateur detectives, she's dead." He shook his head. "Congratulations, ladies. It looks like you've got your friend off the hook. I just hope you can live with the price." He got to his feet and walked to the door. Before he left, he turned to them and said, "Don't leave the area before the inquest. I think I'll be wanting you to tell your story to the coroner."

The policemen left the two women alone. Lindsay stared unseeingly out of the window. After a few minutes, Cordelia got up and put her arms round her. Lindsay half-smiled and said, "One of us better ring Gillian and get her to set the wheels in motion to get Paddy freed. Why don't you do it? I don't think I can face it right now. I should have listened to you.

"I'm really sorry about all of this. I've not done you any favours, have I? Not to mention that poor, tortured kid. Me and my big ideas. I've made a right balls-up of this from start to finish."

Cordelia kissed her forehead. "Don't blame yourself. She chose to kill Lorna. You didn't make her. Everybody seems to be forgetting that side of the story. And she chose to kill herself rather than face up to the consequences. She'd have sat back and let Paddy be destroyed if you hadn't acted. And in spite of what Dart said, I'm not so sure they'd have taken you seriously if you'd gone to them. They'd probably have accused you of wasting police time. So don't go blaming yourself."

Lindsay sighed deeply and turned her face away. "I can't help feeling responsible for the way things have turned out. That's clearly what Pamela Overton thinks as well as Dart. And Cartwright. How's he going to feel? She was all he had. Oh shit . . . why does everything have to be such a mess?"

19

There was no champagne to welcome Paddy Callaghan back to Longnor House on Sunday morning. After the due process of law had been carried out, Gillian drove Paddy back from the remand centre. Cordelia had cooked a lavish Indian meal, and when Paddy walked through the door she was greeted with hugs, kisses, tears, cold lager and the aroma of curry spices. After the emotional reunion, Lindsay walked over to the main building to tell Pamela Overton Paddy was back. The headmistress hurried off immediately to see Paddy in her rooms and Lindsay, who now felt even more uncomfortable in her presence, took the opportunity to file an exclusive story on Paddy's release, complete with interview, to the *Clarion*.

After she had dictated the story, she spoke to the newsdesk. "Lindsay here, Duncan. The copy for my exclusive on the girls' school murder should be dropping on your desk any minute now, I've left a number where you can reach me if there are any queries."

"I've just got it in front of me now, kid. Not a bad piece of work. Mind you, you've taken long enough over it; it should be good. When do I get you back working properly again?"

"If you gave me a job instead of shifts, you'd know the answer to that. I'm supposed to be in on Wednesday at one o'clock. So I'll see you then."

"Give you a job? I'd never see you then! I must be paying you too much as it is if you can afford to spend a whole week gadding about in England."

Lindsay laughed. "I'd rather be suffering from an old slave driver like you than doing what I'm doing right now. I've not had a proper night's sleep since I left Glasgow."

Duncan's voice had a chuckle in it. "That was always your problem, Lindsay, mixing business with pleasure. See you Wednesday."

Lindsay sat in the headmistress's study, smoking quietly and turning over the events of the last week yet again. She forced herself to think about the horrors of the previous day. Now that the first shock had subsided she was able to think more objectively about Sarah's suicide and her confession. It struck her that the confession was remarkably bare of essential detail. There was nothing about Paddy's duffel-coat toggle, something known only to the murderer, the handful of people who had actually seen the body, Paddy and the police. In itself, that was hardly world-shaking, thought Lindsay, though it would have made sense for Sarah, in the flow of her confession, to have said something like, "I made the garrotte with the cello string I took from Music 2 in the morning when I was there with Miss Callaghan, and a toggle I took from someone's coat in the cloakroom at Longnor."

Lindsay began to feel faint stirrings of disquiet. The girl hadn't explained how the window catches could easily be opened. It was Lindsay herself who had fleshed out the method of the crime to the police; ironically that would render Sarah's "confession" all the more credible to them. Also, of all the people who had fallen under Lindsay's suspicion, Sarah was one of the least likely to know how long Lorna was to spend in the music room before she went on stage, for she had no involvement with the musical life of the school.

Supposing Sarah hadn't killed Lorna, Lindsay speculated. Supposing she believed her father had killed Lorna—leaving aside

for the moment whether he had or not. If she had reasons for
thinking he was guilty, and that he was close to being discovered,
would she have killed herself to protect him? That was the sixty-
four-thousand-dollar question, Lindsay realised. Considering what
she knew of the girl's character, from her own observation and
from the comments of others, she thought it was a distinct possibility. The girl worshipped her father. The only other anchor in
her life was the school and her relationship with her fellow pupils,
which had been dealt a hard blow by events at the craft fair. Most
girls would have shrugged the matter off then and there, but Sarah
had reacted rather extremely. She seemed, by choice, to be a very
isolated girl. So it might well have been that she would rather have
sacrificed herself than see her father arrested for murder.

Lindsay sighed deeply. Part of her said, drop it, leave it
be. Paddy was free, free and cleared. But the other part of her
refused to let go. Her newspaper training had heightened the
tenacious determination in her to get to the bottom of things
and not to be fobbed off with half an answer. Now doubts had
wormed their way into her head and she was afraid they were
going to give her no peace.

She shook her head vigorously, like a dog emerging from
a stream, crushed her cigarette out and walked briskly back to
Longnor, hoping that diving back into the celebrations would
drive her doubts away. Pamela Overton had gone by the time
she returned, and Gillian Markham was standing by the door
with her coat on.

She turned to Lindsay and smiled. "I'm glad you're back,"
she said. "I'm off now to let you get on with your celebrations,
but I wanted to thank you for all the work you've done on
Paddy's behalf. I know this business has been pretty terrible; on
the positive side, however, Paddy's name has been cleared, and
that's largely due to the efforts of you and Cordelia."

Paddy interrupted. "That goes for me too. If we'd relied
on the police to clear this business up, I'd still be rotting in jail.
So thanks, both of you."

Lindsay blushed and shook her head. "Maybe we did do that. But I cocked the whole thing up in the end. I was so excited by what we'd found out that I ignored Cordelia's good sense, and I have to accept responsibility for what happened to Sarah. It'll stay with me for a long time. Maybe it will make me stop and think twice about some of the stunts I get up to. But the people who deserve at least as much thanks as me and Cordelia are Pamela Overton and you, Gillian, yourself. If Pamela hadn't been so convinced of your innocence in the first place that she demanded our help, I don't think it would have occurred to Cordelia or me to get involved in the way we did. And you've been pretty exceptional too, Gillian—I can't think of many lawyers who would go along with the unconventional routine we've been pulling over the last week. End of speech. Now, will someone give me a beer?"

Gillian said goodbye and left the three of them sitting round the fire with their meal. They ate in a companionable silence for the main part, and it was only after they sat back with coffee that Paddy demanded to know the full story of their investigations. Between them, Lindsay and Cordelia managed to give her a full rundown.

There was a hush while Paddy took in all they had to tell. "What a waste!" she sighed at last. "So much loyalty. So much love. And two horrible deaths out of it. And what for? A bunch of bloody playing fields, which Cartwright will almost certainly pick up since I can't see us raising the money now. Oh God, I think I'll get a job in some grotty inner-city comprehensive where nobody cares that much about anything, let alone a few acres of green."

"You'd hate that, and you know it," Lindsay retorted, "so what about some inner-city comprehensive where people do care and need what you can give them?"

Paddy burst out laughing. "I'm hardly out of prison and already you're lecturing me. I give up, Lindsay, I give up!"

Their general laughter was interrupted by a knock at the door. Paddy groaned. "Sounds like everything's back to normal already." She called, "Come in!"

Caroline's head appeared round the door. "Sorry to interrupt," she said. "But we just wanted to tell you how pleased we all are to have you back with us. We all knew you didn't do it, and we missed not having you about the place. It just wasn't the same having Sherlock Holmes and Watson keeping an eye on us. I say, Miss Callaghan, you should have seen them in action. Extremely tough cookies."

"That will do, Caroline," said Paddy, smiling. "Thank you for your kind words. I'll do the rounds later on, so you'll be able to check for yourselves that I'm still in one piece."

"Okay, Miss Callaghan. We've all been a bit worried about you. It's good to see prison hasn't ground you down."

"Caroline—on your way!"

The girl grinned and vanished. "I swear her grin hangs around after her, like the Cheshire Cat," Cordelia muttered.

Caroline wasn't the only visitor. As the afternoon wore on, most of the members of the staff popped in briefly to congratulate Paddy on her release. But the atmosphere remained muted, for no one could forget that a girl had died. After a couple of hours, Paddy suggested that they all go for a walk up the hill behind the school. As they set off, Lindsay spotted Jessica Bennett walking through the trees from the main building. On an impulse she said, "You two go ahead, I'll catch you up. I just want to have a few words with Jessica. Nothing important, just a little point I want to clear up for my own satisfaction."

Cordelia shook her head with an air of amused tolerance. "You're never content, are you? All right, but don't be long or you'll never catch us up."

"Don't be so sure of that," said Paddy. "After a week's incarceration, I feel totally flabby." They walked off, leaving Lindsay to wait by the door for the girl.

When Jessica spotted Lindsay, she smiled broadly, "Hi," she said. "I hear Miss Callaghan's been released. It's wonderful news, isn't it? I'm so glad you were able to find out what really happened."

Lindsay smiled wanly. "I'm glad she's back. But I seem to have done as much harm as good. Listen, Jessica, can you spare me a couple of minutes? There's something I want to ask you, just to settle something in my own mind."

The girl frowned slightly. "But I thought it was all cleared up now?"

"Come in a minute," said Lindsay, leading the way into Paddy's sitting-room. "There are a couple of details I was wondering about. It's being a journalist. I'm like a dog with a bone."

Jessica sat down. "All right. Ask what you want and I'll try to answer."

"It's my own fault. I should have asked you this when I spoke to you before. But I let myself be sidetracked when you told us where you found Miss Callaghan and what frame of mind she seemed to be in. Daft of me—because I asked everyone else what I'm going to ask you now. I had a feeling it might be important. All I wondered was if you saw Sarah at all on Saturday night, and if so, when and where."

"Is that all?" she said, sounding relieved. "I actually saw her a couple of times. When I went to get my coat to go across to Main Building to get Miss Callaghan, Sarah was just going out of Longnor. She had her anorak on and she was wearing track suit bottoms and trainers."

"What time was that?"

"It must have been about a quarter past seven. I remember looking at my watch and thinking that was good because I'd be able to find Miss Callaghan before the concert started. Then, when we came back, I went back into the cloakroom to hang my coat up. That must have been just after half-past seven—say, twenty-five to eight. Sarah was sitting in the cloakroom, just staring into space, I tried to talk to her, but she just shrugged me off and I saw her going back upstairs. I suppose she was going back to her room. It's terrible to think of it now—she must have just come back from killing Lorna then, mustn't she?"

Lindsay was non-committal, trying not to show that what the girl had said was significant. She thanked Jessica for her help and as gently as possible got rid of her. She sat at Paddy's desk with her head in her hands. What she had just been told made her thoughts race furiously round her head. How could Sarah have killed Lorna between seven fifteen and seven thirty-five? Although that part of the school grounds overlooked by the music-room windows was normally dark and deserted at that time of the evening, on the night of the murder it had been busy: cars were being parked and people were walking to the concert. It would not have been feasible to have carried out that murderous climb until the area had been quiet again—in other words, till seven-thirty. And Lindsay couldn't believe the murderer would have taken any chances till the concert was under way, to muffle any sounds coming from the music room.

So that left her two choices. James Cartwright. And Anthony Barrington. If she had to pick one on the basis of what she already knew, she would have opted for Cartwright every time, but it wasn't that simple. If she went to Inspector Dart with her latest suspicions, she was sure she'd get extremely short shrift. And approaching Cartwright himself on the day after his daughter had killed herself was something she couldn't face. She thought back to her first few weeks as a journalist, when she had discovered how much she hated the ghoulish task of talking to bereft relatives, trying to collect pictures from them. Now she would do almost anything to avoid those assignments. She knew journalists who could cope in that situation, but the grief of strangers was something she still found painful and embarrassing, especially after Frances's death. She asked herself how, carrying the extra weight of responsibility for this death, she could walk into Cartwright's house and start asking the questions she needed answers to.

That left Anthony Barrington. It could do no harm to talk to him, she reasoned. If he was innocent, she could eliminate him—which would leave her virtually certain of Cartwright's guilt. And if he wasn't innocent she would have avoided a crass encounter with Cartwright.

She made her decision then and there. She glanced at her watch. If she drove fast, she could be at Barrington's Welsh home by six. She grabbed a piece of paper and wrote, "Had to go out on business. Sorry—back about nine. If the office rings, tell them I'm on the road and I'll phone in later." She didn't want either Paddy or Cordelia to know that pursuit of the truth was still gnawing at her like a maggot.

But luck wasn't on her side. Just as she was leaving the building, Cordelia jogged back down the path. "I came back to see what was holding you up," she said. "Paddy's nattering to one of her colleagues so I thought I'd collect you. Coming?"

Lindsay shook her head. "I've got to go out," she muttered. "I've left you a note."

"What do you mean? Don't be so mysterious! Where are you off to?"

Lindsay sighed. "If you must know. I'm going to see Anthony Barrington." She looked like a sulky child caught stealing chocolate.

"Oh Lindsay," Cordelia groaned, "why can't you just leave it alone? Look, Paddy's free. Sarah has confessed. The police are satisfied. Why can't you be?"

"Because it doesn't seem right to me," she replied stubbornly. "You didn't read that suicide note. I did and I don't believe Sarah killed Lorna. For a start, the note was too long. It's as if she was trying to convince us that she'd done it. But it was also short on detail. There was nothing in it that wasn't common knowledge. I'm convinced that she killed herself because she thought her father had done it and she couldn't face living with that."

"But if Sarah killed herself because she thought her father was guilty, why not go to see him? Why go to see Barrington?"

"I'm going to see Barrington, because that's what we were intending to do as the next logical step. Besides, it's a softer option than Cartwright just now."

"You're crazy," Cordelia retorted angrily. "Can't you just accept that it's all over and you've made a mistake? You don't have to be perfect, you know. No one expects you to be infallible."

"I wasn't wrong, damn it," Lindsay exploded, "I'm bloody certain Sarah didn't kill Lorna. It's not enough any more just to clear Paddy. Not for me, anyway. There's someone walking around out there who committed murder. I don't think that's a very healthy state of affairs, do you?"

"No, but why should it be you that's got to put it right? Call the police, tell Dart what you think. That's how you should do it. Haven't you learned anything from what's happened?"

"Oh yes," said Lindsay, her voice heavy with sarcasm, "and Dart's going to pay a lot of attention to me, isn't he? No, I'm going to talk to Barrington. That's that."

They stood glaring at each other. Cordelia broke the silence with a sigh. "Well, I'd better come with you, hadn't I? We don't want you walking into a potential murderer's front room on your own, do we?"

But Lindsay, thoroughly roused, was in no mood for olive branches. "I don't need a minder," she stated. "I've been looking after myself in dodgy situations for a long time now. I think I'll manage it on my own. See you later."

She turned on her heel and walked over to her car without looking back. When she glanced behind in her rear-view mirror, Cordelia had gone. Lindsay smacked her fist against the steering wheel.

"Why do I do it? Why the hell do I do it?"

20

Just before six, Lindsay left the main trunk road she'd been following through Wales and turned north up a terrifying single-track road with a series of hairpin bends and sheer drops down the mountainside. Lindsay was only glad it was twilight and she couldn't see the extent of the precipitous slopes. Eventually the road climbed to a tiny village consisting of a post office, a pub, a chapel and a handful of cottages. Other houses straggled up the hillside. Lindsay pulled up and took another look at the scrap of paper with Barrington's address. Plas Glyndwr, Llanagar. No wonder the Welsh got fed up with the English and their weekend cottages, thought Lindsay. The invaders even pinched the best Welsh names.

She set off slowly, trying without success to find the house. Carrying on up the road, however, as she came round a particularly awkward blind bend, she found Plas Glyndwr. Lindsay braked sharply. This was no weekend cottage. It was a four-square, large family house, set behind banks of rhododendrons with a fair-sized lawn and big kitchen garden to one side. A dark blue Daimler was parked in front of the house and an elderly Ford Cortina sat outside the side door. "Oh well, in for a penny, in for a pound," she muttered to herself as she reversed the MG up the drive.

She got out and rang the bell by the front door. A full minute passed before it was opened by a woman in her fifties wearing a voluminous wrapround apron. She had flour on her hands and smudges on one cheek. She looked surprised to see Lindsay.

"Can I help you?" she inquired, her Welsh accent evident even in those few words.

"I'd like to see Mr Barrington, if he's at home," said Lindsay.

"And who shall I say is calling?"

"My name is Lindsay Gordon," she replied. "He won't recognise the name, but I know his daughter Caroline. I won't take up much of his time."

"Wait here a moment," she said and disappeared, shutting the door firmly behind her. She was back within thirty seconds. "Come in," she said, leading Lindsay in.

As they walked through the hall, Lindsay noticed that the only distraction came from framed Ordnance Survey maps of the region hanging on the walls. The woman showed Lindsay into an airy sitting-room, furnished unpretentiously with large chairs upholstered in well-worn William Morris Liberty prints. Anthony Barrington was sitting at a big roll-top desk by the window, a tumbler of whisky in his hand. He looked remarkably like the photograph in Caroline's room. He was wearing a baggy Aran sweater, old corduroy breeches, thick socks and sheepskin slippers. His eyebrows were raised quizzically as he rose to greet Lindsay.

"Good evening, Miss Gordon, is it? Do sit down. My housekeeper tells me you're a friend of Caroline's. What has my mad daughter been up to this time to drag you out into the middle of nowhere?"

"Thanks for seeing me, Mr Barrington. Caroline hasn't been up to anything she shouldn't have. It's not exactly Caroline I wanted to talk to you about, though she's involved indirectly."

His eyebrows shot up again in surprise. "Oh?" he said speculatively. "You do know my daughter, I take it?"

Lindsay smiled. "Oh yes, I know Caroline. She's a remarkable girl. You must be proud of her. She'll go far with that lively mind. But it's more to do with the school. Last week, Pamela Overton asked me to do something related to the murder of Lorna Smith-Couper."

Lindsay's words seemed to hang grimly in the air. Anthony Barrington remained completely unmoved at the sound of a name that must have taken him by surprise.

"And what exactly do you imagine that has to do with me?" Lindsay found him distinctly intimidating as he towered above her.

"If I could just explain. Last week the police arrested Caroline's housemistress for the murder. Miss Overton asked me and another friend of Miss Callaghan's if we would make some inquiries into the matter, since she believed Paddy was innocent and she knew that I felt the same way. I don't know how much you know about the events of the last few days?"

He studied her carefully before answering. "I read in this morning's papers that a girl at the school had killed herself and that the police were investigating a connection between her and the murder. I rang Caroline this morning about it, since I was naturally concerned, and she told me that Sarah Cartwright confessed to the murder. As a result, Miss Callaghan has been freed. Or so the school gossip goes. I would have thought that meant an end to it. I don't quite understand what you are doing here."

Lindsay sighed. "I'm not completely convinced that Sarah was responsible for Lorna's death. I know the police are satisfied, but there are nagging doubts at the back of my mind. I suppose now that Paddy's free I should be satisfied. But I want to be sure there's not still a killer on the loose. Forgive me if I seem melodramatic. Now, I only discovered a couple of days ago that you were about on the day of the murder and I wondered if you had noticed anything out of the ordinary?"

"What on earth can you mean by that?" he said, a note of vexation in his voice.

"This week, I discovered that the murder was committed in such a way that it required certain preparations to be made in advance, made, in fact, at about the time you were dropping Caroline off after your afternoon out . . . Obviously the police have questioned most of the people who were around at the time but I don't think they've gone to the lengths I have because they were sure they had the person responsible. I just wondered if you had seen anything unusual."

"I see," he said, seeming to relax. "By the way, I'm not being very hospitable. Would you like a drink?"

"No thanks, I've got the car," said Lindsay, glad of the excuse not to accept a drink from a man she still feared could be a murderer. "Now, when you dropped Caroline off, what exactly did you do, can you remember?"

"We got to Derbyshire House about half-past five—quarter to six—that sort of time. I drove her up to Longnor House in the Daimler. I got out with her and went up to her room to collect some family photographs and came down more or less right away, because it was nearly time for her to have dinner. Then I drove back to my hotel."

"Did you go straight back to the hotel?"

"Of course I did! When I got there, I sat in the car for about half an hour listening to the end of a Bartók concert on the radio."

"You misunderstood me," said Lindsay, congratulating herself that she was beginning to get somewhere on establishing opportunity. "I meant, did you come straight down the drive the way you came in, or did you by any chance drive round by the building site?"

"The building site? Oh, you mean where they're putting up the squash courts? No, why on earth should I have? They're way beyond the trees. I suppose it might have been logical to turn left and go round the back of the house to rejoin the main drive but I simply went right, back the way I'd come. It was more

or less dark by then and there were quite a lot of girls going off
to dinner. I didn't want to chance hitting any of them with the
car so I avoided the back of the main building as far as possible.
Does that answer your question?"

"Yes, thank you. You were aware of what was happening
at the school that night, weren't you?"

"Caroline had mentioned the concert, yes."

"I'm surprised you didn't stay for it, since you seem to enjoy
music enough to sit in the car on a cold night listening to the
end of a piece of Bartók," said Lindsay casually.

He looked sharply at her. "I had a lot of work to do. And
besides, the programme didn't appeal to me," he retorted.

Never give two excuses when one will do, thought Lindsay. The mark of the lie. "The programme or the soloist?" she
coolly asked. "I know a certain amount about your relationship
with Lorna, you see."

"If you know anything about it at all, you will also know
that it finished a long time ago," he replied, anger giving his
voice a sharp edge.

"Caroline has spoken very freely to me about the affair and
your reactions to it," said Lindsay, keeping calm.

"How dare you question my daughter about a family matter!" he exploded, "I'm damned certain Pamela Overton gave
you no brief to subject her pupils to such disgusting prying."

"Caroline volunteered most of the information. She seemed
to think that uncovering a murderer's identity was rather more
important than personal feelings. Don't think it gives me any
pleasure to rake up the sordid details of people's private lives.

"And I have to tell you, I think your daughter is a damn
sight more honest than you are. You've given me a version of
events that I know isn't strictly true. You were seen in your car at
Derbyshire House at about twenty past seven. Now, you weren't
at the concert and your car was gone fifteen minutes later. The
police don't know this yet, but it's made me wonder what you
were up to—and I'm sure they'll wonder too. While you claim

to have been listening to Bartók, you could have been killing Lorna. You may find this outrageous, but it seems to me that there's a stronger case against you than ever there was against Paddy Callaghan—and they arrested her."

Throughout this speech, Anthony Barrington had looked profoundly astonished. In any other circumstances, his expression would have provoked laughter, with his open mouth, his bewildered expression and his raised eyebrows. The silence was almost tangible, but before it could become oppressive, he found his tongue.

"How dare you!" he roared. "My God, you've a nerve. First you interrogate my daughter—and you haven't heard the last of that, I can assure you. Then you walk into my house as bold as brass and accuse me of murder, with no evidence whatsoever to support some crack-brained theory. Do you think the police are fools? If they're satisfied, maybe it's because they've got evidence. Evidence! Do you know what the word means? It means something more substantial than accusing a man of murder just because he changed his mind about going to a concert.

"Pamela Overton must have taken leave of her senses, letting an idiot like you loose on something like this. Now, get out of here before I call the police and have you arrested. And if I ever hear you've repeated this insane accusation to anyone else I'll have a writ for slander on you so fast your tiny mind will go into a flat spin. Just take yourself out of my house—and don't ever go near my daughter again or you will be truly sorry."

There was nothing for it but to go. She piled into the car, all dignity gone, and found that her hands were shaking. She glanced back at the house to see Barrington silhouetted in the doorway, shouting and waving his fist at her. She shot down the drive and hurtled back down the narrow road with scant regard for the tortuous bends. Once on the main road, she stopped at the first lay-by and lit a cigarette.

She tried to sort through her impressions of the hair-raising interview. She realised she had mishandled the situation and wished she'd brought Cordelia along for moral support. As far as eliminating him was concerned, there had been nothing offered in the way of proof. But unless Anthony Barrington was a first-class actor, Lindsay would stake her life on his innocence. It suddenly dawned on her that that was exactly what she had done by bowling up to his front door alone. It sent a chill through her. "I really have been bloody stupid from the very start over this," she thought. "Still, I'm further forward than I was. I don't believe that outrage was faked—and it says something that he admitted to having gone back to the school because he'd changed his mind about the concert. I wonder what made him feel he couldn't go through with it once he'd steeled himself to coming back? Oh well, I guess I'll never know."

She set off for the long drive back to Derbyshire, stopping only to check with the *Clarion* newsdesk that there were no queries on her copy. While she was in the phone box, on impulse she decided to phone Cordelia and tell her she would definitely be back by nine.

She got straight through to Paddy and was immediately bombarded with questions. She refused to supply any details of her humiliation, promising to fill them in when she returned. Once she got Cordelia on the line she said, "Don't say anything to Paddy yet, but I've just come from an extremely heavy scene with Barrington."

"I'm not surprised," she replied stiffly. "What exactly happened?"

"I'll tell you later." She sighed. "Suffice it to say that it never happens like this in books. Your fictional detective never gets thrown out of rich men's houses with threats of slander. I think in future I'll stick to being a journo. At least journalism more or less lives up to its own mythology."

Cordelia laughed softly and said, "You mean you really are a promiscuous alcoholic who spends her life running into crowded newsrooms yelling, 'Hold the front page'?"

"But of course," Lindsay replied. "Pour me a drink, pass me a woman and a cigarette while I knock out a world exclusive. I'll see you later, okay?"

She made better time on the return journey as there was little traffic about. Two hours of hard driving with Joan Armatrading blasting out of the stereo had made her feel better. She got out of the car singing and noticed with surprise that a police car was drawn up next to Paddy's Land Rover. As she walked towards the door of the house, two uniformed officers got out of the car and intercepted her.

The elder of the two, a sergeant, said, "Miss Lindsay Gordon?"

"That's right. What's the problem?"

"Inspector Dart has asked me to bring you along to the police station. There are one or two things he wants to have a word with you about."

She forced a taut smile to her lips and said in a voice that struggled to stay casual, "I don't suppose I have a great deal of choice?"

The sergeant studied her, saying nothing. She shrugged and said, "Very well. Shall we go?"

They travelled the short journey to the police station in silence. The car pulled up by a long, low building above the town centre. Lindsay followed the policemen inside to a large hallway with a reception desk closed off by partitions of frosted glass. The sergeant left her to wait with the constable and disappeared through a side door. From the reception area she could hear the low murmur of voices. Lindsay wondered what Dart could possibly want with her now.

A couple of minutes passed before the sergeant reappeared. It felt longer. "Come with me, please," he said. "The Inspector's waiting for you."

They walked together down a long corridor. Even on a Sunday evening the station seemed busy. There were lights on throughout the building and people appeared in doorways and bustled along the corridors. They stopped before an unmarked door and the sergeant knocked. It was opened by Dart's silent young sidekick. He stood back for her to enter and the two uniformed men departed.

Inspector Dart was sitting behind a cluttered desk. He glanced up at her, shook his head wearily and said, "Some coppers get to spend Sunday night at home with their feet up watching *Dirty Harry* on the video. Other poor sods get dragged out because they happen to get tangled up in cases that throw up right stupid bastards. Guess which category I come into, Miss Gordon?"

Lindsay said nothing. Her silence clearly exasperated him. He went on. "I could say, I suppose you're wondering why I had you brought here tonight. But that would be a pretty silly thing to say to someone who thinks she's smarter than the whole of Derbyshire Constabulary. I think you know very well why you're sitting here tonight.

"I've had a complaint about your activities. A very strongly worded complaint from a very irate gentleman who alleges that you virtually accused him of committing murder. Not even an unsolved murder, at that. A murder to which an eighteen-year-old girl confessed before she killed herself in an extremely unpleasant and painful way. Now I don't know what the hell you think you're playing at, but this gentleman told me a great deal about your little chat. I presume you know what I'm talking about? Or are there some more people scattered round the countryside that you've been accusing of murder? Well?"

"I suppose Anthony Barrington's been on the phone," said Lindsay resignedly. She was thankful that her journalistic experiences over the last few years had destroyed any awe and respect she had ever felt for the police. It made the interview a little easier to deal with at the end of a draining day.

"He has indeed, Miss Gordon. And from what he says, you really have been playing silly buggers this time. Isn't it enough to drive one girl to suicide? Don't you think that's sufficient mayhem for one weekend?"

"That's unfair. Sarah did what she did for her own reasons, which I suspect had little to do with me. But I managed to work out what really happened last Saturday night—which is more than you and your men achieved."

They glowered at each other across the desk. When Inspector Dart spoke again, he sounded calmer, "I'm at a loss to know what you're playing at. I want an explanation."

"If you treated people in an adult and reasonable way, you might get explanations more often. But every time I've spoken to you, all I've had is hostility and aggression. That, together with the fact that you locked up my best mate for a crime she had nothing to do with, means you shouldn't be surprised that if I've got any ideas at all about this business, I want to check them out myself before I entrust them to you."

He got up from the desk and walked round behind her. She refused to turn round to face him. His voice sounded tired. "The last thing the police want is to be made fools of. In this force, we're not stupid and we're not bent. We are, by and large, a bunch of honest coppers doing our damnedest to clear up the messes that the inadequate, the criminal and the plain bloody stupid leave behind them.

"If in the process we upset the likes of you then that's tough luck. You can look after yourself; you're not some pathetic little wimp. So don't expect us to fall over ourselves being nice.

"But you've proved that, even though you've done some incredibly stupid, naive and dangerous things over the last week, you've got a brain. So I'd like to know what happened tonight, and why.

"And before you start, just let me say again how bloody naive and stupid you've been. Just suppose Anthony Barrington *had* been a killer. You went off there on your own. You might like to think you'd have been able to deal with that situation, but I'm not so sure. A person who has killed has broken a fundamental human taboo. Once broken, the taboo loses all force. The next kill is easier. And if your life lies between a killer and safety, it's not worth much. This is real life, you know, not some kind of game. You could have been as dead as Lorna Smith-Couper by now."

Lindsay nodded slowly, feeling an enormous weariness sweeping over her. "It occurred to me afterwards. I'm afraid that I get carried away when I get gripped by an idea. However, I think I've reached the point where I have to tell you what I think happened last Saturday night."

21

Lindsay walked out of the police station and breathed the cold night air deeply. It tasted clean after the stuffiness of Inspector Dart's office. She sighed profoundly, knowing that she still had work to do before she could sleep. The interview had been trying and far from satisfactory. She walked across the deserted market place to a phone box and dialled Paddy's number. It was Cordelia who answered.

"Where are you?" she demanded. "Do you know what time it is? You said you'd be back by nine. The police have been here looking for you. I've been worried sick."

Lindsay allowed herself a lopsided wry smile. "You sound like my bloody mother," she replied. "I got caught up, that's all. I'll tell you about it later. I've got one more thing to do, and I'm not sure how long it'll take me. Will you wait with Paddy till I get back?"

Cordelia caught the serious tone in Lindsay's voice. "Are you all right?" she asked anxiously.

"Yeah, I'm fine; just a bit tired, that's all. I only rang so you wouldn't be worried. See you later."

"All right. Take care, now. I'll wait up for you."

Lindsay put the phone down quickly. The concern in Cordelia's voice hurt too much. She didn't want to do what she was

going to do but she couldn't see any alternative. That didn't take
the fear away, however. She left the phone box and quickly walked
the half mile to their hotel. She ran upstairs to their room and let
herself in. She pulled out her miniature tape recorder from her
holdall and checked the batteries. She broke open a fresh pack of
tiny cassettes and inserted one. Finally, she did a check for voice
level with the machine in her jacket pocket. Satisfied that her
equipment was working properly, she took a last look round the
hotel room. She thought of writing a note to Cordelia in case
anything happened to prevent her safe return, but then dismissed
the idea as melodramatic, turned on her heel and marched back
downstairs. It took her a couple of minutes to get her bearings,
then she set off to walk to James Cartwright's house.

The street was quiet and empty except for a few parked cars.
Lindsay shivered when a strong gust of wind caught her face as
she turned into Cartwright's drive. There was a light burning
in the hall, and a smudge of light on the lawn at the side of the
house which Lindsay guessed came from the ground-floor office
where she and Cordelia had interviewed Cartwright before.

On the doorstep, she set the tape recorder for voice-
automated recording and rang the doorbell. Some time elapsed
before it opened, framing Cartwright against the strong light
from within. He looked tired and dishevelled, as if he'd gone to
seed overnight and as he spoke, his sour gin breath hit Lindsay.
"What the hell do you want?" he demanded angrily.

"I want to talk to you. About Sarah," said Lindsay quietly.

"You? What the hell do you think you've got to say that I
would want to listen to? My daughter's dead, thanks to you, and
now you want to talk to me about her? You can piss off." He
moved to close the door, but Lindsay was quicker and pushed
her body into the gap.

"That might be what the police have told you, but you and I
know a different story, don't we? If anybody drove Sarah to slash
her wrists, it wasn't me. I know the truth, Cartwright, and I want

to talk to you about it. You can take your pick. Either we talk about it now or I go to the police and talk about it with them."

He looked suspiciously at her. The blurred look left his features as comprehension drove the effect of the drink away. "I don't know what you mean," he replied belligerently. Lindsay said nothing. "Oh, for Christ's sake, you'd better come in. I don't want a scene on the doorstep," he sighed.

"You've got a bloody cheek," he complained bitterly as he led her down the hall to the office. Once there he rounded on her. "Sit down. Now what's all this crap about the police?"

"I thought I'd like to put a proposition to you," said Lindsay. "Forget about blaming me for Sarah's death. It'll go down fine with anybody else, but it won't wash with me."

His expression was calculating. "And what's that supposed to mean?"

Lindsay managed to maintain the tough façade she had adopted, though inwardly she was quaking with fear. "Last Saturday night. Saturday's not been a lucky day for you lately, has it? First Lorna, then Sarah."

A flash of genuine pain crossed his face. "You're not fit to speak her name," he spat.

"Leave it out, Cartwright," Lindsay replied. "I know how Lorna was murdered, which, thanks to the conversation I had yesterday with Inspector Dart, is getting to be common knowledge. But only you and I know who murdered her."

A new wariness appeared in Cartwright's face. "Sarah confessed, you know. Not easy for me to believe, but my daughter did that to try to save my business."

"Save it for the funeral oration, Cartwright. Though, funnily enough, those are the first true words you've spoken in this whole sorry business. Sarah did just that. She confessed to save both your business and your neck. She was bright enough to know that alive her 'confession' wouldn't stand up to a five-minute police interview. There were too many details of the killing she simply didn't know. And the reason for that is that it wasn't Sarah who killed Lorna. It was you."

He sat and stared at her, his hands balling into fists on the desk top. "You must be mad. I've got an alibi. The police have checked. It was Sarah, God damn it, it was Sarah!"

"I've checked it out too. And it's not tight enough. Lorna was killed between half-past seven and twenty to eight. You could just have done it on the basis of the times you were actually seen in the two pubs. Sarah couldn't have done it, though. By twenty-five to eight she was in Longnor. That only leaves you with the necessary knowledge and skill to assemble that scaffolding and kill Lorna."

"You can't prove that. If you could, or thought you could, you'd be telling the cops, not me." He got to his feet and started pacing about the office restlessly.

"I can prove that Sarah couldn't have done it. I've got a witness who will swear to where Sarah was at the crucial time. You've had it, Cartwright. So listen to my proposition."

His lips curled in a sneer. "You're talking rubbish. But let's hear this so-called proposition. If it's blackmail you're after, forget it. I haven't got a bloody penny."

"I got involved in this business because Paddy Callaghan was arrested. Since then, a lot of people have had a very shitty time because of you. I think it's only fair that you should make it up to them in some small way. So all I'm asking is a written undertaking that you will withdraw from all negotiations concerning the purchase of Derbyshire House's playing fields. When I get that, I'll forget everything I ever knew about Lorna's murder. Do we have a deal?"

He continued to pace back and forth. "If I pull out, which I might say is because of the way I feel about my Sarah's death, what guarantee do I have that you're not going to go around spreading these slanderous lies about me?"

"Why should I say anything? I'll have got what I want."

"And what's to stop you coming back any time in the future and making more demands?"

"You'll just have to take my word for that."

His seemingly aimless striding around had brought him to within a few feet of Lindsay's chair. Suddenly he lunged at her. Caught by surprise, she could only struggle feebly as his weight overturned the chair and pinned her to the floor. His hands were round her throat, squeezing. She could feel the bursting pressure in her chest as her lungs fought for air. Just as she felt her head start to swim, his hands came away as he jerked her to her feet and pulled his arm round her throat in a half-nelson. She gulped air desperately as he pulled her back so hard that her toes scrabbled to stay on the floor. With his free hand, he picked up a stiletto paper knife from the desk top. He held it to her temple and growled, "That's what I think of your lousy proposition, Miss Gordon. Now I'm going to let go of your neck. And you're not going to move a muscle. One move and this goes straight into your smart little brain. If you're clear about that, say yes."

Lindsay swallowed hard and croaked, "Yes," through a dry throat. He let her go and moved surprisingly quickly round in front of her.

"Walk backwards towards that other desk. One step at a time."

She stumbled backwards until she backed painfully into the metal edge of the desk. He moved so close she could smell the combination of stale gin and sweat. She could feel bitter vomit rising in her throat and swallowed it back with effort. He reached beyond her and picked up a roll of coloured plastic tape. "Now turn around and walk slowly to the chair by the wall. The one with the arms." Lindsay obeyed, bewitched by the knife that was now pricking into her neck just below her ear. When she reached the chair, he punched her roughly into it and handed her the tape. "Use your left hand to tape your right wrist to the arm of the chair," he told her. "And make a good job of it." Lindsay did what she was told like an automaton. Only now was her numbed mind beginning to come out of shock and beginning to reason. Not that that was much help, since she couldn't think of anything that could be effective against this animal with the knife.

He watched her carefully, and picked his moment well for the next part of his operation. His hand darted out and grabbed her left wrist. Without breaking the tape he swiftly taped her free hand to the chair, throwing the knife on to the floor.

Lindsay tried to kick him as he bent over her, but her foot only glanced off his shin. He started with the pain and reacted swiftly with a hard slap to the head that Lindsay felt the length of her spine. "Bitch," he spat. "Try that again and I'll kill you here and now. And don't think I'm bluffing. That was Lorna Smith-Couper's mistake." He moved to the side of the chair and pushed it away from the wall. He came round behind her and started going through the pockets of her jacket. He removed the tape recorder triumphantly. "I thought you might have one of these," he crowed. "I'm not daft, you know." He opened the machine and pulled out the cassette. He walked over to a metal bin and began to draw the tape viciously out of its plastic cassette. When he reached the end of the tape, he took a cigarette lighter from his desk and set fire to the tape, which blazed briefly then died.

"Thought you'd got me, didn't you?" he gloated. "Well, you were wrong. Now I've got you. And you're not going to live long enough to tell your little tale to anybody else. This bloody land was worth killing once for. It's got to be worth killing twice for it."

Lindsay found her voice. "Make that three times. You as good as killed Sarah as well."

"Don't say that," he almost screamed. "I know why Sarah died. It was because of your meddling. If you'd kept your nose out of this nobody would have ever known anything about that bloody scaffolding. It was you that killed my daughter, you bitch."

"Keep thinking that if it helps. But one day you're going to have to face the fact that Sarah preferred to die rather than live with a murderer."

A cunning look crept across his face. "You're trying to make me lose my temper, to give you a chance of coming back at me. Well, it won't work. Where's your car? Is it outside?"

Surprised by the change in tack, Lindsay blurted out, "No, it isn't."

"Where is it then?"

Lindsay couldn't work out why the question was being asked, but some instinct for self-preservation made her keep her mouth shut.

He moved back to face her. "I asked where your bloody car is."

"Find out your bloody self," Lindsay retorted. Before the words were out of her mouth, his hand slashed at her face again. Pain blotted out her consciousness for a moment. When she could sense anything again, she tasted blood and felt her mouth beginning to swell. Her left eye felt on fire. She shook her head to clear it.

"Where's your car?"

He grasped the little finger of her left hand and began to bend it backwards. Lindsay gritted her teeth as the pain flooded through her arm. "It's at the school," she gasped.

He let go. "All the better. No one will have noticed it here. We'll go and collect it a little later on. You're going to have a nasty accident. Driving away from the school. There's a lot of really bad bends up on the Cat and Fiddle road. Somebody who doesn't know their way around and likes to drive fast could easily have a fatal accident up there. Don't worry, you won't feel a thing. A bump on the head, that's all. I'll drive you up there in your own car and we'll send it over the side. Shame you don't like wearing a seatbelt, isn't it?"

Lindsay stared at him with pure hatred. "You bastard," she said, her words slurring slightly.

He moved towards her again. But before he could reach her the door burst open and Inspector Dart ran into the room followed by half a dozen uniformed officers. "Police!" he yelled. "Stop right there, Cartwright. Okay, lads, take him." They rushed towards him in a body. Cartwright picked up the fallen chair Lindsay had been sitting on previously and hurled it at the approaching policemen, then threw himself through the window. He'd reckoned without Dart's foresight. He dived, bleeding, straight into the arms of Dart's sergeant and another group of uniformed men. He thrashed out blindly but it was only a matter of seconds before they overpowered him, handcuffed him and hustled him off to a waiting police van.

While the struggle was going on, Dart crouched behind Lindsay's chair and picked the tape away from her wrists. She felt herself close to tears and collapse, but she was determined not to give way in front of the policeman. "You took your bloody time," she complained weakly. "I was beginning to think the radio mike had packed in when he jumped me."

"You did well," Dart said as he helped her to her feet and lit a cigarette for her. "We picked it all up loud and clear. I took the precaution of having a shorthand writer take it all down as well as taping it, just in case. We wanted to let him hang himself good and proper, since he seemed reluctant to make anything amounting to an admission. Probably because he guessed you were wired. That was a good idea of yours to take your own tape recorder. It put him right off his guard after he'd disposed of that. Now we can probably get him for attempted murder on you as well."

"Terrific. That makes me feel it's all been worthwhile," said Lindsay ironically. "Now, could one of your lads take me back to Derbyshire House? I've had enough for one day."

"We'll need a full statement from you. But that can wait till the morning. Don't you think you should go down to the hospital and get checked over?"

Lindsay shook her head. "There's nothing broken. I'd know if there was. I'm just bruised and shaken. Nothing a good night's sleep won't put more or less right. But thanks for the belated concern," she added. She walked out of the room on very nearly steady legs.

A few minutes later the police car drew up outside Longnor House. Lindsay glanced across at her car. It seemed many hours since she'd left it. She glanced at her watch and was astonished to see it was barely past midnight. "I'll never feel the same about that car again," she said to the policeman with her. "If that bastard had had his way, it would have been my coffin. Tell the Inspector I'll see him tomorrow about noon."

The door into the house was locked. Lindsay's shoulders sagged. It was the last straw. She leaned against the wall of the porch and studied the bells. Housemistress. Senior Mistress. Junior Mistress. She pressed the top bell and prayed for Paddy.

PART V

CODA

22

It was just after nine the following morning when Paddy pulled back the curtains in her bedroom and turned to look at the waking figure in her bed. Lindsay's sleep-rumpled hair suited a disreputable appearance that included a black eye, a split and swollen lip and a badly bruised jaw. She opened her eyes and winced as the pain hit her. Paddy brought her a glass of orange juice and smiled anxiously. "How are you feeling?" she inquired.

"Like I've been run over by a truck," Lindsay replied crossly. "I'm sure that bastard Dart deliberately let Cartwright work me over."

"I don't know what you're talking about, you know," Paddy complained. "You staggered in here last night looking as though you'd been mugged, told us everything was all right, demanded a large Scotch and a bed and refused point-blank to tell us a bloody thing more until you'd slept. Cordelia has been going out of her head with worry. I couldn't get her to bed till gone three. Really, Lindsay, you are the pits."

Lindsay attempted a scowl, then thought better of it. "Sorry. I had just had more than enough for one day. Anyway, shouldn't you be teaching? Isn't that what they pay you for?"

"I've managed to off-load my classes for today on the grounds that I'm nursing an invalid journalist. So if Pamela Overton comes across, try to look sick."

"That won't be hard. Where's Cordelia?"

"Upstairs, I presume. I've given her the guest room. She was sufficiently anaesthetised by the time she went to bed to sleep half the morning if we let her."

"Where did you sleep, then?"

"On the sofa. After prison comforts, it seemed like the Ritz."

"Sorry I spoilt your homecoming."

"Never mind that. Just tell me what the hell has been going on!"

"When I've had a shower and Cordelia's here. Not till then. I'm not going over the whole thing twice."

Paddy wasn't happy with this answer, but Lindsay was adamant, insisting on washing and dressing immediately. Paddy left to fetch Cordelia, and Lindsay winced her way to the bathroom, where she let the hot water soothe away some of the aches from her battered body.

When she emerged, Cordelia was pacing the living-room. She rushed to Lindsay and hugged her. For the first time since she'd woken up, Lindsay forgot her pain. "Don't ever scare me like that again," Cordelia murmured. "Thank God you're all right." Paddy looked mildly astonished, then discreetly exited to the kitchen to brew more coffee.

When she returned, the two lovers were sitting together, Lindsay with her bruised head on Cordelia's shoulder. She sat up to relate the events of the previous evening. Just the telling of it was enough to make her shiver with horror. And the effect on Paddy and Cordelia was no less chilling.

"You must be crazy, Lindsay," Cordelia cried. "Going in there on your own. You could have been killed. You should have taken me with you."

Lindsay shook her head, "No, this was one thing that had to be done solo. There's no way Cartwright would have opened up at all if there had been two of us. He wouldn't have fallen for the line I took. He'd simply have tried to brazen it out. So I had to trust Dart to take care of me.

"He'd fitted me out with a very good radio microphone, so that was transmitting everything said and done in the room. The cops were sitting outside in a troop of unmarked police cars with a van parked in the next-door neighbour's drive behind the shrubbery. And for extra security, Dart's sergeant was outside the office window with one of those limpet microphones.

"Dart was very quick at getting the operation together once I'd convinced him it was the only way to do it. He wouldn't hear of it to begin with, but I told him if he wouldn't help me, I'd do it on my own and the only way he could stop me was to throw me in the cells. He finally relented when I pointed out that eventually I'd be back on the streets again, and I'd go straight to Cartwright and confront him. At least when the case comes to trial I'll have a wonderful exclusive to flog—How I Caught The Girls' School Killer."

"Yes. The scars will probably have healed by then," said Cordelia drily.

"I'm sorry to be a bore," said Paddy, "but you'll have to bear with me. Don't forget, I've not been party to all these discussions you've had in the course of the past week. Someone has yet to explain to me exactly what has been going on. Starting from the murder."

Lindsay took a deep breath and began. "I now know how precarious James Cartwright's financial position was. He admitted last night he didn't have a brass farthing. Inspector Dart told me he'd made some bad property deals lately. He had already raised a lot of capital on the strength of his time-share scheme and it was absolutely crucial that the playing fields deal succeeded. Had he not pulled it off, he would have been forced into liquidation and bankruptcy. He couldn't face that prospect; he enjoyed his lifestyle too much. And he was worried about losing Sarah's affection and respect if he couldn't give her the life she was used to.

"He tried to bribe Lorna not to play that night. Even though the tickets had already been sold, if Lorna had pulled out, a lot of people would have been looking for their money back. And it would have completely discredited any further attempt to raise the money. But Lorna wouldn't hear of it. She was enjoying herself far too much watching people being upset by her presence. Also, in spite of herself, I think she did care about the school. And she had sufficient integrity as an artist not to let her public down. So she refused, and in deeply insulting terms. He was thwarted and also very angry. That's when he thought of trying to murder her. He had reached the end of his tether, something Lorna couldn't have known. He was desperate enough to be dangerous.

"He knew the school layout very well. So, when everyone was at dinner, he went to the music room and helped himself to a cello string. He was probably wearing his driving gloves, because the police haven't found any prints. He probably also checked that the window catches were still easy to manipulate. Then he fetched the scaffolding and set it up.

"He dashed back to the Woolpack and bought a pint. He must have downed it in a oner, because by about twelve minutes past seven he was back at the school. He went to Longnor—I guess because he knew the cloakroom was near the door and it would be quieter than the main building—and helped himself to a toggle, presumably having realised by then that the string was sharp enough to cause bad cuts even through gloves if he used it on its own. That's almost certainly when Sarah saw him. I think she was probably coming downstairs to go for a walk at the time, or to go down to the gym to do some exercises, perhaps.

"I'm guessing a bit now. But I think she followed him, catching up with him as he was preparing the garrotte or climbing up the fire escape to the scaffolding. He sent her back telling her to forget she'd seen him.

"Then, of course, he killed Lorna. He had to leave the scaffolding on the kitchen roof because he was running out of time to keep up the alibi he'd set himself. Of course, once the murder was common knowledge, Sarah must have realised her father was implicated. The girl must have been under colossal strain all last week. I suppose your arrest made things even worse for her, Paddy. Then when she heard about our experiments with the scaffolding, she must have felt sure the net was closing around her father.

"She must have realised that the lie she'd told the police about you in the music room would be found out. Incidentally, I don't think she lied out of particular malice—at that stage, after all, it wasn't clear that the police were going to arrest you. I think she was just trying to cloud the issue in every conceivable way possible. I think what drove her to commit suicide was a combination of factors. She knew her father was a killer and she couldn't bear it, but she still wanted to protect him, and the only way she could do that was to kill herself. Just confessing wouldn't have been enough. She'd never have been able to make up a story that would have satisfied the police. And she probably felt that if she gave herself up to the police, the very thing that she was trying to avoid would happen—her father would give himself up to protect her.

"As it was, I'm not altogether sure he would have done. He was happy enough for her to carry the blame after her death. That's what I find most inhuman about him." She paused to pour out more coffee. "God, my throat is sore. I'm amazed there are hardly any bruises on it. I thought he was going to kill me."

Paddy looked puzzled. "But everyone seemed to be satisfied after Sarah's death that the whole thing had been cleared up. What made you think you knew better?"

"Apart from a general sense of superiority, she means," said Cordelia with a rather grim smile.

"I finally got on the right track when I asked Jessica Bennett a question we should have asked her when we first interviewed her. When I saw her yesterday I wanted to ask her if she'd seen Sarah at all on that Saturday evening—just for my own satisfaction, I suppose, though I did have one or two doubts about Sarah's confession. It seemed so superficial, so lacking in feeling and detail. But Jessica's answer put Sarah out of the running. She said she'd seen Sarah going out of Longnor at about quarter past seven.

"And at the crucial time when the murder must have been committed to avoid any comings and goings, Jessica saw Sarah in the cloakroom. She tried to talk to her. But Sarah went straight upstairs. Jessica didn't see her again that night.

"That removed Sarah from the list of suspects. But it put her father right back into the frame. However, Anthony Barrington still seemed a possibility, and I thought on balance I'd prefer to talk to him. Barrington gave me such a hard time, I was convinced he was innocent. He was too outraged to be guilty. And then, of course, he called Dart and I was hauled off to the nick.

"And the rest you know," she said, closing her eyes as a wave of tiredness hit her.

She forced her eyes open again. "I've got to go and give the police a statement at noon. And then, if you don't mind, Paddy, I want to go home. I've got work to go to on Wednesday, and I could do with a day's sleep."

"I understand," said Paddy. "I'll never be able to pay you and Cordelia back for what you've done for me. But come back soon and see us again, promise?"

Lindsay grinned but said, "Ouch! I must stop doing that. I'll come soon if you guarantee no hassles."

"I guarantee it." They smiled at each other, relaxed again after the upheavals of the last ten days.

"I'll drive you back to Glasgow," said Cordelia, "you're far too tired to hammer up the motorway on your own. Besides, I think we've got one or two things to talk about."

Paddy's eyebrows had shot up. "Well, well, well," she marvelled. "I see some good has come out of all this."

"Surprised?" demanded Cordelia.

"Before we get into all of that, I need to phone my newsdesk," said Lindsay apologetically. "Sorry. Since I've got to go down the cop shop this morning, if I don't put over a story nice and early my life won't be worth living on Wednesday. Can I use the phone?"

Paddy grinned at Cordelia. "How does it feel to play second fiddle to a news story?"

Cordelia pulled a face. "I don't think I want to get used to the idea. Maybe Lindsay could change her priorities . . . just a bit?"

Lindsay dialled the number. "Yeah, yeah, okay, Cordelia. I'll work on it. But tomorrow, eh, please . . . Hello? Duncan? Lindsay here. I've got a real belter for you this morning . . ."

COMMON
MURDER

For my father

ACKNOWLEDGEMENTS

Thanks to: Helen for keeping us laughing at Greenham; Andrew Wiatr for advice on computers (any errors are mine); Diana for all the constructive criticism; Lisanne and Jane for their hard work; John and Senga, Laura and Ewan for their hospitality at the crucial point; Sue Jackson for her inimitable skills; Henry the lawyer for letting me pick his brains; and Linzi.

1

"This is murder," Lindsay Gordon complained, leaning back in her chair and putting her feet up on the desk. "I can't bear it when there's nothing doing. Look at us. Eight p.m. on the dynamic newsdesk of a national daily. The night news editor's phoning his daughter in Detroit. His deputy's straining his few remaining brain cells with the crossword. One reporter has escaped to the pub like a sensible soul. Another is using the office computer to write the Great English Novel . . ."

"And the third is whingeing on as usual," joked the hopeful novelist, looking up from the screen. "Don't knock it, Lindsay, it's better than working."

"Huh," she grunted, reaching for the phone. "I sometimes wonder. I'm going to do a round of calls, see if there's anything going on in the big bad world outside."

Her colleague grinned. "What's the problem? Run out of friends to phone?"

Lindsay pulled a face. "Something like that," she replied. As she opened her contacts book at the page with the list of police, fire and ambulance numbers she thought of the change in her attitude to unfettered access to the office phone since she'd moved from her base in Glasgow to live with her lover Cordelia in London. She had appreciated quiet night shifts in

those days for the chance they gave her to spend half the night
chattering about everything and nothing with Cordelia. These
days, however, it seemed that what they had to say to each other
could easily be accommodated in the hours between work and
sleep. Indeed, Lindsay was beginning to find it easier to open
her heart to friends who weren't Cordelia. She shook herself
mentally and started on her list of calls.

On the newsdesk, Cliff Gilbert the night news editor finished his phone conversation and started checking the computerised newsdesk for any fresh stories. After a few minutes, he
called, "Lindsay, you clear?"

"Just doing the calls, Cliff," she answered.

"Never mind that. There's a bloody good tip just come in
from one of the local paper lads in Fordham. Seems there's been
some aggro at the women's peace camp at Brownlow Common.
I've transferred the copy into your personal desk. Check it out,
will you?" he asked.

Lindsay sat up and summoned the few paragraphs on to
her screen. The story seemed straightforward enough. A local
resident claimed he'd been assaulted by one of the women from
the peace camp. He'd had his nose broken in the incident, and
the woman was in custody. Lindsay was instantly sceptical. She
found it hard to believe that one of a group pledged to campaign
for peace would physically attack an opponent of the anti-nuclear
protest. But she was enough of a professional to concede that her
initial reaction was the sort of knee-jerk she loved to condemn
when it came from the other side.

The repercussions unfolding outside Fordham police station
made the story interesting from the point of view of the *Daily
Clarion* newsdesk. The assaulted man, a local solicitor called
Rupert Crabtree, was the leader of Ratepayers Against Brownlow's Destruction, a pressure group dedicated to the removal
of the peace women from the common. His accusation had
provoked a spontaneous demonstration from the women, who
were apparently besieging the police station. That in its turn

had provoked a counterdemonstration from RABD members outraged at the alleged attack. There was a major confrontation in the making, it appeared.

Lindsay started making phone calls, but soon hit a brick wall. The police station at Fordham were referring all calls to county headquarters. Headquarters were hiding behind the old excuse: "We can make no statement yet. Reports are still coming in." It was not an unusual frustration. She walked over to Cliff's desk and explained the problem. "It might be worth taking a run down there to see what the score is," she suggested. "I can be there in an hour at this time of night, and if it is shaping up into a nasty, we should have someone on the spot. I don't know how far we can rely on the lad that filed the original copy. I've got some good contacts at the peace camp. We could get a cracking exclusive out of it. What do you think?"

Cliff shrugged. "I don't know. It doesn't grab me."

Lindsay sighed. "On the basis of what we've got so far, we could be looking at a major civil disturbance. I'd hate the opposition to beat us to the draw when we've got a head start with my contacts."

"Give your contacts a bell, then."

"There are no phones at the camp, Cliff. British Telecom have shown an incomprehensible reluctance to install them in tents. And besides, they'll probably all be down the cop shop protesting. I might as well go. There's sod all else doing."

He grinned. "Okay, Lindsay, go and take a look. Give me a check call when you get there. I'll see if we can get any more information over the phone. Remember your deadlines—there's no point in getting a good exclusive if we can't get it in the paper."

"What about a pic man?"

"Let me know if you need one when you get there. I seem to remember there's a local snapper we've used before."

Five minutes later, Lindsay was weaving through the London traffic in her elderly MG roadster. She drove on automatic pilot while she dredged all she knew about the peace camp to the surface of her mind.

She'd first been to the camp about nine months before. She and Cordelia had made the twenty-mile detour to Brownlow Common one sunny May Sunday after a long lunch with friends in Oxford. Lindsay had read about the camp in one of the Sunday papers, and had been intrigued enough by the report to want to see it for herself. Cordelia, who shared Lindsay's commitment to opposing the nuclear threat, had been easily persuaded to come along on that initial visit, though she was never to share Lindsay's conviction that the camp was an effective form of protest. For Cordelia, the channels of dissent that came easiest were the traditional ones of letters to the *Guardian* and MPs. She had never felt comfortable with the ethos of the camp. Cordelia always felt that she was somehow being judged and found wanting by the women who had made that overwhelming commitment to the cause of peace. So she seldom accompanied Lindsay on later visits, preferring to confine her support to handing cash over to Lindsay to purchase whatever necessities the camp was short of, from lentils to toilet chemicals. But for that first visit, she suspended her instinctive distrust and tried to keep her mind open.

The peace camp had started spontaneously just over a year before. A group of women had marched from the West Country to the American airbase at Brownlow Common to protest at the siting of US cruise missiles there. They had been so fired by anger and enthusiasm at the end of their three-week march that they decided to set up a peace camp as a permanent protest against the nuclear colonisation of their green unpleasant land.

Thinking back to that early summer afternoon, Lindsay found it hard to remember what she'd expected. What she had found was enough to shatter her expectations beyond recall. They had turned off the main road on to a leafy country lane. After about a mile and a half, the trees on one side of the road suddenly stopped. There was an open clearing the size of a couple of football pitches, bisected by a tarmac track that led up to a gate about 250 yards from the road. The gate was of heavy steel bars covered with chain-link fencing and surmounted by savage angled spikes wrapped with barbed wire. The perimeter fence consisted of ten-foot-tall concrete stanchions and metal-link fencing, topped by rolls of razor wire. More razor wire was laid in spirals along the base of the fence. The gate was guarded by four British soldiers on the inside and two policemen on the outside. A sign declared, "USAF Brownlow Common."

In the distance, the long low humps of the missile silos broke the skyline. Three hundred yards inside the perimeter fence were buildings identifiable as servicemen's quarters—square, concrete blocks with identical curtains. From beyond the wire, they looked like a remand centre, Lindsay had thought. They provided a stark contrast to the other human habitation visible from the car. Most of the clearing outside the forbidding fence had been annexed by the peace women. All over it were clusters of tents—green, grey, orange, blue, brown. The women were sitting out in the warm sunshine, talking, drinking, cooking, eating, singing. The bright colours of their clothes mingled and formed a kaleidoscope of constantly changing patterns. Several young children were playing a hysterical game of tig round one group of tents.

Lindsay and Cordelia had been made welcome, although some of the more radical women were clearly suspicious of Lindsay's occupation and Cordelia's reputation as a writer who embodied the Establishment's vision of an acceptable feminist. But after that first visit Lindsay had maintained contact with the camp. It seemed to provide her with a focus for her flagging political energies, and besides, she enjoyed the company of the peace women. One in particular, Jane Thomas, a doctor who had given up a promising career as a surgical registrar to live at the camp, had become a close and supportive friend.

Lindsay had come to look forward to the days she spent at Brownlow Common. The move to London that had seemed to promise so much had proved to be curiously unsatisfying.

She had been shocked to discover how badly she fitted in with Cordelia's circle of friends. It was an upsetting discovery for someone whose professional success often depended on that mercurial quality she possessed which enabled her to insinuate herself virtually anywhere. Cordelia, for her part, clearly felt uncomfortable with journalists who weren't part of the media arts circus. And Cordelia was no chameleon. She liked to be with people who made her feel at home in the persona she had adopted. Now she was wrapped up in a new novel, and seemed happier to discuss its progress with her friends and her agent than with Lindsay, who felt increasingly shut out as Cordelia became more absorbed in her writing. It had made Lindsay feel uncomfortable about bringing her own work problems home, for Cordelia's mind always seemed to be elsewhere. Much as she loved and needed Cordelia, Lindsay had begun to sense that her initial feeling that she had found a soulmate with whom she occasionally disagreed was turning into a struggle to find enough in common to fill the spaces between the lovemaking that still brought them together in a frighteningly intense unity. Increasingly, they had pursued their separate interests. Brownlow Common had become one of Lindsay's favourite boltholes.

But the camp had changed dramatically since those heady summer days. Harassment had sprung up from all sides. Some local residents had formed Ratepayers Against Brownlow's Destruction in an attempt to get rid of the women who created in the camp what the locals saw as an eyesore, health hazard and public nuisance. The yobs from nearby Fordham had taken to terrorising the camp in late-night firebomb attacks. The police were increasingly hostile and heavy-handed in dealing with demonstrations. What media coverage there was had become savage, stereotyped and unsympathetic. And the local council had joined forces with the Ministry of Defence to fight the women's presence through the civil courts. The constant war of attrition coupled with the grim winter weather had changed the camp both physically and spiritually. Where there had been green grass, there was now a greasy, pot-holed morass of reddish-brown clay. The tents had vanished, to be replaced with benders—polythene sheeting stretched over branches and twine to make low-level tepees. They were ugly but they were also cheap, harder to burn and easier to reconstruct. Even the rainbow colours the women wore were muted now that the February cold had forced them to wrap up in drab winter plumage. But more serious, in Lindsay's eyes, was the change in atmosphere. The air of loving peace and warmth, that last hangover from the sixties, had been heavily overlaid with the pervading sense of something harder. No one was in any doubt that this was no game.

It was typically ironic, she thought, that it needed crime to persuade the *Clarion* that the camp was worth some coverage. She had made several suggestions to her news editor about a feature on the women at the peace camp, but he had treated the idea with derision. Lindsay had finally conceded with ill grace because her transfer to the job in London was a relatively recent achievement she couldn't afford to jeopardise. The job hadn't quite turned out the way she'd expected either. From being a highly rated writer who got her fair share of the best assignments, she had gone to being just another fish in the pool of reporters. But she remembered too well the years of hard-working, nail-biting freelancing before she'd finally recovered the security of a wage packet, and she wasn't ready to go back to that life yet.

Jane Thomas, however, encouraged her to use her talents in support of the camp. As a result, Lindsay had rung round her magazine contacts from her freelance days and sold several features abroad to salve her conscience. Thanks to her, the camp had had extensive magazine coverage in France, Italy and Germany, and had even featured in a colour spread in an American news magazine. But somewhere deep inside, she knew that wasn't enough. She felt guilty about the way she had changed since she'd decided to commit herself to her relationship with Cordelia. She knew she'd been seduced as much by Cordelia's comfortable lifestyle as by her lover's charm. That had made it hard to sustain the political commitment that had once been so important to her. "Your bottle's gone, Gordon," she said aloud as she pulled off the motorway on to the Fordham road. Perhaps the chance for redemption was round the next corner.

As she reached the outskirts of the quiet market town of Fordham, her radio pager bleeped insistently. Sighing, she checked the dashboard clock. Nine-fifteen. Forty-five minutes to edition time. She wasted five precious minutes finding a phone box and rang Cliff.

"Where are you?" he said officiously.

"I'm about five minutes away from the police station," she explained patiently. "I'd have been there by now if you hadn't bleeped me."

"Okay, fine. I've had the local lad on again. I've said you're *en route* and I've told him to link up with you. His name's Gavin Hammill, he's waiting for you in the lounge bar of the Griffon's Head, in the market place, he says. He's wearing a Barbour jacket and brown trousers. He says it's a bit of a stalemate at present; anyway, suss it out and file copy as soon as."

"I'm on my way," Lindsay said.

Finding the pub was no problem. Finding Gavin Hammill was not so simple. Every other man in the pub was wearing a Barbour jacket and half of them seemed to be alone. After the second failure, Lindsay decided to buy a drink and try again. Before she could down her Scotch, a gangling youth with mousy brown hair and a skin problem inadequately hidden by a scrubby beard tapped her on the shoulder and said, "Lindsay Gordon? From the *Clarion*? I'm Gavin Hammill, *Fordham Weekly Bugle*."

Far from relieved, Lindsay smiled weakly. "Please to meet you, Gavin. What's the score?"

"Well, both lots are still outside the police station but the police don't seem to know quite how to play it. I mean, they can't treat the ratepayers the way they normally treat the peace women, can they? And yet they can't be seen to be treating them differently. It's kind of a standoff. Or it was when I left."

"And when was that?"

"About ten minutes ago."

"Come on then, let's go and check it out. I've got a deadline to meet in twenty minutes."

They walked briskly through the market place and into the side street where a two-storey brick building housed Fordham police station. They could hear the demonstration before they saw the demonstrators. The women from the camp were singing the songs of peace that had emerged over the last two years as their anthems. Chanting voices attempted to drown them out with "Close the camp! Give us peace!"

On the steps of the police station, sat about forty women dressed in strangely assorted layers of thick clothing, with muddy boots and peace badges fixed to their jackets, hats and scarves. The majority of them looked remarkably healthy, in spite of the hardships of their outdoor life. To one side, a group of about twenty-five people stood shouting. There were more men than women, and they all looked as if they ought to be at home watching "Mastermind" instead of causing a civil disturbance outside the police station. Between the two groups were posted about a dozen uniformed policemen who seemed unwilling to do more than keep the groups apart. Lindsay stood and watched for a few minutes. Every so often, one of the RABD group would try to push through the police lines, but not seriously enough to warrant more than the gentlest of police manhandling. These attempts were usually provoked by jibes from one or two of the women. Lindsay recognised Nicky, one of the camp's proponents of direct action, who called out, "You're brave enough when the police are in the way, aren't you? What about being brave when the Yanks drop their bombs on your doorstep?"

"Why aren't the cops breaking it up?" Lindsay asked Gavin.

"I told you, they don't seem to know what to do. I think they're waiting for the superintendent to get here. He was apparently off duty tonight and they've been having a bit of bother getting hold of him. I imagine he'll be able to sort it out."

Even as he spoke, a tall, uniformed police officer with a face like a Medici portrait emerged from the station. He picked his way between the peace women, who jeered at him. "That him?" Lindsay demanded.

"Yeah. Jack Rigano. He's the boss here. Good bloke."

One of the junior officers handed Rigano a bullhorn. He put it to his lips and spoke. Through the distortion, Lindsay made out, "Ladies and gentlemen, you've had your fun. You have five minutes to disperse. If you fail to do so, my officers have orders to arrest everyone. Please don't think about causing any more trouble tonight. We have already called for reinforcements and I warn you that everyone will be treated with equal severity unless you disperse at once. Thank you and goodnight."

Lindsay couldn't help grinning at his words. At once the RABD protesters, unused to the mechanics of organised dissent, began to move away, talking discontentedly among themselves. The more experienced peace women sat tight, singing defiantly. Lindsay turned to Gavin and said, "Go after the RABD lot and see if you can get a couple of quotes. I'll speak to the cops and the peace women. Meet me by that phone box on the corner in ten minutes. We'll have to get some copy over quickly."

She quickly walked over to the superintendent and dug her union Press Card out of her pocket. "Lindsay Gordon, *Daily Clarion*," she said. "Can I have a comment on this incident?"

Rigano looked down at her and smiled grimly. "You can say that the police have had everything under control and both sets of demonstrators were dispersed peacefully."

"And the assault?"

"The alleged assault, don't you mean?"

It was Lindsay's turn for the grim smile. "Alleged assault," she said.

"A woman is in custody in connection with an alleged assault earlier this evening at Brownlow Common. We expect to charge her shortly. She will appear before Fordham magistrates tomorrow morning. That's it." He turned away from her abruptly as his men began carrying the peace women down the steps. As soon as one woman was carried into the street and the police returned for the next, the first would outflank them and get back on to the steps. Lindsay knew the process of old. It would go on until police reinforcements arrived and outnumbered the protesters. It was a ritual dance that both sides had perfected.

When she saw a face she recognised being dumped on the pavement, Lindsay quickly went over and grabbed the woman's arm before she could return to the steps. "Jackie," Lindsay said urgently. "It's me, Lindsay, I'm doing a story about the protest, can you give me a quick quote."

The young black woman grinned. She said, "Sure. You can put in your paper that innocent women are being victimised by the police because we want a nuclear-free world to bring up our children in. Peace women don't go around beating up men. One of our friends has been framed, so we're making a peaceful protest. Okay? Now I've got to get back. See you, Lindsay."

There was no time for Lindsay to stay and watch what happened. She ran back to the phone box, passing a police van loaded with uniformed officers on the corner of the marketplace. Gavin was standing by the phone box, looking worried.

Lindsay dived into the box and dialled the office copytakers' number. She got through immediately and started dictating her story. When she had finished, she turned to Gavin and said, "I'll put you on to give your quotes in a sec, okay? Listen, what's the name of this woman who's accused of the assault? The lawyer will kill it, but I'd better put it in for reference for tomorrow."

"She comes from Yorkshire, I think," he said. "Her name's Deborah Patterson."

Lindsay's jaw dropped. "Did you say . . . Deborah Patterson?"

He nodded. Lindsay was filled with a strange sense of unreality. Deborah Patterson. It was the last name she expected to hear. Once upon a time it had been the name she scribbled idly on her notepad while she waited for strangers to answer their telephones, conjuring up the mental image of the woman she spent her nights with. But that had been a long time ago. Now her ghost had come back to haunt her. That strong, funny woman who had once made her feel secure against the world was here in Fordham.

2

Lindsay stroked the four-year-old's hair mechanically as she rocked her back and forth in her arms. "It's okay, Cara," she murmured at frequent intervals. The sobs soon subsided, and eventually the child's regular breathing provided evidence that she had fallen asleep, worn out by the storm of emotions she'd suffered. "She's dropped off at last," Lindsay observed to Dr Jane Thomas, who had taken charge of Cara after her mother's dramatic arrest.

"I'll put her in her bunk," Jane replied. "Pass her over." Lindsay awkwardly transferred the sleeping child to Jane, who carried her up the short ladder to the berth above the cab of the camper van that was Deborah's home at the peace camp. She settled the child and tucked her in then returned to sit opposite Lindsay at the table. "What are your plans?" she asked.

"I thought I'd stay the night here. My shift finishes at midnight, and the boss seems quite happy for me to stop here tonight. Since it looks as if Debs won't be using her bed, I thought I'd take advantage of it and keep an eye on Cara at the same time if that sounds all right to you. I'll have to go and phone Cordelia soon, though, or she'll wonder where I've got to. Can you stay with Cara while I do that?"

"No sweat," said Jane. "I was going to kip down here if you'd had to go back to London, but stay if you like. Cara's known you all her life, after all. She knows she can trust you."

Before Lindsay could reply, there was a quiet knock at the van's rear door. Jane opened it to reveal a redheaded woman in her early thirties wearing the standard Sloane Ranger outfit of green wellies, needlecord jeans, designer sweater and the inevitable Barbour jacket.

"Judith!" Jane exclaimed, "Am I glad to see you! Now we can find out exactly what's going on. Lindsay, this is Judith Rowe, Deborah's solicitor. She does all our legal work. Judith, this is Lindsay Gordon, who's a reporter with the *Daily Clarion*, but more importantly, she's an old friend of Deborah's."

Judith sat down beside Lindsay. "So it was you who left the note for Deborah at the police station?" she asked briskly.

"That's right. As soon as I found out she'd been arrested, I thought I'd better let her know I was around in case she needed any help," Lindsay said.

"I'm glad you did," said Judith. "She was in a bit of a state about Cara until she got your message. She seemed calmer afterwards. Now, tomorrow, she's appearing before the local magistrates. She's been charged with breach of the peace and assault resulting in actual bodily harm on Rupert Crabtree. She's going to put her hand up to the breach charge, but she wants to opt for jury trial on the ABH charge. She asked me to tell you what happened before you make any decisions about what I have to ask you. Okay?"

Lindsay nodded. Judith went on. "Crabtree was walking his dog up the road, near the phone box at Brownlow Cottages. Deborah had been making a call and when she left the box, Crabtree stood in her path and was really rather insulting, both to her and about the peace women in general. She tried to get past him, but his dog started growling and snapping at her and a scuffle developed. Crabtree tripped over the dog's lead and crashed face first into the back of the phone box, breaking his nose. He claims to the police that Deborah grabbed his hair and smashed his face into the box. No witnesses. In her favour is the fact that she phoned an ambulance and stayed near by till it arrived.

"It's been normal practice for the women to refuse to pay fines and opt for going to prison for non-payment. But Deborah feels she can't take that option since it would be unfair to Cara. She'll probably be fined about twenty-five pounds on the breach and won't be given time to pay since she'll also be looking for bail on the assault charge and Fordham mags can be absolute pigs when it comes to dealing with women from the camp. She asked me to ask you if you'd lend her the money to pay the fine. That's point one."

Judith was about to continue, but Lindsay interrupted. "Of course I will. She should know that, for God's sake. Now, what's point two?"

Judith grinned. "Point two is that we believe bail will be set at a fairly high level. What I need is someone who will stand surety for Deborah."

Lindsay nodded. "That's no problem. What do I have to do?"

"You'll have to lodge the money with the court. A cheque will do. Can you be there tomorrow?"

"Provided I can get away by half past two. I'm working tomorrow night, you see. I start at four." She arranged to meet Judith at the magistrates' court in the morning, and the solicitor got up to leave. The night briefly intruded as she left, reminding them all of the freezing February gale endured by the women outside.

"She's been terrific to us," said Jane, as they watched Judith drive away. "She just turned up one day not long after the first court appearance for obstruction. She offered her services any time we needed legal help. She's never taken a penny from us, except what she gets in legal aid. Her family farms on the other side of town and her mother comes over about once a month with fresh vegetables for us. It's really heartening when you get support from people like that, people you'd always vaguely regarded as class enemies, you know?"

Lindsay nodded. "That sort of thing always makes me feel ashamed for writing people off as stereotypes. Anyway, I'd better go and phone Cordelia before she starts to worry about me. Will you hold the fort for ten minutes?"

Lindsay jumped into the car and drove to the phone box where the incident between Deborah and Crabtree had taken place though it was too dark to detect any signs of the scuffle. A gust of wind blew a splatter of rain against the panes of the phone box as she dialled the London number and a sleepy voice answered, "Cordelia Brown speaking."

"Cordelia? It's me. I'm down at Brownlow Common on a job that's got a bit complicated. I'm going to stay over. Okay?"

"What a drag. Why is it always you that gets stuck on the out-of-towners?"

"Strictly speaking, it's not work that's the problem." Lindsay spoke in a rush. "Listen, there's been a bit of bother between one of the peace women and a local man. There's been an arrest. In fact, the woman who's been arrested is Deborah Patterson."

Cordelia's voice registered her surprise. "Deborah from Yorkshire? That peace camp really is a small world, isn't it? Whatever happened?"

"She's been set up, as far as I can make out."

"Not very pleasant for her, I should imagine."

"You've hit the nail on the head. She's currently locked up in a police cell, so I thought I'd keep an eye on little Cara till Debs is released tomorrow."

"No problem," Cordelia replied. "I can get some more work done tonight if you're not coming back. It's been going really well tonight, and I'm reluctant to stop till my eyes actually close."

Lindsay gave a wry smile. "I'm glad it's going well. I'll try to come home tomorrow afternoon before I go to work."

"Okay. I'll try to get home in time."

"Oh. Where are you off to? Only, I thought you were going to be home all week."

"My mother rang this evening. She's coming up tomorrow to do the shops and I promised I'd join her. But I'll try to be back for four."

"Look, don't rush your mother on my account. I'll see you tomorrow in bed. I should be home by one. Love you, babe."

A chill wind met her as she stepped out of the phone box and walked quickly back to the car. She pictured her lover sitting at her word processor, honing and refining her prose, relieved at the lack of distraction. Then she thought of Deborah, fretting in some uncomfortable, smelly cell. It wasn't an outcome Lindsay had anticipated all those years before when, a trainee journalist on a local paper in Cornwall, she had encountered Deborah at a party. For Lindsay, it had been lust at first sight, and as the evening progressed and drink had been taken, she had contrived to make such a nuisance of herself that Deborah finally relented for the sake of peace and agreed to meet Lindsay the following evening for a drink.

That night had been the first of many. Their often stormy relationship had lasted for nearly six months before Lindsay was transferred to another paper in the group. Neither of them could sustain the financial or emotional strain of separation, and soon mutual infidelities transformed their relationship to platonic friendship. Not long after, Lindsay left the West Country for Fleet Street, and Deborah announced her intention of having a child. Deborah bought a ruined farmhouse in North Yorkshire that she was virtually rebuilding single-handed. Even after Lindsay moved back to Scotland, she still made regular visits to Deborah and was surprised to find how much she enjoyed spending time with Deborah's small daughter. She felt comfortable there, even when they were joined for the occasional evening by Cara's father Robin, a gay man who lived near by. But Lindsay and Deborah never felt the time was right to revive their sexual relationship.

After she had fallen for Cordelia, Lindsay's visits had tailed off, though she had once taken Cordelia to stay the night. It had not been a success. Deborah had been rebuilding the roof at the time, there was no electricity and the water had to be pumped by hand from the well in the yard. Cordelia had not been impressed with either the accommodation or the insouciance of its owner. But Lindsay had sensed a new maturity in Deborah that she found appealing.

Deborah had clearly sensed Cordelia's discomfort, but she had not commented on it. She had a willingness to accept people for what they were, and conduct her relationships with them on that basis. She never imposed her own expectations on them, and regarded her reactions to people and events as entirely her responsibility. It would be nice, thought Lindsay, not to feel that she was failing to come up to scratch. Time spent with Deborah always made her feel good about herself.

Back at the van, she brought in a bottle of Scotch from the car and poured a nightcap for herself and Jane.

"Are you all right, Lindsay?" Jane asked.

Lindsay's reply was drowned out by a roar outside louder, even, than the stormy weather. It was a violent sound, rising and falling angrily. Lindsay leaped to her feet and pulled back the curtain over the van's windscreen. Fear rose in her throat. The black night was scythed open by a dozen brilliant headlamps whose beams raked the benders like prison-camp searchlights. The motorbikes revved and roared in convoluted patterns round the encampment, sometimes demolishing benders as they went. As Lindsay's eyes adjusted to the night, she could make out pillion riders on several of the bikes, some wielding stout sticks, others swinging heavy chains at everything in their path. It was clearly not the first time the women had been raided in this way, for everyone had the sense to stay down inside the scant shelter the benders provided.

Lindsay and Jane stood speechless, petrified by the spectacle. The van's glow seemed to exert a magnetic effect on three of the bikers and their cyclops lamps swung round and lit it up like a follow-spot on a stage.

"Oh shit," breathed Lindsay as the bikes careered towards the van. She leaned forward desperately and groped round the unfamiliar dashboard. What felt like agonising minutes later she found the right switch and flicked the lights on to full beam. The bikes wavered in their course and two of them peeled off to either side. The third skidded helplessly in the mud and slithered into a sideways slew on the greasy ground. The rider struggled to his feet, mouthing obscenities, and dragged himself round to his top-box. Out of it he pulled a large plastic bag which he hurled at the van. The women instinctively dived for the floor as it slammed into the windscreen with a squelching thud. Lindsay raised her head and nearly threw up. The world had turned red.

All over the windscreen was a skin of congealing blood with lumps of unidentifiable material slowly slithering down on to the bonnet. Jane's head appeared beside her. "Oh God, not the pigs' blood routine again," she moaned. "I thought they'd got bored with that one."

As she spoke, the bikes revved up again, then their roar gradually diminished into an irritated buzz as they left the camp and reached the road.

"We must call the police!" Lindsay exclaimed.

"It's a waste of time calling the police, Lindsay. They just don't want to know. The first time they threw blood over our benders, we managed to get the police to come out. But they said we'd done it ourselves, that we were sensation seekers. They said there was no evidence of our allegations. Tyre tracks in the mud don't count, you see. Nor do the statements of forty women. It doesn't really matter what crimes are perpetrated against us, because we're sub-human, you see."

"That's monstrous," Lindsay protested.

"But inevitable," Jane retorted. "What's going on here is so radical that they can't afford to treat it seriously on any level. Start accepting that we've got any rights and you end up by giving validity to the nightmares that have brought us here. Do that and you're half-way to accepting that our views on disarmament are a logical position. Much easier to treat us with total contempt."

"That's intolerable," said Lindsay.

"I'd better go and check that no one's hurt," Jane said. "One of the women got quite badly burned the first time they fire-bombed the tents."

"Give me a second to check that Cara's okay and I'll come with you," Lindsay said, getting up and climbing the ladder that led to Cara's bunk. Surprisingly, the child was still fast asleep.

"I guess she's used to it by now," Jane said, leading the way outside.

It was a sorry scene that greeted them. The headlights of several of the women's vehicles illuminated half a dozen benders now reduced to tangled heaps of wreckage, out of which women were still crawling. Jane headed for the first aid bender while Lindsay ploughed through the rain and wind to offer what help she could to two women struggling to salvage the plastic sheeting that had formed their shelter. Together all three battled against the weather and roughly re-erected the bender. But the women's sleeping bags were soaked and they trudged off to try and find some dry blankets to get them through the night.

Lindsay looked around. Slowly the camp was regaining its normal appearance. Where work was still going on, there seemed to be plenty of helpers. She made her way to Jane's bender, fortunately undamaged, and found the doctor bandaging the arm of a woman injured by a whiplashing branch in the attack on her bender.

"Hi, Lindsay," Jane had said without pausing in her work. "Not too much damage, thank God. A few bruises and cuts, but nothing major."

"Anything I can do?"

Jane shook her head. "Thanks, but everything's under control."

Feeling slightly guilty, but not wanting to leave Cara alone for too long, Lindsay returned to the van. She made up the double berth where Jane had shown her Deborah normally slept.

But sleep eluded Lindsay. When she finally dropped off, it was to fall prey to confusing and painful dreams.

✦

Cara woke early, and was fretful while Lindsay struggled with the unfamiliar intricacies of the van to provide them both with showers and breakfast. Luckily, the night's rain had washed away all traces of the pigs' blood. Of course, the keys of the van were with Deborah's possessions at the police station, so they had to drive into town in Lindsay's car.

Fordham Magistrates Court occupied a large and elegant Georgian town house in a quiet cul-de-sac off the main street. Inside, the building was considerably less distinguished. The beautifully proportioned entrance hall had been partitioned to provide a waiting room and offices and comfortless plastic chairs abounded where Chippendale furniture might once have stood. The paintwork was grubby and chipped and there was a pervasive odour of stale bodies and cigarette smoke. Lindsay felt Cara's grip tighten as they encountered the usual odd mixture of people found in magistrates' courts. Uniformed policemen bustled from room to room, up and down stairs. A couple of court ushers in robes like Hammer Horror vampires stood gossiping by the WRVS tea stand from which a middle-aged woman dispensed grey coffee and orange tea. The other extras in this scene were the defeated-looking victims of the legal process, several of them in whispering huddles with their spry and well-dressed solicitors.

For once, Lindsay felt out of her element in a court. She put it down to the unfamiliar presence of a four-year-old on the end of her arm, and approached the ushers. They directed her to the café upstairs where she had arranged to meet Judith. The solicitor was already sitting at a table, dressed for business in a black pinstripe suit and an oyster grey shirt. She fetched coffee for Lindsay and orange juice for Cara, then said, "I'd quite like it if you were in court throughout, Lindsay. How do you think Cara will cope if we ask a friendly policeman to keep an eye on her? Or has she already acquired the peace women's distrust of them?"

Lindsay shrugged. "Best to ask Cara." She turned to her and said, "We're supposed to go into court now, but I don't think you're allowed in. How would it be if we were to ask a policeman to sit and talk to you while we're away?"

"Are you going to get my mummy?" asked Cara.

"In a little while."

"Okay, then. But you won't be long, will you, Lindsay?"

"No, promise."

They walked downstairs to the corridor outside the courtroom and Judith went in search of help. She returned quickly with a young policewoman who introduced herself to Cara.

"My name's Barbara," she said. "I'm going to sit with you till Mummy gets back. Is that all right?"

"I suppose so," said Cara grudgingly. "Do you know any good stories?"

As Lindsay and Judith entered the courtroom, they heard Cara ask one of her best questions. "My mummy says the police are there to help us. So why did the police take my mummy away?"

The courtroom itself was scarcely altered from the house's heyday. The parquet floor was highly polished, the paintwork gleaming white. Behind a table on a raised dais at one end of the room sat the three magistrates. The chairwoman, aged about forty-five, had hair so heavily lacquered that it might have been moulded in fibreglass and her mouth, too, was set in a hard line. She was flanked by two men. One was in his late fifties, with the healthy, weather-beaten look of a keen sailor. The other, in his middle thirties, with dark brown hair neatly cut and styled, could have been a young business executive in his spotless shirt and dark suit. His face was slightly puffy round the eyes and jowls and he wore an air of dissatisfaction with the world.

The court wound up its summary hearing of a drunk and disorderly with a swift £40 fine and moved on to Deborah's case.

Lindsay sat down on a hard wooden chair at the back of the room as Deborah was led in looking tired and dishevelled. Her jeans and shirt looked slept in, and her hair needed washing. Lindsay reflected, not for the first time, how the law's delays inevitably made the person in police custody look like a tramp.

Deborah's eyes flicked round the courtroom as a uniformed inspector read out the charges. When she saw Lindsay she flashed a smile of relief before turning back to the magistrates and answering the court clerk's enquiry about her plea to the breach of the peace charge. "Guilty," she said in a clear, sarcastic voice. To the next charge, she replied equally clearly, "Not guilty."

It was all over in ten minutes. Deborah was fined £50 plus £15 costs on the breach charge, and remanded on bail to the Crown Court for jury trial on the assault charge. The bail had been set at £2,500, with the conditions that Deborah reported daily to the police station at Fordham, did not go within 200 yards of the Crabtree home, and made no approach to Mr Crabtree. Then, the formalities took over. Lindsay wrote a cheque she fervently hoped would never have to be cashed which Judith took to the payments office. Lindsay returned to Cara, who greeted her predictably with, "Where's my mummy? You said you'd get her for me."

Lindsay picked up the child and hugged her. "She's just coming, I promise." Before she could put Cara down, the child called, "Mummy!" and struggled out of Lindsay's arms. Cara hurtled down the corridor and into the arms of Deborah who was walking towards them with Judith. Eventually, Deborah disentangled herself from Cara and came over to Lindsay. Wordlessly, they hugged each other.

Lindsay felt the old electricity surge through her, and pulled back from the embrace. She held Deborah at arms' length. "Hi," she said.

Deborah smiled. "I didn't plan a reunion like this," she said ruefully.

"We'll do the champagne and roses some other time," Lindsay replied.

"Champagne and roses? My God, you've come up in the world. It used to be a half of bitter and a packet of hedgehog-flavoured crisps!"

They laughed as Judith, who had been keeping a discreet distance, approached and said, "Thanks for all your help, Lindsay. Now you'll just have to pray Deborah doesn't jump bail!"

"No chance," said Deborah. "I wouldn't dare. Lindsay's motto used to be 'Don't mess with the messer,' and I don't expect that's changed.

Lindsay smiled. "I've got even tougher," she said. "Come on, I'll drop you off at the camp on my way back to London."

They said goodbye to Judith and headed for the car park. Deborah said nonchalantly to Lindsay. "You can't stay, then?"

Lindsay shook her head. "Sorry. There's nothing I'd rather do, but I've got to get back to London. I'm on the night shift tonight."

"You'll come back soon, though, won't you, Lin?"

Lindsay nodded. "Of course. Anyway, I'm not going just yet. I expect I can fit in a quick cup of coffee back at the van."

They pushed through the doors of the courthouse and nearly crashed into two men standing immediately outside. The taller of the two had curly greying hair but his obvious good looks were ruined by a swollen and bruised nose and dark smudges beneath his eyes. He looked astonished to see Deborah, then said viciously, "So you're breaking your bail conditions already, Miss Patterson. I could have you arrested for this, you know. And you wouldn't get bail a second time."

Furious, Lindsay pushed forward as Deborah picked up her daughter protectively. "Who the hell do you think you are?" she demanded angrily.

"Ask your friend," he sneered. "I'm not a vindictive man," he added. "I won't report you to the police this time. When the Crown Court sentences you to prison, that will be enough to satisfy me."

He shouldered his way between them, followed by the other man, who had the grace to look embarrassed.

Deborah stared after him. "In case you hadn't guessed," she said, "that was Rupert Crabtree."

Lindsay nodded. "I figured as much."

"One of these days," Deborah growled, "someone is going to put a stop to that bastard."

3

The alarm clock went off at a quarter to six. Lindsay rolled on to her side, grunting, "Drop dead, you bastard," at the voice-activated alarm Cordelia had bought her to replace the Mickey Mouse job she'd had since university. She curled into a ball and considered going back to sleep. The early Saturday morning start to her weekend at the peace camp that had seemed such a good idea the night before now felt very unappealing.

But as she hovered on the verge of dozing off, she was twitched into sudden wakefulness as Cordelia's finger ends lightly traced a wavy line up her side. Cordelia snuggled into her and kissed the nape of her neck gently. Lindsay murmured her pleasure, and the kisses quickly turned into nibbles. Lindsay felt her flesh go to goose pimples; thoroughly aroused she twisted round and kissed her lover fiercely. Cordelia pulled away and said innocently, "I thought you had trouble waking up in the morning?"

"If they could find an alarm clock that did what you do to me, there would be no problem," Lindsay growled softly as she started to stroke Cordelia's nipples. Her right hand moved tentatively between Cordelia's legs.

Cordelia clamped her thighs together, pinning Lindsay's hand in place. "I've started so I'll finish," she murmured, moving her own fingers unerringly to the warm, wet centre of Lindsay's pleasure.

The feeling of relaxation that flooded through Lindsay afterwards was shattered by the alarm clock again. "Oh God," she groaned. "Is that the time?"

"What's your hurry?" Cordelia asked softly.

"I promised I'd be at Brownlow really early. There's a big action planned for today," Lindsay replied sleepily.

"Oh, for Christ's sake, is that all you think about these days," Cordelia complained, pulling away from Lindsay. "I'm going for a bloody shower." She bounced out of bed before Lindsay could stop her.

"I wasn't finished with you," Lindsay called after her plaintively.

"I'll wait till your mind's on what you're doing, if it's all the same to you," came the reply.

※☆☞

It was just after seven when Lindsay parked alongside the scruffy plastic benders. She had tried to make her peace with Cordelia, but it had been fruitless. Now Cordelia was on her way to spend the weekend with her parents, and Lindsay was keeping the promise she'd made to Deborah three weeks before. She parked her MG between a small but powerful Japanese motorbike and a 2CV plastered with anti-nuclear stickers. If they ever stopped making 2CVs, she mused, the anti-nuclear sticker makers would go out of business. She cut her engine and sat in silence for a moment.

It was a cool and misty March morning, and Lindsay marvelled at the quiet stillness that surrounded the encampment. The only sign of life was a thin trickle of smoke coming from the far side of the rough circle of branches and plastic. She got out of the car and strolled over to Deborah's van. The curtains were drawn, but when Lindsay tried the door, she found it unlocked. In the gloom, she made out Deborah's sleeping figure. Lindsay moved inside gingerly and crouched beside her. She kissed her ear gently and nearly fell over as Deborah instantly woke, eyes wide, starting up from the bed. "Jesus, you gave me a shock," she exploded softly.

"A pleasant one, I hope."

"I can't think of a nicer one," said Deborah, sitting up. She pulled Lindsay close and hugged her. "Put the kettle on, there's a love," she said, climbing out of bed. She disappeared into the shower and toilet cubicle in the corner of the van, leaving Lindsay to deal with the gas rings.

Lindsay thought gratefully how easy it was to be with Deborah. There was never any fuss, never any pressure. It was always the same since they had first been together. They slipped so easily into a comfortable routine, as if the time between their meetings had been a matter of hours rather than months or weeks. Lindsay always felt at home with Deborah, whether it was in a Fordham courtroom or a camper van.

Deborah reappeared, washed and dressed, towelling her wavy brown shoulder-length hair vigorously. She threw the towel aside and settled down with a mug of coffee. She glanced at Lindsay, her blue eyes sparkling wickedly.

"You picked the right weekend to be here," she remarked.

Lindsay leaned back in her seat. "Why so?" she asked, "Jane told me it was just a routine blockade of the main gate."

"We're going in. Through the wire. We think it should be possible to get to the bunkers if we go in between gates three and four. The security's not that wonderful over there. I suppose any five-mile perimeter has to have its weak spots. The only exposed bit is the ten yards between the edge of the wood and the fence. So there will be a diversion at the main gate to keep them occupied while the others get through the wire. And it just so happens that there's a Channel 4 film crew coming down anyway today to do a documentary." Deborah grinned broadly and winked in complicity at Lindsay.

"Good planning, Debs. But aren't you taking a hell of a risk with the assault case already hanging over you? Surely they'll bang you up right away if they pick you up inside the fence?"

"That's exactly why we've decided that I'm not going in. I'm a very small part of the diversion. Which is why it's good that you're here. Left to my own devices, I'd probably find myself carried along with the flow. Before I knew it, I'd be back in clink again." Deborah smiled ruefully. "So, since I presume you're also in the business of keeping a low profile, we'll have to be each other's minder. Okay?"

Lindsay lit a cigarette and inhaled deeply before she replied. "Okay. I'd love to go along with the raiding party to do an 'I' piece, but given my bosses' views on peace women, I guess that's right out of the question."

"You can help me sing," said Deborah. She leaned across the table to Lindsay, grasped her hand tightly and kissed her. "My, but it's good to be with you, sister," she said softly.

Before Lindsay could reply, Cara's dark blonde head and flushed cheeks suddenly appeared through the curtains. As soon as she realised who was there, she scrambled down the ladder to hurl herself on Lindsay, hugging her fiercely before turning to Deborah. "You didn't tell me Lindsay was coming," she reproached her.

"I didn't tell you because I wasn't sure myself and I didn't want both of us to be disappointed if she couldn't make it. Okay?"

The child nodded. "What are we having for breakfast? Have you brought bacon and eggs like you promised last time?"

"I managed to smuggle them past the vegetarian checkpoint on the way in," Lindsay joked. "I know you're like me, Cara, you love the things that everybody tells you are bad for you."

"You really are a reprobate, aren't you," Deborah said, amused. "I know you like taking the piss out of all the vegetarian nonsmokers, but don't forget that a lot of us are veggies from necessity as much as choice. I love the occasional fry-up, but beans are a hell of a lot cheaper than bacon. Not everyone has the same sense of humour about it as I do."

"Don't tell me," Lindsay groaned. "Cordelia never stops telling me how people like me who love red meat are causing the distortion of world agriculture. Sometimes I feel personally responsible for every starving kid in the world."

Impatient with the conversation, Cara interrupted. "Can we have breakfast, then?"

By the time they had eaten the bacon, eggs, sausages and mushrooms that Lindsay had brought, the camp had come to life again. Women were ferrying water from the standpipe by the road in big plastic jerry cans while others cooked, repaired benders or simply sat and talked. It was a cold, dry day with the sun struggling fitfully through a haze. Lindsay went off to see Jane and found her sitting on a crate, writing in a large exercise book. She looked tired and drawn.

"Hi, Doc. Everything fine with you?"

Jane shrugged. "So so. I think I'm getting too close to all this now. I'm getting so wrapped up in the logistics of the camp I'm forgetting why I'm here. I think I'm going to have to get away for a few days to put it back into perspective."

"There's always a bed at our place if you need a break." Jane nodded as Lindsay went on, "Debs says you can fill me in with the details of today's invasion plan."

Jane outlined the intended arrangements. Nicky was leading a raiding party of a dozen women armed with bolt-cutters. They would be waiting in the woods for a signal from the lookout post that the diversion at the main gate was attracting enough attention from camp security to allow them to reach the fence and cut through the wire. What followed their entry into the base would be a matter for their own judgment but it was hoped that they'd make it to the missile silos. The diversion was timed for noon, the main attraction for fifteen minutes later.

"You should keep out of the front line," she concluded. "Help Deborah with the singing. Keep an eye on her too. We don't want her to get arrested again. It would be just like her to get carried away and do something out of order. I imagine that a few of the local coppers know perfectly well who she is and wouldn't mind the chance to pick her up and give her a hard time. Crabtree is pretty buddy-buddy with the local police hierarchy according to Judith. Understandably enough, I suppose. So do us all a favour unless you desperately want to take on Cara full-time—keep the lid on Deborah."

By late morning there was an air of suppressed excitement around the camp. The television crew had arrived and were shooting some interviews and stock background shots around the benders. It wasn't hard for Lindsay to suppress her journalistic instincts and avoid them. She was, after all, off duty, and since the *Clarion* had no Sunday edition, she felt no guilt about ignoring the story. She noticed Jane and a couple of other long-standing peace campers having a discreet word with the crew, which had included a couple of unmistakable gestures towards the long bunkers that dominated the skyline.

At about midday, Deborah came looking for her. Leaving Cara and three other children in the van with Josy, one of the other mothers living at the camp, they joined the steady surge of women making for the main gate. About forty women were gathered round. A group of half a dozen marched boldly up to the sentry boxes on either side of the gate and started to unwind the balls of wool they carried with them. They wove the wool around the impassive soldiers and their sentry boxes, swiftly creating a complex web. Other women moved to the gates themselves and began to weave wool strands in and out of the heavy steel mesh to seal them shut. Deborah climbed on top of a large concrete litter bin just outside the gates and hauled Lindsay up beside her. Together they started to sing one of the songs that had grown up with the camp and soon all the women had joined in.

Inside the camp the RAF police and behind them the USAF guards came running towards the gate. On the women's side, civil police started to appear at the trot to augment the pair permanently on duty at the main gate. The film crew were busy recording it all.

It looked utterly chaotic. Then one of the women let out an excited whoop and pointed to the silos. There, silhouetted against the grey March sky, women could be seen dancing and waving. Alerted by her cries, the film crew ran off round the perimeter fence, filming all the while. Inside the wire, the military turned and raced across the scrubby grass to the bunkers constructed to house the coming missiles.

Outside the base the women calmly dispersed, to the frustration of the police who were just getting into the swing of making arrests. Lindsay, feeling as high as if she'd just smoked a couple of joints, jumped down from the litter bin and swung Deborah down into her arms. Like the other women around them they hugged each other and jumped around on the spot, then they bounced away from the fence and back towards the main road. A tall man stood at the end of the camp road. On the end of a lead was a fox-terrier. A sneer of scorn spoiled his newly healed features.

"Enjoy yourself while you can. Miss Patterson. It won't be long before I have you put some place where there won't be much to rejoice over." His threat uttered, Crabtree marched on down the main road away from the camp. Lindsay looked in dismay at Deborah's stunned face.

"Sadistic bastard. He can't resist having a go every time he sees me," said Deborah. "He seems to go out of his way to engineer these little encounters. But I'm not going to let him get the better of me. Not on a day like today."

4

The women had gathered in the big bender that they used for meeting and talking as a group. Lindsay still couldn't get used to the way they struggled to avoid hierarchies by refusing to run their meetings according to traditional structures. Instead, they sat in a big circle and each spoke in turn, supposedly without interruption. The euphoria of the day's action was tangible. The film crew were still around, and not even the news that the dozen women who had made it to the silos had been charged with criminal damage and trespass could diminish the high that had infected everyone.

But there was a change in attitude since Lindsay had first encountered the peace women. It was noticeable that far more women were advocating stronger and more direct action against what they perceived as the forces of evil. She could see that Jane and several other women who'd been with the camp for a long time were having a struggle to impress upon others like the headstrong Nicky the need to keep all action nonviolent and to minimise the criminal element in what they did. Eventually, the meeting was adjourned without a decision till the following afternoon.

The rest of the day passed quickly for Lindsay who spent her time walking the perimeter fence and picking up on her new friendships with women like Jackie. Lindsay appreciated the different perspectives the women gave her on life in Thatcher's Britain. It was a valuable contrast with the cynical world of newspapers and the comfortably well-off life she shared with Cordelia. Jackie and her lover Willow, both from Birmingham, explained to Lindsay for the first time how good they felt at the camp because there was none of the constant pressure of racial prejudice that had made it so difficult for them to make anything of their lives at home. By the time Lindsay had eaten dinner with Cara and Deborah, she knew she had made a firm decision to stay. By unspoken consent, Deborah took Cara off to spend the rest of the night with her best friend Christy in the bender she shared with her mother Josy. When she returned, she found Lindsay curled up in a corner with a tumbler of whisky.

"Help yourself," said Lindsay.

Deborah sensed the tension in Lindsay. Carefully she poured herself a small drink from the bottle on the table and sat down beside her. She placed a cautious hand on her thigh. "I'm really glad to be with you again," she said quietly. "It's been a long time since we had the chance to talk."

Lindsay took a gulp of whisky and lit a cigarette. "I can't sleep with you," she burst out. "I thought I could, but I can't. I'm sorry."

Deborah hadn't forgotten the knowledge of Lindsay that six hectic months had given her. She smiled. "You haven't changed, have you? What makes you think I wanted to jump into bed with you again?" Her voice was teasing. "That old arrogance hasn't deserted you."

Outrage chased incredulity across Lindsay's face. Then her sense of humour caught up with her and she smiled. "Touché. You never did let me get away with anything, did you?"

"Too bloody true I didn't. Give you an inch and you were always half-way to the next town. Listen, I didn't expect a night of mad, passionate lovemaking. I know your relationship with Cordelia is the big thing in your life. Just as Cara is the most important thing in my life now. I don't take risks with that, and I don't expect you to take risks with your life either."

Lindsay looked sheepish. "I really wanted to make love with you. I thought it would help me sort out my feelings. But when you took Cara off, I suddenly felt that I was contemplating something dishonest. You know? Something that devalued what there is between you and me."

Deborah put her arm round Lindsay's tense shoulders. "You mean, you'd have been using me to prove something to yourself about you and Cordelia?"

"Something like that. I guess I just feel confused about what's happening between me and her. It started off so well—she made me feel so special. I was happy as a pig. Okay, it was frustrating that I was living in Glasgow and she was in London. But there wasn't a week when we didn't spend at least two nights together, often more, once I'd got a job sorted out.

"We seemed to have so much in common—we liked going to the same films, loved the theatre, liked the same books, all that stuff. She even started coming hill-walking with me, though I drew the line at going jogging with her. But it was all those things that kind of underpinned the fact that I was crazy about her and the sex was just amazing.

"Then I moved to London and it seemed like everything changed. I realised how much of her life I just hadn't been a part of. All the time she spent alone in London was filled with people I've got the square root of sod all in common with. They patronise the hell out of me because they think that being a tabloid hack is the lowest form of pond life.

"They treat me like I'm some brainless bimbo that Cordelia has picked up. And Cordelia just tells me to ignore it, they don't count. Yet she still spends great chunks of her time with them. She doesn't enjoy being with the people I work with, so she just opts out of anything I've got arranged with other hacks. And the few friends I've got outside the business go back to Oxford days; they go down well with Cordelia and her crowd, but I want more of my life than that. And it never seems the right time to talk about it.

"About once a fortnight at the moment I seriously feel like packing my bags and moving out. Then I remember all the good things about her and stay."

Lindsay stopped abruptly and leaned over to refill her glass. She took another long drink and shivered as the spirit hit her. Deborah slowly massaged the knotted muscles at the back of her neck. "Poor Lin," she said. "You do feel hard done by, don't you? You never did understand how compromise can be a show of strength, did you?"

Lindsay frowned. "It's not that. It just seems like me that's made all the compromises—or sacrifices, more like."

"But she has too. Suddenly, after years of living alone, doing the one job where you really need your own space, she's got this iconoclast driving a coach and horses through her routines, coming in at all hours of the day and night, thanks to her wonderful shift patterns, and hating the people she has to be nice to in order to keep a nice high profile in the literary world. It can't be exactly easy for her either. It seems to me that she's got the right idea—she's doing what she needs to keep herself together."

Lindsay looked hurt. "I never thought I'd hear you taking Cordelia's side."

"I'm not taking sides. And that reaction says it all, Lin," Deborah said, a note of sharpness creeping into her voice. "I'm trying to make you see things from her side. Listen, I saw you when the two of you had only been together six months, and I saw you looking happier than I'd ever seen you. I love you like a sister, Lin, and I want to see you with that glow back. You're not going to get it by whingeing about Cordelia. Talk to her about it. At least you're still communicating in bed—build on that, for starters. Stop expecting her to be psychic. If she loves you, she won't throw you out just because you tell her you're not getting what you need from her."

Lindsay sighed. "Easier said than done."

"I know that. But you've got to try. It's obviously not too late. If you were diving into bed with me to prove you still have enough autonomy to do it, I'd say you were in deep shit. But at least you're not that far down the road. Now, come on, drink up and let's get to bed. You can have Cara's bunk if you can't cope with sharing a bed with me and keeping your hands to yourself."

"Now who's being arrogant?"

Lindsay stood by the kettle waiting for it to boil, gazing at Deborah who lay languidly in a shaft of morning sunlight staring into the middle distance. After a night's sleep, the clarity she had felt after the conversation with Deborah had grown fuzzy round the edges. But she knew deep down she wanted to put things right between her and Cordelia, and Deborah had helped her feel that was a possibility.

She made the coffee, and brought it over to Deborah. Lindsay sat on the top of the bed and put her arms round her friend. Lindsay felt at peace for the first time in months. "If things go wrong when it comes to court, I'd like to take care of Cara, if you'll let me," she murmured.

Deborah drew back, still holding Lindsay's shoulders. "But how could you manage that? With work and Cordelia and everything?"

"We've got a crèche for newspaper workers' kids from nine till six every day. I can swap most of my shifts round to be on days and I'm damn sure Cordelia will help if I need her to."

Deborah shook her head disbelievingly. "Lindsay, you're incredible. Sometimes I think you just don't listen to the words that come out of your mouth. Last night, you were busily angsting about how to get your relationship with Cordelia back on an even keel. Now today you're calmly talking about dumping your ex-lover's child on her. What a recipe for disaster that would be! Look, it's lovely of you to offer, and I know she'd be happy with you, but I hope that won't be necessary. We'll look at the possibilities nearer the time and I'll keep it in mind. What counts is what's going to be best for her. Now, let's go and get Cara, eh? She'll be wondering where I am." They found Cara with Jane, and after a bread and cheese lunch the four of them went for a walk along the perimeter fence. Lindsay and Cara played tig and hide-and-seek among the trees while Jane and Deborah walked slowly behind, wrangling about the business of peace and the problems of living at Brownlow.

They made their way back to the camp, where the adults settled down in the meeting bender for a long session. Three hours later, it had been agreed that the women charged the day before should, if they were willing, opt for prison for the sake of publicity and that a picket should be set up at the gate of Holloway in their support. Jane offered to organise the picket. Lindsay thought gratefully that at least that way her friend could make a small escape without offending her conscience. It had been a stormy meeting and Lindsay was glad when it was over. Even though she had by now experienced many of these talking-shops, she never failed to become slightly disillusioned at the destructive way women could fight against each other in spite of their common cause.

Deborah went off to collect Cara and put her to bed and Lindsay joined Willow and Jackie and their friends in their bender. There were a couple of guitars and soon the women were singing an assortment of peace songs, love songs and nostalgic pop hits. Deborah joined them and they sat close. Lindsay felt she couldn't bear to wrench herself away from the sisterhood she felt round her. Sentimental fool, she thought to herself as she joined in the chorus of "I Only Want to Be with You."

Just after ten the jam session began to break up. Most of the women left for their own benders. Lindsay and Deborah followed. "I'm going to have a word with Jane about the Holloway picket," said Lindsay. "You coming?"

"No, I'll see you at the van."

"Okay, I'll not be long."

Deborah vanished into the darkness beyond the ring of benders to where the van was parked near the road. Lindsay headed for Jane's makeshift surgery and found the harassed doctor sorting through a cardboard box of pharmaceutical samples that a sympathetic GP had dropped off that evening. She stopped at once, pleased to see Lindsay in spite of her tiredness, and began to explain the picket plans. Although Lindsay was itching to get back to Deborah, it was after eleven when she finally set off to walk the fifty yards to the van.

The first thing that caught her eye as she moved beyond the polythene tents was bright lights. Now that the army had cleared the ground round the perimeter fence, it was possible to see the temporary arc lights from quite a distance. That in itself wasn't extraordinary as workmen occasionally sneaked in a night shift to avoid the picketing women.

She stopped dead as she caught sight of three figures approaching the camp, silhouetted against the dim glow from the barracks inside the fence. Two were uniformed policemen, no prizes for spotting that. The third was a tall, blond man she had noticed in the area a couple of times before. Her journalistic instinct had put him down as Special Branch. She was gratified to find that instinct vindicated. She glanced around, but the only other women in sight were far off by a campfire. Most of them had already gone to bed.

Lindsay had no idea what was going on, but she wanted to find out. The best way to do that was to stay out of sight, watch and listen. She crouched down against the bender nearest her and slowly worked her way round the encampment, trying to outflank the trio who were between her and the lights. When she reached the outer ring of tents, she squatted close to the ground while the three men passed her and headed for Jane's bender with its distinctive red cross. Lindsay straightened up and headed for the lights, keeping close to the fringes of woodland that surrounded the base. As she neared the lights, she was able to pick out details. There were a couple of police Landrovers pulled up on the edge of the wood. Near by, illuminated by their headlamps and the arc lights, were a cluster of green canvas screens. Beyond the Landrovers were three unremarkable saloon cars. A handful of uniformed officers stood around. Several people in civilian clothes moved about the scene, vanishing behind the screens from time to time.

Lindsay moved out of the shelter of the trees and approached the activity. She had only gone a few yards when two uniformed constables moved to cut off her progress. Her hand automatically moved to her hip pocket and she pulled out the laminated yellow Press Card which in theory granted her their co-operation. She flashed it at the young policemen and made to put it away.

"Just a minute, miss," said one of them. "Let's have a closer look if you don't mind."

Reluctantly, she handed the card over. He scrutinised it carefully; then he showed it to his colleague who looked her up and down, noting her expensive Barbour jacket, corduroy trousers and muddy walking boots. He nodded and said, "Looks okay to me."

"I'm here writing a feature about the camp," she said. "When I saw the lights, I thought something might be doing. What's the score?"

The first constable smiled. "Sorry to be so suspicious. We get all sorts here, you know. You want to know what's happening, you best see the superintendent. He's over by the Landrover nearest to us. I'll take you across in a minute, when he's finished talking to the bloke who found the body."

"Body?" Lindsay demanded anxiously. "What is it? Accident, murder? And who's dead?

"That's for the super to say," the policeman replied. "But it doesn't look much like an accident at this stage."

Lindsay looked around her, taking it all in. The scene of the murder was like a three-ring circus. The outer ring took the form of the five vehicles and a thinly scattered cordon of uniformed police constables. Over by one of the Landrovers, a policewoman dispensed tea from a vacuum flask to a nervous-looking man talking to the uniformed superintendent whom Lindsay recognised from the demonstration outside the police station. She crossed her fingers and hoped the victim was no one from the camp.

The temporary arc lights the police had rigged up gave the scene the air of a film set, an impression exaggerated by the situation, part of a clear strip about fifteen yards wide between a high chain-link fence and a belt of scrubby woodland. It was far enough from any gates to be free of peace campers. The lamps shone down on the second ring, a shield of tall canvas screens hastily erected to protect the body from view. Round the screen, scene-of-crime officers buzzed in and out, communicating in their own form of macabre shorthand.

But the main attraction of the circus tonight was contained in the inner circle. Here there were more lights, smaller spotlights clipped on to the screens. A photographer moved round the periphery, his flash freezing for ever the last public appearance of whoever was lying dead on the wet clay. Could it be one of the women from the camp lying there? Superintendent Rigano said a few words to the man, then moved back towards the scene of the crime. The constable escorted Lindsay across the clearing, being careful, she noted, to keep between her and the tall canvas screens. Once there, he secured the attention of the superintendent, whom Lindsay recognised from their earlier encounter outside Fordham police station. "Sir, there's a journalist here wants a word with you," the constable reported.

He turned to Lindsay, fine dark brows scowling over deep-set eyes. "You're here bloody sharpish," he said grudgingly. "Superintendent Rigano, Fordham Police."

"Lindsay Gordon, *Daily Clarion*. We met at the demonstration after Deborah Patterson's arrest. I happened to be at the camp," she replied. "We're doing a feature comparing the peace camps at Brownlow and Faslane," she lied fluently. "I saw the lights and wondered if there might be anything in it for me."

"We've got a murder on our hands," he said in a flinty voice. "You'd better take a note. It would be a pity to screw up on a scoop." Lindsay obediently pulled out her notebook and a pencil.

"The dead man is Rupert Crabtree." The familiar name shocked Lindsay. Suddenly this wasn't some impersonal murder story she was reporting. It was much closer to home. Her surprise obviously registerd with Rigano, who paused momentarily before continuing. "Aged forty-nine. Local solicitor. Lives up Brownlow Common Cottages. That's those mock-Georgian mansions half a mile from the main gate of the camp. Bludgeoned to death with a blunt instrument, to wit, a chunk of drainage pipe which shattered on impact. Perhaps more to the point, from your side of things, is the fact that he was chairman of the local ratepayers' association who were fighting against that scruffy lot down there. It looks as if there was a struggle before he was killed. Anything else you want to know?"

Lindsay hoped her relationship with "that scruffy lot down there" was not too obvious and that she was putting up a sufficiently good performance in her professional role as the single-minded news reporter in possession of a hot exclusive. "Yes. What makes you think there was a struggle?"

"The mud's churned up quite a bit. And Crabtree had drawn a gun but not had the chance to fire it."

"That suggests he knew his life was at risk, doesn't it?"

"No comment. I also don't want the gun mentioned just yet. Any other questions?"

She nodded vigorously. "Who found the body?"

"A local resident walking his dog. I'm not releasing a name and he won't be available for interview in the foreseeable future."

"Any suspects? Is an arrest likely within the next few hours? And what was he doing on the common at this time of night?"

Rigano looked down at her shrewdly. "No arrest imminent. We are actively pursuing several lines of enquiry. He was walking the bloody dog. He usually did this time of night. Well-known fact of local life."

"Any idea of the time of death?" she asked.

Rigano shrugged expressively. "That's for the doctors to tell us. But without sticking my neck out, I can tell you it was probably some time between ten and eleven o'clock. I hope you've got an alibi," he said, a smile pulling at the corners of his mouth. "Come and have a quick look." He strode off, clearly expecting her to follow. She caught up with him at the entrance to the screens.

"I'd rather not, if you don't mind," she said quickly.

His eyebrows shot up. "Happy to dish the dirt, not so happy to see the nastiness?"

Lindsay was stung by his sardonic tone. "Okay," she said grimly. He led her through the gap in the screens.

She would not have recognised Rupert Crabtree. He lay on his front, the wet March ground soaking the elegant camel hair coat and the pinstripe trousers. His wellingtons were splashed with vivid orange mud, as were his black leather gloves. The back of his head was shattered. Blood matted his hair and had spattered over the fragments of a two-foot-long piece of earthenware water pipe which had clearly broken under the force with which it had been brought down on the skull. A few feet away, a handgun lay in the mud. Lindsay felt sick. Rigano took her arm and steered her away. "You'll be wanting to get to a phone," he said, not unkindly. "If you want to check up on our progress later on, ring Fordham nick and ask for the duty officer. He'll fill you in with any details." He turned away, dismissing her.

Slowly, Lindsay turned her back on the depressing camouflage of death. And at once, her mind was torn away from murder. Across the clearing, the trio she had seen earlier were returning. But now there were four people in the group. She felt a physical pain in her chest as she recognised the fourth. As their eyes met Lindsay and Deborah shared a moment of pure fear.

5

For a moment, Lindsay stood stock still, the journalist fighting the friend inside her. This was an important story, she had the edge on the pack and she needed to call the office as soon as possible. Logically, she knew there was little she could do for Deborah as the police Landrover carried her off. That didn't stop her feeling an overwhelming rage that translated itself into the desire for action. Abruptly, she turned back to the scene of the crime and found Rigano. Forcing herself to sound casual she elicited the information that Deborah had not been arrested but was assisting police with their enquiries. End message. Lindsay turned and started to run back to the van.

Once out of the circle of light, she was plunged into darkness. Tripping over tree roots and treacherous brambles, she stumbled on, her only guide the distant glow of the campfire and the dim light from a few of the benders. At one point she plunged headlong over a rock and grimly picked herself up, covered in mud. Cursing, she ran on till she reached the camp. As she reached the benders, she realised that several knots of women had gathered and were talking together anxiously. Ignoring their questioning looks, she made straight for the van, where she burst in, gasping for breath, to find Jane sitting over a cup of coffee. She took one look at Lindsay and said, "So you know already?"

"How's Cara? Where is she?" Lindsay forced out.

"Fast asleep. The coppers were very quiet, very civil. But the van mustn't be moved till they've had a chance to search it." She was interrupted by a knock on the door. Lindsay leaned over and opened it to find a policewoman standing on the threshold.

"Yes?" Lindsay demanded roughly.

"I've been instructed to make sure that nothing is removed from this van until our officers arrive with a search warrant," she replied.

"Terrific," said Lindsay bitterly. "I take it you've no objection to me moving a sleeping child to where she won't be disturbed?"

The policewomen looked surprised. "I don't see why you shouldn't move the child. Where is she?"

Lindsay pointed up to the curtained-off bunk. She turned to Jane and said, "I'll take Cara to Josy's bender. She'll be all right there."

Jane nodded and added, "I'll stay here to make sure everything's done properly."

Lindsay smiled. "Thanks. I've got to get to the phone." Then, with all the firmness she could muster, she said to the police officer, "I'm a journalist. I've got the details of the story from Superintendent Rigano, and I intend to phone my office now. I'll be back shortly. Till then, Dr Thomas is in charge here."

She climbed the ladder and folded Cara into her arms. The child murmured in her sleep but did not wake. Lindsay carried her to Josy, then ran as fast as she could to the phone box. She glanced at her watch and was amazed to see it was still only half past midnight. Her first call was to Judith Rowe. When the solicitor surfaced from sleep, she promised to get straight round to the police station and do what she could.

Next, Lindsay took a deep breath and put in a transfer charge call to the office. The call was taken by Cliff Gilbert himself. "Listen," she said. "There's been a murder at Brownlow Common. I've checked it out with the cops locally and the strength of it is that the leader of the local opposition to the women's peace camp has been found with his head stoved in. I've got enough to file now, which I'll do if you put me on to copy. I'll also get stuck in to background for tomorrow if you think that's a good idea."

Cliff thought for a moment. Lindsay could almost hear the connections clicking into place to complete the mental circuit. "You've got good contacts among the lesbian beanburger brigade down there, haven't you?"

"The best. The prime suspect seems to be an old pal of mine."

"What shift are you on tomorrow?"

"Day off."

"Fine. Take a look at it if you don't mind and check in first thing with Duncan. I'll leave him a note stressing that I've told you to get stuck in. And Lindsay—don't do anything daft, okay?"

"Thanks, Cliff. How much do you want now?"

"Let it run, Lindsay. All you've got."

There followed a series of clicks and buzzes as she was connected to the copytaker. She recited the story off the top of her head, adding in as much as she knew about Crabtree and his connection with the camp. "A brutal murder shocked a women's peace camp last night," she began.

Then, at nearly two o'clock she made her final call. Cordelia's sleepy voice answered the phone. "Who the hell is it?"

Lindsay swallowed the lump that had formed in her throat at the sound of the familiar voice. She struggled with herself and tried to sound light. "It's me, love. Sorry I woke you. I know you'll be tired after driving back from your parents', but I'm afraid I've got a major hassle on my hands. There's been a murder down here. Rupert Crabtree the guy whose face Debs is supposed to have rearranged—he's been killed. The cops have pulled Debs. I don't think they're going to charge her. I know I said I'd be home tomorrow lunchtime, but I don't know when the hell I'll make it now."

"Do you want me to come down?"

Lindsay thought for a moment. The complication seemed unnecessary. "Not just now, I think," she replied. "There's nothing either of us can really do till I know more precisely what's happening. I simply wanted to tell you myself so you wouldn't panic when you heard the news or saw the papers. I'll ring you later today, all right?"

"All right," Cordelia sighed. "But look after yourself, please. Don't take any chances with a murderer on the loose. I love you, don't forget that."

"I love you too," Lindsay replied. She put the phone down and walked back to the camp. She opened the door to the van, forgetting momentarily about the police. The bulky presence of two uniformed men searching the van startled her.

"What the hell are you doing?" she demanded angrily.

"We'll be as quick as we can," said the older of the two, a freckle-faced, grey-haired man with broad shoulders and a paunch. "We have a warrant. Your friend said it was all right," he added, nodding towards Jane.

"I'd forgotten you'd be doing this." Lindsay sighed as she collapsed into the comfortable armchair-cum-driver's seat.

True to the constable's word, they departed in about fifteen minutes with a bundle of clothing. Lindsay poured a large whisky for Jane and herself.

"I could do without another night like this," Lindsay said. "I don't know what it is about my friends that seems to attract murder."

Jane looked puzzled. "You mean this happens often?"

"Not exactly often. About two years ago, a friend of mine was arrested for a murder she didn't commit. Cordelia and I happened to be on the spot and got roped in to do the Sam Spade bit. That's when the two of us got together—a mutual fascination for being nosy parkers."

"Well, I hate to say it, but I'm glad you've had the experience. I think you could easily find yourself going through the same routine for Deborah."

Lindsay shook her head. "Different kettle of fish. They've not even arrested Debs, never mind charged her. I'm pretty sure they don't have much to go on. It's my guess that Debs will be back here by lunchtime tomorrow if Judith's got anything to do with it. Let's face it, we all know Debs is innocent and I'm sure the police will find a more likely suspect before the day's out. They've just pulled her in to make it look good to anyone who's got their beady eyes on them. Now I'm going to bed, if you'll excuse me."

In spite of Lindsay's exhaustion she did not fall asleep at once. Crabtree's murder had set her thoughts racing in circles. Who had killed him? And why? Was it anything to do with the peace camp, or was Debs's connection with him purely coincidental? And what was going to happen to Debs? Lindsay hated being in a position where she didn't know enough to form reasonable theories, and she tossed and turned in Debs's bed as she tried to switch off her brain. Finally she drifted into a deep and dreamless sleep, which left her feeling neither rested nor refreshed when she awoke after nine.

After a quick shower, she emerged into a mild spring day with cotton-wool clouds scudding across the sky to find the camp apparently deserted. Puzzled, Lindsay glanced over at the big bender used for meetings; it seemed that was where the women had gathered. She decided to take advantage of the quiet spell by phoning the office and checking the current situation with the police.

Her first call was to the police HQ in Fordham. She asked for Rigano and was surprised to be put straight through to him. "Superintendent Rigano? Lindsay Gordon here, *Daily Clarion*. We met last night at Brownlow . . ."

"I remember. You were quick off the mark. It's been hard to get away from your colleagues this morning. Now, what can I do for you?"

"I wondered where you were up to. Any imminent arrest?"

"You mean, are we going to charge your friend? The answer is, not at the moment. Off the record, we'll be letting

COMMON MURDER   309

her go later this morning. That's not to say I'm convinced of
her innocence. But I can't go any further till I've got forensics.
So you can say that at present good old Superintendent Rigano
is following several lines of enquiry, but that the woman we
have been interviewing is being released pending the outcome
of those enquiries. Okay?"

"Fine. Do you mind if I drop in on you later today?"

"Please yourself," he said. "If I'm in, I'll see you. But I don't
know what my movements will be later, so if you want to take
a chance on missing me, feel free."

Lindsay put the phone down, thoughtful. Her experience
with the police during the Paddy Callaghan case had fuelled
her ingrained mistrust of their intelligence and integrity. But in
her brief encounter with Rigano she had felt a certain rapport
which had not been dispelled by their telephone conversation.
She had surprised herself by her request to call in on him and
now she felt slightly bewildered as to what on earth she would
find to discuss with him once Debs was released.

But that was for later. Right now she had the unpleasant task
of talking to Duncan Morrison, the *Daily Clarion*'s news editor
and the man responsible for her move to London. She put the call
in and waited nervously to be connected to her boss. His voice
boomed down the line at her. "Morning, Lindsay," he began. "I
see from the overnight note that you're back in that nest of vipers.
Still, you did a good job last night. We beat everyone else to the
draw and that's the way I want to keep it. It's of interest for us
in terms of the link with the peace camp, okay, so let's keep that
in the front of our minds. What I want from you by noon is a
good background piece about the camp, a few quotes from the
loony lefties about this man Crabtree and his campaign. I don't
have to spell it out to you?" Lindsay fumed quickly as the venom
of his prejudices ran over her. "I also want to be well up on the
news angles too. Try for a chat with the widow and family or his
colleagues. And try to overcome your natural prejudices and stay
close to the cops. Now, what's the score on all that?"

Lindsay somehow found her tongue. She was aware that she should know better than to be surprised by Duncan's about-turn when faced with a strong news story, but she still couldn't help being a little taken aback that he was now hassling her for a background piece on the camp. She stammered, "The cops are releasing the woman they held for questioning. She's Deborah Patterson, the woman charged with assaulting him last month. I don't know what the legal implications are as yet—I should imagine that with his death the prosecution case automatically falls, but whether that releases us immediately from *sub judice* rules, I don't know."

"As far as the news feature's concerned, no problem. Also, I'm hoping to see the copper in charge of the case again this afternoon, so I can let you have whatever he says. I'll try the family but I don't hold out much hope. They're a bit too well clued-up about Her Majesty's gutter press to fall for the standard lines. But leave it with me."

"Fine. Normally on one this big, I'd send someone down to help you out, but you're the expert when it comes to the lunatic fringe, so I'll leave you to it." Patronising shit, she thought, as he carried on. "We've got a local snapper lined up, so if you've got any potential pics, speak to the picture desk. Don't fall down on this one, Lindsay. File by noon so I can see the copy before I go into morning conference. And get a good exclusive chat with this woman they're releasing. If the lawyers say we can't use it, we can always kill it. Speak to you later."

The phone went dead. "Just what I love most," Lindsay muttered. "Writing for the waste-paper bin." She walked back to the van and made herself some coffee and toast before she sat down and began to put her feature together. She had only written a few paragraphs when there was a knock at the van door.

"Come in," she called. Jane entered, followed by Willow and another woman whom Lindsay knew only by sight.

"The very people I wanted to see," she exclaimed. "My newsdesk has said I can do a piece about the camp reaction to

Crabtree's campaign. So I need some quotes from you about how you are here for peace and while you didn't have any sympathy for his organisation, you wouldn't ever have stooped to violence, etc., etc. Is that all right?"

Willow grinned. "We'll have to see about that," she replied. "But first, we've got something to ask you. We've just had a meeting to discuss this business. We've decided we need to safeguard our interests. Already there have been reporters round here and we don't like the attitude they've been taking. That leaves us with a bit of a problem. We need someone who can help us deal with the situation. It's got to be someone who understands why none of us could have done this, but who also knows the way the system works. It looks like you're the only one who fits the bill."

The third woman chimed in. "It wasn't a unanimous decision to ask you. Not by a long chalk. But we're stuck. Personally, I don't feel entirely happy about trusting someone who works for a paper like the *Clarion*, but we don't have a lot of choice. Deborah's already been picked up, and even if she's released without charges, the mud's been slung and it will stick unless we can get our point of view across."

Lindsay shrugged. "I do know how the media works. But it sounds more like you're looking for a press spokeswoman, and that's not a job I can really do. It gives me a serious conflict of interest."

The third woman looked satisfied. "I thought you'd say that," she said triumphantly. "I knew that when the chips were down you'd know which side your bread was buttered."

Needled, Lindsay said, "That's really unfair. You know I want to do everything I can. Deborah's been my friend for years. Look, I can help you project the right kind of image. But don't expect miracles. What I do need if I'm going to do that is total co-operation. Now I know there are women here who would die before they'd help a tabloid journo, but from those of you who are willing to help I need support."

Jane replied immediately. "Well, I for one am willing to trust you. The articles you've written abroad about the camp have been some of the most positive pieces I've seen about what we're doing here. You're the only person capable of doing what we need that we can any of us say that about."

"I'll go along with that," Willow added. "I'll pass the word around that you're on our side."

"Care to supply some quotes before you go?" Lindsay asked as Willow and the other woman seemed about to leave.

"Jane can do that. She's good with words," Willow said over her shoulder as they went out, closing the van door on Jane and Lindsay.

"There was something else I wanted to discuss with you," Jane said hesitantly. "I know a lot of the women would disagree with me, so I didn't raise it at the meeting. But I think we need someone to investigate this on our behalf. We are going to be at the centre of suspicion over this, and while they've got us as prime candidates, I don't think the police will be looking too hard for other possible murderers. Will you see what you can find out?"

For the second time that morning, Lindsay was taken aback. "Why me?" she finally asked. "I'm not any kind of detective. I'm a journalist, and there's no guarantee that my interests aren't going to clash with yours."

Jane parried quickly. "You told me you'd cleared a friend of a murder charge. Well, I figure if you did it once, you can do it again. Those features you wrote for the German magazine seem to have a feel for the truth, even if you don't always choose to report it. You can talk to the cops, you can talk to Crabtree's family and friends. None of us can do that. And you're on our side. You can't believe Deborah's guilty. You of all people can't believe that."

Lindsay lit a cigarette and gazed out of the window. She really didn't want the hassle of being a servant of two masters. Jane sat quiet but Lindsay could feel the pressure of her presence. "All right," she said, "I'll do what I can."

By noon Lindsay had dictated her story and spoken to Duncan who, never satisfied, started to pressurise her about an interview with Deborah. Disgruntled, she was walking back from the phone box when a car pulled up alongside. Suddenly Lindsay found herself enveloped in a warm embrace as Deborah jumped out of the car. Nothing was said for a few moments. Judith leaned over from the driver's seat and called through the open door, "I'll see you up at the camp," before driving off.

"Oh, Lin," Deborah breathed. "I was so afraid. I didn't know what was going on. The bastards just lifted me, I couldn't even do anything about Cara. I've been so worried. I haven't slept, haven't eaten—Thank God you had the sense to get Judith on to it straight away. God knows what I wouldn't have confessed to otherwise, just to get out of there. There was a big blond Special Branch bloke, but he was no big deal, they're always too busy playing at being James Bond. But the superintendent is so fucking clever. Oh Lin . . ." And the tears came.

Lindsay stroked her hair. "Dry your eyes, Debs. Come on, Cara will be wanting you."

Deborah wiped her eyes and blew her nose on Lindsay's crumpled handkerchief then they walked back to the camp arm in arm. As soon as they came into view, Cara came charging towards them. Behind her, to Lindsay's astonishment, came Cordelia, looking cool and unflustered in a designer jogging suit and green wellies, her black hair blowing in the breeze.

As mother and daughter staged a noisy and tearful reunion, Cordelia greeted Lindsay with a warm kiss. "I couldn't sit in London not knowing what was happening," she explained. "Even if there's nothing I can do, I had to come."

Lindsay found a smile and said, "It's good to see you. I appreciate it. How long can you stay?"

"Till Wednesday lunchtime. Jane's filled me in on what's been happening. What's the plan now that you've been appointed

official Miss Marple to the peace women? Do I have to rush off
and buy you a knitting pattern and a ball of fluffy wool?"

"Very funny. I'm not entirely sure what I'm supposed to
be doing. But I'll have to speak to Debs about last night. I've
already warned her not to talk to anyone else. Of course, Duncan
wants me to do the chat with her, but the lawyer will never let
us use a line of it. I suppose I should have a crack at the family
too. I've got a good contact, the copper who's handling things
at the moment, a Superintendent Rigano. I'm going to see him
this afternoon. Let's go and have a pint and I'll fill you in."

Lindsay swallowed the emotional turmoil triggered off by
Cordelia's appearance and told her lover all she knew about the
murder over a bowl of soup in the nearest pub that accepted peace
women customers—nearly three miles away. Cordelia was fired
with enthusiasm and insisted that they set off immediately in her
car for Brownlow Common Cottages which, in spite of their
humble name, were actually a collection of architect-designed
mock-Georgian mansions.

There could be no mistaking the Crabtree residence. It was
a large, double-fronted two-storey house covered in white stucco
with bow windows and imitation Georgian bottle-glass panes.
A pillared portico was tacked on to the front. At the side stood
a double garage, with a fifty-yard drive leading up to it. In front
of the house was a neatly tended square lawn which had been
underplanted with crocuses, now just past their best. The road
outside was clogged on both sides by a dozen cars, the majority
new. At the wrought-iron gate in the low, white-painted wall
stood a gaggle of men in expensive topcoats. A few men and
women stood around the cars looking bored. Every few minutes,
one reporter peeled off from a group and ambled up the drive to
ring the door bell. There was never any reply, not even a twitch
of the curtains that hid the downstairs rooms from view.

"The ratpack's out in force," Lindsay muttered as she
climbed out of the car and headed for her colleagues. She soon
spotted a familiar face, Bill Bryman, the crime man from the

London Evening Sentinel. She greeted him and asked what was happening.

"Sweet FA," he replied bitterly. "I've been here since eight o'clock, and will my desk pull me off? Will they hell! The son answered the door the first time and told us nothing doing. Since then it's a total blank. If you ask me, they've disconnected the bell. I've told the office it's a complete waste of time, but you know news editors. Soon as they get promoted, they have an operation on their brains to remove all memory of what life on the road is all about."

"What about the neighbours?"

Bill shook his head wearily. "About as much use as a chocolate chip-pan. Too bloody 'okay yah' to communicate with the yobbos of the popular press. Now if you were to say you were from the *Tatler*—though looking at the outfit, I doubt you'd get away with it." Lindsay looked ruefully at her clothes which still bore the traces of her headlong flight the night before, in spite of her efforts to clean up. "You been down the peace camp yet?" he added. "They're about as much help as this lot here."

"So I'd be wasting my time hanging around here, would I?"

"If you've got anything better to do, do it. I'd rather watch an orphanage burn," Bill answered resignedly with the cynicism affected by hard-boiled crime reporters the world over. "I'll be stuck here for the duration. If I get anything, I'll file it for you. For the usual fee."

Lindsay grinned to herself as she returned to the BMW. As they pulled away, Lindsay noticed the tall blond man she'd tagged as Special Branch when she'd seen him at the camp. He was leaning against a red Ford Fiesta on the fringes of the press corps, watching them.

"To Fordham nick," she said to Cordelia. "And stop at the first public toilet. Desperate situations need desperate remedies."

6

Lindsay emerged from the public toilet on the outskirts of Fordham a different woman. Before they left the camp she had retrieved her emergency overnight working bag from the boot of her car, and she was now wearing a smart brown dress and jacket, chosen for their ability not to crease, coupled with brown stilettos that would have caused major earth tremors at the peace camp. Cordelia wolf-whistled quietly as her lover got back into the car. "You'll get your lesbian card taken away, dressing like that," she teased.

"Fuck off, she quipped wittily," Lindsay replied. "If Duncan wants the biz doing, I will do the biz."

At the police station, Lindsay ran the gauntlet of bureaucratic obstacles and eventually found herself face to face with Superintendent Rigano. They exchanged pleasantries, then Lindsay leaned across his desk and said, "I think you and I should do a deal."

His face didn't move a muscle. He would have made a good poker player if he could be been bothered with anything so predictable, thought Lindsay. When he had finished appraising her, he simply said, "Go on."

Lindsay hesitated long enough to light a cigarette. She needed a moment to work out what came next in this sequence of unplanned declarations. "You had Deborah Patterson in here for twelve hours. I imagine she wouldn't even tell you what year it is.

"They'll all be like that," she continued. "They've gone past the 'innocents abroad' stage down there, thanks to the way the powers that be have used the police and manipulated the courts. Now, they have a stable of sharp lawyers who don't owe you anything. Several of the peace women have been in prison and think it holds no terrors for them. They all know their rights and they're not even going to warn you if your backside is on fire.

"So if you want any information from them, you're stymied. Without me, that is. I think I can deliver what you need to know from them. I'm not crazy about the position I find myself in. But they trust me, which is not something you can say about many people who have a truce with the Establishment. They've asked me to act as a sort of troubleshooter for them."

He looked suspicious. "I thought you were a reporter," he said. "How have you managed to earn their trust?"

"The women at the camp know all about me. I've been going there for months now."

He could have blustered, he could have threatened, she knew. But he just asked, quietly, "And what's the price?"

Glad that her first impression of him hadn't been shattered, Lindsay replied, "The price is a bit of sharing. I'm a good investigative reporter. I'll let you have what I get, if you'll give me a bit of help and information."

"You don't want much, do you?" he complained.

"I'm offering something you won't get any other way," Lindsay replied. She doubted she could deliver all she had promised, but she reckoned she could do enough to keep him happy. That way, she'd get what she and the women wanted.

He studied her carefully and appeared to come to a decision. "Can we go off the record?" he asked. Lindsay nodded. His response at first appeared to be a diversion. "He was an influential man, Rupert Crabtree. Knew most of the people that are supposedly worth knowing round these parts. Didn't just know them to share a pink gin with—he knew them well enough to demand favours. Being dead seems to have set in motion the machinery for calling in the favours. I'm technically in charge of the CID boys running this at local level. But CID are avoiding this one like the plague. And other units are trying to use their muscle on it.

"Our switchboard has been busy. I'm under a lot of pressure to arrest your friend. You'll understand that, I know. But I'm old-fashioned enough to believe that you get your evidence before the arrest, not vice versa. That wouldn't have been hard in this case, if you follow me.

"I happen to think that she didn't kill him. And I'm not afraid to admit I'll need help to make that stick. You know I don't need to make deals to achieve that help. Most coppers could manage it, given time and a bit of leaning. But I don't have time. There are other people breathing down my neck. So let's see what we need for a deal."

Lindsay nodded. "I need access to the family. You'll have to introduce me to them. Suggest that I'm not just a newspaper reporter. That I'm working on a bigger piece about the Brownlow campaign for a magazine that will feature an in-depth profile of Crabtree—a sort of tribute."

"Are you?"

"I can be by teatime. Also point out to them that it will get the pack off their back and end the siege. I'll be taping the conversation and transcribing the tapes. You can have full access to the tapes and a copy of the transcripts."

"Are you trying to tell me you think it was a domestic crime?"

"Most murders are, aren't they? But I won't know who might have killed him till I've found out a lot more about his life. That means family, friends, colleagues and the peace women will all have to open up to me. In return, any of the peace women you want to talk to, you tell me honestly what it's about and I'll deliver the initial information you need. Obviously, you'll have to take over if it's at all significant, but that's got to be better for you than a wall of silence."

"It's completely unorthodox. I can't run an investigation according to the whim of the press."

"Without my help, I can promise you all you'll find at the camp is a brick wall. Anyway, you don't strike me as being a particularly orthodox copper."

He almost smiled. "When do you want to see the family?" he asked.

"Soon as possible. It really will get the rest of the press off the doorstep. You'll have to tell my colleagues at the gate that the family asked expressly to talk to a *Clarion* reporter or you'll get a load of aggravation which I'm sure you could do without."

"Are you mobile?"

"The BMW cabriolet outside."

"The fruits of being a good investigative reporter seem sweeter than those of being a good copper. Wait in the car." He rose. The interview was over.

Slightly bewildered by her degree of success, Lindsay found her way through the labyrinthine corridors to the car park, feeling incongruous in her high heels after days in heavy boots, and slumped into the seat beside Cordelia, who looked at her enquiringly.

"I think perhaps I need my head examined," Lindsay said. "The way I've been behaving today, I think it buttons up the back. I've just marched into a superintendent's office and offered to do a deal with him that will keep Debs out of prison, get me some good exclusives and might possibly, if we all get very lucky indeed, point him in the right direction for the real villain. Talk about collaborating with the class enemy. Mind you, I expected him to throw me out on my ear. But he went for it. Can you believe it?"

Lindsay outlined her conversation with Rigano. When she'd finished, Cordelia asked, "Would he be the one who looks like a refugee from a portrait in the Uffizi?"

"That's him. Why?"

"Because he's heading this way," she said drily as Rigano's hand reached for Lindsay's door. Lindsay sat bolt upright and wound down the window.

"Open the back door for me, please," said Rigano. "I believe we may be able to do a deal."

Lindsay did as she was told and he climbed in. A shadow of distaste crossed his face as his eyes flicked round the luxurious interior. "Drive to Brownlow Common Cottages," he said. "Not too fast. There will be a police car behind you."

Cordelia started the car, put it in gear, then, almost as an afterthought, before she released the clutch, she turned round in her seat and said, "I'm Cordelia Brown, by the way. Would it be awfully unreasonable of me to ask your name?"

"Not at all," he replied courteously. His face showed the ghost of a smile. "I am Superintendent Giacomo Rigano of Fordham Police. I'm sorry I didn't introduce myself. I've grown so accustomed to knowing who everyone is that I forget this is not a two-way process. Because I knew who you were, I assumed you knew me too."

"How did you know who I was?" she demanded, full of suspicion. She never seemed to remember that, as the writer of several novels and a successful television series, she was a minor celebrity. It had often amused Lindsay.

As usual, Rigano took his time in replying. "I recognised you from your photographs." He paused, and just before Cordelia could draw again on her stock of paranoia, he added, "You know, on your dust jackets. And, of course, from television."

Fifteen-love, thought Lindsay in surprise. They drove off and Lindsay swivelled round in her seat. "What's the deal, then?"

"I've just spoken to Mrs Crabtree. She wasn't keen, but I've persuaded her. I'll take you there and introduce you to her. Then I'll leave you to it. On the understanding that I can listen to the tapes afterwards and that you will give me copies of the transcript as agreed. In return, I need to know who was at the peace camp last night and where each woman was between ten and eleven. If you can give me that basic information, then I know who I need to talk to further."

"Okay," Lindsay agreed. "But it'll be tomorrow before I can let you have that."

"Then tomorrow will have to do. The people who want quick results will have to be satisfied with the investigation proceeding at its own pace. Like any other investigation."

"Yes, but to people round here, he's not quite like any other corpse, is he?" Cordelia countered.

"That's true," Rigano retorted. "But while this remains my case, he will simply be a man who was unlawfully killed. To me, that is the only special thing about him."

That must endear you to your bosses, Cordelia thought. Just what is Lindsay getting into this time? Maverick coppers we don't need.

Cordelia steered carefully through the crowd of journalists and vehicles that still made the narrow road in front of Brownlow Cottages a cramped thoroughfare. Lindsay noticed the blond watcher was no longer there. At the end of the Crabtrees' drive, Rigano wound down the window and shouted to the constable on duty there, "Open the gate for us, Jamieson!"

The constable started into action, and as they drove inside, Lindsay could see the looks of fury on the faces of her rivals. As soon as the car stopped, Rigano got out and gestured to Lindsay to follow him. He was immediately distracted by journalists fifty yards away shouting their demands for copy, Lindsay took advantage of the opportunity to lean across and say urgently to Cordelia, "Listen, love, you can't help me here. I want us to work as a team like we did before. Would you go back to the camp and see if you can get Jane to help you sort out this alibi nonsense that Rigano wants? And make it as watertight as possible. Okay?"

"We have a deal," said Cordelia, with a smile. "As the good superintendent says."

"Great. See you later," Lindsay replied as she got out of the car and joined Rigano standing impatiently on the doorstep.

"Mrs Crabtree's on her own," he remarked. "There were some friends round earlier but she sent them away. The son, Simon, is out. He apparently had some urgent business to see to. So you should have a chance to do something more than ask superficial questions to which we all know the answers already."

He gave five swift raps on the door knocker. Inside, a dog barked hysterically. As the door opened Rigano insinuated himself into the gap to block the view of the photographers at the end of the drive. Using his legs like a hockey goal-keeper he prevented an agitated fox-terrier taking off down the drive to attack the waiting press eager to snatch a picture of Rupert Crabtree's widow. Lindsay followed him into a long wide hallway. Rigano put his hand under Mrs Crabtree's arm and guided her through a door at the rear of the hall. The dog sniffed suspiciously at Lindsay, gave a low growl and scampered after them.

Lindsay glanced quickly around her. The occasional tables had genuine age, the carpet was dark brown and deep, the pictures on the wall were old, dark oils. This was money, and not *arriviste* money either. Nothing matched quite well enough for taste acquired in a job lot. Half of Lindsay felt envy, the other half contempt, but she didn't have time to analyse either emotion. She reached into her bag and switched on her tape recorder, then entered the room behind the other two.

She found herself in the dining room, its centrepiece a large rosewood drum table, big enough to seat eight people comfortably. Against one wall stood a long mahogany sideboard. The end of the room was almost completely taken up by large french windows which allowed plenty of light to glint off the silver candlesticks and rosebowl on the sideboard. On the walls hung attractive modern watercolours of cottage gardens. Lindsay took all this in and turned to the woman sitting at the table. Her pose was as stiff as the straight-backed chair she sat in. At her feet now lay the dog, who opened one eye from time to time to check that no one had moved significantly.

"Mrs Crabtree, this is Miss Lindsay Gordon. Miss Gordon's the writer I spoke to you about on the phone. She's to write a feature for *Newsday*. I give you my word, you can trust her. Don't be afraid to tell her about your husband," Rigano said.

Emma Crabtree looked up and surveyed them both. She looked as if she didn't have enough trust to go round, but she'd hand over what she had in the full expectation that it would be returned to her diminished. Her hair was carefully cut and styled, but she had not been persuaded either by husband or hairdresser to get rid of the grey that heavily streaked the original blonde. Her face showed the remnants of a beauty that had not been sustained by a strong bone structure once the skin had begun to sag and wrinkle. But the eyes were still lovely. They were large, hazel and full of life. They didn't look as if they had shed too many tears. The grief was all being carried by the hands, which worked continuously in the lap of a tweed skirt.

She didn't try to smile a welcome. She simply said in a dry voice, "Good afternoon, Miss Gordon."

Rigano looked slightly uncomfortable and quickly said, "I'll be on my way now. Thank you for your co-operation, Mrs Crabtree, I'll be in touch." He nodded to them both and backed out of the room.

Emma Crabtree glanced at Lindsay briefly, then turned her head slightly to stare through the windows. "I'm not altogether sure why I agreed to speak to you," she said. "But I suppose the superintendent knows best and if that's the only way to get rid of that rabble that's driving my neighbours to distraction, then so be it. At least you've not been hanging over my garden gate all day. Now, what do you want to know?"

Her words and her delivery cut the ground from under Lindsay's feet. All the standard approaches professing a spurious sympathy were rendered invalid by the widow's coolness. The journalist also sensed a degree of hostility that she would have to disarm before she could get much useful information. So she changed the tactics she had been working out in the car and settled on an equally cool approach. "How long had you been married?" she asked.

"Almost twenty-six years. We celebrated our silver wedding last May."

"You must have been looking forward to a lot more happy years, then?"

"If you say so."

"And you have two children, is that right?"

"Hardly children. Rosamund is twenty-four now and Simon is twenty-one."

"This must have come as an appalling shock to you all?" Lindsay felt clumsy and embarrassed, but the other woman's attitude was so negative that it was hard to find words that weren't leaden and awkward.

"In many ways, yes. When the police came to the door last night, I was shaken. Though the last thing that I would have expected was for Rupert to be bludgeoned to death taking Rex for his bedtime stroll."

"Were you alone when the police arrived with the news?"

She shook her head. "No. Simon was in. He'd been working earlier in the evening, he rents a friend's lock-up garage in Fordham. He's got all his computing equipment there. He's got his own computer software business, you know. He commutes on his motorbike so he can come and go as he pleases."

At last she was opening up. Lindsay gave a small sigh of relief. "So the first you knew anything was amiss was when the police came to the door?"

"Well, strictly speaking, it was just before they rang the bell. Rex started barking his head off. You see, the poor creature had obviously been frightened off by Rupert's attacker and he'd bolted and come home. He must have been sitting on the front doorstep. Of course, when he saw the police, he started barking. He's such a good watchdog."

"Yes, I'd noticed," Lindsay replied. "Forgive me, Mrs Crabtree, but something you said earlier seems to me to beg a lot of questions."

"Really? What was that?"

"It seemed to me that you implied that you're not entirely surprised that your husband was murdered. That someone should actively want him dead."

Mrs Crabtree's head turned sharply towards Lindsay. She looked her up and down as if seeing her properly for the first time. Her appraisal seemed to find something in Lindsay worth confiding in.

"My husband was a man who enjoyed the exercise of power over people," she said after a pause. "He loved to be in control even in matters of small degree. There was nothing that appealed to Rupert so much as being able to dictate to people, whether over their plea on a motoring offence or how they should live their entire lives.

"Even when shrouded in personal charm of the sort my husband had, it's not an endearing characteristic. Miss Gordon, a lot of people had good cause to resent him. Perhaps Rupert finally pushed someone too far . . ."

"Can you think of anyone in particular?" Lindsay asked coolly, suppressing the astonishment she felt at Mrs Crabtree's open admission but determined to cash in on it.

"The women at the peace camp, of course. He was determined not to give up the battle against them till every last one was removed. He didn't just regard it as a political pressure campaign. He saw it as his personal mission to fight them as individuals and as a group and wear them down. He was especially vindictive towards the one who broke his nose. He said he'd not be satisfied till she was in prison."

"How did you feel about that mission of your husband's? How did it affect you?" Lindsay probed.

Mrs Crabtree shrugged. "I thought he was doing the right thing to oppose the camp. Those women have no morals. They even bring their children to live in those shocking conditions. No self-respecting mother would do that. No, Rupert was right. The missiles are there for our protection, after all. And that peace camp is such an eyesore."

"Did it take up a lot of your husband's time?"

"A great deal. But it was a good cause, so I tried not to mind." Mrs Crabtree looked away and added, "He really cared about what he was doing."

"Was there anyone else who might have had a motive?"

"Oh, I don't know. I've no idea who might hold a professional grievance. But you should probably talk to William Mallard. He's the treasurer of Ratepayers Against Brownlow's Destruction. He and Rupert were in the throes of some sort of row over the group's finances. And he'd be able to tell you more about Rupert's relations with other people in the group. There was one man that Rupert got thrown out a few weeks ago. I don't know any details, I'm afraid. Does any of this help?"

"Oh yes, I need to get as full a picture as possible. Your husband was obviously a man who was very active in the community."

Emma Crabtree nodded. Lindsay thought she detected a certain cynicism in her smile. "He was indeed," she concurred. "One could scarcely be unaware of that. And for all his faults, Rupert did a lot for this area. He was very good at getting things done. He brooked no opposition. He was a very determined man, my husband. Life will be a lot quieter without him." For the first time, a note of regret had crept into her voice.

Lindsay brooded on what had been said. It seemed to her that it was now or never for the hard questions. "And did his forcefulness extend to his family life?" she pursued.

Mrs Crabtree flashed a shrewd glance at her. "In some ways," she replied cautiously. "He was determined the children shouldn't be spoilt, that they should prove themselves before getting any financial help from him. Rosamund had to spend three years slaving away in restaurants and hotel kitchens before he'd lend her enough to set up in business on her own. Then Simon wanted to set up this computer software company. But Rupert refused to lend him the capital he needed. Rupert insisted that he stay on at college and finish his accountancy qualifications. But Simon refused. Too like his father. He went ahead with his business idea, in spite of Rupert. But of course, without any capital, he hasn't got as far as he had hoped."

"Presumably, though, he'll inherit a share of his father's money now?" Lindsay pursued cautiously.

"More than enough for his business, yes. It'll soften the blow for him of losing his father. He's been very withdrawn since . . . since last night. He's struggling to pretend that life goes on, but I know that deep down he's in great pain."

Her defence of her son was cut off by the opening of the dining-room door. Lindsay was taken aback. She failed to see how anyone could have entered the house without the dog barking as it had when she and Rigano arrived. She half turned to weigh up the new arrival.

"I'm back, mother," he said brusquely. "Who's this?"

Simon Crabtree was a very tall young man. He had his father's dark curling hair and strong build, but the impression of forcefulness was contradicted by a full, soft mouth. Lindsay suddenly understood just why Emma Crabtree was so swift to come to his defence.

"Hello, darling," she said. "This is Miss Gordon. She's a journalist. Superintendent Rigano brought her. We're hoping that now all the other journalists will leave us alone."

He smiled, and Lindsay realised that he had also inherited his slice of Rupert's charm. "That bunch? They'll go as soon as they've got another sensation to play with," he said cynically. "There was no need to invite one in, mother." He turned to Lindsay and added, "I hope you've not been hassling my mother. That's the last thing she needs after a shock like this."

"I realise that. I wanted to know a bit about your father. I'm writing a magazine feature about the camp, and your father played an important role that should be recognised. I need to talk to everyone who's involved and your mother kindly agreed to give me some time. In return, I've promised to get rid of the mob at your gate. A few quotes should persuade them to leave," Lindsay replied, conciliatory.

"You'd be better employed talking to those women at the peace camp. That way you'd get an interview with my father's murderer, since the police don't seem to be in any hurry to arrest her."

"I'm not sure I understand what you mean," Lindsay said.

"It's obvious, isn't it? One of those so-called peace women had already assaulted my father. It doesn't take much intelligence to work it out from there, does it?" Lindsay wondered if it was grief that made him appear so brusque.

"I can understand why you feel like that," she sympathised. "I'm sure your father's death has upset you. But at least now you'll be able to afford to set up your business properly. That will be a kind of tribute in a way, won't it?"

He shot a shrewd look at Lindsay. "The business is already set up. It's going to be successful anyway. All this means is that I can do things a bit quicker. That's all. My father's death means more to me than a bloody business opportunity. Mother, I don't know why you brought this up." Turning back to Lindsay he added. "I'm going to have to ask you to leave now. My mother is too tired to deal with more questioning." He looked expectantly at his mother.

The conditioned reflex built up over the years of marriage to Rupert Crabtree came into play. Simon had come into his inheritance in more ways than one. "Yes," she said, "I think I've told you all I can, Miss Gordon. If you don't mind."

Lindsay got to her feet "I'd like to have a few words with your daughter, Mrs Crabtree. When will she be home?"

"She doesn't live here any more. We're not expecting her till the funeral," Simon interjected abruptly. "I'll show you out now." He opened the door and held it open. Lindsay took the hint and thanked the widow routinely.

In the hall, with the door closed behind them, Lindsay tried again. "Your father's death has obviously upset you. You must have cared for him very deeply."

His face remained impassive. "Is that what you've been asking my mother about? Oh well, I suppose it's what the masses want to read with their cornflakes. You can tell your readers that anyone who knew my father will realise how deeply upset we all are and what a gap he has left in our lives. Okay?" He opened the front door and all but shoved her through it. "I'm sure you've already got enough to fabricate a good story," was his parting shot as he closed the door behind her.

She flipped open her bag, switched off the tape recorder and headed off down the drive to offer a couple of minor tit-bits to her rivals.

7

Bill Bryman had offered to drive Lindsay the mile back to the peace camp principally because he thought he might be able to prise more information from her than the bare quotes she had handed out to the pack. He was out of luck. Neither gratitude nor friendship would make Lindsay part with those pearls she had that were printable. But as she left the Crabtrees' house, she noticed that the Special Branch man with the red Fiesta was back, which added indefinably to her eagerness to leave the scene. So she had frankly used Bill's car as a getaway vehicle to escape her colleagues and any watching eyes. As soon as he pulled up near the van, she was off. There was hardly a sign of life at the camp, and she realised a meeting must be in progress. Clever Cordelia, she thought.

She struggled through the mud in her high heels to Cordelia's car and retrieved her other clothes. Back at the van, she changed into jeans and a sweater then set off jogging down the road towards the phone box on the main road, in the opposite direction to Brownlow Common Cottages. She had deliberately chosen the further of the two boxes in the neighbourhood to avoid being overheard by any fellow journalists hanging around waiting to talk to their offices. To her relief the box was empty. She rang the police at Fordham to check that there were no new developments, then got through to the *Clarion*'s copy room. She dictated a heavily edited account of her interview with Emma and Simon Crabtree, coupled with an update on the case.

When she was transferred to the newsdesk, Duncan's voice reverberated in her ear. "Hello, Lindsay. What've you got for me?"

"An exclusive chat with the grieving widow and son," she replied. "Nobody else got near them, but I had to give a couple of quotes to the pack in exchange for the exclusive. You'll see them from the agency wire services, probably. Nothing of any importance. Any queries on the feature copy I did earlier?"

"No queries, kid. Your copy has just come up on screen and it looks okay. Any progress on the exclusive chat with the bird who broke his nose?"

Lindsay fumed quietly. How much did the bastard want? "Hey, Duncan, did you know that women get called birds because they keep picking up worms? I doubt if I'll get anything for tonight's paper on that. The woman concerned is still a bit twitchy, you know? First thing tomorrow, though. I'll file it before conference. And I've got another possible angle for tomorrow if the lawyers won't let us use the interview. Apparently there were one or two wee problems with Crabtree's ratepayers' association. Possible financial shenanigans. I'm going to take a look at that, okay?" Lindsay couldn't believe she was taking control of the conversation and the assignment, but it was actually happening.

"Fine," Duncan acknowledged. "You're the man on the spot, that sounds all right to me. Stick with it, kid. Speak to me in the morning." The line went dead. Man on the spot, indeed. She made a face at the phone and set off at a leisurely pace to the camp.

As the benders came into sight, she saw that things were no longer quite so quiet. Outside the meeting tent were several figures. As she got closer, Lindsay could distinguish Cordelia, Jane, Deborah, Nicky and a couple of other women. There seemed to be an argument in progress, judging by the gestures and postures of the group. Lindsay quickened her pace.

"Lindsay!" Jane exclaimed. "Thank goodness you're here. Maybe you can sort this mess out."

Cordelia interrupted angrily. "Look, Jane, I've said already, there's nothing *to* sort out. Just count me out in future."

"Look, just calm down, all of you," soothed Deborah. "Everybody's taking this all so personally. It's not any sort of personality thing. It's about the principle of trust and not reneging on the people you've entrusted something to. You know?"

"Are you saying I'm not to be trusted?" Cordelia flashed back.

"Personally, I don't think either of you are," Nicky muttered.

"It's really nothing to do with you, Cordelia," Jane replied in brisk tones. "The women find it very hard to trust people they see as outsiders and they used up all their available goodwill on Lindsay."

Exasperated, Lindsay demanded, "Will someone please tell me what the hell is going on?"

The others looked at each other, uncertain. Cordelia snorted. "Typical," she muttered. "Everything by committee. Look, Lindsay, it's pretty simple. You asked me to sort out the alibis for you and your pet policeman. I figured the quickest and most logical way to do it was get everyone together. So I got Jane to call a meeting. Which eventually got itself together only to decide that I wasn't right-on enough for them to co-operate with. So I upped and left, which is where you find us now."

Lindsay sighed. Jane said with no trace of defensiveness, "I think that's a bit loaded, Cordelia. The women didn't like someone they perceive as an outsider calling a meeting and making demands. We had enough difficulties getting agreement on asking Lindsay for help. Maybe you could have been a bit less heavy. I still think they'll be okay if you both explain to them why we need the information to protect ourselves and to protect Deborah. Right now, it's seen as being simply a case of us doing the police's job for them and exposing ourselves to groundless suspicion."

Cordelia scowled. "You can do all the explaining you want, but you can leave me out of the negotiations. I've had it. I'm going back to London," she said, and stalked off towards her car.

"How childish can you get?" Nicky asked airily of no one in particular.

"Shut it," Lindsay snarled. "Why the hell did nobody help her? Debs, could you and Jane please go and talk them down in there? I want a word with Cordelia before she goes. I'll be back as soon as I can." She ran off in Cordelia's wake and caught up with her before she could reach the car.

Lindsay grabbed her arm, but Cordelia wriggled free. Lindsay caught up again and shouted desperately, "Wait a minute, will you?"

Cordelia stopped, head held high. "What for?"

"Don't take off like this," Lindsay pleaded. "I don't want you to go. I need you here. I need your help. It's perfectly bloody trying to deal with this situation alone. I've got to have a foot in both camps. Nobody really trusts me either; you know I'm just the lesser of two evils, both for the women and for the police. Don't leave me isolated like this."

Cordelia continued to stare at the ground. "You're not isolated, Lindsay. If you go into that meeting, you won't be humiliated like I was. It's not enough with these women to have your heart in the right place. You've got to have the right credentials too. And my face just doesn't fit."

"It's not like that, Cordelia. Don't leave because there was one hassle between you." Lindsay reached out impulsively and pulled Cordelia close. "Don't leave me. Not now. I feel . . . I don't know, I feel I'm not safe without you here."

"That's absurd," Cordelia replied, her voice muffled by Lindsay's jacket. "Look, I'm going back to London to get stuck into some work. I'm not mad at you at all. I simply choose not to have to deal with these women solely on their terms. All right? Now don't forget, I want to know where you are and what you're doing, okay? I'm worried about you. This deal you've done with Rigano could get really dangerous. There are so many potential conflicts of interest—the women, the police, your paper. And you should know from experience that digging the dirt on murderers can be dangerous. Don't take any chances. Look, I think it will be easier for you to deal with the peace women if I'm not around. But if you really need me, give me a call and I'll come down and book myself into a hotel or something."

Lindsay nodded and they hugged each other. Then Cordelia disengaged herself and climbed into the car. She revved the engine a couple of times and glided off down the road, leaving a spray of mud and a puff of white exhaust behind her. Lindsay watched till she was long gone, then turned to walk slowly back to the meeting tent.

She pushed aside the flap of polythene that served as a door and stood listening to Deborah doing for her what someone with a bit of sense and sensitivity should have done for Cordelia. Deborah finally wound up, saying, "We've got nothing to hide here. We asked Lindsay to help us prove that. Well, she can't do it all by herself. When she asks us for help, or sends someone else for that help, we should forget maybe that we have some principles that can't be broken or suspicions we won't let go, or else we're as bad as the ones on the other side of that wire."

Lindsay looked round. The area was crowded with women and several small children. The assortment of clothes and hairstyles was a bewildering assault on the senses. The warm steamy air smelled of bodies and tobacco smoke. The first woman to speak this time was an Irish woman; Lindsay thought her name was Nuala.

"I think Deborah's right," she said in her soft voice. "I think we were unfair the way we spoke before. Just because someone broke the conventions of the camp was no reason for us to be hostile and if we can't be flexible enough to let an outsider come in and work with us, then heaven help us when we get to the real fight about the missiles. Let's not forget why we're really here. I don't mind telling Lindsay everything I know about this murder. I was in my bender with Siobhan and Marieke from about ten o'clock onwards. We were all writing letters till about twelve, then we went to sleep."

That opened the floodgates. Most of the women accepted the logic of Nuala's words, and those who didn't were shamed into a reluctant co-operation. For the next couple of hours, Lindsay was engaged in scribbling down the movements of the forty-seven women who had stayed at the camp the night before. Glancing through it superficially, it seemed that all but a handful were accounted for at the crucial time. One of that handful was Deborah who had gone on alone to the van while Lindsay talked to Jane. No one had seen her after she left the sing-song in Willow's bender.

Trying not to think too much about the implications of that, Lindsay made her way back to the van. She looked at her watch for the first time in hours and was shocked to see it was almost eight o'clock. She dumped the alibi information then went down to the phone box yet again. She checked in with the office only to find there were no problems. She phoned Cordelia to find she had gone out for dinner leaving only the answering machine to talk to Lindsay. She left a message, then she checked in with Rigano.

"How is our deal progressing?" he asked at once.

"Very well. I'll have the alibi information collated by morning and I should have a fairly interesting tape transcribed for you by then. Tomorrow, I'm going to see William Mallard. Do I need your help to get in there?"

"I shouldn't think so. He's been giving interviews all day. The standard hypocrisy—greatly admired, much missed, stalwart of the association." She could picture the expression of distaste on his mouth and thought a small risk might be worth the taking.

"Any mention of the financial shenanigans?" she enquired.

"What financial shenanigans would they be, Miss Gordon?"

"Come, come, Superintendent. You live here, I'm just a visitor, after all. There must have been talk, surely."

"I heard they had a disagreement but that it had all been cleared up. The person you want to talk to in the first instance is not Mallard but a local farmer called Carlton Stanhope. He was thoroughly disenchanted with the pair of them."

"Do you think he'll play for an interview? That's just the sort of person I need to crack this," Lindsay said.

"I don't know. He's not as much of a stick-in-the-mud as a lot of them round here. He's been helpful to me already. He might be persuaded to talk to you off the record. Being outside his circle, he might tell you a bit more than he was prepared to tell a policeman. And, of course, you could pass that on to me, unofficially, couldn't you?"

"Any chance of you helping me persuade him?" In for a penny, thought Lindsay.

There was a silence on the other end of the phone. Lindsay crossed her fingers and prayed. Finally, Rigano spoke. "I'll ring him tonight and fix something up. I'm sure if I ask him, he'll give you all the help he can. Besides, he might even enjoy meeting a real journalist. How about half past ten tomorrow morning in the residents' lounge of the George Hotel in Fordham?"

"Superintendent Rigano, you could easily become a friend for life. That will do splendidly. I'll see you then."

"Oh, there won't be any need for me to be there. But I'll see you at ten o'clock in my office with the information you've gathered for me so far. Goodnight, Miss Gordon."

⚜

By the time she got back to the camp, Lindsay was exhausted and starving. She made her way to Jane's bender, where she found her deep in conversation with Nuala. Jane looked up, grinned at her and said, "Cara's with Josy's kids. Deborah's in the van cooking you some food. You look as if you could do with it too. Go on, go and eat. And get a good night's sleep, for God's sake. Doctor's orders!"

Lindsay walked back to the van, realising that she was beginning to find it hard to remember life outside the peace camp with real houses and all their pleasures. But the thought was driven from her head as soon as she opened the van door. The smell that greeted her transported her back into the past. "Bacon ribs and beans," she breathed.

Deborah looked up with a smile. "I got Judith to whizz me round Sainsbury's this morning. Cooking your favourite tea's about all I can do to thank you for all you've done."

"Wonderful," said Lindsay, "I'm starving. Is it ready now?"

Deborah stirred the pot and tried a bean for tenderness. "Not quite. About fifteen minutes."

"Good, just long enough for you to tell me your version of events on the night of the murder during the crucial time for which you have no alibi. Care to tell me exactly what you did?"

Deborah left the stove and sat down at the table. She looked tired. Lindsay took pity, went to the fridge and took out a couple of coolish cans of lager. Both women opened their beer and silently toasted each other. Then Deborah said, "I'm afraid you're not going to like this very much.

"After I left you, I came back to the van and made sure Cara was sleeping quietly. I was just about to brew up when I remembered I wanted to get hold of Robin. He's staying at my place just now. We did a deal. I said he could stay rent free if he did the plumbing for me. I've never been at my best with water. It's the only building job I always try to delegate. Anyway, I'd been thinking that I wanted him to plumb in a shower independent of the hot water system.

"So I thought I'd better let him know before he went any further and I decided to phone him."

Lindsay broke in. "But your house isn't on the phone."

"No. But if I want to get hold of Robin, I ring the Lees. They've got the farm at the end of the lane. They send a message up with the milk in the morning telling Rob to phone me at a particular time and number. It works quite well. So I went to the phone."

"Which box did you go to?"

"The wrong one from our point of view. The one nearer Brownlow Common Cottages."

"Will the Lees remember what time it was when you phoned?"

"Hardly. No one answered. They must have been out for the evening. So I just came straight back and made a brew."

"Did you see anything? Hear anything?"

"Not really. It was dark over by the perimeter fence anyway. I thought I might have seen Crabtree walking his dog, but it was quite a bit away, so I wasn't sure."

Lindsay sat musing. "Any cars pass you at all?"

"I don't remember any, but I doubt if I would have noticed. It's not exactly an unusual sight. People use these back lanes late at night to avoid risking the breathalyser."

Lindsay shrugged. "Oh, Debs, I don't know. I just can't seem to get a handle on this business."

Deborah smiled wanly. "You will, Lin, you will."

Later, fortified by a huge bowl of bacon and beans, Lindsay settled down to work. It took her over an hour to transcribe the tape, using her portable typewriter. Next came the even more tedious task of typing up her notes of the camp women's alibis. It was after midnight before she could put her typewriter into its case and concentrate again on Deborah, who was curled up in a corner devouring a new feminist novel.

"You look like a woman who needs a hug," said Deborah, looking up with a sympathetic smile.

"I feel like a woman who needs more than a hug," Lindsay replied, sitting down beside her. Deborah put her arms round Lindsay and gently massaged the taut muscles at the back of her neck.

"You need a massage," she said. "Would you like me to give you one?"

Lindsay nodded. "Please. Nobody has ever given me back rubs like you used to."

They made up the bed, then Lindsay stripped off and lay face down on the firm cushions. Deborah undressed and took a small bottle of massage oil from a cupboard. She rubbed the fragrant oil into her palms and started kneading Lindsay's stiff muscles.

Lindsay could feel warmth spreading through her body from head to foot as she relaxed.

"Better?" Deborah asked.

"Mmm," Lindsay replied. She had become aware of Deborah's body against hers. She rolled over and lightly stroked Deborah's side. "Thank you," she said, moving into a half-sitting position where she could kiss Deborah.

Deborah slid down beside her and their two bodies intertwined in an embrace that moved almost immediately from the platonic to the passionate, taking them both by surprise. "Are you sure about this, Lin?" Deborah whispered.

For reply, Lindsay kissed her again.

8

The morning found Lindsay in good humour as she breezed into the police station at Fordham. She had dived into the local Marks and Spencer and bought a new pair of smart mushroom coloured trousers and a cream and brown striped shirt that matched her brown jacket. She felt she looked her best and was on top of things professionally. The events of the night before were fresh in her memory, and for as long as she could put Cordelia out of her mind, she felt good about what had happened with Deborah too.

Her benign mood lasted for as long as it took her to reach the reception counter. At a desk at the back of the office she spotted a now familiar blond man flicking through some papers. Lindsay frowned as the SB man glanced up at her. Pressing the bell for service, she turned her back to wait. By the time the duty constable responded, the man had disappeared.

Rigano didn't keep her waiting. As soon as she sat down in his office, he attacked. "We've turned up a witness who saw Deborah Patterson walking down the road towards the camp at approximately ten forty-five."

"In that case, Deborah's statement won't come as a surprise to you," Lindsay retorted. "It's all here, Superintendent. Where she went, when and why." She put two files on the desk. "This one: the peace women. That one: Emma and Simon Crabtree."

He smiled coldly. "Thank you. It might have made things a little simpler if Miss Patterson had chosen to make her statement when she was here, don't you think?" Lindsay shrugged. "Anyway, I've spoken to Stanhope. He's expecting you in the George."

Lindsay deliberately lit a cigarette, ignoring the implicit dismissal. "Do you know where I can get hold of Rosamund Crabtree?" she enquired. "I didn't have the chance to get that information from Mrs Crabtree."

"Don't know why you want to see her," Rigano grumbled. "The way this case seems to be breaking, we're going to have to take another long hard look at Miss Patterson. But if you really feel it's necessary, you'll probably be able to catch up with her at work. She and a partner run this vegetarian restaurant in London. Camden Town. Rubyfruits, it's called."

"Rubyfruits?" Lindsay exclaimed. "Quick, ring Arthur Koestler."

He looked at her uncomprehendingly. "Funny sort of a name, eh?" he said.

"It isn't that, it's just the small-world syndrome striking again."

"You know it?"

Lindsay nodded. "Fairly well. We go there quite a lot."

"You surprise me. I wouldn't have put you down as one of the nut cutlet brigade. Anyway, you're going to be late for Carlton Stanhope, and I wouldn't recommend that. I'd like to hear how you get on. If you're free at lunchtime, I'll be in the snug at the Frog and Basset on the Brownlow road. Now run off and meet your man."

Lindsay got to her feet. "How will I recognise him?" she asked.

Rigano smiled. "Use your initiative. There won't be that many people in the residents' lounge at half past ten on a Tuesday morning, for starters. Besides, I've described you to him so I don't imagine there will be too many problems of identification."

Lindsay scowled. "Thanks," she muttered on her way to the door. "I'll probably see you later in the pub. Oh, and by the way, do tell your Special Branch bloodhound to stop following me around. I'm not about to do a runner." She congratulated herself on her smart response. She would remember that arrogance later.

⚬⚬⚬

Ripe for takeover by the big boys, thought Lindsay as she entered the George Hotel. The combination of the faded fifties decor and odd touches of contemporary tatt was an unhappy one. She could imagine the prawn cocktail and fillet steak menu. A neon sign that looked like a museum piece pointed up a flight of stairs to the residents' lounge. Lindsay pushed open the creaky swing door. The chairs looked cheap and uncomfortable. The only occupant of the room was pouring himself a cup of coffee. Lindsay's heart sank. So much for Rigano's assumption that they'd have the place to themselves, for the young man sprawled leggily in an armchair by the coffee table didn't look like a farmer called Carlton Stanhope.

He wore tight blue jeans, elastic-sided riding boots and an Aran sweater. His straight, dark blond hair was cut short at the sides, longer at the back, and had a floppy fringe that fell over his forehead from its side parting. He didn't look a day over twenty-five. He glanced over at Lindsay hesitating by the door and drawled, "Miss Gordon, do sit down and have a cup of coffee before it gets cold."

As he registered the surprise in her eyes, he smiled wickedly. "Not what you expected, eh? You thought a Fordham farmer called Carlton Stanhope who was a sidekick of Rupert Crabtree was bound to be a tweedy old foxhunter with a red face and a glass of Scotch in the fist, admit it! Sorry to disappoint you. Jack Rigano really should have warned you."

Lindsay's mouth wavered between a scowl and a smile. She sat down while Stanhope poured her a cup of coffee. "Do say something," he mocked. "Don't tell me I've taken your breath away?"

"I was surprised to see someone under fifty, I must say. Other than that, though, I can't say I'm greatly shocked and stunned. Don't all young gentlemen farmers dress like you these days?"

"*Touché*," he replied. "And since you're not what I expected of either a journalist or a peace woman, I'd say we're probably about quits. You see, Miss Gordon, we moderate men are just as much subject to stereotyping as you radical women."

Lindsay felt a hint of dislike in her response to him. She reckoned he knew himself to be a highly eligible young man; but she gave him credit for trying to build on his physical charm with an entertaining line in conversation. His manner irritated rather than appealed to her, but that didn't stop her acknowledging that it would normally find its admirers. "Superintendent Rigano seemed to think you might be able to fill me in on some background about Ratepayers Against Brownlow's Destruction."

"Jack says you're doing the investigative crime reporter bit over Rupert's death. He seems to think you're a useful sort of sleuth to have on his side, so I suppose I'm the quid pro quo," he observed.

"I appreciate the help," she responded. "I'm sure you've got more important things to be doing—drilling your barley or whatever it is farmers do in March."

"Lambing, actually. My pleasure, I assure you. Now, what exactly is it you want to know?"

"I'm interested in RABD. How did you come to get involved with it?" Lindsay asked. She found her cigarettes and offered Stanhope the packet. He dismissed it with a wave of his hand as he began his story.

"Let's see now . . . I got involved shortly after it was formed. That must have been about six or seven months ago, I guess. I hadn't been back in the area long. My father decided he wanted to bow out of the day-to-day hassle of running the farm, so he dragged me back from my job with the Forestry Commission to take over what will one day be mine. That is, what the bank and the taxman don't get their hands on.

"Anyway, to cut a long story short, I was appalled when I arrived back home and found these women camped on the common. I mean, Brownlow Common was always a place where people could walk their dogs, take their sprogs. But who'd actually want to take their offspring for a walk past that eyesore? All that polythene and earth-mother cooking pots and lesbians hugging each other at the drop of a hat or any other garment. Grotesque, for those of us who remember what a walk on the common used to be like.

"Also, say what you will about the Yanks, their base has brought an extraordinary degree of prosperity to Fordham. It's cushioned the local people against the worst excesses of the recession. And that's not something to be sneezed at."

He paused for breath, coffee and thought. Lindsay dived in. "Was it actually Rupert Crabtree who recruited you, then?"

"I don't know if recruit is quite the word. You make him sound like some spymaster. I was having dinner with my parents at the Old Coach restaurant, and Rupert was there with Emma—Mrs Crabtree, you know? Anyhow, they joined us for coffee and Emma was complaining about how ghastly it was to have this bloody camp right on the doorstep and Rupert was informing anyone who'd care to listen that he was going to do something about it and that anyone with any civic pride left would join this new organisation to get rid of the women at the camp for good and all."

Lindsay looked speculatively at the handsome, broad-shouldered young man. It would be nice to shake that self-assurance to its roots. But not today. "That sounds a bit heavy duty," she simply said.

"Oh no, nothing like that. No, RABD was all about operating within the law. We used the local press and poster and leaflet campaigns to mobilise public opinion against the camp. And of course, Rupert and a couple of other lawyers developed ways of harassing them through the courts using the by-laws and civil actions. And whenever they staged big demos, we'd aim to mount a token counter-demonstration, making sure the media knew."

"In other words, peaceful protest within the law?"

"Absolutely."

"Just like the peace women, in fact?" Avoiding Stanhope's glance Lindsay screwed out her cigarette in the ashtray. "So, tell me about the in-fighting at RABD."

He looked suddenly cautious. "We don't want all this to become public knowledge."

Lindsay shrugged. "It already is. All sorts of rumours are flying round," she exaggerated. "It's better to be open about these things, especially when the world's press is nosing about, otherwise people start reading all sorts of things into relatively minor matters. You don't want people to think you've got something to hide, do you?"

Stanhope picked up the coffee jug and gestured towards Lindsay's cup "More coffee?" He was buying time. When Lindsay declined the offer he poured coffee into his own cup. "It's not quite that simple, though, is it?" he demanded. "We're talking about a murder investigation. Something one would happily have gossiped about in a private sort of way last week can suddenly take on quite extraordinary connotations after a man has been murdered. I know I seem to take everything very lightly, but in fact I feel Rupert's death strongly. We didn't always see eye to eye—he could be bloody irritating, he was so arrogant at times—but he was basically an absolutely straight guy and that's something I find I have to respect. So I'm wary of pushing something he cared about into an area where it could become the subject of public scorn."

Lindsay groaned inwardly. Scruples were the last thing she needed. She had to get something out of Stanhope to provide a fresh lead for the next day's paper, at the very least. And she needed to get it fast, before Duncan could start screaming for copy on Debs. She had foolishly thought that an interview set up by Rigano, with all the force of his authority, would be an easy answer. She set about overcoming Stanhope's objections. It took less persuasion than she anticipated and she suspected he had simply put her through the hoops in order to salve his conscience. And she managed to elicit the useful information that he had been alone in the lambing shed at the time of the murder.

"There were two things that might interest you," he said. "One, a lot of people knew about. The other, only a handful of people. So, while I don't mind what you do about the first matter, I want to be left well out of anything to do with the second. Okay?"

Lindsay nodded. "Okay."

"I really don't want to be brought into this as your source. I mean it," he added.

"I said okay," Lindsay replied. "I'll cover your back."

He sighed. "The first concerns a man called Paul Warminster. He's local. He owns a couple of gents' outfitters in Fordham. He joined RABD shortly after I did and was always mouthing off against the women. He wasn't happy with the way our campaign was being run.

"He said we should take the fight into the enemy territory instead of simply reacting to them. He always speaks in that sort of jargon. I suspect he must have been in the Pay Corps or something like it in the war. He thought we should be actively banning them from shops, pubs, cinemas, the lot. He thought also that we should be harassing them in the town—insulting them, jostling them, generally making life hard for them.

"Rupert always managed to keep the lid on him till about a month or so ago. Paul stood against him in the election for chair and made the most scurrilous attack on him. He ended up by saying that Rupert was so wishy-washy that he was lucky the motorbike gangs weren't throwing pigs' blood on *his* house.

That, I'm afraid, was his big mistake. Our group has always utterly repudiated the thugs who terrorise the women at the camp. But I'd certainly heard mutterings that perhaps Paul wasn't as quick to condemn as one would expect, if you catch my drift. As I said, this was all common knowledge.

"Well, Rupert was duly re-elected with a thumping majority and he announced that since Paul's policies and attitudes had been so soundly defeated at the ballot box, it would seem there was no place for him within the group. It didn't actually leave Paul any option except resignation. So out he stormed, making sure we all knew he was right and Rupert was wrong. He didn't actually make any threats, but the inference was there to be taken."

"Okay, Mr Stanhope. And the second incident?"

"Call me Carl, please. I'm not old enough yet for Mr Stanhope." He radiated charm at her.

She felt like throwing up over his clean jeans. But she didn't even grind her teeth as she said, "Okay, Carl. The second incident?"

"Look, I really meant what I said about keeping my name out of this. If I thought you'd drop me in it I'd shut up now . . ."

"No, no," said Lindsay, "I'll forget you told me. Just give me the details."

"I was told this by someone I can't name. But I'm certain it's true, because it's referred to in the agenda for next week's meeting, though not in any detail that would make clear what it's about. William Mallard is the treasurer of RABD. He's a local estate agent. We're quite a wealthy organisation. We need to be because we try to fight civil court actions, which costs an arm and a leg. But we are a popular cause locally, and all our fund-raising is well supported by the locals. And we've had some financial donations from outside the area too."

"So at any given time, there's a few hundred in the kitty, is that what you're trying to say?" Lindsay interjected, frustrated.

"More like a few thousand," he said. "Rupert was a bit concerned that we weren't using our money properly—you know, that we should be keeping it in a high interest account instead of a current one. Mallard wouldn't agree. Now, being an awkward sort of bloke Rupert thought his reaction was decidedly iffy. So, armed with the latest treasurer's report, he zapped off to the bank and demanded a chat with the manager. The upshot was that instead of there being about seven thou in the account, as the report stated, there was barely five hundred.

"Rupert blew a fuse. He hared off to see Mallard and confront him. They apparently had a real up and downer. Mallard claimed he'd simply been doing what he always did with large lumps of money in his care, to wit, dumping them in high interest, seven-day accounts. But he couldn't show Rupert the money then and there. Rupert accused him of speculating with the RABD's money and pocketing the profits—Mallard's known for having a taste for the stock market, you see.

"Anyway, Rupert went off breathing fire. Next thing is, the following day, Mallard came to see Rupert, with evidence that the missing six and a half grand was all present and correct. But this didn't satisfy Rupert once he'd slept on it; he was baying for blood. He'd had time to think things through and realised that at some point Mallard must have forged Rupert's signature to shift the cash, since a cheque required both signatures. He told Mallard he was going to raise the matter at the next meeting and let the association decide who was in the wrong. Mallard was apparently fizzing with rage and threatening Rupert with everything from libel actions to—" He broke off, then stumbled on, "to you name it."

"Murder perhaps? Cosy little bunch, aren't you?" Lindsay remarked. "The wonder of it is that it's taken so long for someone to get murdered."

He looked puzzled. "I don't think that's quite fair," he protested.

"Life isn't fair," she retorted, getting to her feet. "At least, not for most people. Who's got the files now, by the way? I'll need to see them."

He shrugged. "Mallard, I guess."

"Could you call him and tell him Jack Rigano wants him to co-operate?" she asked.

"Look, I told you I didn't want to be connected with you on this," he protested.

"So tell him the request came from Rigano. Otherwise you've wasted your breath talking to me, haven't you?"

He nodded reluctantly. "Okay," he said.

Lindsay was at the door when he spoke again. "Jack says you'll be talking to a lot of people in Rupert's immediate circle?"

"That's right. It all helps to build up the picture."

"Will you be seeing his daughter Ros?"

Lindsay nodded. "I'm hoping to see her one evening this week," she replied.

"Will you say hello from me? Tell her I hope the business is going well and any time she's down home, she should give me a call and we'll have a drink for old times' sake."

"Sure, I didn't realise you knew Ros Crabtree."

"Everyone knows everyone else around here, you know. Ask Judith Rowe. Ros and I were sort of pals in the school holidays when we were growing up. You know the routine—horses, tennis club."

Lindsay grinned, remembering the summers of her youth fishing for prawns with her father in the thirty-foot boat that was his livelihood. "Not quite my routine, Carl, but yes, I know what you mean. Was she your girlfriend, then?"

He actually blushed. "Not really. We spent a lot of time together a few years ago, but it was never really serious. And then . . . well, Ros decided that, well, her interests lay in quite other directions, if you follow me?"

"I'm not entirely sure that I do."

"Well, it rather turned out that she seems to prefer women to men. Shame, really. I think that's partly why she moved away from home."

"You mean her parents were hostile about it?"

"Good God, no! They knew nothing about it. Rupert Crabtree would never have put up the money for her restaurant if he'd thought for one minute she was gay. He'd have killed her!"

9

"No, Duncan, I can't write anything about the RABD yet. I've only got one guy's word for it, and half of that's second-hand," Lindsay said in exasperation. "I should be able to harden up the ratepayers' routine by tomorrow lunchtime."

"That'll have to do then, I suppose," Duncan barked. "But see if you can tie it up today, okay? And keep close to the cops. Any sign of an arrest, I want to be the first to know. And don't forget that interview with the suspect woman. Keep ahead of the game, Lindsay."

The line went dead. Lindsay was grateful. The interview with Stanhope had produced more than she'd anticipated and she'd spent the rest of the morning trying to set up meetings with Mallard and Warminster. But neither could fit her in till the next day, which left her with a hole in the news editor's schedule to fill and nothing to fill it with except for the one interview she didn't want to capitalise on. The fact that she was no stranger to living on her wits didn't mean she had to enjoy it. The one thing she wasn't prepared to admit to herself yet was that the job was increasingly turning into something she couldn't square either with her conscience or her principles. After all, once she had acknowledged the tackiness of the world she loved working in, how could she justify her continued determination to take the money and run?

It was half past one by the time she reached the Frog and Basset, a real ale pub about two miles out of the town in the opposite direction to Brownlow. She pushed her way through the crowd of lunchtime drinkers into the tiny snug, which had a hand-lettered sign saying, "Private Meeting" on the door. The only inhabitant was Rigano, sitting at a converted sewing-machine table with the remains of a pint in front of him. He looked up at her. "Glad you could make it," he said. "I've got to be back at the station for two. Ring the bell on the bar if you want a drink. Mine's a pint of Basset Bitter."

Lindsay's eyebrows rose, but nevertheless she did as he said. The barman who emerged in response to her ring scuttled off and returned moments later with two crystal-clear pints. Lindsay paid and brought the drinks over in silence. Rigano picked up his and took a deep swallow. "So was Carlton Stanhope a help?"

Lindsay shrugged. "Interesting. There seems to have been something going on between Crabtree and the treasurer, Mallard."

Rigano shook his head. "Don't get too excited about that. It's only in bad detective novels that people get bumped off to avoid financial scandal and ruin."

Stung, Lindsay replied, "I'm not so sure about that. There are plenty of cases that make the papers where people have been murdered for next to nothing. It all depends how much the murderer feels they can bear to lose."

"And did Carlton Stanhope come up with anyone else that you think might have something to lose?"

Lindsay shrugged. "He mentioned someone called Warminster."

"A crank. Not really dangerous. All mouth and no action."

"Thanks. And have you got anything for me? I could do with a bone to throw to my boss."

Rigano took another deep swig of his beer. "There's not much I can say. We're not about to make an arrest, and we're pursuing various lines of enquiry."

"Oh come on, surely you can do better than that, What about CID? What are they doing? Who's in charge of that end of things?"

Rigano scowled, and Lindsay felt suddenly threatened. "I'm in charge," he answered grimly. "I'll keep my end of the deal, don't worry. I've set you up with Stanhope, haven't I? I gave you the whereabouts of the daughter, didn't I? So don't push your luck."

Frustrated, she drank her drink and smoked a cigarette in the silence between them. Then, abruptly, Rigano got to his feet, finishing his drink as he rose. "I've got to get back," he said. "The sooner I do, the nearer we'll be to sorting this business out. Keep me informed about how you're getting on." He slipped out of the snug. Lindsay left the remains of her drink, and drove back to the camp.

She parked the car and went to the van, which was empty. She put the kettle on, but before it boiled the driver's door opened and Deborah's head appeared. "Busy?" she asked.

Lindsay shook her head. "Not at all," she replied. "Actually, I was about to come looking for you. I need your help again."

Deborah made herself comfortable. "All you have to do is ask. Been on a shopping spree? I can't believe all these frightfully chic outfits came out of that little overnight bag."

"I had to find something to wear that makes me look like an efficient journo. Your average punter isn't too impressed with decrepit Levi's and sweatshirts. Anything doing that I've missed?"

"Judith is coming to see me at three o'clock."

Lindsay poured out their coffee and said, "Is it about the assault case?"

"That's right," Deborah confirmed. "She wants to explain exactly what the situation is. I think she's had some news today.

Or an opinion or something. Now, what was it you wanted from me? Nothing too shocking, I hope."

"I need you to have dinner with me tonight. In London."

Deborah looked surprised. "I thought Cordelia was in London? Doesn't she eat dinner any more?"

"For this particular dinner, I need you. We are going to a bijou vegetarian restaurant called Rubyfruits."

"You're taking me to a dykey-sounding place like that? On your own patch? And you're not worried about who you might run into? Whatever happened to keeping it light between us?"

Lindsay grimaced. "This is business, not pleasure. Rubyfruits is run by Ros Crabtree, our Rupert's daughter. The dyke that Daddy didn't know about, apparently. And I need you there to tell me if you saw anything of Ros or her partner around Brownlow recently. Okay?"

As Deborah agreed, Judith's car drew up outside.

She looked every inch the solicitor in a dark green tweed-mixture suit and a cream open-necked shirt. But behind the façade she was clearly bursting with a nugget of gossip that threatened to make her explode, and she was quite shrewd enough to realise that dumping it in Lindsay's lap was guaranteed to provide it with the most fertile ground possible.

"You look like the cat that's had the cream," Lindsay remarked.

"Sorry, terribly unprofessional of me. We solicitors are not supposed to show any emotion about anything, you know. But this is such a wonderful tale of dirty linen washing itself in public, I can't be all cool and collected about it. A wonderful piece of gossip and the best of it is that it's twenty-four carat truth. Now Lindsay, if you're going to use this, you certainly didn't get it from me, all right?"

Lindsay nodded, bored with yet another demand for anonymity. When she was a young trainee reporter, it had always made the adrenalin surge when people required to be Deep throats. But cynical experience of the insignificance of ninety per cent of people's revelations had ended that excitement years ago. Whatever Judith had to say might merit a few paragraphs. But she would wait and hear it before she let her pulse race.

"Rupert Crabtree's will is with one of the partners in the building next to ours. Anyway, the junior partner is by way of being a pal of mine and he's managed to cast an eye over the will. And you'll never guess who gets ten thousand pounds?"

Lindsay sighed. "Ros Crabtree? Simon?"

Judith shook her head impatiently. "No, no. They each get one third of the residue, about fifty thousand each. No, the ten thousand goes to Alexandra Phillips. Now isn't that extraordinary?" She was clearly disappointed by the blank stares from her audience. "Oh Lindsay, you must know about Alexandra. You're supposed to be looking into Rupert Crabtree. Has no one told you about Alexandra? Lindsay, she was his mistress."

That last word won Judith all the reaction she could have wished. Lindsay sat bolt upright and spilt the remains of her coffee over the table. "His mistress?" she demanded. "Why the hell did nobody tell me he had a mistress?"

Judith shrugged. "I assumed you knew. It wasn't exactly common knowledge but I guess most of us lawyers had a notion it was going on. Anyway, I rather think it was cooling off, at least on Alexandra's side."

Lindsay counted to ten in her head. Then she said slowly and clearly, "Tell me everything you know about the affair, Judith. Tell me now."

Judith looked surprised and hurt at the intensity of Lindsay's tone. "Alexandra Phillips is about twenty-five. She's a solicitor with Hampson, Humphrey and Brundage in Fordham. She does all the dogsbody work, being the practice baby. She's a local girl, used to be friendly with Ros Crabtree, in fact. I know her through the job and also because she and Ros used to kick around with my younger sister Antonia. Anyway, Alexandra came back to Fordham about eighteen months ago and almost as soon as she got back, Rupert pounced. He asked her out to dinner at some intimate little *Good Food Guide* bistro that none of his cronies would be seen dead patronising. He spun the line that he wanted to give her the benefit of his experience and all that blah. And being more than a little impressionable, dear Alexandra fell for his line like an absolute mug. This much I know because she confided in me right at the start. I warned her not to be a bloody fool and to see him off sharpish, which earned me the cold shoulder and no more confidences.

"But I saw his car outside her flat on a few occasions and the will obviously indicates an ongoing situation. However, there's been a whisper of a rumour going round Antonia's crowd that Alexandra was looking for a way out. There was a very definite suggestion that she rather fancied another fish to fry. Sorry, no names. I did ask Antonia, but she's pretty sure that Alexandra hasn't spilled that to anyone."

"Great," said Lindsay, getting to her feet and pulling on her jacket. "Come on then, Judith."

Judith looked bewildered. "Where?"

"To wherever Alexandra hangs out. I want to talk to her, and the sooner the better before the rest of the world gets the same idea."

"But we can't just barge in on her without an appointment. And besides, I came here to talk to Deborah about her pending court case."

"Oh God," said Lindsay in exasperation. "Yes, of course. But after that we've just got to see Alexandra Phillips as soon as possible."

Judith, looking startled and apprehensive, rattled machine-gun sentences at Deborah. Following the demise of the sole prosecution witness, she told her, the police could offer no evidence against Deborah in the Crown Court and the case would therefore fall since she had made no admissions of guilt. It was unlikely that the police would be able to find an eye-witness at that late stage, particularly since they were pursuing that line of enquiry with something less than breathtaking vigour.

"Except in so far as it overlaps with the murder enquiry," Lindsay muttered nonchalantly.

"Thanks for the reassurance," Deborah remarked. "Why don't you two run off now and prevent the police from making too many mistakes about me?"

Judith rose hesitantly. "Are you sure this is a good idea? I mean, Alexandra is something of a friend, or at least a friend of the family. I can't imagine she's going to take too kindly to us barging in and demanding answers about Rupert . . ."

"Look at it this way." said Lindsay. "Events are conspiring to force Debs into Rigano's arms as the obvious and easy villain. Debs is your client. Therefore you'd be failing in your professional duty if you didn't explore every possible avenue to establish her innocence. Isn't that so?"

Judith nodded dubiously. "I suppose so," she conceded. "But it doesn't mean I feel any better about going through with it." Lindsay treated Judith to a hard stare. The solicitor pursed her lips and said, "Oh, come on then. If we go now, we'll probably catch her at the office. I think it would be easier from every point of view if we saw her there."

It took them nearly twenty minutes to reach Alexandra's office thanks to Judith's driving, rendered doubly appalling by her apprehensions about the approaching interview. Her nervousness grew in the fifteen minutes they spent in the waiting room of Hampson, Humphrey and Brundage while Alexandra dealt with her last client of the day. When they were eventually summoned by buzzer, Judith bolted into the office with Lindsay behind her. Barely bigger than a boxroom, Alexandra Phillips's office was dominated by filing cabinets and a standard-sized desk which looked enormous in the confined space.

Yet the surroundings did not diminish its occupant. Alexandra was stunning. Lindsay instantly envied Rupert Crabtree and despised herself for the reaction. The woman who rose to greet them, was, Lindsay estimated, about five foot nine tall. Her hair was a glossy blue-black, cut close to a fine-boned head dominated by almond-shaped luminous brown eyes. Her skin was a healthy glowing golden. Hardly the typical English rose, thought Lindsay. The clothes weren't what she expected either. Alexandra wore a black velvet dress, fitting across the bust, then flaring out to a full swirling skirt. She should have had all the assurance in the world, but it was painfully obvious that self-possession wasn't her long suit. There were black smudges under the eyes and she looked as if tears would be a relief. The exchange of greetings had been on the formal side, and Judith threw a pleading look at Lindsay, expecting her to take over from there.

Lindsay took pity and launched in on an explanation. "Judith has a client called Deborah Patterson." Alexandra's eyebrows flickered. "I can see the name means something to you. Debs is one of my oldest and closest friends and the way things are going at the moment it looks as if she's likely to stand accused of Rupert Crabtree's murder, which I can assure you she did not do. Judith and I are determined to see that the charge won't stick, which is why I'm sticking my nose in where it's not wanted."

Alexandra looked puzzled. "I don't actually understand either your status or what you want with me."

"I'm sorry," said Lindsay, "you do deserve a better explanation than that. I've no official status," she went on. "I'm a journalist. But as it happens my first concern with this business is not to get good stories but to make sure Debs stays free. I'm also co-operating to some degree with the police on behalf of the women at the peace camp. I find that people don't always want to tell things to the police in case too much emphasis gets placed on the wrong things and innocent people start to appear in a bad light. All I'm trying to do, if you like, is to act as a sort of filter. Anything you want kept within these four walls stays that way until I get the whole picture sorted out and I can be fairly sure of what's important and what isn't."

"It's called withholding evidence from the police in the circles I move in," Alexandra countered. "I still don't understand what brings you to me."

The last thing Lindsay wanted was to start putting pressure on the young solicitor, but it appeared that in spite of Alexandra's seeming vulnerability, that was what she was going to have to do. "Rupert Crabtree's will is going to be public knowledge soon. If the police haven't already been here, they will be. And so will reporters from every paper in the land. You can bet your bottom dollar they aren't going to be as polite as me. Now, you can try to stall everyone with this disingenuous routine, but eventually you'll get so sick of it you'll feel like murder.

"Or you can short-circuit a lot of the hassle by talking to me. I'll write a story that doesn't make you look like the Scarlet Woman of Fordham. You can go away for a few days till the fuss dies down. You'll be yesterday's news by then, if you've already talked once. And by talking frankly to me, you can maybe prevent a miscarriage of justice. Now, I know you had been having an affair with Rupert Crabtree for over a year, and I know you were trying to get out of that situation. Suppose you tell me the rest?"

Alexandra buried her head in her hands. When she lifted her face her eyes were glistening. "Nice to know who your friends are, Judith," she said bitterly.

"Judith has done the best thing she could for you by bringing me. She could have thrown you to the wolves for the sake of her client, but she did it decently." Lindsay said with a gentleness that was a sharp contrast to her previous aggression.

"You're not one of the wolves?"

"No way. I'm the pussy cat. Don't think Judith has betrayed you. There will be plenty of others happy to do that over the next few days."

Alexandra gave a shuddering sigh. "All right. Yes, I was Rupert's mistress. I'm not in the least ashamed of that."

"Tell me about him," Lindsay prompted.

Alexandra looked down at her desk top and spoke softly. "He was wonderful company, very witty, very warm. He was also a very generous lover. I know you might find it hard to believe that he was a gentle man if all you've heard is the popular mythology. But he was very different when he was with me. I think he found it refreshing to be with a woman who understood the intricacies of the job."

Lindsay prodded tentatively. "But still you wanted to end it. Why was that?"

Alexanda shrugged. "There seemed to be no future in it. He always made it clear that he would never leave his wife, that his domestic life was one he was not unhappy with. Well, I guess I felt that I wanted more from a long-term relationship than dinners in obscure restaurants and illicit meetings when he could fit them in. I loved him, no getting away from that, but I found I needed more from life. And just when I was at that low ebb, I fell in with someone I knew years ago, someone very different from Rupert, and I realised that with him I could have a relationship that held out a bit more hope for permanence."

"And you told Rupert it was all over?"

Alexandra smiled wryly. "It's easy to see you didn't know Rupert. He had a phenomenal temper. When he raged, he did it in style. No, I didn't tell him it was all over. What I did say was that I was going to have to start thinking about my long-term future. That one of these days I was going to want children, a full-time husband and father for them, and since Rupert wasn't able to fit the bill, we'd better face the fact that sooner or later I was going to need more."

"And what was his reaction to that?" Lindsay asked gently.

"He seemed really devastated. I was taken aback. I hadn't realised how deep I went with him. He asked me—he didn't beg or plead, he'd never forget himself that much—he asked me to reconsider my options. He said that recently everything he had put his trust in seemed to have failed him and he didn't want that to happen to us. He said he wanted time to reconsider his future in the light of what I'd said. That was on Saturday. Time's the one thing he never expected not to have. You know how I found out he was dead? I read it in the papers. I'd been sitting watching television while he was being murdered." Her voice cracked and she turned away from them.

Lindsay found it easy to summon up the set of emotions she'd feel if she read of Cordelia's death in her morning paper. She swallowed, then said, "I'm sorry to go on pushing you. But I need to know some more. Do you know what he meant when he said everything he'd trusted had failed him? What was he referring to?"

Alexandra blew her nose and wiped her eyes before she turned back towards them. "He said Simon had let him down. That he wasn't the son he wanted. He sounded very bitter, but wouldn't say what had provoked it. He seldom discussed family matters with me, though he did say a couple of weeks ago that he'd found something out about Ros that had upset him so much he was seriously considering taking his investment out of her restaurant. I asked him what it was because I've known Ros since we were kids, and I suspected he'd finally found out that she's a lesbian."

"You knew about that?"

"Of course. I was one of the first people she told. I've not seen much of her since then, because I felt really uncomfortable about it. But I'd never have uttered a word to Rupert about it. I knew what it would do to him. But I suspect that that was at the root of his anger against Ros.

"And he was terribly upset about the Ratepayers' Association. He'd discovered that the treasurer was up to something fishy with the money. Instead of there being a large amount, about seven thousand in the current account, there was barely five hundred pounds. Rupert confronted the treasurer with his discovery, and he couldn't account for the difference satisfactorily. Rupert was convinced he'd been using it to speculate in stocks and shares and line his own pockets. So he was bringing it up at the next meeting which I'm told would have been stormy, with Rupert baying for blood."

Suddenly her words tripped a connection lurking at the back of Lindsay's brain. The combination of a repeated phrase and a coincidence of figures clicked into place. "Carlton Stanhope," she said.

Alexandra looked horrified. "Who told you?" she demanded. "No one knew. I made sure no one knew. I wouldn't hurt Rupert like that. Who told you?"

Lindsay smiled ruefully. "You just did. You were unlucky, that's all. I had a talk with Carlton this morning. He told me the William Mallard story. The figures he gave me were identical to those you gave me, and figures are an area where people are notoriously inaccurate. Also, you used a couple of identical phrases. It had to be you who told him. And the only person you'd be likely to tell would be someone very close to you. By the way, I wouldn't bother trying to hide it from the police. I suspect they already know; it was they who pointed me in his direction as a source of good information on Rupert."

"If they question me, I'll tell them the truth," Alexandra said, in control of herself again. "But I don't want to discuss it with you. I've said more than enough to someone who has no business interfering."

Lindsay shrugged. "That's your decision. But there's one more thing I have to ask. It's really important. Was Rupert in the habit of carrying a gun?"

Alexandra looked bewildered. "A gun?" she demanded incredulously.

"I'm told, a high-standard double-nine point two two revolver, whatever that is. He was carrying it when he was killed."

Alexandra looked stunned. "But why? I don't understand. Do you mean he knew he was at risk?"

"It looks like it. Did you know he had a gun? I'm told it was registered to him. Perfectly in order."

Alexandra shook her head slowly. "I never saw him with a gun. My God, that's awful. He must have been so afraid. And yet he said nothing about it. Oh, poor, poor Rupert."

"I'm sorry you had to know," said Lindsay. "Look, if you change your mind and want to talk a bit more, you can always reach me through Judith," she added, moving towards the door.

"Oh, and by the way," she added as Judith rose to follow her, "when did you tell Carlton what Rupert had said about rethinking the future? Was it on Saturday night? Or was it Sunday morning?" She didn't wait for the answer she suspected would be a lie. The look of fear in Alexandra's eyes was answer enough.

10

Lindsay drove down the motorway at a speed that would have seemed tame in a modern high-performance car. In the soft-top sports car it was terrifying. Deborah was relieved that Lindsay's lecture on the current state of play was absorbing enough to occupy her brain. "So you see," Lindsay complained, "Alexandra has opened a completely new vista of possibilities. But the more I find out, the less I know. I don't think I'm really cut out for this sort of thing. I can't seem to make sense of any of it."

"That doesn't sound like you, Lin," Deborah said with a smile. "Just be logical about it. We now know there were a fair few people less than fond of Rupert. Let's run through them. Think out loud."

"Okay," Lindsay replied. "One: his son Simon. For reasons unknown, he was in bad odour. It sounds like more than his assertion of the right to independence by opening up his computer firm. But how much more, we don't know. Yet.

"Two: his daughter Ros. For some unspecified reason, Rupert was seriously considering disinvestment. Now that may or may not be an effective weapon in the war against apartheid, but it sure as hell must be a serious threat to a small restaurant just finding its feet. Hopefully tonight will answer our questions about Ros. But the middle classes being what they are, five will get you ten that Daddy's disenchantment with daughter was deviance of the dykey variety.

"Three: Emma Crabtree. Our Rupert marched off on Saturday to think about his future. What we don't know is whether he told Emma about Alexandra; whether he'd decided he wanted a divorce and whether that prospect would have delighted or dismayed a woman who isn't the most obviously grieving widow I've ever encountered. A lot of questions there.

"Four: Alexandra. She's scared of his temper, she's afraid that he's not going to let her go without a very unpleasant fight. And she's had enough of him, she wants Stanhope. Personally, I'm disinclined to suspect her, though she seems to have no alibi. She did genuinely seem too taken aback by the gun to be a real candidate." She paused to gather her thoughts.

"Go on," Deborah prompted.

"Five: Carlton Stanhope. Alexandra undoubtedly told him of Crabtree's reaction. He may have figured that making an enemy of as powerful a bastard as Crabtree was not a good move and that murder might even have been preferable. Or it may have been that he felt the one sure way of keeping Alexandra was to get rid of the opposition. Depends how badly he wants Alexandra. I have to say that the bias I feel in her favour operates in the opposite direction as far as he's concerned. I took a real dislike to him, and he's got no alibi either.

"And finally, our two prize beauties from RABD. Mallard might have thought, knowing what a fair man Crabtree was, that his speculations would die with his chairman. And Warminster sounds dotty enough to opt for violence as a means of securing his takeover of RABD. What do you think, Debs?"

Deborah thought for a moment. "You realise you haven't established opportunity for any of them?"

"That is a bit of a problem. I know the police have been pursuing their own enquiries. Maybe I can persuade Rigano that it's in the best interests of his investigation to swap that info for what I've got. Such as it is. Mind you, by the time I've flammed it up a bit, maybe he'll buy it as a fair exchange."

"You also left me off the list of suspects. I should be on it."

Lindsay laughed. "Even though you didn't do it?"

"You don't know that because of facts. You only know it because of history and because we're lovers again. Don't discount the theory that I might have seduced you in order to allay your suspicions and get you on the side of my defence. So I should be on that list till you prove I didn't do it."

Lindsay looked horrified. "You wouldn't!"

"I might have. If I were a different person."

"Okay," Lindsay conceded with a smile. "But I don't reckon that you had put Rupert Crabtree into such a state of fear that he was carrying a gun to protect himself. He must have been armed because he feared a murderous attack."

"Or because he intended to kill the person he was meeting."

Lindsay threw a quick glance at Deborah, caught off guard by this flash of bright logic. She forced herself to examine Deborah's fresh insight.

Eventually, she countered it, tentatively at first and then more assuredly as she reached the end of the motorway and followed the route to Camden Town. "You see," she concluded, "he didn't need to kill you. He was going to get all the revenge he needed in court."

Deborah pondered, then blew Lindsay's hypothesis into smithereens as they approached Rubyfruits. "Not necessarily," she said thoughtfully. "Everyone says he was a fair man. He also had a degree of respect for the law, being a solicitor. Now, supposing in the aftermath of the shock of the accident, he genuinely thought I had attacked him, and on the basis of that genuine belief he gave the statement to the police that triggered the whole thing off. In the interim, however, as time has passed, his recollection has become clearer and he's realised that he actually tripped over the dog's lead and I had nothing to do with it. Now, what are his options? He either withdraws his evidence

and becomes a laughing-stock as well as exposing himself to all
sorts of reprisals from a libel suit—"

"Slander," Lindsay interrupted absently.

"Okay, okay, slander suit, to being accused of wasting police
time, all thanks to me. Or he perjures himself, probably an
equally unthinkable option for a man like him. His self-esteem
is so wounded by this dilemma that he becomes unhinged and
decides to kill me in such a way that he can claim self-defence.
So he starts carrying the gun, biding his time till he gets me
alone. Think on that one, Lin. Now, we're here. Let's go eat."
And so saying, she jumped out of the car.

Lindsay caught up with her on the cobbled road outside the
restaurant which occupied the ground floor of a narrow, three-
storey brick building in a dimly lit side street near the trendy
Camden Lock complex of boutiques, restaurants and market
stalls. It stood between a typesetting company and a warehouse.
A red Ford Fiesta turned into the street and they both stepped
back to avoid it as it cruised past the restaurant. Lindsay grabbed
Deborah's arm. "As a theory, it's brilliant," she blurted out. "But
in human terms, it stinks. You didn't do it, Debs."

Deborah smiled broadly and said, "Just testing." She pushed
open the door and moved quickly into the restaurant to avoid
Lindsay's grasp. They were greeted by a young woman with
short blonde hair cut in a spiky crest.

"Hello, Lindsay," she said cheerfully. "I kept you a nice
table over in the corner."

"Thanks, Meg." They followed her, Lindsay saying, "This
is Debs, Meg. She's an old friend of mine."

"Hi Debs. Nice to meet you. Okay. Here's the menu, wine
list. Today's specials are on the blackboard, okay?" And she was
gone, moving swiftly from table to table, clearing and chatting
all the way to the swing doors leading into the kitchen.

Deborah looked around, taking in the stripped pine, the
moss green walls and ceiling and the huge photographs ranging
predictably from Virginia Woolf to Virginia Wade. She noticed

that the cutlery and crockery on each table was different and appeared to have come from junk shops and flea markets. The background music was Rickie Lee Jones turned low. The other tables were also occupied by women. "I can just see you and Cordelia here," Deborah commented. "Very designer dyke."

"Cut the crap and choose your grub," Lindsay ordered.

"Get you," muttered Deborah. They studied the menus and settled for Avocado Rubyfruits. ("Slices of ripe avocado interleaved with slices of succulent Sharon fruit, garnished with watercress, bathed in a raspberry vinaigrette") followed by Butter Beanfeast ("Butter beans braised with organically grown onions, green peppers and chives, smothered in a rich cheese sauce, topped with a *gratinée* of stoneground wholemeal breadcrumbs and traditional farm cheddar cheese") with choose-your-own salads from a wide range of the homely and the exotic colourfully displayed on a long narrow table at the rear of the room. To drink Lindsay selected a bottle of gooseberry champagne.

"My God," Deborah exploded quietly when Meg departed with the order, "I hadn't realised how far pretentiousness had penetrated the world of healthy eating. This is so over the top, Lin. Are there really enough right-on vegetarian women around to make this place a going concern?"

"Don't be too ready to slag it off. The food is actually terrific. Just relax and enjoy it," Lindsay pleaded.

Deborah shook her head in affectionate acceptance and sat back in her chair. "Now tell me," she demanded, "Since you hang out so much in this bijou dinette, how come you don't have the same intimate relationship with Ros Crabtree that you have with Meg?"

"It's very simple. Meg runs around serving at table. Meg answers the phone when you book. Meg stands and natters over your coffee. Ros, on the other hand, must be grafting away in the kitchen five nights a week. She's too busy cooking to socialise, even with people she knows. And by the end of the evening, I'd guess she's too exhausted to be bothered making polite social chit-chat with the customers. It's hard work cooking for vegetarians. There's so much more preparation in Butter Beanfeast than in Steak au Poivre."

Before Deborah could reply, their avocados appeared. Deborah tried her food suspiciously, then her face lit up. "Hey this is really good," she exclaimed.

When Meg returned to clear their plates and serve the champagne, Lindsay made her move.

"That was terrific, Meg. Listen, we'd like to have a word with Ros. Not right now, obviously, but when she's through in the kitchen. Do you think that'll be okay?"

Meg looked surprised. "I suppose so. But . . . what's it all about, Lindsay? Oh, wait a minute . . . You're a reporter, aren't you?" Her voice had developed a hostile edge. "It's about her father, isn't it?"

"It's not what you think," Deborah protested. "She's not some cheap hack out to do a hatchet job on you and Ros. You know her, for God's sake, she's one of us."

"So what *is* it all about then?" The anger in her voice transmitted itself to nearby tables, where a few faces looked up and studied them curiously.

Deborah took a deep breath. "I'm their number one suspect. I've already had one night in the police cells and I don't fancy another. Lindsay's trying her damnedest to get me off the hook and that means discovering the real killer. I'd have thought you and Ros would be interested in finding out who killed her father."

"Him? The only reason I'd want to know who killed him is so that I could shake them by the hand. Look, I'm not too impressed with what you've got to say for yourselves, but I will go ask Ros if she'll talk to you." She marched off and returned a few minutes later with their main courses, which she placed meticulously before them without a word.

They ate in virtual silence, their enjoyment dulled. Meg silently removed their plates and took their order for biscuits, cheese and coffee.

By half past ten and the third cup of coffee, Lindsay was beginning to despair of any further communication from the kitchen. The tension had dried up conversation between her and Deborah. The evening she'd been looking forward to had somehow become awkward and difficult. Then, a tall, broad woman emerged from the kitchen and exchanged a few words with Meg, who nodded in their direction. The woman crossed the room towards them. She was bulky, but she looked strong and sturdy rather than flabby. Her hair was short and curly, her face pink from the heat of the kitchen. Like her brother, Ros Crabtree strongly resembled their father. She wore a pair of chef's trousers and a navy blue polo shirt. In her hand was a brandy bowl with a large slug of spirit sobbing up the sides of the glass.

She pulled a chair up and said without preamble, "So this is the sleuth. The famous Cordelia Brown's girlfriend. Accompanied, unless I am mistaken, by the brutal peace woman who goes around beating up helpless men." She smiled generously. "Enjoy your dinner?"

"As always," Lindsay answered, stung by being defined as an adjunct to Cordelia.

"But tonight you came for more than three courses and a bottle of country wine."

"We hoped you would help us," Deborah stated baldly. "Lindsay's trying to clear my name. I'm afraid that if there isn't an arrest soon, I'll be charged, just so they can be seen to be achieving something."

"We also thought you would have an interest in seeing your father's killer arrested," Lindsay added.

Ros laughed. "Look, I have no feelings about my father one way or the other. I neither loved him nor hated him but I'm sorry about the way he died. I was glad to be out of his house but frankly, the notion of getting some atavistic revenge on the person who killed him leaves me unmoved. You're wasting your time here."

Lindsay shrugged. "So if it matters that little to you, why not talk to me, answer my questions? It could make a lot of difference to Debs."

"I can't think of anything I could tell you that would be of the slightest use. But I suppose I owe something to the woman who cost my father his precious dignity and a broken nose. Oh, the hell with it, ask what you want. If I feel like answering, I will." She swallowed a generous mouthful of brandy, seemingly relaxed.

"I'll ask the obvious question first. Where were you on Sunday night between ten p.m. and midnight?" Lindsay asked.

"Oh dear, oh dear, we have been reading all the snobbery with violence detective novels, haven't we?" The mockery in Ros's voice was still good-natured, but it was obvious that the veneer was wearing thin. "I was here on Sunday night. We have a flat above the restaurant. I think I was reading till about eleven. Then I went to bed and I was woken up just after midnight when my mother phoned to tell me about my father's death."

"I suppose Meg can back you up?"

"As it happens, no. Meg was on her way back from South-ampton. She'd been visiting her parents. She didn't get home till about half past midnight. So I don't have much of an alibi, do I? No one phoned till mother, I phoned no one. You'll just have to take my word for it." She grinned broadly.

"I'm surprised you didn't go down to Brownlow as soon as you heard the news. I mean, with your mother to comfort and all that . . . ?" Lindsay sounded offhand.

"Acting nonchalant cuts no ice with me, darling. I can spot the heavy questions without you signposting them. Why didn't I dash off home to Mummy? For one thing, I have a business to run. On Mondays, I go to the market and see what's look-ing good. On that basis I plan the special dishes for the week.

We also do all the bookkeeping and paperwork on Mondays. I simply couldn't just vanish for the day. It'll be hard enough fitting the funeral in. That's not as callous as it sounds. My father cared about this business too. But more importantly than all of that, I'm not at all sure I'd be the person to comfort my mother."

"Why's that?"

"Because I'm not the weepy, sentimental sort. I'm far too bloody brisk to be much of a shoulder to cry on. I'm afraid I'd be more inclined to tell her to pull herself together than to provide tea and sympathy."

"So it's nothing to do with her attitudes to you being a lesbian? Oh, but of course, they didn't know, did they? Or so Carlton Stanhope reckons. Mind you, I always figure that parents know a lot more than they let on," said Lindsay, her eyes on a distant corner of the room.

"You've talked to Carl?" Suddenly Ros had become guarded.

"He sends his best wishes. He's seeing Alexandra Phillips these days, you know," Lindsay replied.

"How nice for him. She used to be a lovely girl when I knew her. I hope she treats him better than I did. Poor Carl," she said ruefully. "But to go back to what he said to you. He was right, as far as he was aware. They really didn't know. I'd kept it well under wraps. Let me explain the history. After I'd decided my career lay in the catering trade, my father was always keen that I should set up in business on my own when I'd done the training and got the experience. Meg and I did a proper business plan based on the costings for this place and I presented it to him as a good investment. He lent me twenty thousand pounds at a nominal rate of interest so we could get the project off the ground. He'd never have done that much if he'd even suspected. I suppose my cover was never blown because I'd spent so much time studying and working away from home, and when I was home, there were always old friends like Carl around to provide protective colouring. It was really funny when we launched Rubyfruits—we had to have two opening nights. One with lots of straight friends that we could invite the parents to and another with the real clientele."

Lindsay lit a cigarette. "It sounds like you had a lot to be grateful to him for?"

Ros shrugged. "In some ways. But we were never really close. He was always at arm's length, somehow. With all of us. As if his real life happened somewhere else. The office, I suppose. Or one of his causes." The edge of bitterness in her voice was apparent even to Ros herself. She softened her tone and added, "But I guess I owe this place to him. I'm sorry he's dead."

"Then he didn't carry out his threat to take his money back?" Lindsay's casual words dropped into a sudden well of silence. Ros's face wouldn't have looked out of place on Easter Island.

"I have no idea what you're talking about," she declared. "No idea at all."

"I'm told that he'd recently become disillusioned with you, that he was minded to take his money out of this business as a token of his disappointment. You really should tell me about it in case I go away with the wrong idea. And you not having much of an alibi. My news editor would like that story a lot."

Ros stared hard at Lindsay. "Well, well," she muttered bitterly, "So much for lesbian solidarity. You're not the pushover I took you for, are you? Fancy me thinking that anyone who tagged along on Cordelia's coat-tails could be toothless. All right. Since you obviously know enough to make a bloody nuisance of yourself, I'd better tell you the rest.

"Ten days ago I had a phone call from my father. He informed me that he was instructing his bankers to recover the twenty thousand he'd lent me. He refused to say why, or even to say anything else. So I rang my mother to see if she knew what the hell was going on. And she wouldn't say either.

"So I jumped on the bike and bombed down to the old homestead where I squeezed out of Mamma what it was all about. To cut a long story short, it was all down to my perfectly bloody little brother. You know he's got this business in computer software? Well, he had to start it on a shoestring, against my father's advice. Father wanted different things for Simon, and that was the end of the story as far as he was concerned. He wouldn't even listen when one of Simon's teachers came to see him and told us that Simon was the best computer programmer he'd ever encountered. Apparently, he was hacking into other people's systems by the time he was in the third form. Anyway, Simon got off the ground somehow and he's at the stage now where it's make or break, expand or fold, and he needs an injection of cash. God knows where he got the money to get this far, but he was determined that the next chunk of capital should come from Father, on the basis that he'd lent me money for the business and it was only right that he should do the same for Simon.

"Dad refused absolutely. He said I'd proved myself, which Simon still had to do before he could come chasing around for hard-earned handouts. Mum said they were going at it hammer and tongs then Simon blew a fuse and said something along the lines of how appalling it was that Father was prepared to finance a pair of lesbians running a restaurant for queers and he wouldn't finance his only son in a legitimate business. Mum says there was a ghastly silence then Simon walked out. Father apparently wouldn't say a thing, just went off in the car. She thinks he came up here to see for himself. And the next day—bombshell."

"I thought it must have been something like that," Lindsay said. "So I suppose that put you right in the cart."

"Until the death of my father, that's what you're getting at, isn't it? Not quite that easy, I'm afraid. You see, we've been doing better than we projected. It knocked some of our personal plans on the head, like new furniture for the flat, but we've simply transferred to a bank loan. We can just afford the extra interest. Any money from my father's will, unless he's cut me out of that too, will be an absolute godsend, there's no getting away from that. But we could have managed without it. I had no need to kill him. Now, you've got what you came for. Is there anything else before I get you the bill?"

"Just one thing. Any idea why your father was carrying a gun?"

"Carrying a gun? I knew nothing about that. No one said anything to me about a gun!"

"The police are trying to keep it fairly quiet. A point two two revolver."

"I can't begin to think why he had his gun with him. He used to be a member of a small-arms shooting club at Middle Walberley. But he hadn't been for . . . oh God, it must be eight years. He gave it up because he didn't have time enough for practising and he could never bear to do anything unless he did it to perfection. I didn't even know he'd kept his gun. I can't believe he had enemies—I mean, not the sort you'd have to arm yourself against. Wow, that really is weird." For the first time, she looked upset. "Somebody must have really got to him. That's horrible." She swallowed the remains of her brandy and got to her feet. "I'll get Meg to bring your bill." She vanished through the swing door at the back of the restaurant followed by Meg, whose eyes had never left them during the interview.

Lindsay rubbed her forehead with her fingertips. Deborah reached out and took her hand. Before they could speak, Meg re-emerged from the kitchen and strode over to them. By now, they were the centre of attention for the few diners remaining. "Have this meal on me," Meg said angrily. "Just so long as you don't come back here again. Now go. I mean it, Lindsay. Just get out!"

11

The head office of Mallard and Martin, Estate Agents, Auctioneers and Valuers, was at the far end of the main street in Fordham. The retail developers who have turned every British high street into undistinguished and indistinguishable shopping malls had not yet penetrated that far down the street, and the double-fronted office looked old-fashioned enough to appeal to the most conservative in the district. Lindsay, dressed to match the office in her new outfit, studied the properties in the window with curiosity. She noticed several houses in the vicinity of Brownlow Common were up for sale. But their prices didn't seem to be significantly lower than comparable houses in other areas. She pushed open the door and as she entered, a sleek young woman in a fashionably sharp suit rose and came over to the high wooden counter.

"Can I help you?" she enquired.

"I'm due to see Mr Mallard," Lindsay explained. "My name's Lindsay Gordon."

"Oh yes, he's expecting you. Do come through." The woman raised a flap in the counter and showed Lindsay through into Mallard's own office. He got up as Lindsay was ushered in and genially indicated a chair. Mallard was a short, chubby man in his fifties, almost completely bald. He wore large, gold-rimmed spectacles and tufts of grey hair stuck out above his ears, making him look like a rather cherubic owl. He smiled winningly at Lindsay. "Now, young lady," he said cheerfully, "you're a reporter, I think you said?"

"That's right. But I'm not just looking for stories. I believe Carlton Stanhope rang to pass on Superintendent Rigano's request?"

"He did indeed." He smiled. "Always delighted to help an attractive young lady like yourself. Mr Stanhope tells me you've been able to give the police some assistance concerning dear Rupert's death? A dreadful tragedy, quite, quite dreadful."

Lindsay decided she did not care for this bouncing chauvinist piglet. But his seeming garrulity might be something she could turn to her advantage. She smiled at him. "Absolutely. I have been able to come up with some quite useful information so far. And of course, not all of it is passed directly to the police. I mean, a lot emerges in these affairs that has no bearing on the main issue. It would be a pity to cloud matters with irrelevant information, wouldn't it? So if people are open with me, I can often get to the bottom of things that would otherwise cause a lot of wasted police time. If you see what I mean?" She let the question hang in the air.

"So you want to find out how well I knew Rupert, who his friends were, if he made enemies through RABD, that sort of thing? That's what Mr Stanhope said," Mallard replied hastily.

"Not exactly," Lindsay replied. "Though I would like to look through the RABD records. I think Mr Stanhope arranged that with you?"

Mallard nodded vigorously. "They're all upstairs in a little office I put at the disposal of the organisation. You can take as long as you want, you'll have the place to yourself. We've got nothing to hide, you know, though obviously we don't want our future plans made public. That would put an end to our strategies against those . . . those harpies down there," he said, his geniality slipping as he referred to the peace women.

"I rather thought there were one or two matters you'd prefer to keep to yourself, Mr Mallard," Lindsay remarked idly.

"No, no, we're not at all secretive. We're perfectly open, no conspiracies here."

An odd thing to say, Lindsay thought. "No conspiracies, perhaps, but one or two disagreements."

"Disagreements?" He looked apprehensive.

"Paul Warminster?"

"Oh, that," he muttered, looking uncomfortable. "Yes, that was a little unfortunate. But then, it only supports what I was saying to you about being open. We're not extremists in RABD, just people concerned about our local community and the environment our families live in. We don't want to be involved in anything at all violent. That's what Paul Warminster felt we should be doing. He wanted us to be some kind of vigilante band, driving these awful women away by force. We were glad Rupert had the strength to stand up to him. That sort of woman isn't going to go away because you throw them out physically. If we'd gone ahead and taken violent action, the next day there would have been twice as many of them. No, Rupert was right."

"And do you think Paul Warminster resented what he did?"

"No question about that, young lady. He was furious."

"Furious enough for murder?"

Mallard's smile this time was sickly. "I'm sure nobody in our circle, not even someone with Paul Warminster's views, would resort to murder." He made it sound like a social solecism.

"But someone in Rupert Crabtree's circle did just that."

Mallard shook his head. "No. Those women are to blame. It certainly wasn't Paul Warminster. He had nothing to gain. Even with Rupert out of the way, he'll never win control of RABD and its membership. He must know that. He's not a fool."

"I'm happy to take your word for it," Lindsay flattered. "Now, if I might see those papers?" She got to her feet.

"Of course, of course," he said, rising and bustling her out of the room. They climbed two flights of stairs, Mallard chatting continuously about the property market and the deplorable effect the peace camp was having on house prices in the neighbourhood of the common.

"But houses at Brownlow seem about the same price as similar houses near by," Lindsay commented.

"Oh yes, but they used to be the most highly sought after in the area, and the most expensive. Now it takes a lot of persuasion to shift them. Well, here we are."

They entered a small office containing a battered desk, several upright chairs and a filing cabinet. "Here you are, m'dear." Mallard waved vaguely around him. He unlocked the filing cabinet. "Chairman's files and my files in the top drawers. Minutes in the second. Correspondence in the third and stationery in the bottom drawer. Look at anything you please, we've no guilty secrets."

"Will you be in your office for a while? I might come across some things I want to clarify."

"Of course, of course. I shall be there till half past twelve. I'm sure you'll be finished by then. I'm at your disposal." He twinkled another seemingly sincere smile at her and vanished downstairs.

Lindsay sighed deeply and extracted two bulging manila folders from the top drawer of the filing cabinet. They were both labelled "Ratepayers Against Brownlow's Destruction. Chairman's File." In red pen, the same hand had written "1" and "2" on them. She sat down at the desk and opened her briefcase. She took out a large notepad, pen and her Walkman. She slotted in a Django Reinhardt tape and started to plough through the papers.

The first file yielded nothing that Lindsay could see. She stuffed the papers back into it and opened the second file. As she pulled the documents out, a cassette tape clattered on to the desk. Curious, she picked it up. The handwritten label, not in

Crabtree's by now familiar script, said, "Sting: *The Dream of the Blue Turtles*." Surprised, Lindsay put it to one side and carried on working. When her own tape reached the end, she decided to have a change and inserted the Sting tape. But instead of the familiar opening chords she heard an alien sequence of hisses, bleeps and sounds like radio interference. Lindsay knew very little about information technology. But she knew enough to realise that although this tape was mislabelled, it was actually a computer programme on tape. And fed into the right computer, it might explain precisely what it was doing in Rupert Crabtree's RABD file. She remembered the computers she had seen downstairs and wondered if that was where Mallard stored the real information about RABD's finances.

She worked her way quickly through the financial records, making a few notes as she went. It seemed to be in order, though the book-keeping system seemed unnecessarily complex. Finally she skimmed through the minutes and correspondence. "Waste of bloody time," she muttered to herself as she neatly replaced everything. The cassette tape caught her eye, and she wondered again if it might hold the key to the questions Crabtree had been asking about money. She threw the computer tape into her briefcase along with her own bits and pieces and headed downstairs for the confrontation she'd been geared up to since breakfast. As she rounded the corner of the stairs, she noticed a man coming out of Mallard's office. From above, she could see little except the top of his head of greying, gingery hair and the shoulders of his tweed jacket. By the time she reached the bottom of the stairs, he had gone.

Mallard's office door was ajar and she stuck her head round. "Can I come in?" she asked.

"Of course, of course, m'dear," he answered her, beaming. "I expect you've had a very boring morning with our papers."

"It has been hard work," Lindsay admitted. "I'm surprised you haven't got the lot on computer, with Simon Crabtree being in that line of business."

Mallard nodded. "Couldn't agree more, m'dear. But Rupert wouldn't hear of it. Lawyers, you see. Very conservative in their methods. Not like us. Our front office may look very traditional. But all the work gets done in the big office at the back—where our computers are. The latest thing—IBM-compatible hard-disk drives. I actually bought them on Simon's advice. But Rupert didn't trust them. He said you could lose all your work at the touch of a button and he felt happier with bits of paper that didn't vanish into thin air. Typical lawyer—wanted everything in black and white."

"There was one other thing I wanted to ask you about."

"Ask away, m'dear, ask away."

"Why was Rupert Crabtree going to raise your handling of RABD funds at the next meeting?"

Mallard flushed, but managed to freeze his smile in place as he replied, "Was he?"

"You know he was. The two of you had a row about it, and he said the association should decide."

"I don't know where you've got your information from, young lady, but I can assure you nothing of the sort took place." Mallard attempted to stand on his dignity. "We had a very harmonious relationship."

"Not according to my sources. Two separate people have told me the whole story, and I believe the police are aware of it. I already have enough to write a story. It's obviously doing the rounds locally. Hadn't you better put the record straight, give me your version of events before your reputation gets shredded beyond repair?"

He dropped the geniality and looked shrewdly at Lindsay. "Young lady, even if *you* seem blissfully unaware, I'm sure your newspaper has lawyers who understand all about libel. If you are thinking of printing any sort of story about me, you had better be extremely careful."

"We don't have to print a story about you for your reputation to be destroyed. Local gossip will see to that. All I have to write is that police are investigating alleged misappropriation of funds by one of the officials of a local organisation in connection with Rupert Crabtree's death," Lindsay replied.

Mallard paused, sizing her up. Then, after a long enough pause to render himself unconvincing, he smiled again and said, "Really, there's no need for all of this. I've told you that we've got nothing to hide in RABD. That goes for me personally too. Now, you've obviously heard some grossly distorted version of a conversation between Rupert and me. There's no reason on earth why I should attempt to explain to you, but because I'm concerned there should be no misunderstanding, I'll tell you all about it.

"We hold a substantial amount of money on behalf of our members. Most of it is for legal expenses and printing costs. As treasurer, I'm responsible for the money, and I know how important it is these days to make money work. Obviously, the more money we have, the better able we are to fight the good fight. Now, Rupert was checking something on the bank statements and he realised there was far less in the account than he thought there should be. He was always prone to jump to conclusions, so he came round here in a great taking-on, demanding to know where the money was. I explained that I had moved it into the currency markets, an area I know rather a lot about. I was simply maximising our returns. Rupert was perfectly satisfied with my explanation. And so he should have been since I had succeeded in making a substantial profit."

"Then why was he raising the matter at the next meeting?"

"Why? So that I could pass on the good news to the membership, of course. Rupert felt it was a matter for congratulation, m'dear."

His glibness lowered his credibility still further in Lindsay's eyes. She was determined to get him on the run, and she racked her brains to find some leverage in what Stanhope or Alexandra had said. "But how did you move the money without Crabtree's knowledge? Surely that needed his signature?"

A momentary gleam of hatred flashed at Lindsay. "Of course, of course, my dear girl. But Rupert had actually signed it among a pile of other papers for his signature and had simply not registered what it was. Easy to do that when you're signing several bits of paper."

"I wouldn't have thought that was the action of a conscientious lawyer. But you seem to have an answer for everything, Mr Mallard."

His smile was genuine this time. "That's because I have nothing to hide, m'dear. Now, if that is all, I do have work to do . . ."

"One more thing. Since you've nothing to hide, perhaps you could tell me where you were on Sunday night from about ten?"

This time, Mallard couldn't keep the smile in place. "That's none of your business," he snapped.

"You're right. But I expect you've told the police already? No? Oh well, I'm sure they'll be round soon to ask. Superintendent Rigano's very interested in who I've been talking to . . ."

Lindsay felt she was doing battle. Mallard gave in. "I was at home all evening."

"Which is where, exactly?"

He shifted in his seat. "Brownlow Common Cottages. Four doors away from the Crabtrees actually."

Lindsay smiled. "Convenient. Alone, were you?"

He shook his head. "My wife was in. She . . . she almost always *is* in. She has MS, you see, confined to a wheelchair."

Nothing's ever simple, thought Lindsay. Poor woman, stuck in a wheelchair with him. She waited, then he went on. He was clearly a man who felt uncomfortable with silence.

"I put her to bed about ten. So her evidence after that could only be negative—that she didn't hear me go out or come in, that she didn't hear my car. I have no idea why I'm telling you all this," he added petulantly.

"Haven't you, Mr Mallard?" Lindsay enquired. "Thanks very much for your time." She abruptly rose and walked out.

The woman in the front office looked up in surprise as she swept through. Lindsay marched down the main street to the car park where she'd left the MG, irritated that she hadn't broken Mallard's self-possession. She hadn't even thought to ask him who he thought the murderer was. But she knew deep down that the only answer she would have received was the utterly predictable one: "those peace women." And that would have made no difference to her own gut reaction to Mallard, namely that of all the people she'd spoken to so far, he was her favourite suspect. He had opportunity, she'd established that. He looked sturdy enough to cope with the means. And he had motive aplenty. A rumour with Rupert Crabtree behind it would be enough to terminate a man's career in a small town like Fordham when that career depended on trust. And Mallard clearly couldn't afford that, especially not with a wife whose disability gave him another pressing reason for maintaining a comfortable lifestyle.

She drove off, checking her mirrors for Rigano's blond SB man. There was no sign of the red Fiesta. She pulled into the traffic to keep the appointment she'd made with Paul Warminster and following his directions, left Fordham in the opposite direction to Brownlow. Surburban streets gave way to more rural surroundings. Chocolate-box countryside, thought Lindsay, struck as she was occasionally with a sharp pang of longing for the sea lochs and mountains of her native landscape. A couple of miles out of the town, she pulled off the main road into a narrow country lane. Soon she came to a thatched cottage attached to a converted cruck barn. The garden was a mass of daffodils and crocuses with occasional patches of bright blue scilla. A powerful motorbike was parked incongrously by the side of the barn. Lindsay got out of the car and walked up a path made of old weathered brick.

The door was opened by a tall spare man in his late forties. His gingery hair was lank and greying, his face weather-beaten to an unattractive turkey red and a network of fine lines radiated from the corners of his lively blue eyes. In his tweed jacket with the leather patches he looked more like a gamekeeper than a shopkeeper. With a sudden shock, Lindsay realised this was the man she had seen leaving Mallard's office a short time earlier. Covering her confusion, she quickly introduced herself and established her bona fides with her Press card. Warminster ushered her into a chintzy, low-ceilinged living room with bowls of sweet-smelling freesias scattered around.

"So, you're writing about what local people are doing to put a stop to that so-called peace camp," he said, settling himself in a large armchair.

Lindsay nodded. "I understand you've been quite actively involved in the opposition."

Warminster lit a small cigar as he replied. "Used to be. Probably will be again soon."

"Why is that?" Lindsay asked.

"Had a bit of a run-in with that chap Crabtree, the fellow who was murdered at the weekend, so I hadn't been doing too much lately. Blighter thought he ran Fordham. Perhaps now we'll really get to grips with those left-wing lesbians," he said.

"You weren't happy with the policies of Ratepayers Against Brownlow's Destruction, then?" Lindsay probed.

He snorted. "Could say that. Policies? Appeasement, that's what they were about. And look where that got us in the thirties. We should have been taking the war into their territory, getting them out of their entrenched positions instead of pussyfooting around being nicey-nicey to those bloody communist harridans." Warminster was off and running in what were clearly not fresh fields. As she listened to the tirade, trying to control her feelings of disgust and anger, Lindsay gradually began to understand why violence so often seems a solution.

She pretended to take extensive notes of his speech. There was no need to interrogate Warminster. The only difficulty was getting him to stop. Eventually, he ended up with a rabble-rousing peroration. "Very stirring, sir," Lindsay muttered.

"You think so? That's exactly what I told them on Sunday night in Berksbury. I was speaking there, you know, at the instigation of the local Conservative Party. They staged one of those debates about the issues. Had some woolly vicar in a woolly pullover from CND, the local candidate and me. Well worth the trip, I can tell you."

Lindsay's mind had leaped to attention as soon as Sunday was mentioned. "That was Sunday night just past?" she asked. "The night Crabtree was killed, you mean?"

"That's right. Round about when he bought it, we were having a celebratory drink in the Conservative Club. An excellent night. Didn't get home till the small hours. I must say the hospitality was excellent. Good job I'd taken my wife along to drive me home or I'd never have made it. Sorry she's not in, by the way, gone to visit her sister in Fordham. Now, anything else you want to know?"

It all seemed so innocent. And the alibi appeared sound. But Lindsay didn't like what her instincts told her about Paul Warminster. "I see you've got a motorbike outside. Have you ever come across any of those yobs that have been attacking the peace camp?"

He looked startled. "Of course not," he said. "Why should I have?"

Lindsay shrugged. "I just wondered. I thought since you were into direct action they might have made contact with you."

Warminster shook his head violently. "Absolutely not. Ill-disciplined rabble."

"How do you know that?" Lindsay demanded, pouncing on the inconsistency.

"How do I know what?"

"That they're ill-disciplined. If you've got nothing to do with them, how do you know that?"

He looked angry and flustered. "Heard about it, didn't I? Small place, Fordham, you hear things. Absurd of you to think I'd have anything to do with them. Nearly as incompetent as the RABD softies."

"But you obviously maintain contact with some of your friends in RABD," Lindsay probed.

"What d'you mean by that?" he was now deeply suspicious. His hostility was tipping him over the borderline of rudeness.

"I thought I saw you this morning coming out of William Mallard's office," she said.

"So? The man runs a business. I do business in Fordham. Hardly surprising that we do business together, is it? I can't turn my back on every liberal I meet just because I don't agree with their way of going about things."

Lindsay shook her head. "There's no need to get so het up, Mr Warminster. I just wondered if the business you were doing with Mr Mallard was anything to do with the funding of your direct action group."

Her barb hit Warminster, leaving high spots of colour in his cheeks. "Rubbish," he blustered, "absolute rubbish. Now, if you've nothing more to ask me, I'd be obliged if you'd let me get on. I'm a very busy man." He got to his feet, leaving Lindsay little choice but to follow suit. Standing in the doorway he watched her into her car then turned back into the house as she drove away.

An interesting encounter, thought Lindsay. Warminster might have a rock-solid alibi for Sunday night but a tie-in between himself, Mallard and the bikers looked suspiciously probable. It seemed likely to Lindsay that someone had put those bikers up to their attacks on the camp. If it had been only a single incident, it could have been written off as drunken hooliganism. But the concerted attacks of firebombing, blood throwing and damage to the benders looked like something more sinister. And youths like that wouldn't take those chances without some kind of incentive. Money was the obvious choice. The destination of Mallard's funny money now seemed clear too. Driving thoughtfully back to Brownlow Common, Lindsay wondered just how much it would cost to persuade a bloodthirsty biker to make the escalation from firebombing to murder.

12

As Lindsay joined the tight group round the smoky fire, the conversation faltered. Nicky glowered at her and turned away, but Willow moved to one side of the crate she was sitting on and offered Lindsay a place. "We were just sorting out an action for tonight," Deborah said rather too brightly.

"So you'd better rush off and tell your tame policeman," Nicky muttered loudly.

Lindsay ignored the hostility with difficulty, since it triggered her own qualms of conscience about dealing with Rigano, and asked what was planned. Willow explained. "A few of the women were in court yesterday for non-payment of fines and they've been sent to Holloway as per usual. So we're having a candle-lit procession and silent vigil round the wire tonight. There's a couple of coachloads coming down from London. It might be quite a big action—we've tipped off the TV and radio news so we'll get some publicity."

"And with all you journalists kicking round looking for titbits about that creep Crabtree we might even get some decent newspaper publicity for a change," added Nicky bitterly.

"I shouldn't think so," Lindsay replied acidly. "Why should a candle-lit procession alter all our preconceived notions? You don't still believe in Santa Claus, do you, Nicky?"

"Oh, stop it, you two," protested Deborah. "You're like a pair of kids. If you've nothing constructive to say to each other, then don't waste your breath and our time."

Lindsay got to her feet. "I've got to do some work now, but I'll be back for the demo. What time's it all starting?"

"About seven," Deborah answered. "meet me at gate six, near Brownlow Common Cottages. Will you pass the word on to the other reporters if you see them?"

"Sure," Lindsay said. "If that's not too much like consorting with the enemy."

Deborah gave her a warning look and she grinned back at her as she set off for the van. Lindsay dumped her notebook on the table that dropped down and slotted into the long L-shaped bench at night to form the base of the bed. She opened the tiny fridge set next to the two-ring gas cooker and grill, and took out a pint of milk. She swigged a couple of mouthfuls, then sat down to work. She felt comfortable in the van, a big Ford Transit conversion with enough room to stand up and move around in.

She started to scribble down the outline of her story about the in-fighting in RABD with a sneaking feeling that she'd be lucky to get it into the paper. At the end of the day, it was just a rather silly story about a bunch of grown men behaving like schoolboys, and she suspected that Duncan's sharp news sense would come to the same conclusion. Her growing suspicion that William Mallard was somehow implicated in the murder of Rupert Crabtree was not something she could commit to paper yet. Till then, the RABD story was all she had. At least it was exclusive.

She set off for Fordham, in the MG, on a search for a phone box from which to file her copy. As she drove she remembered the computer tape she'd thrust into her briefcase. It occurred to her that she'd have to find out what computer system Simon Crabtree worked with so she could unravel the contents of the tape, since he'd sorted out Mallard's computers in the first place. The obvious way to find out was to pay a visit to his lock-up garage. But that meant another fencing session with Rigano first.

Finding an empty phone box on the outskirts of the town she read over her copy laboriously, silently wishing for the next phase in computer technology that would reduce the transmission of stories to a few seconds of telephone time, thanks to portable remote terminals. The copy transmitted, she spoke to Duncan, telling him about the evening's procession at the base and squeezing from him agreement that she should file copy on it later.

She rang Rigano. After a long delay that involved explaining her identity to the switchboard, the duty officer and Rigano's sergeant, she was finally connected to her contact. He was abrupt to the point of rudeness. "What is it?" he demanded.

"I need some help," Lindsay replied.

"So what's new? What do you need?"

"Just an address. Simon Crabtree's computer workshop. I want to talk to him on his own territory."

"Try the phone book. I thought you were supposed to be full of initiative."

"I can't try the phone book if I don't know what the company's called, can I?"

There was a brief pause. "Okay. I'll leave a note for you at the front counter. I want to talk to you about what you've been up to. I suspect there's a lot you could tell me that you haven't been passing on. Ring me tomorrow morning before ten," he said and put the phone down.

Puzzled and irritated at having to make a detour to the police station, Lindsay set off. Why didn't Rigano just give her the address over the phone? Why go to all the bother of leaving a note for her to pick up? It surely couldn't be an excuse to get her into the station so he could interview her or he wouldn't have made the arrangement for the next day's phone call. Unless that was a red herring . . . There seemed to be no easy answer.

The envelope she collected from the reception desk in Fordham police station fifteen minutes later, contained the address neatly hand written: Megamenu Software, Unit 23, Harrison Mews, Fordham. Lindsay checked the index on the street map she'd bought. No Harrison Mews, but a Harrison Street on the seedier side of town, near the industrial estate. The mews would probably be an alley round the back, she speculated.

She put the car into gear and routinely checked her rear mirror. What she saw nearly caused an accident. The red Ford Fiesta, driven by the man whom she had labelled Special Branch and who seemed a semi-permanent feature of her landscape, was right behind. Lindsay shot into the traffic without signalling and cursed her lack of familiarity with the terrain. While she concentrated on finding her route across the town centre, she was aware of the Fiesta two cars behind her, and an explanation for Rigano's perplexing telephone manner dawned on her. The man now on her tail might have been with Rigano when she called, which begged the more disturbing question: had Rigano lured her into the station just so that the Special Branch man could follow her? And if so, why was the SB interested in a routine murder? And more importantly, why the hell were they so interested in her?

The heaviness of the traffic and the search for her destination forced her to shelve the question. But as she pulled into a back alley with a roughly painted signboard saying, "Harrison Mews: Megamenu Software This Way," she noticed the red hatchback drive slowly past the narrow entrance. She parked the car up against the wall opposite Unit 23 and pondered. If the blond man was SB, then it went a long way towards explaining why a uniformed copper like Rigano had been left in charge of a major murder investigation instead of a plainclothes CID officer. But since the powers that be were so firmly convinced that Brownlow Common women's peace camp was a nest of subversives with sufficient resources to undermine the whole of western democracy, Lindsay supposed it wasn't really so amazing that the SB were taking such a keen interest in a murder that seemed to have some of its origins in the camp.

Lindsay got out of the car and surveyed Megamenu Software's premises. They scarcely inspired confidence. The double doors had been given a cheap and cheerful coat of pale green paint which was already beginning to flake off. There was a large sign in the same style as the one at the mouth of the alley, proclaiming, "Megamenu Software: We Turn Your Needs into Realities." Plenty of scope for a good PR officer, thought Lindsay cynically, when the budget eventually ran to it. But as she rang the bell beside the small door set in one of the larger pair, she noted with some surprise that no expense had been spared on security. The several locks all looked substantial and in spite of the peeling paint, the doors were solid. She didn't have time to speculate further, for the door was opened abruptly by Simon Crabtree.

He frowned and demanded, "What do you want?"

"A few words," Lindsay replied. "Won't take long, I promise."

"I've got nothing to say to the press," he retorted angrily. "You've had enough mileage out of my mother. Bloody vultures."

Lindsay smiled wryly. "Fair enough. But I'm not really here in my role as bloody vulture. Think of me as a seeker after truth. Your father has been murdered and the police seem keen to put one of my oldest friends in the frame for it. I know she didn't do it, and I'm trying to prove that. All I want is a bit of information."

"Why should I help you? You and your bloody friends are no business of mine." He started to close the door, but Lindsay leaned gently against it.

"You don't owe me anything; but I'd have thought you owe your sister," she replied.

He was clearly taken aback. "Ros? What's she got to do with it?"

"I spent yesterday evening at Rubyfruits. She understood the importance of what I'm trying to do. If you rang her, I'm sure she'd tell you to help. And from what I hear, you've got a few debts to pay in that area."

His frown deepened. "You'd better come in, I suppose."

She followed him inside. It was her turn to be taken aback. Inside the shabby lock-up was a complete high-tech environment. The walls were painted matt grey. There was sound-absorbent carpet tile on the floor and the ceiling was covered with acoustic tiling, relieved only by discreet, low-level lighting. One wall was lined with filing drawers. There were four desks, each with a different type of computer terminal on it, including a small portable one, and two expensive-looking, ergonomically designed desk chairs. Several other pieces of equipment, including a standard cassette player and three printers, were sitting on the desks. In the background, baroque music played softly. Simon stood looking truculently at her as she walked round, desperately trying to memorise the names on the computers.

"Quite a set-up you've got here," she said admiringly. "You must be doing well to afford all this."

"I'm good with computers," he said.

"What sort of software do you produce, then?"

"Mainly programmes for managers. So they can interpret what's going on in the business. Now, what did you mean about my sister?"

"People like me and Ros live our lives on the edges of society. That makes it that little bit harder to achieve things. Ros has managed to get something together. And you blew it out of the water for her by telling your father what the score was. In my book, that means you owe her. And because she perceives herself as being part of a group, that means you owe the women she identifies with. Like my friend Deborah. If you don't agree with that analysis, ring up Ros and ask her yourself." Lindsay stopped abruptly, challenging him to make the phone call she knew would have her thrown out instantly.

Her gamble on his sense of guilt paid off. His scowl didn't lift, but he said grudgingly, "And what would you want to know?"

Lindsay hastily searched for a question that would justify her presence. "I wanted to know about his routine with the dog—was it something he always did at around the same time? Would someone have been able to rely on him being on the common with the dog at that time?"

Simon shrugged. "Not really. Rex always gets a walk any time between ten and midnight, depending on all sorts of things like the weather, what's on the box, who's at home. It wasn't always my father who took him out. I did sometimes too. So if someone had been lying in wait, they might have had to hang around for hours on more than one occasion. If I'd been home earlier on Sunday, it could just as well have been me that walked him."

"So you think it's more likely that he met someone by arrangement?"

"Not necessarily. It might have been a chance meeting that turned nasty."

Lindsay recalled Crabtree's distinctive figure. "Your father would have been easy to recognise at a distance and chase after if you were looking for a chance encounter. After all, Deborah thought she spotted him from quite a way off on the night he died, when he was walking the dog," she added. "And she wasn't even on the common. She was walking back from the phone box." Simon shrugged. "But he was carrying a gun, Simon," Lindsay continued. "Surely that suggests he was expecting trouble?"

Simon paused to think. "Yes, but maybe he was just expecting trouble in a general way and had started carrying the gun when he took Rex out last thing."

Lindsay shook her head in disbelief. "This is rural England, not the New York subway. People don't wander round with guns just because they think someone might give them a hard time. If he was genuinely afraid of being attacked, if he'd been threatened in any serious way, surely he'd have gone to the police?"

Simon shrugged. "Don't ask me. It would probably have given him a buzz to confront someone with his gun and then turn them over to the cops. And I think he was genuinely frightened by those peace women. Especially after that one attacked him."

Lindsay shook her head. "I can't believe he thought the peace women were coming after him," she said. "It must have been something else. He said nothing?"

"No. And if you've no more questions, I'd appreciate the chance to get back to work," he replied.

"Okay. Thanks for the time. I'm sure Ros will appreciate your solidarity," she threw over her shoulder as she left.

Back in the car, she scribbled down the names of the computers she had seen and drove off, keeping an eye out for the red Fiesta. But her rear-view mirror was clear, so she stopped at the first phone box she came to. Typically, it was prepared to allow 999 calls only. Three boxes later, she found one that would accept her money, and she dialled an Oxford number. She was quickly connected with a friend from her student days, Annie Norton, a whizz-kid in computer research.

After an exhaustive exchange of gossipy updates while she pumped coins into the box, Lindsay wound her way round to the point of the call. "Annie, I need your help on an investigation I've got tangled up with," she tossed into a gap in the conversation.

"If it's anything to do with Caroline Redfern's much publicised love-life, my lips are sealed," Annie replied.

"No, this is serious, not chit-chat. It's about computers. I've acquired a cassette tape that I think is a computer programme. It could have been made on any one of five computers, and I need to know what it says. Can you help?"

"A cassette tape? How extraordinary. We're talking real computers here, are we, not video games?"

"I think so, yes."

"Hmm. No indication of what language it's in?" Annie asked.

"English, I suppose."

"No, no, what computer language—BASIC, FORTRAN, ALGOL, etc., etc."

"Oh," said Lindsay, bewildered. "No, nothing at all, unless there's a computer language called "Sting: *The Dream of the Blue Turtles.*"

"You what? Are you serious?"

Lindsay laughed. "No, that's what's written on the cassette, that's all."

"And what computers are we talking about?"

"An Apple Macintosh, an IBM, an Apricot, an Amstrad and a Tandy."

"A Tandy? Little lap-top job, would fit in a briefcase? With a flip-up screen?"

"Yes, that's right."

Annie sighed in relief. "That explains the tape. It's probably been transferred from one of the other machines," she mused. "It should be fairly simple to run it through our Univac and read it for you. When can you get it to me?"

"I could drop it off in an hour or so—I'm only down the road in Fordham."

"Tremendous. We could have dinner together if you fancy it."

Lindsay was tempted. She had reached the point where she wanted more than anything to walk away from the conflict of interests with the peace camp, the police and the job. She felt guilty about two-timing Cordelia, and was unsure how she felt about Debs. But she had promised to be at the vigil and she had to keep that promise. She could just fit in the round trip to Oxford if she didn't hang about too long with Annie. "Sorry," she said. "But I'm working tonight. Maybe when I pick it up again, yeah? How long will it take you?"

"Hard to say. A day? Two, maybe, if it's not something obvious. If the person who's made it is a real computer buff, which he or she presumably is, if they really use those four systems to their full potential, then it could be a bit subtle. Still, a nice bit of hacking makes a pleasant change. I'll see you again in about an hour, then. You know where to find me?"

"Sure, I remember. I'll be with you soon as possible." Lindsay rang off and was about to leave the box when she realised she hadn't spoken to Cordelia since her angry departure on Monday. Her mind had been too occupied with Crabtree and Debs for her to pay attention to her lover's needs. It wouldn't be an easy call, for Lindsay knew she'd have to lie about what had happened with Debs. The phone wasn't the place for confessions. And Cordelia would be quite justifiably hurt that Lindsay hadn't made time for her. Especially with Deborah Patterson back on the scene. The stab of guilt made her rake through her pockets for more change and she hastily dialled their number. On the fourth ring, the answering machine picked up the call. "Oh shit," she muttered as she listened to her own voice instructing her to leave a message. After the tone, she forced a smile into her voice and said, feeling foolish as she always did on their own machine, "Hello, darling, it's me. Wednesday afternoon. Just a check call to let you know I'm okay. Duncan's leaving me here on the murder story because of my peace camp contacts, so God knows when I'll be home. Probably not till after the funeral, or an arrest, whichever comes first, I'll try to ring tonight. Love you. Bye." She put the phone down with relief and set off for Oxford.

13

Deborah was waiting impatiently by the gate six encampment for Lindsay. Already, most of the women taking part in the vigil were in place. The traffic on the main road back from Oxford and the need to change into more suitable clothes had delayed Lindsay enough for her to have missed the procession, but she could see that there were not sufficient numbers there to encircle the base holding hands, so they had spread out along as much of the perimeter as they could cover, with gaps of about fifty yards between them. The flicker of candles, feeble against the cloudy winter night, was gradually spreading.

Deborah hustled Lindsay along the muddy clearing by the fence for half a mile till they reached their agreed station, a corner of the fence near a deep drainage ditch. They kissed goodbye, then Lindsay walked on round the corner to her position.

She turned towards the base, where the buildings and bunkers were floodlit against the enemy—not the red menace, but the monstrous regiment, she thought. She turned back and peered towards the nearest flame. She could just make out the silhouette of the next woman in the vigil and in the distance she could hear the faint sound of singing. She knew from experience that it would soon work its way round to her like Chinese whispers. She had been pleasantly surprised to see that for once the police and military presence were fairly low key. She hadn't seen any journalists, but assumed they would all be down by the main gates, reluctant to stagger through the mud unless it became absolutely necessary. She smiled wryly. At least her story would have the unmistakable air of verisimilitude.

She took her Zippo lighter from her jacket pocket and flicked the flame into life. She hadn't remembered to ask Debs for a candle, so the lighter would have to do. She stamped her feet to keep the circulation going and started mentally planning her story.

Her thoughts were interrupted by a short scream, which was cut off by a squelching thud and the sound of crashing in the undergrowth. It came from Deborah's direction. Before she had time to think, she was charging back round the corner in the fence towards her lover. In her panic, she forgot about the drainage ditch and plunged headlong into it, twisting her ankle in an explosion of pain as she fell. But instead of landing in muddy water, she fell on something soft and yielding. Lindsay pushed herself away and fumbled with the lighter which she'd somehow managed to hang on to. The little flare of light was enough to show her a sight that made her heart lurch.

Deborah lay face down in the ditch, blood flowing from a gaping wound in the left side of her head. "Oh my God," moaned Lindsay, as she struggled upright. "Debs, Debs," she cried, fighting back tears of panic as she grabbed her by the shoulders. She remembered all the rules of first aid that instruct not to move victims with head wounds. But Deborah would drown if left lying face down in the mud. So she pulled at her left shoulder till she managed to turn her on her side. Lindsay pulled her scarf off and gently wiped the mud from Deborah's face. She gritted her teeth and cleared the silt from her nose and mouth and checked if she was still breathing by putting her ear to Deborah's mouth. She could feel nothing. "Debs, Debs, breathe, you bastard, breathe," she muttered desperately, pummelling Deborah's chest. After a few moments that felt like an eternity, she was rewarded by a spluttering cough as Deborah retched. Lindsay, herself facing nausea, checked her lover was still able to breathe in spite of her unconsciousness, then stood upright, yelling for help at the top of her voice.

It seemed hours before another couple of women appeared with a torch, looking bewildered.

"Get help, get help!" Lindsay almost screamed. "Debs has been attacked. Get the bloody police. We need an ambulance."

The next half hour was a blur of action as first police and then ambulancemen arrived and rushed Deborah to hospital. Lindsay realised how serious the situation was when a young constable helped her into the ambulance and she found herself racing through the lanes with flashing lights and siren.

At Fordham General, the stretcher on which Deborah's immobile body lay was immediately hurried away on a trolley with the policeman still in attendance. Lindsay sat, exhausted, wet and filthy on the steps of the casualty unit, smoking a battered cigarette. She was numb with fear for Deborah. One of the ambulancemen stopped to speak to her on the way back to his vehicle. "You did well, back there," he said. "Your friend might have died if you hadn't got her head out of the mud. Just as well you kept your head."

Lindsay shook her head. "I didn't keep my head. I panicked. I just acted on pure instinct. I was so afraid I'd lost her. How is she? Do you know?"

He shrugged. "Not out of the woods yet. But they're good in there. You should go inside in the warm, you'll get a chill out here. Get yourself a cuppa."

Lindsay nodded wearily. "Yeah." She got to her feet as he climbed back into the ambulance. As she turned to go a heavy hand clapped her on the shoulder. It belonged to a reporter she recognised by sight.

"What's the score?" he demanded. "We heard someone had been attacked, but the cops are saying nothing." Lindsay stared at him uncomprehendingly. "Come on, Lindsay," he pressed. "Don't be selfish. I've only got half an hour to close copy time on the next edition. You've had every bloody other exclusive on this job. Give us a break."

She wanted more than anything to put a fist in his face. Instead, she simply said, "Fuck off," and turned on her heel, shaking his hand loose. But the incident had reminded her that there was something she could do to put a bit of distance between the attack and her emotions. She walked like a zombie into the hospital, asked a passing nurse where the nearest phone was and transferred the charges to the *Clarion* newsdesk. Luckily, Cliff Gilbert took the call himself.

"Lindsay here, Cliff," she said, speaking very slowly. "Listen. I'm in no fit state to write copy, but there's a very good story going on here and I've got chapter and verse on it. If I give you all the facts, can someone knock it into shape?"

"What?" he exclaimed. "What the hell's the matter with you? Are you pissed?"

"Look, someone's just tried to kill one of my best friends. I'm exhausted, I'm wet, I'm probably in shock and I'm at the end of my rope. I need help."

He realised from her voice as much as her words that Lindsay was serious. "Okay, Lindsay," he said. "I'm sorry. I'll put you on to Tony and you tell him what he needs for the story. No problem. Do you need back-up? I can get someone down there in an hour. Or a local freelance—"

"I don't want anyone else, Cliff. Maybe you should get some more cover down here, though. I'm through for tonight. Now give me Tony." A series of clicks followed, and Lindsay found herself talking to Tony Martin, one of her reporting colleagues. Cliff had obviously warned him what to expect, for his voice was quiet and coaxing. Lindsay forced the lid on her emotions and stumbled through the events of the evening. At the end of her recital, he asked for the number of the police station and the hospital. Her mind was a blank.

"Never mind," he said. "Listen, I'll make sure they put your by-line on this. It's a helluva story. I hope your mate pulls through. But you go and get yourself a stiff drink. You sound as if you need one. Okay?"

"Yeah, okay," she sighed, and put the phone down. Through the door of the booth, she could see other reporters arriving. She knew she couldn't cope with them now, so she turned back to the call box and dialled home. Cordelia picked up the phone on the third ring. Lindsay's voice shook as she said, "It's me. Can you come down?"

"What?" Cordelia demanded. "Now? Whatever's the matter? You sound terrible. What's going on?"

"It's Debs. She's . . . she's been attacked. Someone tried to kill her. I'm at the hospital now. I found her. I really could do with you being here."

There was incredulity in Cordelia's voice. "Someone tried to kill Deborah? How? What happened?"

"There was a candle-lit vigil. We were by the fence, about fifty yards from each other. Someone hit her on the head and left her drowning in a ditch," Lindsay said, on the verge of tears.

"That's awful! Are you okay?"

"Physically, yes. But I'm absolutely drained. I thought she was dead, Cordelia," Lindsay wailed, tears finally coursing down her face. She sobbed helplessly, oblivious to Cordelia's words.

When she managed to control herself again, she could hear her lover's voice soothing her, saying, "Calm down it'll be okay. Why don't you come home now? There's nothing more you can do there tonight. I'd come down and get you, but I've had too much wine."

"I can't," Lindsay said numbly.

"Why ever not?" Cordelia asked. "Look, you'd be better off here. You can have a nice hot bath and a drink and try to get a decent night's sleep. Come home, Lindsay. I'll only worry about you otherwise."

"I just can't," Lindsay replied. "There's too much going on here for me to walk away from it all. I'm sorry. I'll ring you in the morning, okay. Thanks for listening. Goodnight, love."

"I'll come down first thing, how's that?"

"No, it's okay, leave it. I'm not sure what I'll be doing or where I'll be. I'll speak to you soon."

"Be careful, Lindsay, please. Ring me in the morning."

Bleakness descended on Lindsay. She stared across the busy casualty department in time to see Rigano shoulder his way through the flapping celluloid doors and head for the desk. He was immediately surrounded by reporters. She became aware that the phone was squawking.

"Lindsay? Are you there?"

"Yes, I'm here. Bye."

She put the phone down, feeling utterly defeated. She left the phone booth but could not face the mêlée round the information desk. She leaned against the wall, shivering slightly in spite of the airless warmth of the hospital. Rigano, whose eyes had been sweeping the room for her, picked her up almost immediately.

"That's it for now," he said brusquely to the crowd of reporters and strode over to her, followed at a few paces by her colleagues. He took her by the elbow and piloted her into a corridor. He stopped briefly and said firmly to their followers, "Go away. Now. Or I'll have the lot of you removed from the hospital altogether." Reluctantly, they backed off and he steered Lindsay into an alcove with a couple of chairs. They sat down.

"She's going to be all right," he said. "There's a hairline fracture of the skull and a big superficial wound. She's lost quite a bit of blood and had stitches, but they say there's no brain damage."

The relief was like a physical glow that spread through Lindsay. "When can I see her?" she asked.

"Tomorrow morning. Come round about nine and they'll let you in. She'll still be heavily sedated, so they tell me, but she should be awake. It'll be a while before we can get any sense out of her, though, so I need to know anything you can tell me about the attack."

Lindsay shrugged. "I don't know anything. I don't even know what she was hit with. What was it?"

"A brick," he replied. "There's any number of them lying around. You use them to pin down the corners of your benders."

"That's ironic," said Lindsay, stifling the hysterical giggle she felt bubbling inside her. "I really can't tell you anything. I heard a short scream—not a long-drawn-out one, quite brief— and a squelch that must have been Debs falling into the ditch. Then I heard what sounded like someone trying to run off through the woodland."

"Can you say in what direction?"

"Not really. It seemed to be more or less dead ahead of me as I ran towards the ditch, but that's the vaguest of impressions and I wouldn't swear to it. I wish I could tell you that I'd seen someone, but even if he'd still been there, I doubt if I would have seen him. There was really no light to speak of."

"Him?"

"Well, it wouldn't have been one of us, would it?"

❦

It was Jane who woke Lindsay at eight the next morning with a pot of hot coffee. Settling herself down on the end of the bunk, she waited patiently for Lindsay to surface. Brought back to the camp by one of Rigano's men, Lindsay had needed several large whiskies before sleep had even seemed a possibility. Now she was reaping the whirlwind.

Jane smiled at her efforts to shake off the stupor and said, "I thought I'd better make sure you were up in time to get to the hospital. I've already rung them—Deborah is out of danger and responding well, they said. Translation—she's been sedated to sleep but her vital signs are looking good. They say it's okay for you to go in, but they don't think Cara should visit yet."

"How is Cara?" asked Lindsay, who felt as if her limbs were wooden and her head filled with cotton wool.

"A bit edgy, but she's with Josy and the other kids so she'll be more or less all right," Jane replied. "She wants her mummy, but at least she's old enough to understand when you say that Deborah's in the hospital but she's going to be all right."

"Do you think we can keep her here and look after her okay, or are we going to have to get something else sorted out?" Lindsay asked anxiously.

Jane smiled. "Don't worry about Cara. She's used to the routine here now. It's better that she's somewhere she can see Deborah as much as possible."

"I'm just worried in case social services find out about her and take her into care," Lindsay said.

"If anyone comes looking for her from the council, we'll deny all knowledge of her and say she's with her father. By the time they sort that little one out, Deborah will be convalescent," Jane reassured her. "Now, drink this coffee and get yourself over to the hospital."

✥

"Five minutes," warned the nurse as she showed Lindsay into a small side room.

Deborah lay still, her head swathed in bandages. There was a tube in her nose and another in her arm. Her face was chalky white and dark bruises surrounded her closed eyelids. Lindsay was choked with a mixture of pity, love and anger. As she moved towards the bed, she sensed another presence in the room and half turned. Behind the door, a uniformed constable sat, notebook poised. He smiled tentatively at her and said, "Morning, miss."

Lindsay nodded at him and sat down by the bed. Reaching out cautiously she took hold of Deborah's hand. Her eyelids flickered momentarily then opened. The pupils were so dilated that her eyes no longer appeared blue. Frowning slightly, as she tried to focus, she registered Lindsay's presence and her face cleared.

"Lin," she said in a voice that lacked all resonance. "It's really you?"

"Yes, love, it's me."

"Cara?"

"She's okay. Josy's in charge, everything's under control."

"Good. I'm so tired, Lin. I can't think. What happened?"

"Somebody hit you. Did you see anyone, Debs?"

"I'm so glad it's really you, Lin. I think I'm seeing ghosts.
I think Rupert Crabtree's haunting me."

"I'm no ghost, Debs. And he can't hurt you. He's out of
your life for good."

"I know, but listen, Lin. It's crazy, I know, but I have this
weird impression that it was Rupert Crabtree who attacked me.
I must be going mad."

"You're not mad, you're just concussed and sedated up to
the eyeballs. It'll all be clear soon, I promise."

"Yes, but I'm sure it was him that I saw. But it couldn't
be, could it? Just like it couldn't have been him I saw walking
his dog on Sunday night. Because he was already dead by then,
wasn't he?"

"What?" Lindsay suddenly stiffened. "You saw him after
he was dead?"

"I told you before that I saw him. But he was walking
towards his house. And he'd already been killed up by the fence.
It's his ghost, Lin, it's haunting me." Her voice was becoming
agitated.

Lindsay stroked her arm. "It's okay, Debs. There's no ghost,
I promise you. You've got to go to sleep now, and when you
wake up, I swear you'll be much clearer. Now close your eyes,
go back to sleep. I'll be back tonight, I promise. No ghosts, just
good old Lindsay."

Her soothing voice lulled the panic from Deborah's face and
soon she was sleeping again. Lindsay rose to go and the policeman followed her. Outside he said, "Could you make head or
tail of that, miss? All that stuff about being attacked by a ghost?"

Lindsay shook her head. "She's delirious, at a guess. It made
no sense to me, officer," she said.

But she knew as she walked away from the ward that she had lied. The echo of her words seemed to pursue her. Deborah's words had triggered off a chain of thought in Lindsay, making a strange kind of sense. At last, vague suspicions were crystallising into certainties. Lindsay felt a growing conviction that Oxford was where the answers lay.

14

Lindsay cursed the one-way system that had turned a city she knew like the back of her hand into a convoluted maze. Wryly she remembered the April Fool's Day joke that had been played by a bunch of maths students when she'd been an undergraduate. They'd worked out that if they reversed just one sign in the traffic system, vehicles would be able to enter but not to leave it. The city had ground to an infuriated, hooting halt by eight in the morning, a problem it had taken the traffic experts till noon to solve. The memory kept Lindsay mildly amused until she finally pulled into the car park at the Computer Sciences Laboratory at eleven. She had stopped only to plead with Duncan for a day off, a request he reluctantly granted after she had delivered a short, first-person piece about her visit to the hospital. Since the *Clarion* had changed the front page to accommodate her story from the night before, the pugnacious news editor was determined to milk their exclusive line for all it was worth. Lindsay had deliberately left out all references to ghosts and stressed Deborah's ignorance of her attacker's identity. Then, with great satisfaction, she switched off her radio pager for the day.

"Lindsay!" exclaimed Annie as she emerged into the reception area looking more like an earth mother than a computer scientist, dressed as she was in a Laura Ashley print. "I thought you were going to phone." She escorted Lindsay through the security doors and down an air-conditioned corridor.

"Sorry," said Lindsay. "It's just that . . . well, I needed to be doing something and I can't get any further till I know what's on that tape."

Annie stopped in her tracks and studied her friend carefully. "What's happened, Lindsay? You look completely out of it. Getting involved with murders doesn't seem to agree with you."

Lindsay sighed. "Can we sit down somewhere? I don't even know where to begin." Annie ushered Lindsay into her office, a tiny cubby hole with a remote terminal dominating it. Lindsay slumped into a low easy chair while Annie sat at her desk. Lindsay lit a cigarette then stubbed it out almost immediately, remembering that it was forbidden in the computer areas.

"Last night, somebody tried to kill her and nearly succeeded. It was me who found her. I thought . . . I thought she was going to die. It was terrible, Annie. Made me realise . . . I don't know . . . how dangerous all of this is. Unless someone equally screwy is out to avenge Crabtree's death it's got to be Crabtree's murderer. But it's too much of a coincidence to believe there are two different killers on the loose. And that means as far as I'm concerned that it's a race against time to prove who really did it before he has another go and succeeds." Annie nodded encouragingly.

"I thought I could rely on the police to get their fingers out," Lindsay went on. "But I don't know, it all seems very strange to me. For some reason it's a uniformed copper who's running the show, not the CID, and there's some guy who's always around who's either Special Branch or something odd. And somehow there doesn't seem to be any urgency about what's going on. This cop, Rigano, *seems* dead straight but even he's not getting the action going. To begin with, he was keen enough to enlist my help and stay abreast of what I was up to. But now it's almost as if he doesn't want me to get any closer to the truth.

"I think I'm beginning to have just an inkling of an idea about who did it but I haven't a clue why and I think the answer, or part of it, is that tape."

Annie grimaced. "Well, add that to the murderer's assumption that Debs will have told you all she knows and you could be the next target. And knowing you, I suppose all this is upfront in the *Daily Clarion?*"

"Sort of. I mean, I've done a couple of exclusives."

Annie thought for a moment. "And?" she prompted.

"And what? Isn't that enough? That I could be next on a killer's hit list?"

"I know you. There's something else. Something personal."

Lindsay gave a tired smile. "I'd forgotten how sharp you can be," she said. "Yes, there is something more. But it seems hellish trivial beside the real problems of people getting hurt and killed. I'm having a difficult time with Cordelia just now. She seems jealous of the time I spend at the camp, especially now Debs is there."

"Hmm," Annie murmured. "She does have a point, though, doesn't she?"

Lindsay looked astonished. "I didn't—"

"You didn't have to, lovey. It's not what you say, Lindsay, it's how you say it. 'Twas ever thus with you. And if it's that obvious to me who hasn't seen you for months, then it must stick out like a sore thumb to Cordelia. She must be feeling very threatened. If I were you, I'd make a point of going home tonight, no matter what other calls you think there are on your time."

Lindsay smiled. "I'd love to do just that. But a lot depends on what you've got to tell me about that tape. I'm convinced that that's where the answers lie."

Annie frowned. "I hope not," she said. She unlocked her desk and took out a pile of printout paper and the tape. "I'm sorry to disappoint you," she said. "I don't think you'll find many answers here."

"You mean you haven't been able to crack it?" Lindsay asked, her voice full of disappointment.

"Oh no, it's not that," said Annie cheerfully. "I won't bore you with the details, but I must thank you for a really challenging task. It took me a lot longer than I thought. I didn't get to bed till three, you know, I was so caught up in this. Whoever constructed that programme knew exactly what he was doing. But it was one of those thorny problems that I can't bear to give up till I've solved it.

"So I stuck with it. And this is what I came up with." She handed Lindsay a sheaf of printout. It consisted of pages of letters and numbers in groups.

"Is this it?" asked Lindsay. "I'm sorry, it's completely meaningless to me. What does it represent?"

"That's what I don't know for sure," Annie admitted. "It may be some encoded information, or that in itself could be the information. But unless you know what it is you're looking for it doesn't take you any further forward in itself. I've never seen anything quite like it, if that's any help."

Lindsay shook her head. "I hoped that this would solve everything. I think I was looking for a motive for murder. But I seem to have ended up with yet another complication. Annie, do you know anybody who might be able to explain this printout?"

Annie picked up her own copy of the printed message and studied it again. "It's not my field and I'm not sure whose it is until I know what it is, if you see what I mean." She sighed. "The only thing that occurs to me, and it's the vaguest echo from a seminar I went to months ago, is that it might possibly be some kind of signals traffic. I don't know for sure, and I can't even put my finger on why I believe that. But that's all I can go on. And I can't put you in touch with anyone who might help because if it is signals intelligence, then the ninety-nine per cent probability is that it's Official Secrets Act stuff. I'm bound by that and so is anyone else who might help. And if I put you in touch, they'll have to report the contact in both directions. Just what have you got yourself into this time, Lindsay?"

Lindsay sighed again. "Deep waters, Annie."

"You should be talking to the police about this."

"I can't, not yet. I don't trust what's going on, I told you."

"Where did this come from, Lindsay? For my own protection, I think you need to tell me a bit more about the provenance of this tape. It all looks extremely dodgy to me."

"I found it in a collection of papers belonging to Rupert Crabtree, the man who was murdered. His son owns a small software house in Fordham. It was in such a strange place, I figured it might be significant. And now, from what you tell me, it could be more than just a clue in a murder mystery. Have you made a copy of the tape?"

Annie nodded. "I always do, as a precaution."

"Then I'd suggest you disguise it as Beethoven string quartets or something and hide it in your tape collection. I'd like there to be a spare in case anything happens to my copy. Or to me."

Annie's eyebrows rose. "A little over the top, surely?"

Lindsay smiled. "I hope so."

"You can make a copy yourself on a decent tape-to-tape hi-fi, you know," Annie remarked in an offhand way. "And you will be going home tonight, won't you?"

Lindsay grinned. "Yes, Annie. I'll be going home. But I've got a couple of things to do first." She stood up. "Thanks for all your work. Soon as all of this is over, we'll have a night out on me, I promise."

"Let's hope those aren't famous last words. Be careful, Lindsay, if this is what I think it might be, it's not kids' stuff you're into." Suddenly she stood up and embraced Lindsay. "Watch your back," she cautioned, as the journalist detached herself and made for the door.

Lindsay turned and winked solemnly at Annie. "Just you watch me," she said.

As she wrestled with the twin horrors of the one-way system and the pay phones of Oxford, Lindsay decided that she was going to invest in a mobile phone whatever the cost. In frustration, she headed out towards the motorway and finally found a working box in Headington. Once installed, she flipped through her contacts book until she found the number of *Socialism Today*, a small radical monthly magazine where Dick McAndrew worked.

She dialled the number and waited to be connected. Dick was a crony from the Glasgow Labour Party who had made his name as a radical journalist a few years earlier with an exposé of the genetic damage sustained by the descendants of British Army veterans of the 1950s atom bomb tests. He was a tenacious Glaswegian whose image as a bewildered ex-boxer hid a sharp brain and a dogged appetite for the truth. Lindsay knew he'd recently become deeply interested in the intelligence community and GCHQ at Cheltenham. If this was a record of signals traffic, he'd know.

Her luck was still with her. Dick was at his desk, and she arranged to meet him for lunch in a little pub in Clerkenwell. That gave her just enough time to go home and swap her bag of dirty washing for a selection of clean clothes. She made good time on the motorway, which compensated for the time she lost in the heavy West London traffic. Being behind the wheel of her MG relaxed her, and in spite of the congested streets she was almost sorry when she turned off by Highbury Fields and parked outside the house.

She checked her watch as she walked through the front door and decided to make time for herself for a change. She stripped off and dived into a blessedly hot shower. Emerging, she carefully chose a crisp cotton shirt and a pair of lined woollen trousers still in the dry-cleaner's bag. She dressed quickly, finishing the outfit off with an elderly Harris tweed jacket she'd liberated from her father's wardrobe. In the kitchen, Lindsay scrawled a note on the memo board: "12.45. Thurs. I intend to be back by eight tonight. If emergency crops up, I'll leave a message on the machine. Love you."

She pulled on a pair of soft grey moccasins, light relief after her boots, and ran downstairs to the street. There she picked up a passing cab which deposited her outside the pub. She shouldered her way through the lunchtime crowds till she found Dick sitting in a corner staring morosely at a pint of Guinness. "You're late," he accused her.

"Only ten minutes, for Chrissake," she protested.

"It's the job," he replied testily. "You get paranoid. What you drinking?" In spite of Lindsay's attempts to buy the drinks, he was adamant that he should pay, and equally adamant that she had to have a pint. "I'm no' buying bloody half pints for an operator as sharp as you," he explained. "If I'm on pints, so are you. That way I'm less likely to get conned."

He returned with the drinks and immediately scrounged a cigarette from Lindsay. "So," he said, "how's tricks? You look dog rough."

"Flattery will get you nowhere, McAndrew. If you must know, I'm in the middle of a murder investigation, my ex-girlfriend is recovering from a homicidal attack, Cordelia's in a huff and Duncan Morrison expects the moon yesterday. Apart from that, life's the berries. Howsabout you?" she snarled.

"Oh well, you know?" He sighed expansively.

"That good, eh?"

"So what have you got for me, Lindsay? What's behind this meet? Must be good or you'd have given me some clue on the phone and chanced the phone-tap guy not being sharp enough to pick it up. Hell mend them."

"It's not so much what I've got for you as what you can do for me."

"I've told you before, Lindsay, I'm not that kind of boy."

"You should be so lucky, McAndrew. Listen, this is serious. Forget the Simon Dupree of the gay repartee routine. I've got a computer printout that I'm told might be coded signals traffic. Could you identify it if it was?"

Dick looked alert and intent. "Where d'you get this from, Lindsay?"

"I can't tell you yet, Dick, but I promise you that as soon as it's all sorted, I'll give you chapter and verse."

He shook his head. "You're asking a lot, Lindsay."

"That's why I came to you," she said. "Want to see it?" He nodded and she handed him the printout. He helped himself to another cigarette and studied the paper. Ten minutes later, he carefully folded it up and stuffed it back in her handbag. "Well?" she asked cautiously.

"I'm not an expert," he said warily, "but I've been looking at intelligence communication leaks for a wee while now. As you well know. And that looks to me like a typical pattern for a US military base. Somewhere like Upper Heyford, Mildenhall."

"Or Brownlow Common?"

"Or Brownlow Common."

"And what does it mean?"

"Oh Christ, Lindsay. I don't know. I'm not a bloody expert in codes. I've got a source who might be able to unscramble it if you want to know that badly. But I'd have thought it was enough for you to know that you're walking around with a print-out of top secret intelligence material in your handbag. Just possessing that would be enough for them to put you away for a long time."

"It's that sensitive?"

"Lindsay, the eastern bloc spend hundreds of thousands of roubles trying to get their hands on material like that. Quite honestly, I don't even want to know where you got that stuff. I want to forget I've ever seen it."

"But if you know what it is, you must have seen other stuff like it."

Dick nodded and took a long draught of his pint. "I've seen similar stuff, yes. But nothing approaching that level of security. There's a system of security codes at the top of each set of groups. And I've never encountered anything with a code rated that high before. It's the difference between Hansard and what the PM tells herself in the mirror in the morning. You are playing with the big boys, Lindsay." He rose abruptly and went to the bar, returning with two large whiskies.

"I don't drink spirits at lunchtime," she protested.

"You do today," he said. "You want my advice? Go home, burn that print-out, go to bed with Cordelia, forget you ever saw it. That's trouble, Lindsay."

"I thought you were a tough-shit investigative journo, the sort that isn't happy unless you're taking the lid off the Establishment and kicking the Official Secrets Act into touch?"

"It's not like pulling the wings off flies, Lindsay. You don't just do it for the hell of it. You do it when you think there's something nasty in the woodpile. I'm not one of those knee-jerk lefties who publishes every bit of secret material that comes my way, like Little Jack Horner saying, 'See what a good boy am I.' Some things should stay secret; it's when that's abused to protect crime and pettiness and sloppiness and injustice and self-seeking that people like me get stuck in," he replied passionately.

"Okay," she said mildly. "Cut the lecture. But take it from me, Dick, something very nasty has been going on, and I've got to get to the bottom of it before it costs any more lives. If I have to use my terrifying bit of paper to get there, I'll do it. There's nothing wrong with my bottle."

"I never said there was. That's the trouble with you, Lindsay—you don't know when it's sensible to get scared."

By silent consent they changed the subject and spent half an hour gossiping about mutual friends in the business. Then Lindsay felt she could reasonably make her excuses and leave. She got back to the three-storey house in Highbury at half past two, with no recollection of the journey through the North

London streets. The answering machine was flashing, but she ignored it and went through to the kitchen to brew a pot of coffee. She had the frustrating feeling that she had all the pieces of the jigsaw but couldn't quite arrange them in a way that made sense. While the coffee dripped through the filter, she decided to call Rigano.

For once, she was put straight through. As soon as she identified herself, he demanded, "Where are you? And what have you been up to?"

Puzzled, she said, "Nothing. I'm at home in London. I visited Deborah this morning and since then I've seen a couple of friends. Why?"

"I want to know what you make of your friend's remark when you saw her in the hospital. My constable thought it might be significant."

"I told him then that I didn't understand it," she replied cautiously.

"I know what you told him. I don't believe you," he retorted.

"That's not my problem," she replied huffily.

"It could be," he threatened. "I thought we were co-operating, Lindsay?"

"If I had any proof of who attacked Deborah, do you think I'd be stupid enough to sit on it? I don't want to be the next one with a remodelled skull, Jack."

There was a heavy silence. Then he said in a tired voice, "Got anything for me at all?"

"These bikers who have been terrorising the camp—I think Warminster and Mallard are paying them."

"Have you any evidence of that?"

Briefly, Lindsay outlined what she had learned the day before. "It's worth taking a look at, don't you think? I mean, Warminster and Mallard both wanted Crabtree out of the way. Maybe they used the yobs they'd already primed for the vandalism."

"It's a bit far-fetched, Lindsay," he complained. "But I'll get one of my lads to take a look at it."

Having got that off her chest, Lindsay got to the point of the call. "Has it occurred to you that there might be a political dimension to this situation?"

His voice became cautious in its turn. "You mean that RABD is only a front for something else? That's nonsense."

"I mean real politics, Jack. Superpowers and spies. The person you're looking for didn't really kill for personal reasons; I think we're looking at a wider motive altogether. Somebody doesn't want us to do that. And that's why I think this investigation has got bogged down in trivial details about peace women's alibis."

"That's an interesting point of view, but that sort of thing is all out of my hands. I'm just a simple policeman, Lindsay. Conspiracy theories don't do much for me. I leave all that to the experts. And you'd be well advised to do the same."

Simple policeman, my foot, thought Lindsay. "Is that a warning, Jack?" she asked innocently.

"Not at all, Lindsay. I'm just telling you as simply as I know how that this case isn't about James Bond, it's about savage responses to petty situations. It's about people carrying offensive weapons for mistaken notions of self-defence. Anything else is out of my hands. Do I make myself clear?"

"So who is that blond man who keeps following me? Special Branch? MI5?"

"If you mean Mr Stone, he's not Special Branch. There's no SB man around here, Lindsay. And no one is following you. I'd know about it if they were. If anyone's being followed, it's not you. You should stop being so paranoid."

Lindsay almost smiled. "Haven't you heard, Jack? Just because you stop being paranoid doesn't mean they're not out to get you."

15

Lindsay raked around in her desk drawer until she found a blank cassette. Going through to the large L-shaped living room where the stereo system with the twin tape decks occupied a corner she set it up to make a copy of the computer tape and sprawled on one of the elegant grey leather chesterfields while she waited for the recording to finish. It was wonderful to lie back on the comfortable sofa surrounded by the restful atmosphere created by Cordelia's unerring talent for interior design, though she felt a pang of guilt when she remembered the squalid conditions back at Brownlow. Lindsay ruefully recalled her feelings when she had first entered Cordelia's domain two years before. She had been overwhelmed with the luxurious interior of the tall house by the park, and it had been months before she got out of the habit of pricing everything around her with a sense of puritanical outrage. Now, it was her home, far more than her Glasgow flat which she rented out to students at a rent that covered her overheads.

She turned over again what Rigano had said. As far as the blond man was concerned, it seemed plain to Lindsay that he was something to do with intelligence, since Rigano had denied so vehemently that he was SB while pointedly ignoring her MI5 allegation. And if Stone wasn't following *her*, that didn't leave many options for the focus of his interests. And that in turn meant she wasn't barking up the wrong tree as far as the existence of wider political implications was concerned. What she couldn't understand was why Rigano was just sitting back and letting it happen without pursuing the same person that she was interested in.

Unless, of course, she was completely wrong and the two strands were unrelated, leaving the murder as a purely personal matter. That would leave the ball firmly in the court of Warminster, Mallard and the putative biker or Alexandra/Carlton. The interest of the security forces could then be explained away as concern about police action jeopardising some operation of theirs. Since Lindsay was still far from clear about the point of killing Rupert Crabtree, either option seemed possible. However, the attempt on Deborah's life seemed logical only if one assumed that it had been made to silence her. And if that was the case, Lindsay argued to herself, how did the murderer know that Debs hadn't already spilled whatever beans she possessed; and if she hadn't, then was she likely to do so now, especially since her silence must have come not from fear but from a failure to recognise what she knew or its importance? Lindsay shook her head vigorously. She was going round in circles.

She mentally replayed her conversation with Rigano again. Something he had said as a throwaway line came back into sharp focus. "It's about people carrying offensive weapons for mistaken notions of self-defence," he had remarked bitterly. Suddenly the jigsaw fell into place. Lindsay jumped to her feet and went to the phone. If Cordelia had been accessible, she would have outlined her theory then and there and waited for the holes to be picked in it. Failing that, she punched in the number of Fordham police station and drummed her fingers impatiently till the connection was made.

"Hello . . . Can I speak to Superintendent Rigano," she demanded. The usual sequence of clicks and hollow silences followed. Then the switchboard operator came back to her and reported that Rigano was out of the building. But Lindsay was not to be deflected.

"Can you get a message to him, please? Will you tell him that Lindsay Gordon rang and needs to talk to him urgently? I'm just setting off to drive to Fordham now, and I'll be at the police station in about an hour and a half, say five o'clock. If he's not back by then, I'll hang on. Got that?"

The woman on the switchboard seemed slightly bemused by Lindsay's bulldozer tactics, but she dutifully repeated the message and promised it would be passed on over the radio. Taking the original cassette tape out of the machine and stuffing it in her pocket, Lindsay left the house, completely forgetting the flashing answering machine and her promise to Cordelia.

She walked round to the mews garage where she kept the car and was soon weaving through the traffic, seeing every gap in the cars ahead as a potential opportunity for queue jumping. Excited as she was by the new shape her thoughts had taken, she forced herself not to think about murder and its motives while she negotiated the busy roads leading to the M4.

She arrived at Fordham police station ten minutes ahead of schedule. The elderly constable on reception desk duty told her Rigano was due back within the next half-hour and that he was expecting her. She was taken through to a small anteroom near his office and a matronly policewoman brought her a cup of tea, freshly brewed but strong. Lindsay found it hard to sit still and chain-smoked through the twenty minutes she was kept waiting. She looked at one cigarette ruefully as she blew smoke at the ceiling. No matter how hard she tried to give up or cut down, at the first crisis she leaped for the nicotine with the desperate fixation of the alcoholic for the bottle.

Rigano himself came to escort her to his room. More cheerful now, there was no sign that he resented her demand to see him. But he seemed determined to keep a distance between them. In his office, there was no sign of his sergeant or any of the other officers to take notes of the interview. Lindsay was disconcerted by that, but nevertheless relieved. What she had to say didn't need a big audience. And if some hard things were going to be said on both sides, it was probably just as well that they should go unrecorded.

"Well," he said, indicating a chair to her as he walked round his desk to sit down. "You seem in a big rush to talk to me now, when you could barely spare me a sentence earlier on. What's caused the big thaw? Surely not my overwhelming charm."

"Partly it's fear," she replied. "I said to you earlier that I'd be a fool if I knew who had killed Crabtree and tried to kill Deborah and persisted in keeping my mouth shut. Well, I think that now I know, and I'm ready to talk."

If she expected him to show signs of amazement or shock, she was disappointed. His eyebrows twitched slightly and he simply said, "That's assuming the two incidents are directly related."

Lindsay was puzzled. "But of course they are. You can't seriously expect anyone to believe that there are two homicidal maniacs running around out there? Deborah was connected to Crabtree while he was alive; in my book, that makes a strong case for a connection when they're both involved in murderous attacks in the same place within days of each other."

"The attack on Deborah Patterson could have been a random attack on one of the peace women by someone who's got a grudge against the camp," he argued mildly.

Lindsay shook her head. "No way. If anyone was going to do that, they'd pick a spot much nearer the road, where they could make a quick getaway. The woods are really dense around where Debs was attacked. That was someone watching and waiting and biding his time, someone who knows enough about the way things work round here to know where to keep his eyes open."

Rigano smiled. He almost seemed to be enjoying their sparring. "All right," he conceded. "I'll grant you the assumption for now that the incidents were connected. Where do we go from there?"

"Do you want the hypothesis or the evidence?"

"I'll have the evidence, then you can give me the theory."

"Item one. A cassette tape. It was among Rupert Crabtree's papers in the RABD files. It's not what it says on the label—it's a recording of signals traffic on a computer that would be of interest both to this country's allies and our enemies." She put the tape on his desk. He picked it up, studied it and put it down again. He nodded encouragingly.

"Item two. Debs thinks she's being haunted by the ghost of Rupert Crabtree. She thinks she saw him walking the dog after he was dead, and she's convinced it was Crabtree who attacked her.

"Item three. There is someone around, the guy you called Mr Stone, who is taking an interest in what's going on. He's not CID. You tell me he's not SB. That means, given the contents of this tape, that he's MI5 or 6. I imagine from what little I know about intelligence that he's MI6 K Branch. They're the ones who keep track of Soviet and satellite state agents, aren't they?"

A trace of the lighter side of his personality flickered across Rigano's face as he smiled and said, "You seem to know what you're talking about."

Lindsay immediately bristled. She was determined not to grant him any rights where she was concerned. "Please don't patronise me. I'm not a little woman who needs patting on the head because she can play the big boys' game."

The shutters came down over his eyes again. "That wasn't my intention," he replied coolly. "Is that the extent of your evidence?"

"There's one more thing. But that's conjecture rather than hard fact. What if Rupert Crabtree's gun was being carried not for defence but for attack?"

For the first time, Rigano looked truly alert, as if she was telling him something he did not know, or something he did not want her to know. "Why should he?" he demanded.

"If I can explain my idea about what really happened, you'll see why he should," Lindsay replied. "Are you prepared to hear me out?"

He glanced at his watch. It was almost half past five. "I've got half an hour," he said. "Will it take longer than that?"

Lindsay shook her head. "It's not a long story. It's not a very edifying one either. Treachery and greed, that's what we're into here, Jack." He nodded and sat back attentive.

"Simon Crabtree is a computer prodigy. He's one of those people who reads a programme like you or I read a page in the newspaper. And he's a hacker. Even when he was at school, they commented on his rare skill at busting into other people's private programmes. No one had any doubt that he should be looking at a future in computers; no one, that is, except his father, who was conservative enough to be determined that his only son should be properly qualified in something. So he refused to help Simon set up his software business.

"I've seen inside that lock-up and while I don't know too much about computers, I'd say that the equipment in there must run into several thousands of pounds, easily. Maybe even five figures. Now, he wouldn't have got that kind of money from a bank, so where did it come from?

"It's my belief that it came from a foreign power. Almost inevitably the Soviets or an East European Soviet satellite. That cassette you've got there contains a recording of signals traffic from a US military base. I don't know enough about these things to swear that it comes from Brownlow, but the chances are that it does, given that I found it among Rupert Crabtree's papers. What I think happened was this. I think that either Simon was scouted by the Soviets, who learned about his hacking skills and his need for capital; or he approached them with the revelation that he had the key to hack into the base's signals computer. I don't think it's been going on too long, if that's any consolation, because he's only had the business up and running for a few months.

"I'm a bit hazy about what happened to put Rupert Crabtree on to the trail; I'd guess that maybe he saw his son behaving suspiciously, or saw him with someone he shouldn't have been with. Either way, he got hold of this tape. I'm still guessing here, but I think he probably did what I did—took it to someone who knows how to crack computer codes and discovered just what I did—that it's top secret signals traffic. Only, for him, the discovery must have been utterly devastating. Here he is, a pillar of the community, a man in the vanguard of an anti-left-wing campaign, and his son's spying for the Ruskies. Also, to be fair, I think from what I've learned about him that it wouldn't just have been the personal disgrace that would have upset him.

"I think he was a patriotic man who genuinely loved his country. I could never have agreed with his politics, but I don't think he was your stereotype fascist on a power trip. I believe that the discovery of what Simon was doing must have shattered him. And something had really got to him, according to Alexandra Phillips. Are you with me so far?"

Rigano said seriously, "It's a very interesting hypothesis. I think your analysis of Crabtree's character is pretty much on the ball. But do go on. I'm fascinated. You've obviously done a lot of digging that you haven't told me about."

Lindsay smiled. "Isn't that what journalists are supposed to do?"

He frowned. "In theory. But not when they've struck deals with me. Anyway, carry on."

"Crabtree's options once he had discovered Simon's treason were fairly limited. He'd realise at once he couldn't ignore it and carry on as if nothing had changed. He couldn't come to you lot because that would completely destroy his life. It would bring his world crashing down about him, and once the press started digging, it would expose all sorts, like his relationship with Alexandra, like RABD's connections with the violent right. It would make it almost impossible for him to go on practising locally. The shame for him and his wife would have been too much and he was too old to think about starting elsewhere.

"He could have confronted Simon with his knowledge and ordered him to stop, with the blackmail that if he didn't he would go to the authorities. But there's no way that could have been done effectively—Rupert had no way of checking that Simon had really stopped. And Simon probably knew his father well enough to realise that he wouldn't have carried through his bluff. So there would have been a stalemate. And it wouldn't have taken much imagination on Crabtree's part to work out what his fate would probably be once Simon reported back to his control that his father knew he was spying.

"The only other option was to dispose of the son whose treachery was putting his family and his country at risk."

Rigano picked up a pencil and started doodling on a sheet of paper by his phone. He looked up. "Tell me more," he said.

"Not much more to tell, is there? Crabtree had a gun. He was licensed for it. He knew how to shoot. But I'd guess that he probably didn't intend to use it unless he had to. He'd have tried to divert suspicion to the peace women so he'd likely have used the gun as a threat and then killed Simon some other way. He arranged to meet Simon on the common to have a private talk. When he pulled the gun, Simon panicked and overpowered him. Then, realising there was nothing else for it, he killed him.

"Then that cool young man went home, bringing the bemused and terrified family dog, which of course explains why the dog was on the doorstep and not howling over the corpse of his master as one would expect. Then Simon stripped off his muddy bike leathers, and put up a good show for when the police arrived. That, by the way, is when Deborah saw him. You must have noticed that he's physically, if not facially, very like his father. Deborah knew Crabtree but not Simon, and she thought it was the father and not the son she saw outlined against the night sky. It was only much later that she realised he must already have been dead by then.

"And appallingly, it was I who tipped Simon off that Deborah had seen him; I said she'd seen his father, but he was quicker to the point than me and immediately knew who Deborah had really got a glimpse of. He understood the significance, and decided Deborah was too high a risk to leave unattended. Hence the attack on her, and hence her conviction that Rupert Crabtree was haunting her. She must have caught a brief, peripheral glimpse of Simon, and subconsciously identified him wrongly. I hope you've still got a guard on her."

Rigano put his pencil down and sighed. "Very plausible," he muttered. "Fits all the facts in your possession."

"It's the only theory that does," Lindsay replied sharply. "Anything else relies on a string of completely implausible coincidences."

"I tend to agree with you," he replied in an offhand way.

"So what are you going to do about it? You've got the evidence there," Lindsay said, pointing at the tape. "You can get your forensic people to examine the clothes Simon was wearing that night. There must be traces."

"I'm going to do precisely nothing about it, except to say, well done, Lindsay. Now forget it," he said coldly.

Lindsay looked at him in stunned amazement. "What?" she demanded, outraged. "How can you ignore what I've just told you? How can you ignore the evidence I've given you? You've got to bring him in for questioning, at least!"

He shook his head. "No," he said. "Don't you understand?"

"No, I bloody don't," she protested bitterly. "You're a policeman. You're supposed to solve crimes, arrest the culprits, bring them to trial. You're quick enough to do people for speeding— suddenly murder is a no-go area?"

"This murder is," he replied. "Why else do you think a uniform is in charge instead of the CID? Why else am I working with two men, a dog and a national newspaper hack? I am supposed to fail."

Lindsay was dumbstruck. It didn't make any sense to her. "I . . . I don't get it," she stuttered.

Rigano sighed deeply. He spoke quietly but firmly. "I shouldn't tell you this, but I feel I owe it to you after the way you've worked through this. Simon Crabtree is part of a much bigger operation that's out of my hands and way over my head. I am not allowed to touch him. If he ran amok in Fordham High Street with a Kalashnikov, I'd have a job arresting him. Now do you understand?"

Lindsay's fury suddenly erupted. "Oh yes, I bloody understand all right. Some bunch of adolscent spymasters think they can get to some tuppenny-ha'penny KGB thug via Simon Crabtree. So it's hands off Simon. And that means it's open season on Deborah. She can't be kept under police guard for ever. Simon doesn't know he's sacrosanct, he'll have another go. And next time Deborah might not be so lucky. You expect me to stand by while an innocent woman is put at risk from that homicidal traitor? Forget it!"

"So what are you going to do about it?"

"I'm a journalist, Jack," she replied angrily. "I'm going to write the story. The whole bloody, dirty story." She got to her feet and made for the door. As she opened it, she said, "But first of all, I'm going to talk to Simon Crabtree."

16

The roar of the MG's engine was magnified by the high walls of Harrison Mews as Lindsay drew up for her showdown with Simon Crabtree. It was a cold, clear night with an edge of frost in the air and she wound down the car window to take a few deep breaths. The alleyway was gloomy, lit only by a few dim bulbs outside some of the lock-ups. The immediacy of her anger had subsided far enough for her to be apprehensive about what she intended to do. She cursed her lack of foresight in failing to bring along her pocket tape recorder. Although she was desperate for the confrontation, she was enough of a professional to realise that the difficulties she would encounter in getting this story into the paper would only be compounded by an unwitnessed, unrecorded interview with Simon. She could try to find the *Clarion*'s back-up team and enlist their help, but she knew she could only expect the most reluctant co-operation from them unless specifically ordered by Duncan. After her string of exclusives, the poor bastard who'd been sent down as back-up was not going to be too inclined to help her out.

She lit a cigarette and contemplated her options. Behind her apprehension lay the deep conviction of all journalists, that somehow they were immune from the risks faced by the rest of the world. It was that same conviction that had made her face

a killer alone once before. She could dive in now, feet first; the
chances were that Simon would deny everything. Even if he
admitted it, she'd have no proof. Then he'd tip off his masters,
she'd be in the firing line, and as sure as the sun rises in the
morning, Duncan would send her back anyway with a photographer to get pictures and a witnessed interview. It wouldn't
matter so much then if he denied it; the office lawyer would be
satisfied that he'd been given a fair crack of the whip. The other
alternative was to leave it for now, go and visit Debs in hospital,
go home and talk it over with Cordelia, and discuss the best
approach with Duncan in the morning. Then everyone would
be happy. Everyone except Lindsay herself, in whom patience
had never been a highly developed character trait.

Sighing, she decided to be sensible. She wound up the
window but before she could start the engine, she saw a Transit van turn into the alleyway and drive towards her. Only its
sidelights were on, and it was being driven up the middle of the
roadway, making it impossible for Lindsay to pass. Instinctively,
she glanced in the rear-view mirror. In the dim glow of her tail
lights, she saw a red Fiesta, parked diagonally across her rear,
preventing any escape by that route. The Transit stopped a few
feet from her shiny front bumper and both doors opened. There
was nothing accidental about this, she thought.

Two men emerged. One was around the six foot mark, with
the broad shoulders and narrow hips of a body builder. He had
thinning dark hair cut close to his head, and his sharp features
with their five o'clock shadow were exaggerated by the limited
lighting. He looked like a tough Mephistopheles. The other was
smaller and more wiry, with a mop of dark hair contorted into
a curly perm. Both wore leather bomber jackets and training
shoes. All this Lindsay absorbed as they moved towards her,
understanding at once that something unpleasant was going to
happen to her. She discovered that she couldn't swallow. Her
stomach felt as if she'd been punched in the middle of a period
pain. Almost without thinking, Lindsay locked the driver's door

as Curly Perm tried the passenger door and Mephistopheles reached her side of the car. He tried the handle, then said clearly and coldly, "Open it."

Lindsay shook her head. "No way," she croaked through dry lips. She was too scared even to demand to be told what was going on.

She saw him sigh. His breath was a white puff in the night air. "Look," he said reasonably. "Open it now. Or else it's a brick through the window. Or, since you've done us the favour of bringing the soft-top, the Stanley knife across this very expensive hood. You choose."

He looked completely capable of carrying out his threat without turning a hair. Unlocking the door, Lindsay suddenly ached for a life with such certainties, without qualms. Immediately, he wrenched the door open and gestured with his thumb for her to get out. Numbly, she shook her head. Then, behind her, another voice chimed in.

"I should do as he asks if I were you." Lindsay twisted in her seat and saw Stone leaning against the car. Somehow it came as no surprise. She even felt a slight sense of relief. At least she could be sure which side had her. You bastard, Jack Rigano, she thought.

Stone smiled encouragingly. "I assure you, you'll be out of that car one way or another within the next few minutes. It's up to you how painless the experience will be. And don't get carried away with the notion of extracting a price in pain from us. I promise you that your suffering will be immeasurably greater. Now, why don't you just get out of the car?" His voice was all the more chilling for having a warm West Country drawl.

Lindsay turned back to Mephistopheles. If he'd stripped naked in the interval, she wouldn't have noticed. What grabbed her attention was the short-barrelled pistol which was pointing unwaveringly at her right leg. The last flickering of defiance penetrated her fear and she said abruptly, "Because I don't want to get out of the bloody car."

Curly Perm marched round the back of the car, past Stone. He took something from his pocket and suddenly a gleaming blade leapt forward from his fist. He leaned into the car as Lindsay flinched away from him. He looked like a malevolent monkey. He waved the knife in front of her, then, in one swift movement, he sliced her seat belt through the middle, leaving the ends dangling uselessly over her. He moved back, looking speculatively at the soft black vinyl roof.

"The first cut is the deepest," said Stone conversationally. "He's very good with the knife. He knows how to cause serious scars without endangering your life. I wonder if Deborah Patterson would be quite so keen then? Or indeed, that foxy lady you live with. Don't be a hero, Lindsay. Get out of the car."

His matter-of-fact air and the use of her first name were far more frightening than the flick-knife or the gun. The quiet menace Stone gave off was another matter. Lindsay knew enough about herself to realise that he was the one whose threats had the power to invest her life with paranoid nightmares. Co-operation seemed the best way to fight her fear now. So she got out of the car. "Leave the keys," said Mephistopheles as she reached automatically for them on the way out.

As she stood up, Stone moved forward and grasped her right arm above the elbow. Swiftly, he fastened one end of a pair of handcuffs round her wrist. "Am I under arrest, or what?" she demanded. He ignored the question.

"Over to the van, please," he said politely, betraying his words by twisting her arm up her back. Stone steered her round to the back of the Transit. Curly Perm opened the doors and illuminated the interior with a small torch. Lindsay glimpsed two benches fixed to the van's sides then she was bundled inside and the other shackle of the cuffs was fixed to one of the solid steel struts that formed the interior ribs of the van. The doors were hastily slammed behind her, casting her into complete darkness, as she asked again, "What's going on? Eh?" There were no windows. If she stretched out her leg as far as she could reach, she could just touch the doors. She could stand almost upright, but couldn't quite reach the opposite side of the van with her arm. It was clear that any escape attempt would be futile. She felt thankful that she'd never suffered from claustrophobia.

Lindsay heard the sound of her MG's engine starting, familiar enough to be recognisable even inside the Transit. Then it was drowned as the van's engine revved up and she was driven off. She had to hold on to the bench to keep her balance as the van lurched. At first, she tried to memorise turnings, but realised very quickly that it was impossible; the darkness was disorientating. With her one free hand she checked through the contents of her pockets to see if she had anything that might conceivably be useful. A handkerchief, some money (she guessed at £30.57), a packet of cigarettes and her Zippo. Not exactly the Count of Monte Cristo escape kit, she thought bitterly. Why did reality never provide the fillips of fiction? Where was her Swiss army knife and her portable office with the scissors, stapler, adhesive tape and flexible metal tape measure? In her handbag, she remembered, on the floor of the MG. Oh well, if she'd tried to bring it, they would have taken it from her, she decided.

The journey lasted for over an hour and a half. Debs would be wondering why she hadn't appeared, thought Lindsay worriedly. And Cordelia would soon start getting cross that she wasn't home when she said she'd be. They'd probably each assume she was with the other and feel betrayed rather than anxious; no hope of either of them giving the alarm. She was beginning to wonder exactly where she was being taken. If it was central London, they should have been there by now, given the traffic at that time of night. But there were none of the stops and starts of city traffic, just the uninterrupted run of a motorway or major road. If it wasn't London, it must be the other direction. Bristol? Bath? Then it dawned. Cheltenham. General Communications Headquarters. It made a kind of sense.

The van was behaving more erratically now, turning and slowing down at frequent intervals. At 8:12 p.m., according to

Lindsay's watch, it stopped and the engine was turned off. She could hear indeterminate, muffled sounds outside, then the doors opened. Her eyes adjusted to the surge of light and she saw they were in an underground car park. The MG was parked opposite them, the red Fiesta next to it. Stone climbed into the van and unlocked the handcuff linking Lindsay to the van. He snapped it round his left wrist and led her out into the car park.

The four of them moved in ill-assorted convoy to a bank of lifts. Stone took a credit-card-sized piece of black plastic from his pocket and inserted it in a slot, which swallowed it. Above the slot was a grey rubber pad. He pressed his right thumb to the pad, then punched a number into a console. The slot spat the black plastic oblong out and the lift doors opened for them. Curly Perm hit the button marked 5 and they shot upwards silently. They emerged in an empty corridor, brightly lit with fluorescent tubes. Lindsay could see half a dozen closed doors. Stone opened one marked K57 and ushered Lindsay in. The other two remained outside.

The room was almost exactly what Lindsay expected. The walls were painted white. The floor was covered with grey vinyl tiles, pitted with cigarette burns. A couple of bare fluorescent strips illuminated a large metal table in the middle of the room. The table held a telephone and a couple of adjustable study lamps clamped to it. Behind the table stood three comfortable-looking office chairs. Facing it, a metal-framed chair with a vinyl-padded seat and back was fixed to the floor. "My God, what a cliché this room is," said Lindsay.

"What makes you think you deserve anything else?" Stone asked mildly. "Sit in the chair facing the table," he instructed. There seemed no point in argument, so she did as she was told. He unlocked the cuffs again and this time fastened her to the solid-looking arm of the chair.

A couple of hours had passed since she had been really frightened, and she was beginning to feel a little confidence seeping back into her bones. "Look," she said. "Who are you, Stone? What's going on? What am I here for?"

He smiled and shook his head. "Too late for those questions, Lindsay. Those are the first things an innocent person would have asked back in that alley in Fordham. You knew too much. So why ask questions now when you know the answers already?"

"Jesus Christ," she muttered. "You people have got minds so devious you think everyone's part of some plot. When you hemmed me in in that alleyway, I was too bloody stunned to come up with the questions that would have made you happy. Why have I been brought here? What's going to happen to me?"

"That rather depends on you," he replied grimly. "Don't go away, now," he added as he left the room.

She was left alone for nearly half an hour, by which time, all her determined efforts to be brave had gone up in the smoke of her third cigarette. She was scared and she had to acknowledge the fact, although her fear was tempered with relief that it was Rigano's masters rather than Simon Crabtree's who were holding her. She wouldn't give much for her chances if it had been the other way round.

Lindsay had just lit her fourth cigarette when the door opened. She forced herself not to look round. Stone walked in front of her and sat down at one corner of the desk, facing her. He was followed by a woman, all shoulders and sharp haircut, who stood behind the desk scrutinising Lindsay before she too sat down. The woman was severely elegant, in looks as well as dress. Her beautifully groomed pepper-and-salt hair was cut close at the sides, then swept upwards in an extravagant swirl of waves. Extra strong hold mousse, thought Lindsay inconsequentially; if I saw her in a bar, I'd fancy her until I thought about running my fingers through that. The woman had almost transparently pale skin, her eyes glittered greenish blue in her fine-boned face. She looked about forty. She wore a fashionably cut trouser suit in natural linen over a chocolate brown silk shirt with mother-of-pearl buttons. As she studied Lindsay, she took out a packet of Gitanes and lit one.

The pungent blue smoke played its usual trick on Lindsay, flashing into her mind's eye a night in a café in southern France with Cordelia, playing pinball, smoking and drinking coffee, and listening to Elton John on the jukebox. The contrast was enough to bring back her fear so strongly she could almost taste it.

Perhaps the woman sensed the change in Lindsay, for she spoke then. "Mr Stone tells me you are a problem," she said. "If that's the case, we have to find a solution." Her voice had a cool edge, with traces of a northern accent. Lindsay suspected that anger or disappointment would make it gratingly plaintive.

"As far as I'm concerned, the problems are all on your side. I've been abducted at gunpoint, threatened with a knife, the victim of an act of criminal damage and nobody has bothered to tell me by whom or why. Don't you think it's a little unreasonable to expect me to bend over backwards to solve anything you might be considering a problem?" Lindsay demanded through clenched teeth, trying to hide her fear behind a show of righteous aggression.

The woman's eyebrows rose. "Come, come, Miss Gordon. Let's not play games. You know perfectly well who we are and why you're here."

"I know he's MI6 K division, or at least I've been assuming he is. But I don't know why the hell I've been brought here like a criminal, or who you are. And until I do, all you get from me is my name."

The woman crushed out her half-smoked cigarette and smiled humourlessly at Lindsay. "Your bravado does you credit. If it helps matters any, my name is Barber. Harriet Barber. The reason you've been brought here, in your words like a criminal, is that, according to the laws of the land, that's just what you are.

"You are, or have been in unauthorised possession of classified information. That on its own would be enough to ensure a lengthy prison sentence, believe me, particularly given your contacts on the left. You were apprehended while in the process of jeopardising an operation of Her Majesty's security forces, another matter on which the courts take an understandably strong line. Superintendent Rigano really should have arrested you as soon as you tossed that tape on his desk."

Thanks a million, Jack, Lindsay thought bitterly. But she recognised that she had begun marginally to relax. This authoritarian routine was one she felt better able to handle. "So am I under arrest now?" she asked.

Again came the cold smile. "Oh no," said Harriet Barber. "If you'd been arrested, there would have had to be a record of it, wouldn't there?"

The fear was back. But the moment's respite had given Lindsay fresh strength. "So if I'm not under arrest, I must be free to go, surely?" she demanded.

"In due course," said Stone.

"Don't be too optimistic, Mr Stone," said Barber. "That depends on how sensible Miss Gordon is. People who can't behave sensibly often suffer unfortunate accidents due to their carelessness. And someone who drives an elderly sports car like Miss Gordon's clearly has moments when impulse overcomes good sense. Let's hope we don't have too many moments like that tonight."

There was a silence. Lindsay's nerve was the first to go and she said, struggling to sound nonchalant, "Let's take the posturing as read and come to the deal. What's the score?"

"There's that unfortunate bravado again," sighed Barber. "We are not offering any deal, Miss Gordon. That's not the way we do things here. You will sign the Official Secrets Act and will be bound by its provisions. You will also sign a transcript of your conversation with Superintendent Rigano this evening, as an insurance policy. You will hand over any copies of that tape still in your possession. And then you will leave here. You will not refer to the events of this evening or to your theories about the murder of Rupert Crabtree to anyone. On pain of prosecution. Or worse."

"And if I don't?"

"The answer to that question is not one that will appeal, believe me. What have you to lose by co-operating with what are, after all, your own country's national interests?"

Lindsay shook her head. "If we started to debate where the national interest really lies, we'd be here a long time, Ms Barber. I've got a more immediate concern than that. I understand that you're not going to let Simon Crabtree be charged with the murder of his father?"

"Superintendent Rigano's indiscretions were quite accurate."

"So that means he stays free until you're ready?"

The woman nodded. "You have a good grasp of the realities, Miss Gordon."

"Then what?"

"Then he will be dealt with, believe me. By one side or the other."

"But not immediately?"

"That seems unlikely. He has—certain uses, shall we say?"

Lindsay lit another cigarette. "That's my problem, you see, Ms Barber. Simon Crabtree is a murderer and I want him out of circulation."

"I'm surprised that the Protestant ethic is still so firmly rooted in you, given how the rest of your lifestyle has rejected it. I didn't expect a radical lesbian feminist to be so adamant for justice," Barber replied sarcastically.

"It's not some abstract notion of justice that bothers me," Lindsay retorted. "It's life and death. The life and death of someone I care about. You see, no one's told Simon Crabtree that he's immune from prosecution. And he thinks that Deborah Patterson has information that will tie him to his father's murder and put him away. For as long as he's on the streets, Deborah Patterson is at risk, and I can't go along with any deal that means there's a chance that she's going to die. So I'm sorry, it's no deal. I've got to tell my story. I've got to put a stop to Simon Crabtree."

"That's a very short-sighted view," Barber responded quietly. "If you don't accept the deal, Deborah will be in exactly the same position of risk that you have outlined."

Lindsay shook her head. "No. Even if I can't get the paper to use the story, I can get her out of the firing line. I can take her away somewhere he'll never find us."

Harriet Barber laughed softly. "I don't think you quite understand, Miss Gordon. If you don't accept our offer, you'll be in no position to take Deborah anywhere. Because you won't be going anywhere. Accidents, Miss Gordon, can happen to anyone."

17

The phone was ringing when Cordelia let herself in, but before she could reach the nearest extension, the answering machine picked up the call. No hurry, she thought, climbing the stairs. She took off her sheepskin, went into their bedroom and swapped her boots for a pair of slippers. She carried her briefcase through to her study, then headed for the kitchen. She put on some coffee to brew, and with a degree of anticipation went to read the note from Lindsay she'd spotted on her way past the memo board. She wished she'd been able to dash down to Brownlow to be with Lindsay when she'd needed her and was gratified when she found that her presumed errant lover was due home within the half hour. Only then did she play back the messages stored on the machine.

All were for Lindsay, and all were from Duncan, increasingly angry as one succeeded another. There were four, the earliest timed at noon, the latest the one she'd nearly picked up when she came in. It was all to do with some urgent query from the office lawyer about her copy, and Duncan was clearly furious at Lindsay's failure to keep in touch. Cordelia sighed. It was really none of her business, but she toyed with the idea of calling Duncan and making soothing noises while explaining that Lindsay was due back at any minute. She got as far as dialling the number of the newsdesk, but thought better of it at the last minute and replaced the receiver. Lindsay wouldn't thank her if she had the effect of irritating Duncan still further, which, knowing him, was entirely possible.

Cordelia poured herself a mug of coffee, picked up the morning paper and ambled through to the living room. She sat down to read the paper, but decided she needed some soothing music and went over to the record and tape collection to select her current favourite, a tape Lindsay had compiled of Renata Tebaldi singing Mozart and Puccini arias. She slotted the tape into the stereo, noting with annoyance that the power was still switched on and that there was an unidentified tape in the other deck. It aroused her curiosity, so she rewound the tape and played it back. The series of hisses and whines puzzled her, but she shrugged and put it down to some bizarre exercise of Lindsay's. She stopped the tape and went back to her coffee and paper to the strains of "Un Bel Di Vedremo."

She was immersed in the book reviews when the phone rang again. She picked it up, checking her watch, surprised to see it was already ten past eight. "Cordelia Brown here," she said.

"Thank Christ somebody answers this phone occasionally!" It was Duncan, sufficiently self-confident not to bother announcing his identity. "Where the hell is she, Cordelia? I've been trying to get hold of her all bloody day. She's got her bloody radio pager switched off too, the silly bitch. I mean, I told her she could have the day off, but she knows better than to do a body-swerve when she's got a story on the go. Where is she, then?"

"I really don't know, Duncan," Cordelia replied. "But I'm expecting her back any minute. She left a note saying she'd be back by eight and she's usually very good about punctuality. I'll get her to call as soon as she gets in, okay?"

"No, it's not okay," he retorted with ill-grace. "But it'll have to do. I'll have her on the dog watch for a month for this. Makes me look a bloody idiot, you know?"

"I'm sorry, Duncan. You know it's not like her to let you down."

"She's got some bloody bee in her bonnet about this peace camp. It was the same over that bloody murder in Derbyshire but at least she was freelance then. She owes me some loyalty for giving her a job. I'll get no proper work out of her till this is cleared up," he complained.

"You don't have to tell me, Duncan," Cordelia sympathised. "I'll get her to call you, okay?"

Cordelia sat for a moment, the first stirrings of worry beginning. Lindsay was pathologically punctual. If her note said "back by eight," then home by eight she'd be, or else she'd have phoned a message through. She always managed it; in the past she'd bribed passing motorists or British Rail porters to make the phone calls on her behalf. Presumably, Lindsay was visiting Deborah, since she'd been so worried about her condition. And there was no point in fretting about that. She was only twenty-five minutes late, after all.

On an impulse, Cordelia went through to Lindsay's desk and checked her card-index file to see if there was any contact number for the peace camp. The only number that seemed to suit her purpose was that of the pub the women used regularly. She keyed in the nine digits and when a man answered, she asked if Jane was in. She was told to hang on and after a few minutes a cautious woman's voice said, "Hello? Who is this?"

"Is that Jane?" asked Cordelia. "This is Cordelia."

"No, it's not Jane. She's not here. Do you need to get a message to her?"

"Yes, I do. It's really urgent. Would you ask her to call Lindsay Gordon's home number as soon as possible, please?"

"No problem. Lindsay Gordon's home number," the voice said. "A couple of the women are going back in five minutes, so they can tell Jane then. She'll get your message in about a quarter of an hour."

Fifteen minutes stretched into twenty for Cordelia. She poured herself a glass of wine, though what she craved was a large Scotch. But she wasn't taking the chance of being over the limit if she had to drive anywhere to rescue Lindsay from some mess or other. After twenty-five minutes, she raked around the house till she found a packet with a couple of Lindsay's cigarettes left in it, and lit one.

The phone had barely rung when Cordelia snatched it up, praying for Lindsay's familiar voice. She was unreasonably disappointed to find Jane on the other end of the line.

"Hi, Cordelia. I got this urgent message to phone Lindsay. Is she there?"

"No," Cordelia sighed. "The message was from me. I'm trying to track her down. She seems to have dropped out of sight, and given the events of the last few days, I'm a bit worried. I don't suppose you know where she's got to?"

"I'm sorry, love, I was hoping this message was from her, to be honest. She was supposed to come to the hospital to see Deborah tonight, but she hasn't shown up. I took Cara in for five minutes to see her mum, and I deliberately left it till towards the end of visiting time to give Lindsay a chance to spend a bit of time with Deborah if she was up to it, but the policeman on duty said Lindsay hadn't been at all. I was pretty amazed because the last thing she said this morning was that she'd see me there tonight," Jane said.

"So when was the last time you saw Lindsay?" Cordelia asked.

"This morning. Not long after nine. She'd been in to see Deborah and I went along for moral support. She came out from seeing Deborah and asked if I could make my own way back to the camp because she'd got to go to Oxford urgently. Look, Cordelia, I wouldn't worry about her. She's probably been held up on something to do with work," Jane reassured her.

"No," Cordelia replied. "Her office are going nutso because she hasn't been in touch with them either. It's odd—she's been back here and left a note since then. God knows where she's gone now. She didn't say why she was going to Oxford, did she? Or who she was going to see?"

"She didn't mention any names, but she did say it was something to do with a computer," said Jane. "I'm sorry I can't be more help."

"No, you've been great," said Cordelia. "Look, if by any remote chance she turns up, will you tell her to phone the office as soon as possible, on pain of death? And me too?"

"Of course I will," said Jane. "I hope you get hold of her soon. She'll probably be chasing some story that's the most important thing in the world to her right now. I'm sure she's okay, Cordelia."

"Yeah, thanks. See you." Cordelia put the phone down. Oxford and computers. That could only mean Annie Norton. She trailed back to Lindsay's desk to try and find a number for Annie. There was nothing in the card-index, and Lindsay's address book listed Annie without a phone number. Cordelia tried directory enquiries, but wasn't surprised, given the way her luck was running, to find that Annie was ex-directory. A trawl through Lindsay's address book produced three other mutual friends who might be able to supply a number for Annie. Predictably, it took her three attempts to get what she wanted.

Annie's phone rang nearly a dozen times before she answered. Her voice was irritable as she gave her number.

"Annie? I'm sorry to interrupt you. It's Cordelia Brown here," she apologised. "I was wondering if by any chance you know where Lindsay is? Did she come to see you this morning by any chance? The thing is she's disappeared, and her office are desperate to contact her."

"I'm sorry, Cordelia, I really have no idea where she might be. Yes, she was here, but she left my office about half past ten, I guess. She gave me no indication of where she was heading then." Annie sounded reluctant to continue the conversation.

"I'm sorry if this is an awkward time . . ." Cordelia trailed off.

"I have some people for dinner, that's all," said Annie.

"I'm just really worried about her, Annie. She never goes walkabout like this. Not when she's got work on. She's far too conscientious. Do you mind me asking, what was it she wanted to know about?"

Annie relented, touched by the concern in Cordelia's voice. "She had left a computer tape with me for analysis, and she came round to collect the results. She did say that she intended to get back to London tonight. This attack on Deborah has taken a lot out of her. I think it frightened her badly."

"I know that," Cordelia replied, "but what was this tape all about? What kind of tape was it?"

"It was an ordinary cassette tape." That made sense, thought Cordelia, remembering the tape in the stereo. "But I think you'd better ask Lindsay what it was about. I'm not in a position to discuss it, Cordelia. I'm sorry, I'm not being obstructive, just cautious. I think there are too many people involved already."

"What do you mean, Annie? You can't leave it at that!"

"I'm sorry. I shouldn't have said as much as I have. Lindsay's mixed up in something that could cause a lot of hassle. I told her she should be talking to the police about it, not me. Maybe she took my advice."

"Jesus, Annie, what the hell's going on? Are you saying she's in danger?"

"Don't worry, Cordelia. I don't imagine for one minute that she's in any danger. She'll be in touch. She could be trying to phone now, for all we know. Take it easy and don't worry. Lindsay's a born survivor. Look, I'd better go now. Tell her to give me a call in the morning, okay?" Annie's tone was final.

"Okay," said Cordelia coldly. "Goodbye." Her anger at Annie's nonchalance had the salutory effect of making her do something to fight her own growing anxiety. She collected the mystery tape, pulled on her boots and sheepskin and ran downstairs. She climbed into the BMW and joined the night traffic. When she reached the motorway, she put her foot down and blasted down the fast lane. "Please God," she said aloud as

she drove. "Please let her be all right." But the appalling fantasy
of Lindsay's death would not be kept at bay by words. Cordelia
was near to tears when she pulled up in the car park of Fordham police station just before ten o'clock. She marched inside,
determined to find out what had happened to Lindsay.

She marched up to the duty officer. "I need to see Superintendent Rigano," she said. "It's a matter of great urgency."

The officer looked sceptical. "I don't know if he's still here,
miss," he stalled. "Perhaps if you could tell me what it's all about
we'll see if we can sort it out."

"Why don't you check and see if he is here? You can tell
him that I need to speak to him about the Deborah Patterson
attack," she responded crisply.

He compressed his lips in irritation and vanished behind
a frosted-glass partition. Five minutes later he reappeared to
say grudgingly, "If you follow me, I'll take you to the Super."

She found Rigano sitting alone at his desk going through
a stack of files. The lines on his face seemed to be etched more
deeply and there were dark shadows under his eyes. "So what is
it now, Miss Brown? Can't Miss Gordon run her own errands?
Or is she just keeping out of my way?"

"I was hoping you might be able to tell me where she is,"
Cordelia enunciated carefully. "She appears to have vanished,
and I rather thought that was police business."

"Vanished? If she's vanished, she's done it very recently. She
was here till about six o'clock. And that's only four hours ago."

Suddenly, Cordelia felt foolish. "She was due home at eight
o'clock. She hadn't phoned by nine. I know that probably sounds
nothing to you, but Lindsay's got a real fetish about punctuality.
She never fails to let me know if she's not going to make it at
a time she's prearranged. Especially when we've not seen each
other for a day or two." Don't dismiss me as a hysterical female,
she pleaded mentally.

"You don't think that you might be overreacting?"

"No. I believe she had some information concerning Rupert Crabtree's death and the attack on Deborah that might have put her in danger. I'm scared, Superintendent. I've got a right to be."

A spasm of emotion crossed his face. But his voice was cool. "Do you know what that information was?"

"Not in detail. But something to do with a computer tape, I believe." He nodded. "Okay. I think we may be a little premature here, but let's make a few enquiries anyway."

She expected him to dismiss her or summon a subordinate, but he picked up his phone and dialled an outside number. "Mrs Crabtree?" he said. "Superintendent Rigano here. I'm sorry to trouble you. Is Simon there by any chance? . . . In London? When did he go, do you know? . . . Yesterday? I see. And you expect him back Saturday. Yes, a computer exhibition. I see. Do you know the number of his stand? You don't? Never mind. No, it's not urgent. Has anyone else been trying to contact him? . . . No? Fine, thanks very much. Sorry to have disturbed you. Good night."

He clicked a pen against his teeth. Then he dialled an internal number. "Davis? Get in here, lad," he demanded. A moment later the door opened and a plain clothes officer in shirtsleeves entered. "Where's Stone?" Rigano asked him abruptly.

"I don't know, sir. He rushed off about six, just before you went out. He's not been back since."

"What do you mean, he rushed off?"

"He came out of his room like a bat out of hell, sir, and ran out to the car park. He took off in that souped-up Fiesta of his."

"Jesus," Rigano swore softly. "I don't believe this. Is his room locked, Davis?"

"I suppose so, sir. He always locks up after himself."

"Okay. Get me the master key from the duty officer. I'm bloody tired of not knowing what's going on in my own station." The young officer looked startled. "Go on, lad, get it." He departed on the double.

"What's going on?" Cordelia asked.

"Sorry, can't say," he replied with an air of such finality that Cordelia couldn't find the energy to challenge him.
There was silence till Davis returned. Then the two men left the
room together. Five interminable minutes passed before Rigano
stormed back into the room. His fury was frightening, his face
flushed a dark crimson. Ignoring Cordelia he grabbed the phone,
dialled a number and exploded into the phone, "Rigano here.
I'm letting you know that I intend to lodge a formal complaint
about Stone. Do you know he's been bugging my office? Not
only has he destroyed this force's credibility over this whole
investigation but now he's taking the law into his own hands.

"Listen, I have good reason to believe that someone could
be in a situation of extreme prejudice thanks to this, and I'm not
going to lie down and die any longer. You'll be hearing from
me formally in the morning." He slammed the receiver down.
His hands were trembling with the force of his rage.

The storm had done nothing to ease Cordelia's growing
fear. Rigano turned to face her and said carefully, "I'm sorry
about that. I think I know where Lindsay is, and I'm not happy
about it." He sighed. "I wish to hell she'd listened to me. Is she
always so damned headstrong?"

"Never mind the bloody character analysis. Where is she?
Who is she with? She's in some kind of trouble, isn't she? What's
going on?" Cordelia almost shouted.

"Yes, she's in trouble. Deep trouble."

"Well, why are we sitting here? Why aren't we doing something about it?"

"I'm going to get her," he said decisively. "It's going to
cause all sorts of bloody aggravation. But I can't leave her to
stew. I can't walk away from it. Miss Brown . . . I suggest you
go home and try not to worry. She should be home by morning.
If not, I'll let you know."

Cordelia could not believe her ears. "Oh no!" she exploded.
"You don't get rid of me like that. If you're going to get Lindsay,

I'm coming too. I will not be fobbed off with all this static. Either you take me along or I'm going to get on the phone to Lindsay's boss and tell him she's been kidnapped by one of your sidekicks. And everything else I know."

"I can't take you with me," he said.

"I'll follow you."

"I'll have you arrested if you try it."

It seemed like stalemate. "I know about the tape," said Cordelia. "I know where there's a copy of the analysis of it, too," she said, guessing wildly about Annie's involvement. "Take me with you or the lot goes to Lindsay's paper. Even if you arrest me, I get to make a phone call eventually. That's all it'll take. And just think what a story it'll make—famous writer sues police for wrongful imprisonment."

He shook his head. "There's no point in all this blackmail, believe me. I give you my word, I'll get her back to you."

"That's not good enough. Something's going on here. And I can't leave it in anyone else's hands. It's too important."

He finally conceded, too worn out to carry on the fight. "All right. You can follow me. But you won't be allowed to come in."

"Why? Where the hell are you going? Where is she?"

"GCHQ Cheltenham, I think."

"What?"

≈≈✦≈≈

It was nearly midnight when they reached the main gates of the intelligence complex. As Rigano instructed, Cordelia parked as unobtrusively as possible about quarter of a mile from the brightly lit gate. She watched as Rigano drove up and, after five minutes, was admitted. Tearing irritably at the cellophane on the packet of cigarettes she'd bought at a petrol station *en route* Cordelia prepared herself for a long vigil. Rigano wasn't exactly her idea of the knight in shining armour. But he was all she'd got.

18

The chirrup of the telephone broke the stalemate in the smoky room. Lindsay was grateful for the note of normality it injected into what had become a completely disorientating experience. Harriet Barber frowned and picked it up. "Barber here," she said coolly. A puzzled look crossed her face and she turned to Stone, handing him the phone. "You'd better deal with this," she ordered.

"Yes? Stone speaking," he said. He listened for a few moments then said, "I'll be right down." He replaced the phone and got to his feet. "I don't understand this, I'm afraid. Are you staying here?" he asked.

"The situation down there is your problem, Stone," she replied icily. "Deal with it. Deal with it quickly."

He left the room.

"I suppose a visit to the loo would be out of the question?" Lindsay asked.

"Not at all."

"You surprise me."

"Provided you don't mind my company."

"What?" Lindsay demanded, outraged.

"We don't take chances with valuable government property," Barber replied easily. "Besides, I thought it might rather appeal to you. Given your . . . inclinations."

Lindsay's face revealed her contempt. "I'd rather eat razor blades," she spat.

"That could be arranged," Barber replied with a faint smile. She pulled a small black notebook from her jacket pocket and made a few notes. Lindsay glowered at her in silence. Long minutes passed before the phone rang again. "Barber here," the woman said again. She listened then said abruptly. "Out of the question. No . . ." She listened again. "He says what?" Anger clouded her eyes. "Well, in that case, you'd better bring him up. I'm not going to forget this whole episode, Stone." She slammed the phone down and stared at Lindsay. She lit another fragrant French cigarette then got up and offered one to Lindsay who accepted gratefully. "We have a visitor, Miss Gordon," Barber said, her voice clipped and taut.

"Who?" the journalist asked wearily.

"You'll see soon enough," was the reply before Barber lapsed into silence again.

Lindsay heard the door open and swivelled uncomfortably round in her chair. A surge of relief flooded through her when she saw an obviously disgruntled Stone hustling Rigano into the room. He stopped on the threshold, his face the stony mask that Lindsay had come to recognise as normal. But when he spoke, the concern in his voice was a distinct novelty. "Are you all right?" he asked, moving slowly towards her. Before she could reply, he spotted the handcuffs and rounded angrily on Stone. "For Christ's sake," he thundered. "She's not one of the bloody Great Train Robbers. What's all this crap?"

Stone looked helplessly at Harriet Barber, who responded immediately. "Mr Stone is not in charge here, Superintendent. I am, and I have no intention of releasing Miss Gordon until we have the assurances from her that we require. I am under no obligation towards you, and you are here out of courtesy only."

The tension between the two of them crackled in the air. "We'll see about that," Rigano replied grimly before turning back to Lindsay. "Are you all right?"

"Considering that I've been kidnapped at gunpoint, threatened with a knife, transported in conditions that would be illegal if I was a sheep, and interrogated by assholes, I'm okay," she answered bitterly. "You got me into this mess, Jack. You shopped me. Now call off the dogs and get me out of it."

"He doesn't have the authority," Barber said.

"We'll see about that as well," Rigano retorted. "But I didn't shop you, Lindsay. That bastard Stone had my office bugged. I have proof of that, and it's already in the hands of my senior officers. You people, madam," he said, turning towards Harriet Barber, "had my men's full co-operation, but that wasn't good enough for you, was it?"

"As things have turned out, it looks as if that was a wise precaution. We haven't had your full co-operation, after all."

"You don't get away with bugging a senior police officer's room, whoever you are, madam."

"Your intervention at this juncture is tedious and utterly pointless, Superintendent. You have satisfied yourself as to the well-being of Miss Gordon and I suggest that you leave now." Barber's tone suggested that she was not accustomed to being thwarted.

But Rigano refused to be intimidated. "Where are we up to, Lindsay? What's the deal?"

"I would advise you not to reply, Miss Gordon. Superintendent, you have no standing here. I strongly advise you to leave."

"You might not think I have any standing here, madam, but I'd have thought you'd welcome *any* intervention that might sort this business out. Now, will someone please tell me what the offer is?"

"It's simple, Jack," said Lindsay. "I sign away all my rights, promise to forget everything I know and Simon Crabtree gets to kill Debs."

Exasperated by the situation spiralling out of her control, Harriet Barber got to her feet and said angrily, "Don't be absurd. Superintendent, we expect Miss Gordon to sign the Official

Secrets Act and to be bound by it. We expect the return of any secret material still in her possession. She will not refer to the events of this evening or to her theories about what has happened at Brownlow to anyone, on pain of prosecution. Not unreasonable, I submit."

"That's the sanitised version," interrupted Lindsay. "What she misses out is that Crabtree stays free to take whatever steps he wants against Debs and that if I write the story I'll be silenced. Permanently."

"No one has threatened your life," Barber snapped.

"Not in so many words," Lindsay agreed. "But we both know that's what we've been talking about."

Rigano shook his head. "This is bloody silly. This is not the Soviet Union. People don't get bumped off because they possess inconvenient knowledge. You're both making a melodrama out of a molehill. Do you really think that any newspaper's going to print her story? For a kick-off, no one would believe her. And besides, you can easily shut up any attempts at publication.

"There's no need to threaten Miss Gordon with dire consequences because she'd never get any editor to take the chance of using this stuff. She's got no evidence except the computer tape and that means bugger all at the end of the day. All you need from her is her signature on the OSA and the return of the tape. You don't need threats."

"But what about Deborah?" Lindsay interrupted. "Crabtree's going to walk away from all this believing she knows something that can put him away. You can't protect her twenty-four hours a day for ever."

Rigano looked puzzled. "I still don't bloody see why you people want Crabtree free. He's a bloody spy as well as a murderer."

Barber frowned. "He has uses at present. He will eventually pay the price for his activities. That I can guarantee."

Rigano jumped on her words. "So surely until that happens you people can put Deborah Patterson into a safe house."

Lindsay shook her head. "I can't trust them to look after her. Their organisation's probably penetrated at every level already without Simon Crabtree hacking his way in. Besides, this lot would do a double-cross tomorrow if it fitted their notion of national security."

"And there's the impasse, Superintendent," Barber said. "She doesn't trust us, and we don't trust her."

Rigano thought for a moment, then said slowly, "There is one way."

⚜

Cordelia counted the cigarettes left in the packet. She fiddled with the radio tuner, trying to find a station that would take her mind off the terrifying possibilities that kept running through her head. She looked at her watch, comparing the time with the dashboard clock. He'd been in there for more than an hour. She lit another cigarette that she knew she wouldn't enjoy and stared back at the dark cluster of buildings in deep shadow under the severe overhead lights that led from the road. As she watched, a tall man came out of the main gate and started walking in her direction. She paid little attention until he stopped by her car expectantly. Wary, she pressed the switch that lowered the window until a two-inch gap appeared. She could see a blond head of hair above a windproof jacket. His eyes glittered as he asked brusquely, "Cordelia Brown?"

"Yes," she answered. An edginess in his manner urged her to caution.

"I have a message for you." He handed her a note.

Cordelia recognised her lover's familiar handwriting and her stomach contracted with relief. She forced herself to focus on the words, and read, "Give the copy of the computer tape to the man who delivers this if you've got it. It's all right. L." She looked up at the man's impassive face. "What's going on? Am I going to see her soon?" she pleaded.

"Looks like it," he said. His voice was without warmth. "The tape?"

She fumbled in her bag and handed him the unlabelled cassette.

"The note as well, please."

"What?" she asked, puzzled.

"I need the note back." Reluctantly, she handed him the scrap of paper.

Cordelia watched him walk towards the gate and gain admission. Unnerved by the brevity of the encounter she lit another cigarette and searched the radio wavebands again.

⋙⋘

The digital clock on the dashboard showed 2:01 when the barrier at the gate rose. Cordelia stared so hard into the pool of light by the gate that she feared the sight of Rigano's car followed by Lindsay's MG was a mirage. She sat bolt upright in her seat, then hurriedly got out of the BMW. When the other two cars reached her, they stopped, and their drivers emerged. Lindsay and Cordelia fell into each other's arms. For once, no words came between them as they clung desperately to each other. Rigano cleared his throat noisily and said, "You promised them I'd have the printout by ten. We'd better get a move on, hadn't we?"

Lindsay disengaged herself from Cordelia's arms and rubbed her brimming eyes. "Okay, okay," she said. "And we have to work out the details of how you keep your end of the bargain. We'd better go back to London in convoy. I hope you're going to give us the benefit of the blue flashing light."

"Is someone going to explain what's been going on?" Cordelia demanded. "I've been sitting here like a lemon half the night, going out of my mind with worry."

"Later," said Lindsay.

"No," said Rigano. "No explanations. That's the deal, remember."

Dawn was fading the streetlights into insignificance by the time they reached Highbury. Cordelia drove off to garage her car while Lindsay went indoors to collect the printout. When she returned Rigano took the papers, saying, "What arrangements do you want me to make?"

Lindsay spoke abruptly. "I need to make some phone calls. If the hospital say it's okay, then I'll act tonight. Unless you hear from me to the contrary, I'll expect your men to be gone by seven. And I don't want anyone following us."

He smiled grimly. "There won't be." Rigano raised his hand in mock salute then turned and walked back to his car as Cordelia arrived at the door. After watching him accelerate out of sight, Lindsay buried her head in Cordelia's shoulder and burst into tears. "I've been so bloody scared," she sobbed. "I thought I'd never see you again."

Cordelia led her indoors and helped her upstairs. Lindsay's muscles felt like jelly and she was shivering. "Tell me about it later," Cordelia said as she undressed her and got her into bed. "Sleep now and we'll talk later." Lindsay fell back on the pillows and fell asleep almost immediately, sprawled across the bed like a starfish. Cordelia looked down at her exhausted face with pity, and decided to sleep in the spare room to avoid disturbing her.

❧❀❧

Lindsay woke at noon to the sound of the phone ringing. She grabbed the receiver and was immediately deafened by a raging Duncan. She lay back and let him rant till he finally ran out of steam. "So what've you got to say for yourself?" he yelled for the third time.

"I was in police custody till six this morning, Duncan," she explained. "I wasn't allowed to make a phone call. They had got it into their heads that I was withholding information concerning the Rupert Crabtree murder and they were giving me the third degree."

The phone crackled into life again as Duncan's rage transferred itself to Fordham police. Again, Lindsay let the storm blow itself out. As he threatened for the fourth time to sue the police and have questions raised in Parliament, Lindsay butted in. "Look, it's all over now, Duncan. It won't serve any purpose to jump up and down about it. Anyway, I'm on the trail of a cracking good exclusive connected to the murder. But I'm going to have to drop out of sight for a couple of days while I get some info undercover and look up a few dodgy contacts. Is that okay?"

"No, it's not bloody okay. What is this exclusive? You don't decide to fuck off chasing whatever rainbows you fancy just because you've had a lucky run with a few stories. Tell me what you're following up and I'll let you know if it's worthwhile."

Lindsay could feel a headache starting somewhere behind her eyes. "I don't exactly know where it's going to lead me, Duncan, but I've discovered that there's an MI5 man involved somehow in the fringes of the murder. I want to dig around a bit and see if I can find out what the intelligence angle is, see what it's all about. I think it could be a belter, Duncan. I've got that feeling about it. One of the coppers has hinted to me that there could be a security angle. But I'll have to keep a low profile. I might be out of touch for a day or two." She kept her fingers crossed that the gamble would pay off. There was a pause.

"Till Monday, then," he said grudgingly. "I want a progress report by morning conference. This is your last chance, though, Lindsay. Piss me about like yesterday again and no excuses will do." The phone crashing down at the other end nearly deafened Lindsay, but she didn't mind. She had got her own way, and Duncan was only indulging in office bravado in order to terrorise her colleagues.

Sighing, she got out of bed and quickly pulled on a pair of jeans and a thick sweater. She pushed her head round the spare room door to see Cordelia apparently sound asleep. It was good to be home again. The events of the last twenty-four hours had convinced her that in spite of her frequent absorption in her own concerns, Cordelia was still totally committed to her. Grabbing a pocketful of change on her way out, Lindsay headed across Highbury Fields. She was going to have to be careful. It was at times like this she could use Cordelia's help but it was too risky to involve anyone else unnecessarily. Lindsay couldn't justify to herself the act of confiding in Cordelia for her own selfish reasons. She put these thoughts to the back of her mind as she reached the phone box. She wanted to be sure these calls weren't going to end up on one of Harriet Barber's phone taps. She called Fordham General Hospital where, under the guise of a close relative, she eventually found a doctor who was prepared to admit that it would now be possible to move Deborah without untoward risk, though he personally would accept no responsibility for this.

There followed a series of phone calls including one to her parents in Argyllshire. She made the necessary arrangements with the minimum of fuss, then headed back home. She put some coffee on, then stripped off and dived under the shower. She spent a long time luxuriating in the hot water, putting off the moment when she would have to waken Cordelia and tell her she was about to go missing without trace again. It wasn't something she relished, particularly since the business of Deborah still lay unresolved between them.

She emerged from the shower and wrapped the towel around herself. In the kitchen, Cordelia was staring moodily into a mug of coffee. Lindsay squeezed past and poured out her own. She reached across the table for a discarded packet of cigarettes and nervously lit up.

Cordelia picked up the morning paper and began to read the front page. Lindsay cleared her throat and said awkwardly, "Thanks for last night. If it hadn't been for you, I don't know what would have happened."

Cordelia shrugged. "Least I could do. I do worry about you, you know. Ready to tell me about it yet?"

"I'd rather wait till it's all sorted, if that's okay. I've got to go away again for a couple of days." Cordelia said nothing, and turned the page of the paper. "We're taking Debs somewhere she'll be safe. Once that's done, I'll be able to tell you the whole story. It's not that I don't trust you—but after last night, knowing how heavy these people can get, I just don't want to expose you to any risks. I don't enjoy being secretive."

"You could have fooled me," Cordelia said with a wry smile. "Okay, Lindsay, you play it your way. When will you be back?"

"I'm not sure. I'll call you when I know."

Lindsay swallowed the remains of her coffee and went back to the bedroom. She dressed quickly, then she threw knickers, socks, shirts and jeans into a holdall, grimacing as she noticed how few clean clothes were left in her wardrobe. Everything else she needed was in the car or Deborah's van already. She finished packing, and turned to find Cordelia standing just inside the room, leaning on the door jamb.

"You are coming back?"

Lindsay dropped her bag and hauled Cordelia into her arms. "Of course I'm coming back."

19

Closing the front door behind her, Lindsay felt weariness creep over her at the thought of the day ahead. She got into the MG, noticing how badly she'd parked only seven hours before. The memory of her ordeal threatened to overwhelm her, so she quickly started the car and shot off. Driving, as usual, restored some of her equanimity and she was fairly calm by the time she reached Brownlow. She went straight to the Red Cross bender and found Jane lying on a pallet reading a novel. Lindsay marvelled once again at the ability of the peace women to indulge in perfectly normal activities in such an outlandish situation. Guiltily breaking in to Jane's much-needed relaxation, Lindsay sketched out what she needed and why. Her sense of urgency transmitted itself to Jane, who agreed to the plan.

Lindsay waited until dusk, then borrowed a 2CV from one of the peace women. Going first to the hospital, she made a brief reconnaissance before heading back to the camp. She linked up with Jane as arranged and hastily they loaded the van with their own bags. Then Lindsay made up the double berth and got Cara ready for bed.

At twenty past seven, Lindsay got into the MG and shot off down the winding lane away from the camp, heading in the opposite direction from the hospital. A quarter of a mile down the road she spotted a set of headlamps in her rear-view mirror. Once she hit the outskirts of the town, she figured, her pursuer, this time in a green Ford Escort, would have to close up or risk losing her. Her calculations proved right. Thanks to her earlier homework she shook off the pursuit by doubling back down an alley and taking a short cut up a one-way street in the wrong direction. Then, driving in a leisurely fashion to a small industrial estate near the motorway, she tucked the MG into a car park behind one of the factory units. Jane was waiting for her in the van. Together they made straight for Fordham General. Lindsay directed Jane into a small loading area at the back of the main hospital building.

Lindsay crouched down beside Cara, who was lying in bed, drifting in and out of sleep. "I want you to promise me you'll stay here very quiet till we get back. We won't be long. We're going to fetch your mummy, but she'll still be very poorly, so you've got to be very gentle and quiet with her. Okay?" Cara nodded. "I promise we won't be long. Try to go back to sleep." She stroked Cara's hair, then joined Jane outside.

They had no difficulty in reaching Deborah's side ward without arousing untoward interest since it was still during visiting hours. Lindsay quickly scouted round to make sure the area was not under surveillance before the pair of them ducked into Deborah's room. In the thirty-six hours since Lindsay had last seen her, Deborah had made a noticeable improvement. She was propped up on her pillows watching television, the deathly white pallor had left her skin and she looked like a woman in recovery mode. Even the drips had been taken out. When they entered, she grinned delightedly. "At last," she said. "I thought you'd all forgotten me."

"Far from it," said Lindsay, going to her and kissing her warmly. "Listen, there's no time to explain everything now. But we've got to get you out of here. The doctors say you can be moved safely, and Jane's promised to take care of you."

Jane nodded, picking up the chart on the end of the bed. "It looks as if your condition is quite stable now," she remarked. "Don't worry, Deborah, you'll be okay with me."

"I don't doubt it, Jane. But what's all this about, Lin? Why can't I stay here? Surely I must be safe enough or the police wouldn't have left me unguarded?"

Lindsay sighed. "I know it looks like I'm being really high-handed about this, but it's because I'm scared for you. You were attacked because Rupert Crabtree's murderer thinks you know something that can compromise him. I'll explain all the details later, I promise, but take it from me that the police won't arrest the person who attacked you. He doesn't know that, though. So you've got to get out of the firing line or he'll have another go.

"I've managed to arrange somewhere for you and Cara to stay for a while till the heat dies down, somewhere no one will find you. I don't trust the police to take care of you, so we're doing it all off our own bat, without their help. Will you trust me?"

"I don't seem to have a lot of choice, do I?" Deborah replied. "But I don't know how you're going to get me out of here. I tried getting out of bed this afternoon. It turned out to be a seriously bad idea."

It was a problem that hadn't occurred to Lindsay. But Jane had already found a solution. "A wheelchair, Lindsay," she said, smiling at the look of dismay on the other's face. "We passed a couple outside the main ward, in an alcove. Can you fetch one while I get Deborah ready?"

Lindsay strolled down the corridor, trying to look nonchalant, till she reached the wheelchairs Jane had spotted. With all the subtlety of Inspector Clouseau, she wrestled one out of the alcove, struggled to release the brake, then shot off back to the side ward. Luckily no one saw her, for she would have aroused suspicion in the most naïve student nurse. Between them, Lindsay and Jane got Deborah into the wheelchair and wrapped a couple of hospital blankets round her. After checking that the coast was clear, they left the room. Jane started to push the wheelchair back the way they'd come, but Lindsay hissed, "No, this way," leading them in the opposite direction. During her earlier visit, she had reconnoitred an alternative route that was quicker and less public. Back at the van it was a matter of moments for Lindsay and Jane to lift Deborah in. Jane settled her into the double berth beside an overjoyed Cara.

Even so short a move had clearly taken its toll on Debs, who looked more tired and pinched than she had done a few moments ago. Jane carefully arranged the pillows under her to give her maximum support, but Deborah could not stifle a low moan as she tried to find a comfortable position for her head. Cara looked scared, but Jane soothed her and persuaded her to lie down quietly at the far side of the bed. Leaving the wheelchair where it stood Lindsay climbed into the driver's seat.

With perfect timing they left the hospital grounds in the middle of the stream of visitors' cars departing from the scene of duty done. Lindsay stayed in the flow of traffic for half a mile or so, then turned off to make a circuitous tour of the back streets of Fordham town centre, keeping a constant check on her mirrors. She trusted Rigano to keep his word, but she felt no confidence that Harriet Barber would do the same. After ten minutes of ducking and diving Lindsay felt satisfied that no one was on their trail and headed back to the MG. She drew up beside the car and turned round to confer.

"We've got a long drive ahead. I anticipate about twelve hours, given the van. We need to take both vehicles so I can leave you the MG. Where you're going, you'll need wheels, and I think I need to borrow the van for a while. I suggest that we swap at the half-way stage, Jane, around Carlisle?"

"Okay, but we'll have to stop at every service area so I can check on Deborah's condition," Jane replied.

"Just where are we going, Lin?" Deborah asked in a tired voice.

"An old school friend of mine has a cottage about ten miles from Invercross, where I grew up. She's a teacher and she's away in Australia at the moment, on a six-month exchange scheme, so I fixed up for you to use the cottage. It's lovely there, ten minutes from the sea. Electricity, bottled gas for cooking, telly, peat fires—all you could ask for. And no one will come looking for you there. Cara can even go to the village school if she wants. It's a small community, but they'll keep their mouths shut about you being there if my mother explains that you're convalescing after an attack and you're scared the man who attacked you is still looking for you."

"My God," said Deborah faintly.

"I'm sorry," said Lindsay. "I had to act quickly. I couldn't just sit back. There was no one else I could trust to make sure you were protected."

"And how long do I have to hide in the heather?"

"That depends. Until Simon Crabtree is dealt with. It could be months, I'm afraid."

"I'll stay as long as you need me," Jane chipped in.

"I can't take all of this in. What has Simon Crabtree to do with me?" Deborah demanded, hugging Cara close. "One minute I'm recuperating in hospital, the next I'm thrust into a remake of *The Three Musketeers* crossed with *The Thirty-Nine Steps*."

"I'll explain in the morning when I'm driving you, I promise," Lindsay replied. "But right now, we should get a move on."

"I'll take the van as far as Carlisle, then," Jane decided.

Lindsay nodded. "That'll be best. And don't push yourself too hard. Any time you need a rest or a coffee, just pull off at the services. I'm used to driving half the night, working shifts like I do; but I don't expect you to do the same."

"Cheeky so-and-so!" muttered Jane. "Have you forgotten the hours junior hospital doctors work? You'll be flaked out long before I will, Lindsay."

"Sorry, I forgot," Lindsay apologised.

The journey seemed endless. Deborah and Cara managed to sleep most of the way, only really waking during the last couple of hours. Lindsay explained the reasons for their flight to Deborah as she drove the last sixty miles down the familiar narrow roads with their spectacular views of the Argyllshire mountains and sea lochs on all sides. Cara was spellbound by the changing scenery and seemed not to be listening to the adult conversation.

Lindsay reached the end of her tale as they arrived in the tiny fishing village of Invercross. A cluster of brightly painted houses and cottages crowded along the harbour. "So here we are," Lindsay concluded. "Right back where I started all those years ago. Only this time, on the run like Bonnie Prince Charlie and Flora Macdonald." She pulled up outside a small, two-storey house on the harbour front. "Wait here a minute, I've got to get the keys."

The woman who opened the door before Lindsay reached it was small and wiry with curly grey hair and eyes that matched Lindsay's. She swept her daughter into her arms, saying, "It's grand to see you. It's been a long time since the New Year. Now, come in and have some breakfast. Bring your friends in. Is Cordelia up with you?"

Lindsay disengaged herself and followed her mother indoors. "No, she's busy. Listen, Mum, I want to get the others settled in at the cottage first, then I'll come back for a meal and a sleep before I get back to London."

"You're not stopping, then?" Her mother's obvious disappointment stabbed Lindsay. "You'll miss your father. He's at the fishing, he'll not be back before the morn's morning."

"I'm sorry, Mum, I'm in the middle of something big. This was a kind of emergency. Have you got Catriona's keys?"

Her mother produced a bunch of keys from her apron pocket. "I got them from Mrs Campbell last night when you phoned. I went up this morning with a few essentials and lit the fire, so they should be comfortable."

Lindsay kissed her. "You're a wee gem, Mum. I'll be back in a couple of hours."

Her mother shook her head, an affectionate smile on her face. "You never stop, do you, lassie?"

Ten hours later, Lindsay was back on the road south. Jane, Deborah and Cara were settled comfortably in the cottage, amply supplied with Mrs Gordon's idea of essentials—bread, butter, milk, eggs, bacon, fish, onions, potatoes and tea. Mrs Gordon had promised to take Jane to sign on the following Monday. If she lied about paying rent, they could fiddle enough to live on. So there would be no need for any part of the official world to know Deborah's whereabouts. Jane thought Lindsay's precautions extreme but she would not be moved.

Lindsay spent the night less comfortably than the three refugees. Her eyes were gritty and sore, her body ached from the jolting of the van's elderly suspension. She finally gave in when even the volume of the stereo couldn't keep her awake and alert. She parked in a lay-by off the motorway where she slept fitfully for five hours before hammering back down to London.

Somewhere around Birmingham, she realised that she'd felt no desire whatsoever to stay in Invercross with Deborah. That realisation forced her to examine what she had been steadfastly ignoring during the traumatic events of the last few days. It was time to think about Cordelia and herself. Why had she felt such an overwhelming need to sleep with Deborah? Did she subconsciously want to end her relationship with Cordelia and was Deborah just a tool she'd used? Until her kidnapping by the security forces, Lindsay had been confused and frightened about her emotions.

But there was no denying the fact that Cordelia had come to her rescue in spite of the problems there had been between them. Driving on, Lindsay gradually came to understand that her relief at seeing Cordelia outside GCHQ had been more than just gratitude. Her own behaviour had been negative in the extreme, and if she wanted to heal the breach between them she would have to act fast. As that thought flickered across her mind, Lindsay realised there was no "if" about it. She knew she wanted to try again with Cordelia. Full of good resolutions, she parked the van outside the house just before noon and rushed in. The house was empty.

Stiff and exhausted, and having lost track of time almost completely, Lindsay ran a sweet-smelling foam bath, put Monteverdi's 1610 Vespers on at high volume and soaked for half an hour. Then, in sweat pants and dressing gown, she sat down at the word processor. Now that Deborah was safe, she had settled her obligations. There was even less honour among the Harriet Barbers of this world than among thieves and journalists, she had now realised. The promises they had made about leaving her alone had been shattered. They had tried their damnedest to follow her. There was only one real insurance left. So she wrote the whole story of Rupert Crabtree's murder and its repercussions, leaving nothing out.

She had barely finished it when she heard the front door slam. Alerted by the music, Cordelia superfluously called, "I'm home." Pink-cheeked from the cold outside, she stopped in the doorway. "Welcome back," she said. Linday picked up the sheaf of paper on the desk and proffered it.

"I promised you an explanation," she said. "Here it is. The uncensored version. It's probably quicker if you read it rather than listen to me explaining it."

Cordelia took the papers. "I missed you," she said.

"I know," Lindsay replied. "And I've missed you, constantly. I'm not very good at being on my own. I tend to get overtaken by events, if you see what I mean."

Cordelia gave a sardonic smile. "I've heard it called a lot of things, but that's a new one on me." There was a silence, as they met in a wary and tentative embrace. Cordelia disengaged herself, saying, "Let me read this. Then we'll talk. Okay?"

"Okay. I'll be in the kitchen when you've finished. The idea of cooking dinner in a real kitchen is strangely appealing after the last few days."

It took Cordelia half an hour to work through Lindsay's account of her investigations. When she had finished, she sat staring out of the window. She could barely imagine the stress that Lindsay had been operating under. Now she could understand, even if she could not yet forgive what she instinctively knew had happened between Lindsay and Deborah. But the most important thing now was to make sure Lindsay's natural inclination to the defence of principle was subdued for the sake of her own safety.

Cordelia found Lindsay putting the finishing touches to an Indian meal. "I had no idea," she said.

Lindsay shrugged. "I wanted so much to tell you," she said. "Not just at the end, but all through. I missed sharing my ideas with you."

"What about Deborah?"

"It's not something you should be worried about, truly."

"So what happens now? I don't mean with you and me, I mean with Deborah? Do we wait till Simon Crabtree is dealt with and then everything returns to normal?"

Lindsay shook her head. "No. Those bastards didn't keep their word. They tried to follow me—you read that, didn't you? So as far as I'm concerned, I'm not just sitting back till I get the all clear from Rigano. The best way to make sure they deal with Crabtree is to force the whole thing into the open. Otherwise it could be months, years till one side or the other decides Crabtree has outlived his usefulness. I don't see why we should all live under a shadow till then. Besides, the guy is a murderer. He'll do it again the next time someone gets close to the truth. And next time it could be me. Or someone else I care about."

"So what are you going to do?"

"I'm going to give the whole story to Duncan. And if he won't use it. I'll give it to Dick McAndrew. Either way, it's going to be published."

"You're crazy," Cordelia protested. "They'll come after you instead of Crabtree. They've got your signature on the Official Secrets Act. And the first journo that fronts Crabtree with your story points the finger straight at you. If our lot don't get you, the Soviets will."

"Don't be so melodramtic," Lindsay replied crossly. "I know what I'm doing."

"And did you know what you were doing when you ended up in Harriet Barber's clutches the other night? I'd have thought you'd have learned more sense by now," said Cordelia bitterly.

"Point taken," Lindsay replied. "But there's no use in arguing, is there? We're starting from different premises. I'm operating on a point of principle as well as self-defence. All you care about is making sure nothing happens to me. That's very commendable and I'd feel the same if our positions were reversed. But I think the fact that people who have committed no crime are hounded into hiding to protect a spy and a killer is too important to ignore simply because revealing it is going to make life difficult for me. I wish I could make you understand."

Cordelia turned away. "Oh, I understand all right. Rigano set you up to do his dirty work and you fell for it."

Lindsay shook her head. "It's not that simple. But I do feel utterly demoralised and betrayed. And I've got to do something to get rid of these feelings, as well as all the other stuff."

Cordelia put her arms round Lindsay. "I just don't want you to get hurt. When you get wound up about something, you completely disregard your own safety."

"Well, I've learned my lesson. This time, I'm going to make sure my public profile is too high for them to come after me," Lindsay retorted. "Trust me, please."

Cordelia kissed her. "Oh, I trust you. It's the other nutters I worry about."

Lindsay smiled. "Let's eat, eh? And then, maybe an early night?"

In the morning, Lindsay smiled reminiscently about their rapprochement the night before as she gathered all her papers together and prepared to set off for an early briefing with Duncan at the office. Before she left, Cordelia hugged her, saying, "Good luck, and take care. I'm really proud of you, you know."

"Yes, I know. I'll see you later."

"I'm afraid I'll be back quite late. I'm sorry, I didn't know you'd be home. I promised William we could work on the script rewrites for the new series tonight," Cordelia apologised.

Lindsay smiled. "No problem. I'll probably be late myself, given the importance of the story. I might even wait for the first edition to drop. I'll see you whenever."

Outside the house, Lindsay hailed a cab and headed for the office. She had barely stepped into the newsroom when Duncan's deputy told her to go straight to the editor's office. His secretary had obviously been briefed to expect her, for Lindsay was shown straight in, instead of being left to cool her heels indefinitely with a cup of cold coffee.

Three men were waiting for her—Duncan, Bill Armitage, the editor, and Douglas Browne, the Clarion group's legal manager. No one said a word of greeting. Lindsay sensed the intention was to intimidate her, and she steeled herself against whatever was to come. "I've brought my copy in," she said, to break the silence. She handed the sheaf of paper to Duncan, who barely glanced at it.

Bill Armitage ran his hands through his thick grey hair in a familiar gesture. "You've wasted your time, Lindsay," he said. "We'll not be using a line of that copy."

"What?" Her surprise was genuine. She had expected cuts and rewrites, but not a blanket of silence.

Duncan replied gruffly, "You heard, kid. We've had more aggravation over you this weekend than over every other dodgy story we've ever done. The bottom line is that we've been made to understand that if we fight on this one it will be the paper's death knell. You're a union hack—you know the paper's financial situation. We can't afford a big legal battle. And I take the view that if we can't protect our staff, we don't put them in the firing line."

Armitage cut across Duncan's self-justification. "We've got responsibilities to the public. And that means we don't make our living out of stirring up needless unrest. To be quite blunt about it, we're not in the business of printing unsubstantiated allegations against the security services. All that does is destroy people's confidence in the agencies that look after our safety."

Lindsay was appalled. "You mean the security people have been on to you already?"

The editor shook his head patronisingly. "Did you really think the mayhem you've been causing wouldn't bring them down about our ears like a ton of bricks? Jesus Christ, Lindsay, you've been in this game long enough not to be so naive. You can't possibly have the sort of cast-iron proof we'd need to run this story."

Lindsay looked doubtful. "I think I have, Bill. Most of it can be backed up by other people and I can get hold of a copy of the computer tape that clinches it all. The cops can't deny what has been going on, either. Superintendent Rigano should be able to back it up."

"Rigano was one of the people who was here yesterday," Browne said heavily. "There will be no help from that quarter. The story must be killed, Lindsay."

"I'm sorry," said Duncan. "I know you worked hard for it."

"Worked hard? I nearly got myself killed for it." Lindsay shook her head disbelievingly. "This story is dynamite," she protested. "We're talking about murder, spying, security breaches, GBH and kidnapping, all going on with the consent of the people on our side who are supposed to be responsible for law and order. And you're telling me you haven't got the bottle to use it because those bastards are going to make life a little bit awkward for you? Don't you care about what they've done to me, one of your own?"

"It's not that we don't care. But there's nothing we can legitimately do," the editor replied. "Look, Lindsay, forget the whole thing. Take a week off, get it into perspective."

Lindsay stood up. "No," she said. "No way. I can't accept this. I never thought I'd be ashamed of this paper. But I am now. And I can't go on working here feeling like that. I'm sorry, Duncan, but I quit. I resign. As of now, I don't work for you any more." She stopped abruptly, feeling tears beginning to choke her. She snatched up the sheaf of copy from the table where Duncan had laid it, turned and walked out of the office. No one tried to stop her.

In the ladies' toilet, she was comprehensively sick. She splashed cold water on her face and took several deep breaths before heading for the offices of *Socialism Today*.

Here there were no security men on the door to challenge her, no secretaries to vet her. She walked straight up to the big room on the second floor where the journalists worked. Dick was perched on the corner of his desk, his back to her, a phone jammed to his ear. "Yeah, okay . . ." he said resignedly. "Yeah, okay. Tomorrow it is then. See you." He slammed the phone down. "Fucking Trots. Who needs them?" he muttered, turning round to reach for his mug of coffee. Catching sight of Lindsay, he actually paled. "Christ! What the hell are you doing here?"

"I've got a story for you," she said, opening her bag and taking out another copy of her manuscript.

"Is it to do with the computer printout?" he demanded.

"Sort of. Among other things. Like murder, kidnap, GBH and spying. Interested?"

He shook his head reluctantly. "Sorry, Lindsay. No can do. Listen, I had the heavies round at my place last night about you. It's a no-no, darling. It may be the best story of the decade, but I'm not touching it."

A sneer of contempt flickered at the corner of Lindsay's mouth. "I expected the big boys at the *Clarion* to wet themselves at the thought of prosecution. But I expected you to take that sort of thing in your stride. I thought you were supposed to be the fearless guardian of the public's right to know?"

Dick looked ashamed and sighed deeply. "It wasn't prosecution they threatened me with, Lindsay. These are not people who play by the rules. These are not pussycats. These are people who know how to hurt you where you live. They were talking nasty accidents. And they knew all about Marianne and the kiddy. I'll take risks on my own account, Lindsay, but I'm not having on my conscience anything that might happen to my wife and child. You wouldn't take chances with Cordelia, would you?"

Lindsay shook her head. Exhaustion surged over her in a wave. "I suppose not, Dick. Okay, I'll be seeing you."

It took her more than an hour to walk back to the empty house. She was gripped by a sense of utter desolation and frustration that she sensed would take a long time to dissipate. There had been too many betrayals in the last week. She turned into their street, just as a red Fiesta vanished round the corner at the far end of the mews behind. That unremarkable event was enough on a day like this to make her break into a run. She fumbled with her keys, clumsy in her haste, then ran upstairs. At first glance, everything seemed normal. But when she went into the living room, she realised that every cassette had been removed from the shelves above the stereo. In the study it was the same story. Lindsay crouched down on the floor against the wall, hands over her face, and shivered as the sense of insecurity overwhelmed her.

She had no idea how long she crouched there feeling utterly defenceless. Eventually the shaking stopped and she got unsteadily to her feet. In the kitchen she put some coffee on, then noticed there was a message on the answering machine. She lit a cigarette and played the tape back.

The voice sounded scared. "Lindsay. This is Annie Norton. I've been burgled. My car has been broken into and my office has also been turned over. I suspect this may have something to do with you since all that has been stolen are cassettes. Whoever was responsible has probably got your phone bugged, so for their benefit as well as yours, for the record, they have now got the only data I had relating to that bloody tape you brought me. I wish you'd bloody warned me you didn't have the sense to leave this alone, Lindsay. You'd better stay away from me till this is all over—I need my security clearance so I can work. Look, take care of yourself. This isn't a game. Be careful. Goodbye."

It was the last straw. Lindsay sat down at the table, dropped her head in her hands and wept till her eyes stung and her sinuses ached. Then she sat, staring at the wall, reviewing what had happened, trying to find a way forward for herself. As the afternoon wore on, she smoked steadily and worked her way down the best bottle of Burgundy she could find in the house.

By teatime she knew exactly what she had to do. She set off across the park for the phone box and started setting wheels in motion.

20

Lindsay waited patiently on hold to be connected, praying that the object of her call would still be at his desk. Even on cheap rate, the phone box was eating £1 coins at an alarming rate. While she hung on, she mentally congratulated Jane for forcing her to examine her conscience about doing something positive to support the peace camp all those months before. If it hadn't been for those features she'd sold abroad then, she wouldn't have built up the contacts she needed now. Her musing was cut short by a voice on the end of the phone.

"*Ja?*"

"Günter Binden?" Lindsay asked.

"*Ja. Wer ist?*"

"It's Lindsay Gordon, Günter. From London."

Immediately the bass voice on the other end of the phone switched to immaculate English. "Lindsay! How good to hear from you. How goes it with you?"

"A bit hectic. That's what I wanted to talk to you about. I've got a wonderful story for you. I'm having problems getting anyone over here to print it because of the national security angle, but it's too important a tale to ignore. So I thought of you."

"Is it another story about the peace camp?"

"Indirectly, yes. But it's really to do with spying and murder."

"Sounds good. Do you want to tell me some more?"

Lindsay started to tell the too-familiar story of recent events. Günter listened carefully, only stopping her to seek clarification when her journalistic idioms became too obscure for him to follow. Lindsay was glad she'd trusted her instincts about approaching him. As well as being the features editor of a large-circulation left-wing weekly magazine that actively supported the Green Party, he had spent two years working in London and understood the British political scene as well as having a first-class command of English. When she reached her kidnapping by the security forces, he exploded.

"My God, Lindsay, why isn't your own paper publishing this? It's dynamite."

"That's precisely why they're backing off. They don't want a legal battle right now for business reasons—the publisher wants to float the company on the stock market later this year, and he wants to present a healthy balance sheet and a good reputation. Also, they've got no stomach for a real fight against the Establishment. If I was offering them a largely unsubstantiated tale about a soap-opera star having a gay affair, they'd go for it and to hell with the risks. But this is too much like the real thing. But let me finish the tale. It gets better, I promise."

Günter held his tongue till Lindsay had finished her recital. Then there was a silence. "What sort of price are you looking for?"

"If I hadn't jacked my job in today, I'd let you have it for free. But I'm going to have to feed myself somehow, and I can't imagine I'm going to find much work in national newspapers. Can you stretch to five thousand Deutschmarks?" Lindsay asked.

"Do you have pictures of this man Crabtree? And of Deborah Patterson?"

"I've got pics of Deborah, and you can get pics of both Simon and Rupert Crabtree through the local paper. I've got a good contact there. And you can do pics of me. What do you say, Günter?"

"How soon can I see copy?"

"I can fax it to you tonight. Have we got a deal?"

"Four thousand. That's as high as I can go. Don't forget, I've got translation to pay for too."

Lindsay paused, pretending to think. "Okay," she said. "Four thousand it is. I'll get the copy on the fax tonight and I'll bring the pics over myself."

"You're coming over?"

Lindsay nodded. "You bet. I want to be well out of the way when the shit hits the fan. And besides, I won't believe it till I actually hold the first copy off the presses in my own hands."

"So how soon can you get here?"

"I can get a night crossing and be with you by tomorrow afternoon. Does that leave you enough time?"

They arranged the rest of the details, then Lindsay hung up gratefully. Returning home, she picked up the bundle of copy she'd wasted her time writing for Duncan and left the house. She made for the tube station, not caring if she was being followed or not. It was already seven o'clock, and the rush hour press of bodies had dissipated. Emerging from Chancery Lane station she walked to the *Clarion* building. Her gamble that word of her departure wouldn't have yet got round paid off: she walked unchallenged into the building and made her way to the busy wire room on the third floor. After a quiet word with the wire room manager, he left her with the fax machine for the price of a few pints. An hour later, she left the building and headed back to Highbury. When she emerged from the tube station, she realised she wasn't able to face the empty house again just yet, so she walked slowly down Upper Street to the King's Head pub. Over a glass of the house red, she turned the situation over in her mind.

The chain reaction she had set in motion would blow Simon Crabtree's cover completely. She wished she could be a fly on the wall when it dropped on Harriet Barber's desk. The only question mark that remained in her mind was which side would get to him first. She suspected the Soviets would be the ones to terminate him; *glasnost* only extended so far. And it would be expedient for MI6 to keep their hands clean for once. But she knew she'd have to keep her head down till she was sure that Simon Crabtree had met the fate he deserved. And that might take a few weeks. A fatal accident following too closely on the heels of her revelations might seem a little too convenient even for the unscrupulous intelligence community.

The only problem that remained was how to find out when Crabtree was removed from circulation. Her first thought was to enlist Jack Rigano's help. He owed her one. As Cordelia had so forcefully reminded her, he had brought her into the frame when forces beyond his control prevented him from doing his job. But he had already stuck his neck out once for her, and the fact that it was he who had been despatched to put the frighteners on the *Clarion* demonstrated where his allegiance lay in the final analysis.

There was one other person Lindsay could ask. It would avoid the danger of providing an interested party with too much information. And provided the storm that the story was inevitably going to raise didn't make him lose his bottle, he'd also be happy to supply information when there was something in it for him. Lindsay searched through the pages of her notebook till she found the page where she'd scribbled Gavin Hammill's number. The pub phone was mercifully situated in a quiet corner, granting her some privacy.

She was in luck. The Fordham reporter was at home for the evening. After the formalities, Lindsay explained what she wanted. "I'm going to be out of the country for a while," she said. "But I need someone to keep an eye on Simon Crabtree for me. I just want to know what he's up to, and if anything untoward happens to any member of the family. If you hear anything at all, especially if he drops out of sight for a few days, you can get in touch with me via a guy in Cologne called Günter Binden."

She gave him Günter's office and home numbers and explained that Günter's magazine would pay him a generous credit for any material he supplied. "They're very generous payers, Gavin," she added. "And they never forget a good source. If you do the biz for them, they'll put work your way. Oh, and if anybody asks why you're interested, don't mention my name."

"Of course not, Lindsay. Thanks for thinking of me."

"Don't mention it. See you around."

The final phone call she made was to reserve a ticket for herself and the van on the midnight crossing to Zeebrugge. The train or the plane would have been more comfortable, but she wanted to be self-sufficient and mobile once she was out of the country.

She wished she could take Cordelia with her, turn the trip into a break for both of them. But she knew it wouldn't work out like that, even supposing Cordelia was able and willing to get to Dover for the midnight ferry. Lindsay knew that the divisions between them needed time and energy from both sides before they could be healed. A mad dash across Europe followed by all the hassles of getting this story on to the streets was no basis for a major reconciliation. Besides, Lindsay didn't know how long she would have to stay away, and Cordelia had other commitments.

It was a quarter past eight when she reached home. She would have to leave in three quarters of an hour. The clothes she had thrown into the washing machine earlier would be dry in half an hour, and it would take her only ten minutes to pack. She had half an hour to write an explanation of her absence for Cordelia. The word processor would be quicker, if more impersonal. But getting the words right was the most important thing.

She started by explaining where she was going and why. That was the easy bit. Now came the part where years of working with words were no help at all.

"I'm going to have to keep my head down after this piece is published. The security services will want to bring charges, and I don't think it will be safe for me to come home till after Simon Crabtree is no longer a threat. I'm going to stay abroad for a while, but I don't know yet where I'll be. I'll let you know as soon as I've sorted things out and maybe you can join me for a while. I'm sorry—I really wanted to spend some time with you. I love you. Lindsay."

She scowled at the screen, deeply dissatisfied with what she had written. But there was no time now for more. She got up and stretched while the letter printed out, then left it by the answering machine. The next fifteen minutes were a whirlwind of throwing clothes, books, papers and maps into a couple of holdalls. She went through to the lounge to pick up some tapes for the journey, forgetting the raid that had left the shelves empty. When she saw the spaces where her music had been, she swore fluently. The shock gave her the extra kick of energy she needed to get out into the night and off to the ferry port.

⚜

Three nights later, Lindsay stood in the press hall in Cologne watching the massive presses flickering her image past her eyes at hundreds of copies a minute. Günter approached, clutching a handful of early copies from the run and an opened bottle of champagne. He thrust a magazine at Lindsay, who stared disbelievingly at the cover. Her own picture was superimposed on a wide-angled shot of the base at Brownlow Common with the peace camp in the foreground. A slow smile spread across her face and she took a long, choking swig from the offered bottle of champagne. "We did it," she almost crowed. "We beat the bastards."

EPILOGUE

Excerpts from the *Daily Clarion*, 11 May 198-.

MISSILES TO GO The Pentagon announced last night that the phased withdrawal of cruise missiles from Brownlow Common will begin in November . . .

DOUBLE TRAGEDY FOR SPY MURDER FAMILY The man at the centre of a German magazine's revelations about Russian spies at American bases in the UK died in a freak road accident last night.

His death was the second tragedy within two months for his family. His father, solicitor Rupert Crabtree, was brutally murdered eight weeks ago.

Simon Crabtree, who had been officially cleared by British security forces of any involvement in espionage, died instantly when his motorbike skidded on a sharp bend and ploughed into the back of a tractor.